Praise for
Matters of Hon

"With snappy dialogue, intelligent prose, and a careful look at the undercurrents of friendship and personal ambitions . . . Begley paints a memorable portrait of lasting friendship and of the strength required to step outside of the expectations that surround each of us."

—*The Rocky Mountain News*

"Begley is one of the best American novelists. . . . [His] terrifically intelligent, moving, and entertaining new novel is not just his best book since *Wartime Lies*. It is also the book that brings his entire achievement as a novelist into focus."

—*New York Sun*

"An idiosyncratic voice . . . Begley has, as always, interesting things to say about class and sex and friendship."

—*The New York Times*

"As the author of eight novels, [Begley] has won wide critical acclaim. . . . Much of his fiction—beginning with his first novel, *Wartime Lies* . . . has been marked by his youth as a Polish Jew who escaped the Nazis and remade himself in America. . . . *Matters of Honor* is another thoughtful reflection on this experience."

—*The Washington Post*

"An elegant novel of enduring friendship . . . The heart of this tragedy of manners is Sam's compelling assessment of class and social cachet in America. . . . Begley finds new and wonderful nuances."

—*Publishers Weekly* (starred review)

"[An] absorbing novel about the nature of identity and the costs of assimilation. . . . Begley uses a lucid prose style to dispassionately eviscerate the upper classes even as he illuminates the true meaning of friendship."

—*Booklist*

MATTERS OF HONOR

Matters of Honor

A Novel

LOUIS BEGLEY

BALLANTINE BOOKS
NEW YORK

2008 Ballantine Books Trade Paperback Edition

Copyright © 2007 by Louis Begley
Reading group guide copyright © 2008 by Random House, Inc.

Published in the United States by Ballantine Books, an imprint of The Random House Publishing Group, a division of Random House, Inc., New York.

BALLANTINE and colophon are registered trademarks of Random House, Inc.
RANDOM HOUSE READER'S CIRCLE and colophon are trademarks of Random House, Inc.

Originally published in hardcover in the United States by Alfred A. Knopf, a division of Random House, Inc., in 2007.

Library of Congress Cataloging-in-Publication Data
Begley, Louis.
Matters of honor / Louis Begley.
p.   cm.
ISBN 978-0-345-49434-4
1. Harvard University—Students—Fiction. 2. Nineteen fifties—Fiction.
3. Jewish college students—Fiction. 4. Friendship—Fiction.
5. Antisemitism—Fiction. 6. Psychological fiction. I. Title.
PS3552.E373M38   2007
813'.54—dc22   2006046581

Printed in the United States of America

www.randomhousereaderscircle.com

2 4 6 8 9 7 5 3 1

In memoriam
F. B. AND D. B.

Les morts, les pauvres morts ont de grandes douleurs ...

BAUDELAIRE, *Les fleurs du mal*

MATTERS OF HONOR

I

This is my first memory of Henry: I stand at the door of one of the three bedrooms of the ground floor suite in the college dormitory to which I have been assigned. At the open window, with his back to me, a tall, slender, red-haired boy is leaning out and waving to someone. He has heard my footsteps, turns, and beckons to me saying, Take a look, a beautiful girl is blowing kisses to me. I've never seen her before. She must be mad.

I went to the window. Not more than ten feet away, a girl standing on the grass was indeed blowing kisses and waving her hand in the direction of our window. Between kisses, she grinned, her mouth made to seem very large by a thick layer of red lipstick. She wore a suit of beige tweed, dark green stockings, and a Tyrolean hat with a little pheasant feather. A couple of paces away from her I saw a middle-aged woman, in darker tweeds and a brown fedora. Something about her—the hat? an air of haughty distinction?—made me think of Ingrid Bergman in *Casablanca*, about to board the plane for Lisbon. I assumed, partly on account of their similar dress, that she was the girl's mother.

Several undergraduates had stopped on the path leading diagonally to the far corner of the Widener and were gawking at the scene. Neither the daughter's antics nor the audience they had attracted seemed to disturb the mother. But after a few more minutes she said something in a voice too low for us to hear, and the girl, having blown one more kiss, threw up her arms in theatrical despair. They strolled away.

I'm in love, sighed the red-haired boy. I want to throw myself at her feet.

Why don't you? I replied, only half kidding. It's not too late. Climb out the window right now and you won't even have to run to catch them.

Oh no, he wailed, I can't. Why did this have to happen today, when I'm not prepared?

As there wasn't a trace of irony in his voice or expression, I should have let the subject drop. Instead, I told him that, while a formal declaration might be premature, no harm could come of his proposing a cup of coffee in the Square.

He shook his head bitterly. I don't dare, he said. Don't you see how splendid she is? Penthesilea in tweeds! None but the son of Peleus could tame her. I am unworthy even of her scorn.

His face was a mask of discouragement.

I suppose that I shrugged. That or perhaps the expression on my face must have told him that I thought he had gone overboard. He recomposed his face into a bland smile and said, I suppose you are one of my roommates. I'm Henry White . . . from New York.

I had met New Yorkers before, mainly at school, although a number of New York families had summerhouses in the vicinity of Lenox, where my parents and I lived, and in the neighboring Berkshire towns of Stockbridge, Great Barrington, and Tyringham. This fellow didn't sound like any of them. He didn't mispronounce. In fact his speech was oddly slow and accurate, except when he got excited, as during the Peleus routine, with a thickness around the edge of words suggesting a dry mouth. It occurred to me that he might be some kind of foreigner, but, if he had an accent, I couldn't identify it. My notions of how foreigners spoke derived at the time exclusively from the movies and the French family with whom I had just spent the summer in a small town north of Paris. That Henry White of New York didn't have a French accent was quite clear.

I confirmed that I was indeed his roommate and, having introduced myself as Sam Standish, examined Henry more closely. His clothes were wrong; they looked brand-new. The jacket and trousers were of an odd color. Other than that, he was a fine-looking fellow. Is Sam short for Samuel? he asked me earnestly. He nodded when I confirmed that this was the case.

I hadn't had lunch and asked whether he would like to have a sandwich with me in the Square. He said that he had already eaten at the Freshman Union. I went out alone.

Courses weren't going to start for another couple of days, but the dormitories were open, and freshman orientation was in progress. I had assured my mother that I could get down to Cambridge by bus, even with my big footlocker. To my surprise, she had insisted that she really wanted to drive me down. But since she and my father were going out to dinner that evening, she wouldn't have lunch with me. She gave me a couple of bills, the cost of lunch for two by her reckoning, and sped off as soon as I had unpacked the car trunk. I had dragged my stuff into the living room of the suite and saw that I wasn't the first to arrive. Someone's luggage was in the middle of the room. Then I stuck my head into one of the bedrooms and came upon Henry.

After a solitary tuna-salad sandwich at Hayes-Bickford, I returned to the dormitory. Henry may have been watching for me at the window. In any event, he opened the door of the suite before I could turn the key in the lock and said he was glad I had come back so soon. He had a practical question he wanted to ask: Did I care which bedroom he took? He had spent the previous night in the one I had found him in but didn't think that gave him any sort of prior claim. He asked me to follow him to the bedroom he wanted and pointed to the right toward a dark brick classroom building shaped like a whale.

That's Sever, he said, an H. H. Richardson design, and over here, right in front of us, is Memorial Church.

I said that he could keep the room. The three bedrooms were all the same size, and I didn't care about the view. That Sever was a masterpiece of late-nineteenth-century American architecture was unknown to me then, but I don't think that knowing it would have made any difference. I didn't expect to spend much time at the window. Henry, very pleased, sat on my desk chair while I unpacked. When I finished, he helped me make the bed.

The ice had been broken, it seemed, so I asked why he hadn't at least spoken to the girl. After all, she was blatantly trying to pick him up. Henry shook his head and said it was out of the question. The timing was fatally wrong. He might have followed her to find out whether she went to Radcliffe, and in which dorm she lived, but his conspicuous red hair ruled that out. People recognized him instantly. If the girl or her mother had turned around and seen him, they'd know it was he and would think he was some kind of nut who couldn't understand a joke. That would have spoiled everything. He would have to wait.

You're nuts, I told him. There is no possible harm in her and her mother's knowing that you'd like to shake the hand of the girl who took the trouble to blow kisses at you.

He shook his head again. Timing, he said, timing. The stars aren't aligned. I have to wait.

It was none of my business, and probably I should have known enough not to insist on a subject that made him uneasy. But as I was condemned to room with Henry for a year, I thought I was entitled to investigate whether he was a pompous jerk or really deranged.

These questions did not preoccupy me long. Within a couple of weeks, Henry decided that we were close friends—a conclusion I had not yet reached—and he began to unburden himself to me about his feelings with such unsparing frankness and volubility that I sometimes found myself wishing I hadn't done whatever had put him so at ease. Unprompted by me, he spoke again about the girl and acknowledged his behavior as peculiar. It wasn't shyness, he insisted, that had stopped him in his tracks, but a conviction that he must make himself suitable first or face inevitable rejection—not only by this girl and her mother but by every other girl he might find attractive.

And it's not just girls, he said, I mean rejected by everyone here! Do you remember the Raymond Massey character in *Arsenic and Old Lace*, the one whom Dr. Einstein, the Peter Lorre character, made into a monster by botching the operation on his face? Raymond Massey is me. I too have been botched. And therefore I say: Dr. Einstein, we must operate again!

I said this was more evidence that he was nuts.

He shook his head and said that observations he had made during just two meals, dinner and lunch, that he had eaten alone at the Union, before I arrived to find him standing at the window, had confirmed his fears. He was hopelessly out of place in this world of creatures like the girl or me for that matter. He had watched the freshmen milling about the place, studied their appearance and manner, and saw no one like him. Certainly no one dressed like him. Or, put another way, no one he would have wanted to know who looked anything like him or had equally disastrous clothes.

While recounting these experiences, he laughed so hard he had tears in his eyes. I didn't know what to make of this and suggested that his survey of the freshman class might not be scientific. Henry said that could be. But as I would come to see, in fact Henry missed little of what went on and, as a rule, remembered everything. For now he granted my point and reduced his claim: the Freshman Union survey had confirmed what he had already realized at home, before leaving for Cambridge, when his mother was packing the things he was to take with him to college. I was by then familiar with them: a sky-blue suit he had worn at his high school graduation, a tan flannel jacket, and two pairs of brown trousers. His mother had chosen every item, and every item was too large because she expected him to grow into it and seemed unwilling to admit that he had reached his full height. He had begged to be allowed to buy his clothes in Cambridge or Boston once he knew how other people dressed, but she wouldn't hear of it: he was too irresponsible and extravagant, and he had no appreciation of quality. Besides, he said, the way she looks at it, it's my father's money and she is entitled to the fun of spending it. That's how she has gotten me to look like an underage bookkeeper.

By that time, I had gotten used to Henry's wardrobe, but when I recalled our first meeting, and the impression he had made on me, I couldn't deny that he had good reason not to want the girl to see him in one of those outfits. Not if he wanted to make the best possible impression.

To go back to that afternoon, after making my bed we inspected the luggage of our missing roommate in the living room. It consisted of a steamer trunk and a large pigskin suitcase, both so scuffed up that they would have seemed proof of exotic travel even without the stickers of the *Normandie, Queen Mary,* and various hotels with resonant names that had been glued to them. The owner, to judge by the tag attached to the trunk handle, was Archibald P. Palmer III. The name was followed by an APO address. My father had been in the service during the war, and APO was a familiar institution. I explained to Henry that we would have an army brat living with us. It wasn't the military postal service, however, that intrigued him. He wanted to know whether we should infer from the Roman numerals that our roommate belonged to high society. He was inclined to think so, based on engagement and wedding announcements he had read in *The New York Times*. It wasn't unusual, he said, to find for instance that Mr. Ebenezer Witherspoon III, the elder son of Ebenezer Witherspoon II, a collector of Americana and a yachtsman, with homes in Cold Spring, Long Island, Manhattan, and Palm Beach, Florida, and great-grandson of Ebenezer Witherspoon, a business partner of Commodore Vanderbilt, was to be married to the daughter of Mr. and Mrs. Sperry Rand IV, with homes in Oyster Bay, Long Island, and likewise Manhattan.

True enough, I told him, but as Roman numerals were not unheard of among less elevated classes, I suggested that we withhold judgment until we had met Mr. Palmer.

We went to dinner at the Union and afterward saw, at the University Theater, a stupid movie that I have completely forgotten. A raucous party was in progress across the hall in the dormitory when we got back. Through an open door, someone yelled an invitation to come in for a drink. Having wormed out of Henry over dinner that he had graduated from some public high school in Brooklyn, I assumed that he might be reluctant to plunge into a room full of boisterous prep school jocks. However, he seemed game to meet them, and we went in. I had one beer before the noise drove me out. On my way to the door I looked around the room for Henry. A drink in hand, he seemed to be managing well enough; in fact he looked as though he were having a good time.

Our third roommate arrived the following day in the late afternoon. I was present when, animated by the importance of getting this sort of thing right, he explained to Henry the origin of his Roman numeral. He had the same first name and middle initial as his father and paternal grandfather. That made him the third, whereas had he been named after his father, without a grandfather or great-grandfather also named Archibald P., he would have been Archibald P. Palmer Jr., like his father, the colonel, and he further explained that, had he been named for a grand-father, without an intervening Archibald P. father, he would have been Archibald P. Palmer II. His own firstborn son would be IV, he had decided, and would be called Quartus by the family. I had the feeling that Archie (that is what he asked us to call him) realized that Henry was after something more than a recitation of rules laid down by Emily Post, but for the moment that was all he seemed inclined to reveal.

The next development, however, was of a nature to reinforce Henry's initial impression of Archie's high social standing. Archie looked up from his trunk, the contents of which he had been transferring very methodi-cally to the chest of drawers, and, stretching, he asked whether it wasn't about time we had a Scotch. We both accepted. He rummaged some more in the trunk, removing several neatly folded sweaters, and brought to the surface a leather case holding silver tumblers and a martini shaker. There was whiskey in a silver hip flask he pulled out from a pocket of the jacket he was wearing. Each of these objects, leather and silver, was marked APP III. Do you fellows take yours neat, he asked, or with a splash of water? I said I would like water, whereupon he handed me the shaker and sug-gested that I get some. When I returned from the communal bathroom at the end of the hallway, Archie measured out the liquor and handed us the tumblers. We sipped while he continued to unpack. Striking items made their appearance, among them a pair of soft, knee-high leather boots which, he explained, had been his father's, and were essential in the jungle for protecting your ankles and calves from mosquitoes, and a black silk kimono with a furious dragon embroidered on its back, likewise appro-priated from his father, who had bought it in Hong Kong and occasion-ally wore it at home instead of a dinner jacket.

Turning to his more ordinary garments, he said, I don't know if you fel-lows like the clothes you've brought with you, but mine won't do. Mother had them made on the cheap. Fine wool and all that, but badly cut. The tailor is an ass.

Henry had been sipping his whiskey as if lost in thought, but hearing this he erupted.

I loathe every single thing I own, he shouted, I loathe it all.

As Henry realized immediately, Archie and I were startled. He apologized. This was the first time he had tasted hard liquor. It had gone to his head.

Think nothing of it, said Archie. He poured us more whiskey and returned to the subject of his mother's avarice. The garments that Archie called his Don Ramón outfits, which he intended to be rid of soon, had been ordered by her from a tailor in Panama City, conveniently near his father's current post in the Canal Zone. Archie pronounced "mother" as "mither," or else referred to his mother as Mater. His father he called Pater. This usage had its origin in the two years he had spent at a boarding school in Scotland, directly after the war, while his father was serving with a corps headquarters in Germany. That, he said, was the extent of his connection with the British Isles, not counting his father's distant forebears. His father was from Texas, born and bred there until he went to West Point. His "mither," half Mexican, was the daughter of an American petroleum engineer who had made his career south of the border, and a local girl. There's a drop of Aztec blood in Mater's family, he announced to us, but not so much that you'd notice. Her parents had sent her to college in San Antonio, and it was there that a newly minted Lieutenant Palmer, home on Christmas leave, met and courted her.

It was time for dinner when Archie at last declared himself satisfied with the organization of his closet and shelves. On our way to the Union, he put to Henry a series of questions I would have liked to ask.

By the way, he said, where do you come from?

Poland.

Oh, and where in Poland?

Krakow.

Great country, Poland, observed Archie, and when did you come to live here, just before the war?

No, in '47.

Really, and where were you during the war?

In Poland.

Your parents as well?

Yes.

He had given these laconic answers pleasantly enough, in an even voice. Nonetheless, Archie had apparently decided that he had gone far enough. He patted Henry on the shoulder and said that someday he would like to hear the whole story of his war experiences. With that we entered the Union, got silverware, which Henry and I, having already eaten there, had learned to put into the breast pocket of our jackets, and got into line to be served the main course.

II

It is said that no one who had not lived under the ancien régime could claim to know the sweetness of life. The dignified comfort of undergraduate life at Harvard in the early 1950s may have become equally unimaginable. There was nothing unusual in my sharing with two roommates a suite in one of the older dormitories composed of a living room I remember as large and three bedrooms, each capacious enough to hold a desk and a couple of chairs in addition to the bed. If we had happened to live in a newer dorm, our suite would have included a bathroom. In our building, the toilets and showers at the end of the hall on each floor were communal. Elderly Irish maids, affectionately referred to as biddies, cleaned and made beds every day except Sunday. For a small payment they also washed socks and underwear. A laundry company sponsored by the university took away sheets and pillowcases and brought them back washed and ironed; I am almost certain that the sight of an undergraduate using a Laundromat was as yet unknown. According to legend, biddies helped themselves to any liquor they found in an undergraduate's room. No such thing ever happened to me. On the other hand, I never failed to offer my biddy a drink, regardless of the hour, if I was there when she arrived. The one who looked after me when I was a junior had an avowed passion for curaçao, and I made sure I always had a bottle on hand. Upperclassmen lodged in houses inspired by the colleges of Oxford and Cambridge and built during the regime of President Lowell, before the war. One of the houses was named for him. Each had a dining room, common rooms, and a library, the quality of which varied from house to house, as well as a resident master and a complement of resident and nonresident tutors. The disappearance of waiters from the house dining room and the Freshman

Union, and the institution of cafeteria-style self-service, were recent and much lamented cost-cutting measures.

In terms of social cachet, no freshman dormitory was better than any other: the annual turnover of the population made it impossible for them to acquire an individual personality. At most, you weighed better plumbing in the new dorms against higher ceilings and bigger rooms in the older buildings. Houses were a different matter. Their characteristics and standing depended on the success of the master's efforts to screen undergraduate applicants and woo tutors of note. Two houses were recognized to be at the top of the social and intellectual pecking order, scholarship and academic success counting for almost everything in one, so that slovenly or eccentric grinds were tolerated if they were high achieving. The talent and accomplishments of many of the tutors and undergraduates in the other house were as great. However, an undergraduate's brilliance did not always assure admission. In his restless search for perfection, the master was guided by instinct, not unlike that by which the captains or *chefs de salle* at the Stork Club, "21," or Maxim's could determine at a glance whether a diner should be let in the door and at which table he should be seated. Like his counterparts in the world of elegant dining, the master aspired to the composition of a social bouquet worthy of a great salon, one that in this case needed to be refreshed each year. He yearned for undergraduates whose personal attributes and ancestry merited the appellation of "American orchids"—which he readily bestowed, for example, on every descendant of John Adams who was not known to have been publicly disgraced. Sons and grandsons of foreign celebrities had an almost equal claim on his imagination, above all when he found it possible to match and mix them to brilliant advantage, as when he pulled off the coup of putting together as roommates the grandsons of the greatest living French painter, a billionaire Eastern potentate, and the most famous of Irish writers. Against my better judgment, in the second semester of our freshman year, when it was necessary to attend to such matters, Henry, Archie, and I applied for admission to that house. I felt uneasy about the project and considered opposing it, but I would have had to disclose my reasons and in the end went along with it. My annoyance took the form of sulking. I hardly opened my mouth during the inter-

views, first with the senior tutor, Thomas Peabody, a medievalist whose
course I was taking, and then with the master. The latter, when we were
admitted into his study, was squirming in an oversize armchair and crossing and recrossing his legs, which he finally tucked under himself. His
questions were all addressed to Henry. He professed to be puzzled and
amused—those words were repeated more than once—by Henry's background, which he pronounced was unusual, as well as by his friendship
with Archie and me.

White, he finally asked, do you feel entirely at ease with your roommates?

Henry was ready for him.

I've never felt entirely at ease with anyone, he answered. I can't imagine
what that would be like.

How extraordinary, cried the master, exactly my own feelings! *Une âme
sœur!*

That outburst of sympathy notwithstanding, a couple of weeks later
Henry and Archie received a letter, signed by Peabody, informing them
that they had been assigned to a dormitory for upperclassmen who had
not been admitted to any of the houses. Of course, the letter continued,
Messrs. White and Palmer would be affiliated with the house for all other
purposes, in particular meals and the use of the library, and, if a suitable
vacancy became available by the beginning of their junior year, or even
later, they would be considered for it. If one took into account only the
quality of the lodgings, this result could be regarded as a blessing, the dormitory in question being a sumptuous edifice dating from the first decade
of the twentieth century. It contained no less sumptuous suites. However, people who cared about such things considered it a warehouse for
deviants. The blow was harsh. It could have made trouble between Henry
and Archie, because Henry believed that without him Archie would have
been accepted. Being a man of honor, Archie took the stand that they
were equally undesirable and could not be budged from it.

In the end, there was no trouble with me either. I had told them, before
all three of us applied to the house, that I would request a single suite, in
preference to sharing a suite with them. The reason I gave was that there
was no chance of our being given three bedrooms and a living room and

so continuing our current living arrangement. Their immediate response was that I could have the room with only one bed, and they would share, but I held firm, although I would have liked to be with Henry. Single suites were rare in the houses, and I had thought of myself as likely to end up in a dormitory for rejects, living alone. I was astonished to be told by Peabody that a junior who had been living in a single suite was withdrawing from the college and that I was welcome to take his place.

The constraints of our cosseted college existence may seem equally unimaginable. They were premised on a tacit conviction that one goal of higher education was to delay sexual activity of the young by encouraging participation in arduous sports and limiting opportunities for private contacts between the sexes. Thus, only male undergraduates lived in the Harvard College dormitories and houses. There were, in fact, no female students at the college, but a formula known as coinstruction installed a small female minority of Radcliffe girls in all courses except astronomy and physical education. The former called for stargazing expeditions that might have afforded opportunities for misconduct. As for the latter, the presence of girls in a men's sports facility was unthinkable. That Radcliffe students were girls, while we were men, was a principle of diction I never heard challenged. Strict regulations, known as parietal rules, governed visits by the other sex to Harvard dormitories and houses. Girls' dormitory rooms were always off-limits; however, you could wait for your date in the ground floor sitting room of her dormitory, a space that I later realized weirdly resembled parlors at the better sort of funeral homes. During our freshman year, girls were allowed in men's dormitories between four and seven in the afternoon; in the years that followed, the hours were gradually lengthened until, by the time I was a senior, on Saturdays—and perhaps Fridays as well—girls were not required to leave before eleven. On the stroke of that hour, couples streamed out of the houses and dormitories with haggard faces and hair wet from the shower, evidence of amatory exertions followed by attention to personal hygiene. Compliance with the rules required also that girls be signed in and signed out on a list maintained by the resident proctor of the dormitory or by the porter of the house. They were to be entertained in the living room of the suite, with the door to the hallway left ajar, so that a proctor or a tutor could, if so inclined, peek in and satisfy himself that nothing more intimate than conversation and its necessary adjuncts, smoking and drinking, could be discerned.

Ever since I first met Henry and Archie, I had marveled—no less I suppose than the cagey housemaster—at the administrative process that, plucking us out from a class of some thousand freshmen, had made us roommates. Were we the last three members of our class for whom lodging had to be found, or were the rooms we were given the only remaining unassigned accommodations? Were such matters settled by a roll of dice on the crimson carpet lining the floor of some assistant dean's office? According to my roommates, neither of them had filled out the college form asking one's preferences with regard to roommates. I had completed and mailed it on time in the envelope provided by the administration, but the only wish I stated was against living with alumni of any of the New England prep schools and in favor of men from other parts of the country. A good half of the class must have met those criteria. I gave as a reason my desire to get to know people of different backgrounds. This was true as far as it went. I had, however, a more urgent, unexpressed motive, which was to stay clear of undergraduates with roots in my native Berkshires and anyone else possibly acquainted with my parents or their reputation. I must have realized that the barrier I hoped to erect was porous. Indeed, had I been more determined, I would have gone to a college far away, perhaps on the West Coast. My parents wouldn't have offered much resistance, although they considered Harvard a feather in their cap. And I certainly wouldn't have trusted the discretion of the one member of my class, George Standish, the son of my father's first cousin, who presumably knew all that I wished to conceal. My parents had told me that he was applying to the college; in due time, they also told me that he had been accepted. My father had even hinted, rather diffidently, that I might propose to George that we room together. I gave him an impudent stare and said that I wasn't eager to be snubbed. Besides, I added, George would have made other arrangements long since. I was right about the second point: George's three freshman-year roommates had all been at school with him and had all been cut from the same estimable bolt of cloth as he.

As to George's discretion, he had given me no cause to judge it one way or the other. Our acquaintance was too slight. Had I been older and more experienced, I might have taken comfort in the fundamental lack of curiosity of most people about the lives of others. I would also have realized that the gossip about my parents was banal and, in all probability, of little interest, except to people who already knew them and their dreary story. No one else of our age would want to hear scuttlebutt about someone like my father, a pleasant enough fellow of good family who had lost or pissed away most of his money, held down a trust officer's job at a small bank in an ugly one-industry town, lived with his wife and only son in an ancestral house too grand for his circumstances, drove an Oldsmobile to work, and played unremarkable golf at the country club. Was his case made any more piquant by the fact that the bank was run by his rich and upstanding first cousin and had been founded by his family, which still owned it? Being the younger cousin's employee was a torment for my father, who, had he been a stronger and less indolent man, might have moved on. But that was not in his nature, and he had stayed. The rest of the stuff was tawdry and equally commonplace, consisting of such particulars as my father's and mother's intake of martinis before lunch and dinner and Scotch and soda after dinner (which consumption was impressive even in their circle), and the rumors of my mother's heavy flirtations or worse with two high-living lushes, Gus Williams, the insurance broker, and Tim Clark, the real estate agent with a distinguished war record. That there might be other couples in Berkshire County with similar ill-kept secrets, and that I thought I could identify two or three of them, was cold comfort, and I do not find unreasonable my revulsion at the thought that a quirk in the admissions process—like the one that had thrown me together with Henry and Archie—could have as easily paired me with someone who might have made me feel his pity or contempt. There was also a new set of circumstances that had rocked me. When I came home for the Easter break during my last year at school, my admission to Harvard College having already become generally known, my parents told me that Mr. Hibble, the lawyer who handled most legal matters for the bank, had asked to see me at his office without them, and that I had better go. I knew Mr. Hibble from the club as a choleric tennis player. My father, with whom he naturally had many contacts, regularly referred to him as a stuffy dunderhead, but that was of no great importance to me. I expected my father to have a low opinion of anyone more successful and better paid than he, particularly if his nose was rubbed with any frequency in the dunderhead's professional accomplishments, real or not. My curiosity about the meaning of this summons, and my parents' categorical endorsement of it, was considerable. Although I hadn't gotten into trouble at school and hadn't had any run-ins with the town police that might require a lawyer's assistance, I didn't think that anything good could come of the meeting.

I appeared at Mr. Hibble's office at the appointed hour and heard him say, after prefatory twaddle about my hard work and success, that he was the trustee of a trust set up by the late Mr. Horace Standish, the head of the family and my grandfather's brother, and, that as such, he had concluded that the time had come to inform me that both my tuition and expenses at college would be paid by the trust, the trust having also paid for the boarding school I had attended. He had more to tell me. I was entitled to distributions from the income of the trust—a substantial amount but one that should not relieve me of the need to earn a living. That limitation was, to his way of thinking, all to the good. In emergencies and for good cause, I might even have access to the capital. I had not been made privy to the trust's existence and terms sooner, he continued, because in his judgment I was too young. Then he dropped the bomb: the purpose of the trust, and the reason for Mr. Standish's generosity, had been to make it financially prudent, indeed possible, for my parents to adopt me when it became clear that they were unable to have children of their own. Mr. Hibble had not used the word "wastrel" in reference to my father and money, but the implication hung in the air like so much smoke from his cigar. The adoption took place at birth, he added, and it had been a blessing for my parents as well as for me. When I recovered my breath, I asked whether he knew whose child I was. He replied that no one knew. At the time, these matters were done in such a way that absolute secrecy was preserved. Forever.

I drove home slowly. As it was the end of the afternoon, I knew that my parents would both be waiting for me, drinks in hand. My father offered me one as well, a gin and tonic, which I accepted. Mother cried, of course. They also offered assurances of their love, which I said were unnecessary. That was the truth. Even when I was most ashamed of them, I recognized that somehow, from beyond the river of booze, they tried their best with me, my mother in her goofy, eyelash-batting way, my father, as in all things, lazy and stiff. One could imagine that very early he had been given an injection of Novocain good for a lifetime. He said that we should carry on as before; we need never again talk about the adoption. Only Mr. Hibble was in on it; no one knew who my other parents could be—he choked a little on that one—and your mother, he said, pointing at her lest I be confused, had taken steps to fool everyone, the family included. How much of this they believed, I couldn't say. Old Mr. Standish, my benefactor, had pulled all the strings. What were the limits of his discretion? Or the discretion of my real parents, if they had been told or had figured out to whom they were handing over their child?

Mr. Hibble's revelations had knocked me for a loop. But a suspect feeling of elation followed the initial shock: knowing there was no biological connection between those two and me was irrepressibly a reason to rejoice. I speculated wildly about whose child I really was. It had to be someone for whom old Mr. Standish had felt responsible. Who that was I could not imagine with my scant knowledge of the family history and ramifications, but various hypotheses might explain my marked resemblance to my father and the other Standishes: my Standish grandfather who died when I was little but whose photographs I had studied; my benefactor, Horace Standish, who died a few years later; his son Jack who ran the bank; and finally my classmate George, Cousin Jack's only son. That resemblance might in itself furnish an additional explanation of my father's having been allowed to hang on to his job at the bank through thick and thin, although there was in addition always the fundamental imperative: a Standish didn't fire a Standish or publicly humiliate him. Then the question was who knew, and how much was known. The more I thought about it, the less I could believe that there had been no talk about my origins. Things must have been said within the family, particularly if, as I speculated without any basis, the trust could not have remained entirely concealed when old Mr. Standish died and his heirs read his will. Worse yet, in the locker room at the club I had heard Mr. Hibble discuss cases he was handling. He was not one to keep his mouth shut. No one had ever made a remark to me hinting that I was some sort of foundling. That could, however, be ascribed to the generally good manners of the Standish family and most of the people we knew. I wasn't sure how much I cared. We had read that year, in my advanced English class, both *The Tempest* and *King Lear.* Confused notions of the blessings and curses of nature as contrasted with nurture, and of bastardy, swirled in my head without resolution. Sometimes I romanticized my new situation. But my dominant desire was for distance and anonymity. I discovered that it was not too late to sign up for a program that would send me to France for the summer. My parents agreed to it without protest, as did Mr. Hibble, when I telephoned to ask whether the trust would provide the financing. Then, once I got to college, I would strive to keep the Berkshire furies at bay.

III

As a rule, Henry spoke with his mother on the telephone three times a week. It was up to him to call, collect. If she grew impatient, she would make the call herself. I knew all about this because I almost always worked in my room rather than the library, and, unless the radio in the living room was turned up loud, I couldn't help overhearing snippets of their conversations. It was thus that I first deduced that there was such a rule. Its nature was later disclosed to me by Mrs. White in the course of many chats when I answered the phone and was obliged to say that Henry was out. Finally, Henry told me about it himself.

I provided the reason for his absence according to the hour: he's at the library, or he went to dinner early, these having proved to be the most likely to be accepted with something like good humor. If by misfortune I admitted that I didn't know where he was or that he had gone to the movies or was out on a date, she would give me the third degree. Once, in the course of a particularly rough interrogation, I heard myself say that I was Henry's roommate, not his keeper. To my astonishment, the crack, which I instantly regretted, didn't slow her down. Perhaps she didn't get it. However, if I was careful and gave the right answer, the conversation was likely to follow a boring but nonmenacing pattern. She would tell me how many hours or days had passed since she had last heard from her only son and implore me to remind Henry that he still had parents who loved him and were anxious about him. Something along the lines of "Aren't your parents dying of worry if you don't call?" was her customary conclusion. I never confessed that, on the contrary, my own mother and father, assuming that I caught them at home on an evening when they were sober, might panic at the sound of my voice, unless I made it clear at once that I was not telephoning in order to report a catastrophe. After I had told them I just wanted to say hello, they might either laugh in disbelief or advise me to go to the infirmary and have my temperature taken.

Perhaps on account of certain oddities of her pronunciation and diction, I was charmed by her occasional efforts to be girlish—so different from my mother's—and by her assumption that we were allies in the struggle to keep her son's affections. She flirted with me, and before long we became telephone friends. She would ask about my parents and my studies, sometimes extending her inquiries to include Archie, with whom her contacts were rare, since he was seldom in the room when she telephoned, and, when he happened to be there, hardly ever picked up the receiver. He claimed that he was bad at taking messages. His own parents, like mine, never called, and he preferred to have his other calls filtered by me. Sometimes Mrs. White threw in a little compliment. For instance, she would say that it was wonderful how I was at my desk all the time, doing my homework. She addressed me as Mr. Roommate, and, although I begged her to call me Sam, she stuck to it.

I wondered what Henry thought of the bare trickle of communication between his roommates and their respective parents. That he had noticed how different our habits were from his was certain; just as he had warned me, he noticed everything. But did he disapprove? Did he take it as a sign that our parents took little interest in us, or that we were callously neglecting our filial duties? I didn't expect any overt disapproval; he was too polite for that. The subject came up, however, one evening, after a movie. He asked point-blank whether I called my parents at hours when he wasn't in the room, or from a pay phone. Otherwise, it would seem that my parents and I were hardly ever in touch. The same question had occurred to him about Archie and his parents. The complications of my home life were what they were, and I wasn't about to explain them to Henry. Instead I told him a half-truth. I said it was probably a matter of habit. I had been sent to boarding school at thirteen, and my parents and I had gotten used to my being away from home. They didn't worry about me.

He interjected: I've never been away from my mother, not until I came here.

I said, My deal is different from yours, that's all. I do call home, but only if something important comes up.

But that means that you've lost touch with your parents.

I replied that I did write to them from time to time, and that my mother wrote to me fairly often with Berkshire news. Henry acknowledged having seen the lavender envelopes addressed in my mother's schoolgirl script, with her return address invariably appearing in the upper-left-hand corner. And I do telephone, I continued, I called her on her birthday only last week.

He returned to relations among parents and sons abruptly the next day, saying that he was obliged to write twice a week and call every two days. I confessed that his mother had already told me about the calls. But it was as though he had not heard me.

If I don't make that call or write that letter, he continued, she makes scenes. She yells at me and yells at my father, because she claims that he isn't strict enough with me. Then he gets pains in his chest and tells her she is driving him to his grave, and she calls to let me have it for making my father sick and breaking up their marriage. The angina is the worst part. I don't want to be responsible for a heart attack. So I write and call, whether or not I feel like it, and whether or not I have anything to say.

Those are difficult conversations, he added after a pause. They're enough to make you hate the telephone.

As an embarrassed auditor of many of them, I couldn't disagree. In a burst of frankness, I told him that sometimes they sounded like quarrels. Henry didn't take offense; he laughed.

All the same, he said, I have to do it. Wondering whether there might be a two-way flow of anxiety in the White family, I asked whether he worried about his parents when he was late making one of those calls.

No, he replied, I don't, although perhaps I should, because of my father. It's really my mother who's a problem. My father doesn't think about me from one end of the week to the other, except when he wishes I were there to chauffeur him or run errands. And of course during the scenes my mother makes about me. She claims that the only reason she stayed with him after the war was that she didn't want to lose me and now she's lost me anyway and somehow that's my father's fault.

He laughed again. I bet he wishes he had told her to shove off and take her precious son with her! Actually, that's unfair. I know he loves me in his own way, whatever that means, but he has other things on his mind. Such as his business and money, and how to tiptoe around my mother. But he doesn't get worked up about me. That's her specialty. I think she really believes that the only way to show love is by imagining catastrophes. She'll say, I can see it: you've been hit by a bus, you've fallen down the stairs and broken your back, your appendix has burst and you're in unbearable pain. I can already see them carrying you away. That's not love; it's some disastrous mutation, the worst form of selfishness.

You've got to see my mother's worrying for what it is, he continued, undeterred by my silence. Some part of it is genuine, but mostly she just wants me to toe the line. She uses the same technique on my father, but that's a whole different story. For instance, if I don't call because I forgot or couldn't bring myself to do it—which does happen—she can shift the blame to me for everything that has gone wrong over there in Brooklyn. She couldn't cook dinner because she was so worried; she dropped the Rosenthal platter on the kitchen floor because she was so nervous; my father had to take his nitroglycerin because right away he noticed the state she was in; she has spent all her time and energy on me, she hasn't been able to make friends. This can go on and on. She worries about my father's angina and weak heart but not enough to go easy on him. Somehow, I'm not made like them: I worry when I have a problem. Then I do something about it. My mother claims I am heartless. Sometimes, when I want to needle them, I tell them they're right, I have no heart and therefore no pains in the chest. You should hear them afterward. The first punitive measure is to stop my allowance. They send it weekly, so it's easier to clamp down, although the ostensible reason is that if they sent it in advance, for instance monthly, I would spend it all in two days. Of course, at a certain point after a big row I begin to feel bad. I want to make up. That means I have to apologize in at least ten different ways. If the transgression is grave, I have to apologize in writing. There is no such thing as taking in the prodigal son without first raking him over the coals.

Henry laughed at his own joke; he had an irritating tendency to do that. In any event, I disliked his tirades and wondered how much this one owed to Dostoyevsky. We were both reading *The Brothers Karamazov,* and Henry had decided that it contained the answers to all the great questions that perplexed him.

My mother had given me a Sheffield tea set she had inherited a couple years ago from her aunt Kitty and some cups and saucers. The electric hot plate and the kettle I had bought on my own initiative. When the tea was ready, we drank in silence until I broke it asking why, if the telephone calls were such a torment, he didn't tell his parents they could save money by limiting the calls to one a week.

That wouldn't work, he said. My father counts every penny, but hanging on to me is a matter of life and death for my mother, so they consider the high telephone bills another inevitable consequence of having allowed me to go to Harvard. You see, they're in a bind. They realize that they couldn't really force me to decline admission on a full scholarship. In fact, it's something they can brag about. But at the same time they can't get over my having left home. They see it as an outrage. He helped himself to another cup of tea and then asked: Did your parents object when you said you wanted to go away to college?

I said they had no practical choice. Even if I had chosen one of the two colleges that were closer to Lenox, I would have still been going away.

He nodded. That was pretty much what Archie had told him about his own case, except that Archie's situation was special anyway, since the Palmers lived on an army base and might be obliged to move from wherever they were on very short notice. By the way, he added, the reason my parents take it so hard is that they think I wanted to come to this place mainly to get away from them. For instance, if I had gone to Columbia, which is in the city and has a very good reputation, I could have lived at home. Even if I had lived in a dormitory, I could have taken the subway home every weekend. They'd have had me tethered. With Harvard, there is no way I can be in Brooklyn every weekend. Ergo, I've rejected them and must atone. But for what and how? That's not a question I have put, but I know what they want: obedience. Obedience in every other respect. That's what torture by the telephone is about, not to mention the rest of the stuff that you don't even know.

I couldn't help telling Henry that he was describing a Hollywood cliché. The only son packs his bags and heads for State U, four hundred miles away. The girl next door has hysterics; the mother weeps but tries hard to be brave; the father makes a stern face and secretly wipes away a tear. Then the kid becomes the captain of the football team. After graduation he marries the girl, all the fraternity brothers show up at the wedding, and everybody lives happily ever after.

Your story, I said, is just a variation on the basic plot, except that you can't throw a long pass. Any kind of pass!

Sure, Henry answered, that's very funny, but we aren't an American family with an American sense of humor. I can tell you that no matter how often my mother goes to the movies and laughs at clichés like that, she will never accept that any such thing should happen to her. Not after everything she's been through, everything she has seen, everything she has lost. Those nice women in the movies have other children and family—parents, sisters, and brothers—and friends, old friends, to talk to and spend time with. Or they have jobs. My mother hasn't got any of that. Except for my father and me, they've all been killed. She says she doesn't have a job because she has no skills. Nobody had ever expected her to work so she never learned to do anything. I don't really believe that. If she really wanted she could be learning how to do something useful right now, but that would mean risking failure, and that's a risk she will not take. My father does work hard all day, and he isn't the most cheerful man in the world. The result is that I'm my mother's only hobby. I'm also one of the better subjects for their quarrels: It's your fault he is like that, no it's yours, he learned it from you, no, it's all those years he spent with you, no, sorry, he's the portrait of your father, and on and on. Certainly, they can fight over me even if I am in Cambridge, but why put on a show with no audience? Besides which, when I also lose my temper, the brawl becomes a world championship event.

He lost me when he added, Please don't misunderstand me. They love me, and I love them.

I managed not to smile and told him I was certain he did.

There was another lengthy silence. When he spoke again he said, Look, leaving home, isn't that a metaphor for leaving the God of your fathers? My mother has latched on to the great metaphorical sense of my act. Brilliant, isn't it? Even she knows that there is a limit to how long they can beat me over the head just for going away to the best college in the country, so she has put my abandonment of my parents on a loftier plane. My father has joined in. They say that my real purpose in leaving them was to stop being a Jew, or anyway to pass as a Gentile, which is something I can't manage with them nearby. So for me, success in denying that I'm a Jew hinges on shutting them out of my life. It's a terrifying interpretation, but they really believe it. He noticed that my eyes were closing from fatigue and said, I'm sorry to have talked your ear off. The truth is that I started this conversation only to be able to say that I envy you. I wish my parents would leave me alone. Why can't they be like your parents? What would be wrong with that? It hasn't done you any harm.

I didn't answer his question. I was realizing that, even if you put aside their peculiarities, my parents were a species with which he had no familiarity. Just as it seemed I had only the most limited understanding of his circumstances. There was no hurry, I thought, he'll have lots of time to learn about me and my kind. Especially if our friendship lasts. I had begun to think that it might. So I said goodnight, and we went to bed.

WHETHER HENRY WAS A JEW was a question Archie and I had discussed more than once without reaching a definite conclusion. Archie agreed with me that the family's having been in Poland during the war was a reason to suppose that he wasn't. We both believed that the Germans had killed all Polish Jews. The name White gave no clue, because it must have been changed. But changed from what? We also agreed that Henry didn't look like a Jew. His address in Brooklyn pointed the other way. Brooklyn, Archie said, was where all the New York Jews lived. That left the fact that Henry was no friendlier with the three known Jews in our dormitory than with anyone else. According to Archie, that meant nothing. Or one could take it as a sign that Henry wanted to pass. At the time that seemed to me a reasonable conclusion. However, now that Henry had told me that he was a Jew I couldn't imagine that in similar circumstances he would be less forthright with Archie. Didn't that blow out of the water the theory that he was trying to pass? It did occur to me that Henry had created the occasion for this particular confession. Looked at in a certain way, it was a piece of stagecraft. He had certainly avoided saying that he was Jewish when Archie grilled him about his background that day we met. He had stopped short of a lie, but what had his intention been?

The only Jew I had known for a long time and thought I knew well was our dentist in Pittsfield, a nice man who had been taking care of my teeth since my first cavity and who had never hurt or scared me. He had a big, richly stocked aquarium in his office, so cleverly placed that you could watch the fish while he drilled, and I think that at one point I was so interested in them that I looked forward to my appointments. I was very much aware of the Jewish family that owned the big Pittsfield department store. Two of the grandchildren, both a couple of grades behind me, had gone to the same country day school as I in Lenox. My parents didn't know their parents or grandparents, probably because they didn't belong to the country club. But even if they had belonged, my mother and father would have kept a respectful distance from them, as they normally would in the case of a much richer or grander member of the club with whom they didn't have a personal connection. It would have been up to the Kaufmanns to make the first move. There were Jewish musicians in the Boston Symphony Orchestra, which performed in the summer at Tanglewood, but I had not had an opportunity to meet any of them. We had no Jewish neighbors. To my knowledge, there weren't any Jews working at the bank. The position of Jews at my boarding school was, by contrast, well established. There were several New York Jews—elegant and rich—among the students, the most notable being the sons of a family of bankers. Members of that family had been coming to the school since the 1920s, and both the infirmary and the science building bore the family name. As it happened, there was no von Stein in my form, which was probably the reason that out of my form I alone made it to Harvard. According to school legend, every von Stein had a guaranteed berth.

For more than a year, the core of my general information about Jews and their problems had come from the film *Gentleman's Agreement*. My mother, who never missed a movie with Gregory Peck, took me to see it in Pittsfield during a school break. My father never went. The next day I borrowed from Womrath's the novel on which the movie was based. The way Jews were treated, the cowardice of practically everyone whom the Gregory Peck character confronted once he began telling people that he was a Jew, it all disgusted me. For reasons unrelated to Jews, I was envious of Gregory Peck, because his simple, affectionate, and courageous mother in the film was exactly the kind of mother I would have liked, and I was envious of his little son, because I wished I had a father like Gregory Peck. I asked my mother whether that was really how Jews were treated. She said she had no personal experience with Jews. Then, during the second semester of my last year at school, in the modern history course, we took up the Germans' slaughter of Jews during the war. The history master, Mr. Ticknor, brought to the classroom a book of photographs taken by American soldiers who had liberated concentration camps, as well as photographs taken by German soldiers in the Warsaw Ghetto and elsewhere in Poland and Russia. This can't have been the first inkling I had of these matters. But what I had read in magazines, or heard in snatches of conversations, apparently had not sunk in. After Mr. Ticknor's course I had to agree with him that mistreatment of American Jews by Americans was a disgrace. As he saw it, Germans had been able to set about exterminating Jews in Europe only because neither they nor the local populations thought Jews were human. It followed that we all had to fight against anti-Semitism. On an impulse unusual in our relations, during a weekend I was spending at home I told my parents about Mr. Ticknor and his views. It was before the Easter vacation, and therefore before my interview with Mr. Hibble. They didn't say Mr. Ticknor was wrong. I wasn't even sure that they were paying attention. However, on my next visit, while my father and I were driving to the club, he observed apropos of nothing that there was no way you could make people love one another. Many people plain didn't like Jews and didn't want them around. Even if they were well behaved and respectable. The same went for Negroes and Catholics, especially Irish and Italian Catholics. For instance, Gummy—the nickname of the club's president, Mr. Gifford Upton Morris—had sworn that he would never allow a Jew to set foot in the club. Of course, no Jew worthy of being invited to the club would want to offend by his presence the president and not a few of the members. For that matter, my father continued, he didn't think a Jew could get a job at the bank or a management position at the General Electric plant in Pittsfield, and certainly not at the big paper mill in Dalton. I asked whether he thought that was fair. He shrugged and pointed out that violence—Germans killing Jews or Southerners lynching Negroes—was one thing, but being allowed to choose with whom you played golf or worked was another. Besides, he added, there are lots of Jews who hire only Jews and prefer to do business with their own kind. In reply, I too shrugged. There was no use arguing with my parents about anything serious. Their minds were on other things. And much as I would have liked to tell him he was full of it, there was something to be said for his views, especially if the Jew was obnoxious. It seemed that many were. Henry was anything but. If I could get past the problem of whether I could in good conscience suggest that he visit me in Lenox when I knew that his presence wouldn't be universally welcomed if the truth were revealed, and if I could be sure that my parents weren't going to have a big row while he was there, it would be a fine project to bring him to the club and introduce him to Gummy. Henry didn't play tennis, but he could hang around the pool, provided he had suitable swimming trunks. Someone at school had told me that Jews wore bathing suits that were like jockey shorts to show off their dicks and balls.

So far as Henry's wanting to pass was concerned, although he had come clean with me, I thought that probably he preferred to have other people think he was a Gentile. That was his business. I didn't admire the impulse but certainly wouldn't hold it against him. I doubted that Archie would either. How Henry would manage it, ducking answers about his accent and his past without some serious lies, was another matter, but that too was his business. It occurred to me in this connection that I was doing a bit of passing myself. What else was it when I let people take me for my parents' son, with all the advantages that being a Standish instead of a Nowak or a Mahoney entailed? True, the situations were different. Standish was my name, and I had no other. Still, to claim that Henry and I were comrades in arms wasn't much of a stretch.

It was probably a week later, over dinner at the Freshman Union, that we returned to what Henry called his Jewism. We had been able to find a table for two, and I felt that we could talk freely about these very personal matters. Enough so for me to ask him whether his parents were right. Was he trying to get away from being a Jew?

There is no such thing, he answered. You are born a Jew and you die a Jew. Hitler proved it.

I said that wasn't true. Jews converted—I cited the example of the New York Jews at my school, who I believed had converted. Anyway, they came to chapel. Or perhaps it was their parents or grandparents who had converted.

You see—he laughed—they might as well not have bothered. You think they're Jews anyway.

He wasn't wrong. I told him that there was a less direct approach. To be precise, right after we met him, Archie and I had wondered whether he was trying to pass. Henry got red in the face, and I feared that our conversations, and perhaps our friendship, were coming to an end. But he answered me very calmly. It's a fact, he said, that I derive no benefit from being Jewish, or any pleasure. It almost got my parents and me killed. A fact that doesn't inspire me to believe in God. It makes me deny him and wish that I weren't one of the chosen, that I hadn't been thrust at birth into this monstrous trap. All the same, so long as there are people who care whether I am a Jew pretending to be a Gentile, I have to remain a Jew, even though inside I feel no more Jewish than a smoked ham. If the question is asked, I'm obliged to say that I'm a Jew—unless the consequence is ending up in a concentration camp or dead. I consider it a debt of honor, an odd one for someone like me, who doesn't believe he owes anything to anybody. Otherwise I've no intention of making a show of being Jewish.

I wasn't sure I understood and must have looked perplexed.

I'll give you an example, he said. When you, Archie, and I met I didn't think I had a duty to say, Hello, hello, I'm Henry White, a Jew. Or to wear a yellow star. I did that, in Krakow.

I told him that was really absurd.

Is it really? What would it have taken for you and Archie not to suspect me of trying to pass? If not a yellow star, then a yarmulke or side locks?

Should I have a business card that says on it "Jew"? Or Untermensch—that's German for subhuman. Incidentally, most of the fights I have with my parents now are about what I'm doing to show that I am a Jew. When I told them about you and Archie, the first thing my mother asked was, Why don't you have Jewish roommates? I said that I hadn't picked you; it just happened. That didn't satisfy her. She said, You could have asked to room with someone Jewish. Sure, I replied, but I didn't, and why should I? I don't think you want to hear the response to that crack. Her next line of attack was: Do they know you are Jewish? I said I wasn't sure, but if they're intelligent enough to be at Harvard they should be able to figure it out, and if they can't, all they have to do is ask me. You want to hear my mother's reply? She said that maybe they're too polite. That really broke me up and I reminded her that you, and maybe Archie as well, have spoken on the telephone with her and my father many times. Does she think that having heard them you have concluded we had come over on the *Mayflower*? Then, I confess, I turned cruel. I said that if she and my father had wanted to leave no doubt that we were Jews, they shouldn't have changed our name. If it were still Weiss, you'd have to be a total moron to think we weren't Jews. Yes, she and Father changed our name after we came here, as quickly as they could. The official reason is that White is an accurate English translation, and everybody knows how to spell it. That's obvious nonsense; there is nothing unusual about Weiss, certainly not in New York. But to answer your interesting question, no, I'm not trying to pass, but I know that some people don't immediately think that I'm Jewish, and I do nothing to disabuse them. Part of it is my name; part of it is that I don't look especially Jewish. But the false impression usually doesn't last long. Because of my accent, mostly they ask where I come from, as Archie did. When I say I'm from Poland, and that I was there during the war, those who have an idea of what went on there may well say to themselves, He can't be Jewish; otherwise, he'd be dead. He must be a regular Catholic Pole who changed his name from something like Wilczuk, and they leave it at that. That's when I wish I were called Weiss or, better yet, Cohen or Levin. There would be no such confusion. People couldn't say I was trying to pull the wool over their eyes. The subject wouldn't have to be discussed. But the people who get fooled are a minority. Either they aren't curious or they don't want to seem nosy. A regular American will follow up with something along the line of: How did you survive? Then the fat is in the fire. In case you're interested, I knew I wasn't fooling you and Archie, and I wasn't trying. That you thought I was is another matter. It hurts. But I don't blame you.

He looked downcast. It's all right, Henry, I told him. There is no problem between you and me. Or between you and Archie. I'm sure of that.

He brightened at that, and we talked about courses and movies until the end of the meal and as we walked through the Yard to the dormitory. Once we were in our living room, however, he said he wanted to continue the conversation we had begun.

You've let the genie out of the bottle, he told me. You might as well know, he continued, that my mother isn't only interested in whether you or Archie or anyone else I know realizes that I'm a Jew, and, if so, how they found out. Keeping me from leaving home—literally or metaphorically—is a more complicated undertaking. You see, they're good parents in their own way. They want me to have a roof over my head and nice clothes, provided my mother picks them. And, of course, an excellent education. They're willing to make financial sacrifices for that, but so far none has been needed. High school was free, and I have a scholarship here. Naturally they want me to succeed, and they want me to have all the right opportunities. But there is a limit. I'm not supposed to fly too high. Dickens might have said I mustn't try to rise above my station. That's a big unarticulated anxiety. Partly it's prudence. We lost everything in the war, and they don't want me to crash. They're always worried about money, even now that my father is doing well in business. I understand that. The other part is the fear that if I fly high and remain up there in the higher sphere, that too will tempt me to leave them. So, the other big issue about you and Archie is whether you're rich. If you are, maybe I shouldn't be spending so much time with you, and maybe you shouldn't be my best friends. You might give me big ideas and teach me bad habits. I've told them that I don't think an army colonel makes as much as my father, and that you don't strike me as rich, though I'm only guessing. Just the same, you might as well know it: in White family shorthand the two of you are Henry's rich Gentile friends.

Stop, I said. I can tell you right now that my parents aren't rich though they certainly wish they were.

He examined me with an air I took to be skeptical. My mother wouldn't necessarily believe you. By the way, she thinks you're very polite in a standoffish Gentile way. Lukewarm, she calls it.

I didn't know what to say or whether I should say anything. Henry had gotten very flushed and was staring at me. Finding the silence uncomfortable, I told him that I liked my conversations with his mother.

Bullshit, he replied. How could you?

I got up from my armchair and went to the toilet. When I returned he said, Forgive me, I am sorry I got so worked up. Let me try to explain. The current refrain is why don't I seek out my own kind instead of hanging out with you and Archie and God knows what other high-society Gentiles. For instance, there are some nice services in Boston I could go to on Friday evenings. One of my father's big customers has a son at Tufts who attends. Go meet him, stay for dinner, and get to know nice Jewish girls. I say to my parents that I've never gone to Friday services in my life before, and I don't see why I should start now, in Boston. You should understand that I don't think for one minute that my father believes in God. On the other hand with his angina he doesn't want to say he doesn't and take chances on what happens after he's dead. Also, both he and my mother are one hundred percent conventional. Some of my father's customers go to a synagogue not far from us. So he goes too, on High Holidays, and he and my mother fast on Yom Kippur. To be more precise, they pretend to each other that they're fasting. I've had to go to the synagogue with my father. Each of those expeditions was humiliating. There I was, not because I believed but because I had been dragged. I wouldn't mind so much if my parents were religious. But my mother, who makes the most fuss, has no religion, unless you accept as a religion the myth about how it was before the war when we were a family of good Jews. I have no memories of our having been good Jews at home in Krakow. Perhaps the war has crowded them out. It doesn't matter: as I keep telling them, if they had wanted me to be observant, they would have had to be sincerely religious and observant themselves and have provided me with that Jewish home she's always carrying on about. They aren't and they didn't: I'm being badgered to go through the motions of a ritual I don't believe in. I'll leave that sort of stuff to the Grand Inquisitor.

The mention of the Karamazovs, whose appearances in his conversation were frequent, cracked me up. All right, he said, what I really mean, and what I tell them when I'm really worked up, is that I can't seek out my own kind because I don't know who they are. Maybe there are no such people. I'm not sure that I'm like anybody else. I won't pretend that I am.

For a moment I pondered the possibility that he was trying to say he might be queer. I didn't think he was—not just because he was so obviously attracted to girls. I just didn't think so. At the same time I was reminded once more that he really was a good deal like me, one difference being that his problems were more obvious and could be blamed mostly on being Jewish.

So what do you intend to do about finding out? I asked.

Nothing, he said. Everything. I am going to remake myself in the image I carry inside me.

What that image might be and how it fit with Poland and the scars the war had left were a mystery. My attempts to probe, whether out of curiosity or compassion, got me only so far. The previous day when, having screwed up my courage, I asked him to tell me something about how he and his parents had survived the war was a good example. He had stared at me and said quietly, A nice lady hid my mother and me. A nice man hid my father.

IV

HENRY'S *non serviam* did not stand in the way of more conventional attempts at transformation. His principal mentor and accomplice was Archie. Archie's disgust with the efforts of his mother's tailor in Panama City endured unabated, as did his conviction that they gave him the "Don Ramón look." All I need, he said, is a pencil-line mustache. A solution to Archie's and Henry's sartorial problems emerged when Archie discovered Keezer's, a Cambridge establishment rich in university tradition, located in the town-and-gown no-man's-land between Prescott Street and Central Square. One could buy there on the cheap, among many other props required for an undergraduate's social ascension, well-cut secondhand tweeds, dinner jackets, and morning coats, often in fine condition. The Keezer brothers' main suppliers were widows of newly deceased faculty members and alumni. A customer was welcome to trade in his own clothes, which is what Archie did with the Panamanian tailor's creations. Whatever his view of their cut, the quality was so high that at the end of the transaction Archie owed Keezer's nothing. It was his plan that Henry engage in the same sort of exchange; his clothes, although off the rack, were also of good quality. Unexpectedly, Henry balked.

I can't, he said. When I go home, my mother will expect me to wear the clothes she bought for me. I'll never hear the end of it if I tell her they've been sold.

They were at an impasse; without a substantial trade-in credit, Henry couldn't pay for what Archie had picked out for him. Unwilling to accept defeat, he made Henry a loan, not a large sum, to be repaid over the balance of the school year. They invited me to the final fitting, Keezer's being expert at even the most improbable alterations. Archie had done well. If clothes made the man, Henry now could pass for an undergraduate who had been to one of the right schools and knew how to dress.

The loan was a sign that Archie was going through one of his flush periods. They didn't last long, but while they did, a good deal of cash was spent at the liquor store on Mount Auburn Street and at Henri IV, a French restaurant on Winthrop Street in vogue among the faculty and more affluent students as well as parents of undergraduates in Cambridge for the weekend. Archie was fond of rituals. One that he adopted that fall was having lunch on Saturdays at the Henri IV with Clara, a Wellesley freshman from San Salvador with whom he could use his excellent Spanish. It was also where he occasionally entertained a girl from a college in Back Bay known for courses in home economics and students with better bodies than brains. Getting her back to her dormitory by ten or eleven in the evening, the hour by which, depending on the day of the week, she had to be signed in, was easier than getting Clara back to Wellesley. He explained to Henry and me that Clara was very Catholic and brought up in the cult of virginity, so the likelihood of getting beyond what he had already attained— when they kissed she let him put his hand under her Pringle sweater and unhook her bra—was discouragingly small. For instance, Clara refused to go into his bedroom, whether or not Henry and I were around, although, if we weren't there, being on the sofa in the living room was acceptable. It followed that we stayed clear of the dormitory until the end of parietal hours when Archie brought her over on Saturday and Sunday afternoons. She was also willing to park with Archie, after dark, on quiet Cambridge or Wellesley streets, or along the Charles. The only problem was that Archie didn't yet own a car. He could borrow one occasionally, but these loans couldn't be arranged often enough to satisfy him or, perhaps, even Clara, and so hardly accelerated his progress. Jeanie, the girl from the junior college across the river, was also Catholic, and Irish to boot, which lowered her in Archie's esteem. Disrespect does away with many a barrier to conquest— in addition to acting as an aphrodisiac. On the afternoon of Jeanie's second visit to our rooms—no suggestion was made that Henry and I withdraw to the Lamont while Archie and Jeanie were behind the closed door of his bedroom—they emerged holding hands, with only a minute or two to spare before girls had to be signed out. I've separated the boy from the man,

Jeanie announced. Archie signaled assent and hustled her out. Being sensitive to manners and diction, he may have felt embarrassed by the form not to say the simple fact of her declaration, which Henry later told me he had found unbearably sexy. Before long, however, Jeanie's availability—she thought nothing of coming to Harvard Square by subway, and never insisted that Archie take her back to Beacon Street even late in the evening—trumped the Salvadorean's well-bred elegance and charm. Archie took to calling Clara only at hours when he knew she wouldn't be in her dormitory, for instance when she had a class. He would leave a message that he had telephoned. Nothing more. Then he stopped calling her altogether. This tactic confused Clara. She took telephone messages seriously, thought they should be returned, and began calling our room to ask what was wrong. Archie never picked up the receiver; his instinct for avoiding calls he didn't want to answer was nearly infallible.

Most often, Clara spoke to me. Sometime after Christmas, she invited me to a record dance at Wellesley. She said she was used to being treated gently, and I was gentle. To jump ahead in time, in the spring of that year, Archie became the owner of a four-door black Nash, the most important feature of which was the fold-down front seat that made a fairly comfortable bed. I borrowed the Nash to take Clara to the Wellesley prom. We were leaving when she whispered that she wouldn't have to sign in at her dormitory by midnight, as the rules required even on that very important occasion. She had told the housemother that she was staying over with a friend in Newton, and had produced the necessary letter from the friend's parents confirming the invitation. We can be out as late as you like, she said. Then she stuck her tongue in my ear. We drove over to the lake and parked, and I put down the car seat. A little later, she wiggled out of her long strapless pink taffeta dress telling me that otherwise it would be ruined. Before dawn, overcoming my panic, she brought us to a simulacrum of mutual fulfillment. It was, she assured me, without damage to her hymen. That summer, she married the eldest son of a coffee-growing family whose plantation abutted the property of her parents. Through the university administration, she got hold of my home address and sent me an invitation to the wedding mass. Naturally, she did not return to Wellesley, and I was relieved of the need to face future relations.

. . .

THE TRANSFORMATION that Archie was undergoing during our freshman year didn't involve only clothes. He wanted to live up to his Roman numeral, with all its connotations for a connoisseur of American society. Mrs. White was on the right track when she supposed that a young man called Archibald P. Palmer III was likely to have rich parents; both she and Henry showed an instinctive grasp of the lore of American old money. Had Mrs. White learned about the checks that Archie received—irregularly but sometimes in substantial amounts—she would have thought herself proved right. In fact, she was mistaken; the money wasn't old, and its source wasn't a family trust. According to Archie, it flowed from his mother's various unglamorous little businesses, most recently the importation and resale of primitive art and antiquities. Nor was Archie related in any demonstrable way to the grand and wealthy Palmers of Chicago. His middle name was humble: Peters. However, he liked the impression produced by his surname and the enhancing Roman numeral and made no effort to dispel it. Faced with a question on the order of "Is Mrs. Potter Palmer your aunt or cousin?" Archie would laugh and say she was neither. No harm was done. People to whom such things mattered, even undergraduates, were too knowledgeable to take it for granted that someone called Morgan must be connected to the banking house, or that there is only one kind of Rockefeller.

At the same time, Archie did exert himself to make clear to undergraduates he considered useful that, although in a sense he came from nowhere, he should be regarded as their social equal. He simply acted on the English principle that a man may be born a gentleman and remain one even if his material circumstances are depressingly modest and he lacks powerful friends. The latter was certainly Archie's case. Unlike the men he wanted to emulate, he had no friends at college with whom he had been to grammar and prep school, there had been no shared vacations in Northeast Harbor or Tucson, and no one knew his mother and father. From his point of view, that was an unfortunate consequence of his father's army career, one that he could and must correct. Accordingly, he believed that as a matter of right he should be asked, at the beginning of our sophomore year, to join one of the final clubs whose quaint buildings on Mount

Auburn Street and its vicinity he had inventoried. He wanted to wear a club tie—the right tie, not all clubs being equal. Among the rewards would be getting his name on the lists compiled by social secretaries, which assured one of invitations to coming-out parties, cotillions, and assemblies. Later, it would be entry into the old-boy network and first-class passage to posh Wall Street firms. Though a romantic, Archie was clear-eyed about practical matters: he didn't shoot for the moon. There were two or three clubs that he realized were simply out of the question however hard he tried. They were also out of reach for all but a few whose fathers, grandfathers, and uncles hadn't been members. The less grand but still respectable clubs, however, should not shun him. The trick was how to make that understood. The usual route, reminding relatives and upper-classmen with whom you had been at school that you were a freshman and implicitly available, was not open to him. No one outside the British Isles had heard of his boarding school in Scotland, and it probably wasn't a household name even there. The military academy in Ohio to which he was sent after his father's posting to the Canal Zone was also obscure. Archie had to fend for himself. Very astutely, he decided to make the most of two of his special skills. In Scotland, he had learned to play rugby—rather effectively, for someone of his slight build. Joining the rugby club, which existed at the fringe of university sports, threw him in with English and Canadian undergraduates and business school students, a number of whom were long on cosmopolitan polish and money. Archie's other trump card was his near-native Spanish. He liked to use it and did well ferreting out events likely to be attended by Latin American students at the college and at neighboring institutions. In the 1950s, a Latino who had been sent to a New England college or, better yet, boarding school was bound to come from a rich and prominent family. Archie had, in fact, met Clara at a program devoted to Mayan art. But, as he gradually realized, the trouble with his amusing rugby players and Hispanics was that very few of them moved in the provincial society of college clubmen that was Archie's goal, or indeed gave a fig about it.

A drinking song popular at the time proclaimed that it's not for knowledge that we came to college but to have fun while we're here. That summed it up for Archie, if you added useful friendships to fun. Little time or energy remained for course work. I thought that was a pity, because he was so very sharp—as quick, I sometimes thought, as Henry. But while Archie truly didn't try or care, Henry's preoccupation was to hide how hard he worked. Those not familiar with his habits were inclined to believe his standard explanation that everything was done at the last minute, in a burst of speed and nighttime cramming. That merely showed how he had adopted, along with all of Archie's other lessons, the precept that there was nothing less charming than being known as a grind, a disgrace worse than all the detested sky-blue suits or tan flannel jackets in Brooklyn. In reality, Henry worked hard and steadily, but almost in secret and on subjects for which he had a passion. Archie had no such passions and had come to believe in light of Henry's successes that one could get along very well doing virtually nothing.

How Jeanie was going to fare in his evolving new world was a question that troubled Archie. At first, he believed that she would do fine if she could acquire a certain veneer, by which he meant a repertory of tricks she could perform at his prompting or when her own sense of the circumstances moved her. One day, just before they disappeared into his bedroom, he said to Jeanie, Go ahead, do "Au clair de la lune." She sang on command, in a pure and self-confident voice, enunciating very well, although she knew no French. When I expressed my admiration, he patted her on the rump and declared that in no time he would have her singing "Auprès de ma blonde" and "La vie en rose." Indeed, one by one, he added to Jeanie's curriculum several Piaf and Trenet hits. You can teach her anything, was his judgment.

In common with the rich Latinos, some of the rugby players had knowledge of several languages, experience of luxurious vacations spent in distant locations, and tales of adventures in legendary brothels. They also had startlingly large allowances, beyond anything I had imagined possible for students of their age. Archie's charm and inventiveness when it came to having fun served him well. He became their mascot and part of a shifting group of debonair figures at after-game cocktail parties, dinners at the Chinese restaurant on Church Street or an Italian restaurant in North Boston, or at the Savoy, listening to Dixieland jazz. Jeanie was indeed a quick study. The men liked her: she was pretty and pleasant, and as she was sleeping with Archie, which defined her status, none of them would have wanted to treat her unkindly. Whether they made passes at her when Archie's back was turned, and how she responded, were unexplored questions. However, her good nature turned out not to be enough. The contrast with the other girls was too great. It made trouble without a word being said, and perhaps some supercilious, wounding remarks were made. Like the men, these girls were rich, but, unlike them, they were snooty about it. In their company, Jeanie seemed like someone whose mother or grandmother could have been one of their grandmother's Irish maids, probably of the more refined kind, who could be trusted with delicate washing and ironing. Such may indeed have been her lineage. But Jeanie had a lot of spunk. She didn't like the position into which she had been thrust and made the break herself. Archie regretted the termination of their sessions in his bedroom. However, to his credit, he made no serious attempt to wheedle her into coming back.

I was a less frequent guest than Henry at parties given by Archie's friends. If they were on a Friday, which was the norm, my Boston Symphony subscription was a cast-iron reason for not attending. Probably I would have stayed away in any event. The talk bored me. I hadn't a doubt that it bored Henry too; however, Archie's friends were a species he wanted to understand, just as he wanted to learn how to hold his liquor, smoke cigars, play poker and bridge, and acquire the other skills that Archie thought were required of a gentleman. But neither those pursuits, nor any of the other ways of wasting time that Henry discovered on his own, seemed to interfere with other, more arduous aspects of his self-transformation. Perhaps the two were more complementary than I understood.

Just before Christmas vacation, Henry told me that he would major in the classics. He gave his parents the news once he got home. The weeklong row that followed didn't surprise him. They wanted him to plant his feet firmly in the American middle class. Becoming a doctor would assure that, but they were willing to settle for the law, since he absolutely refused to study medicine or even go through the motions of taking the required college biology and chemistry courses. His crazy idea of throwing away all his advantages, full college scholarship included, on the literature of two dead languages and a future limited by the meager salary he could expect from teaching—assuming a Jew could get a job teaching classics at a university—was a bad joke, an insult to them. I must admit that I too had been taken aback by his choice. He expected to excel in all circumstances, that much was clear, but if he made this choice he would be competing against undergraduates who had learned their Latin, and in many cases Greek as well, at boarding schools that took great pride in teaching those subjects. They had been taught in the same manner, and often by the same people, as members of Harvard's classics department. I thought that the odds against Henry would be long. Don't worry, he told me, my Latin is pretty good. I asked whether this was learning acquired at his Brooklyn high school. Not at all, he said, over there I was busy learning English. Then where? I asked. In Krakow, he answered impatiently, in Krakow. I shook my head and suggested he didn't know what he was getting into. In reply he said that catching up would require little more than memorization. Besides he had good German, itself still useful for classicists. During the same conversation he mentioned having noticed that the grander Latinos had a way of switching from English to French instead of Spanish when they spoke to each other. Obviously, learning French well was also a sound investment. A fiercely accelerated French-language course was offered in the spring semester; Henry signed up.

One aspect of the row with his parents about Latin and Greek bothered Henry; he thought he had been unfair. They thought that concentrating in the classics would preclude his going to law school after college, and he had done nothing to set them straight. He waited until the last day of vacation to tell them how the system worked. I was paying them back, he said. Why couldn't they leave me alone just once, or, even better, accept that this was a decision I should make? It would have been such a nice change! In return for the last-minute explanation, and a promise that he wasn't burning his bridges and would keep an open mind about the law, he extracted a price: their agreement to send him to Grenoble for the summer. He had heard good things about the university's French-language program.

In this and many other things he was way ahead of me. I hadn't even begun to think of the summer.

V

HENRY MADE NO MOVE to take out the girls who came to parties given by Archie's friends, although he got on with them just fine. He'd back one of them into a corner of a room packed with undergraduates in full cry to have what he called a quiet talk. Tête-à-tête he could be dazzling. He listened carefully to what was said to him or at least gave that impression. He was less good in groups, especially groups of men. His timidity was one reason—he compensated for it by what I called his Penthesilea-meets-son-of-Peleus preciousness—and his utter ignorance of sports was another. He had never been to a baseball game. Archie had dragged him to a couple of football games at Soldiers' Field and tried to explain to him the basics. Henry could discourse on books with great brio, and that is what he presumably talked about with those girls. However, the girls who came to these parties, even if they liked books, intimidated him by their provocative, hard-edged manners and staccato wit, and by their trick of creating an illusion of physical intimacy, of almost being in your arms, an illusion they could dispel as quickly as it had been created. Instead, he had dates with Radcliffe girls Archie called Henry's dogs: sincere and nice girls too fat or too skinny, with legs bowed or shaped like a Percheron's. He made no mystery of why. You can ask them out at the last minute, he explained, you don't have to huff and puff for the privilege of feeling them up, and the risk of rejection is minimal. It was all true, but I thought he was selling himself short. Although he certainly didn't fit the *Stover at Yale* stereotype, he was handsome, and it wasn't his conversation alone that made him fleetingly attractive to the girls at parties given by Archie's friends. I preached the lesson of self-confidence to Henry over and over. He would hear me out very politely. Once, exasperated, I asked whether this was another manifestation of the Jewish problem and, if it was, did he tell the dogs that he was a Jew. Cool as a cucumber, he replied that of course it was, it was all about being Jewish. As to what he told the dogs, he said there was no general rule: it depended on what he was doing with them. I was puzzled. This seemed a departure from his policy neither to deny Jewism nor proclaim it unbidden. Did he kiss or fondle them without saying that he was a Jew, but inform them if something more was in the offing? I said to myself that he surely told them, and right away was shocked by my own attitude. Did it imply that being Jewish was like having untreated gonorrhea?

Sometime before Thanksgiving Henry told me he thought he had found Penthesilea in his humanities course. The cavernous space of Sanders barely held the crowd drawn by lectures of the visiting professor, a well-known and controversial litterateur. So far, Henry had studied the girl only from a distance, but, if it was indeed Penthesilea, he knew her more prosaic name: Margot Hornung. Another girl called Sue, next to whom he usually sat, had told him all about her. They had attended the same girls' school in the city. Henry thought Sue liked him. Yes, she's a dog, he admitted. Sue and he talked before and after class, passed notes to each other, and went for tea and English muffins at Hayes-Bickford. He had never met a bigger gossip. I was curious to hear the tales she told, but Henry said there wasn't any point until I had confirmed the identification. He proposed that I come to Sanders for that purpose the next day. It was a silly idea: we had each had the same opportunity to study her looks. Finally, I gave in, in part because I was curious about the visiting professor. We got to Sanders early, and there were still some empty seats up front, but Henry pulled me along to one of the back rows. When I protested, he said that I'd be able to hear perfectly well. Anyway, that was where Sue sat, and she was saving our places. She turned out to be a pleasant-looking blond who showed braces over tiny yellow teeth when she smiled. Henry sat down between us. The hall was filling up, and I had begun to wonder whether the girl would appear, when Henry poked me and pointed to the door nearest the podium. There she is, he whispered. There was no question about it; it was Penthesilea of green stockings, now in navy-blue socks and penny loafers. I gave him the thumbs-up sign.

I had to go to another class after the lecture and said goodbye to Henry and Sue as soon as we left Sanders. But Henry and I met for lunch at the Union. With her identity confirmed, I thought he would have finally spoken to Margot. He seemed startled at the idea and told me that he certainly hadn't. His plan was to continue to lie low. In fact, he had already gotten Sue to promise never to mention to Margot his name or his interest in her. It was my turn to be surprised. I asked how this squared with wanting to declare his undying love from the moment he first saw Margot.

It doesn't, he fired back. I told you the stars weren't aligned. It was a dumb thing to think and a dumb thing to say, but at least I was smart enough not to do anything of the sort. I don't want to be humiliated.

Archie and Henry hadn't yet reequipped themselves at Keezer's. When Henry confirmed my hunch that his wardrobe was a problem, I let him feel my exasperation. Had he not yet realized that so far no one had rejected him because of the way he was dressed?

How would you know? he replied. Disdain is something you feel in your bones. I know what I feel in mine.

After a pause he said, The immediate problem is whether I should stop seeing Sue. She's very affectionate and nice, but Margot and she live in the same dorm, they spend their time with the same girls. I want to avoid complications. I think I have to drop her—very gently.

I made no comment.

We finished lunch and walked back to the dormitory. On the way he started to tell me what he had learned about Margot. The gist of it was that her parents were rich and elegant enough to be featured regularly in fashion magazines. They were said to know everyone who was famous and important. This made them the subject of a good deal of talk among the other girls at the school and their parents. The details were interesting. Margot's father had been an important banker in Amsterdam before the war. Most people seemed to know he was a Jew. However, the mother was a real American; that is to say she wasn't Jewish. According to school lore, Mr. Hornung had "bought" her when she was a cabaret singer performing at the Pierre, and Margot was born five months later. Both events were café society news in the New York tabloids even though Mr.

Hornung had taken his bride and child back to Holland. He was no fool. Already in 1938, he began transferring his capital and his collections to New York. Then, in June 1939, the family, accompanied by the English nanny who was still with the Hornungs, tranquilly sailed to New York aboard a Cunarder and were reunited with the money and the art. They moved into their present apartment on Park Avenue in time for Margot to go to school that fall. According to Sue, the apartment was like the Frick Collection. Mr. Hornung made a second fortune on Wall Street, which may be the reason they hadn't moved back to Amsterdam.

I sensed it, Henry said, as soon as I saw the mother, I sensed what kind of people they are. None of them would give me the time of day, no matter how I was dressed. I'll have to make Margot my long-term project. In the meantime, I'll stay away. Don't want to screw it up.

I agreed that the mother was glamorous. But was that a reason for a Radcliffe freshman—a Jewish or half-Jewish one at that—to refuse to go out with a Jewish undergraduate she had already tried to pick up? Just because her parents were loaded and knew Picasso and the Windsors?

Henry said, You can't really be that stupid.

I didn't take offense, but our conversation was over. Henry had to go to the library to read a book that was on reserve. However, we returned to the subject of the Hornungs that evening and in the days that followed. As we talked, I learned, in bits and pieces, the war story that Archie had wanted to hear. Henry spoke reluctantly, and I believe that if his mind had not been fixed on Margot he wouldn't have said so much.

Apparently, Henry's father had not been really rich before the war; he had been merely very well-to-do, on the scale of successful Jewish businessmen in Poland, one that, Henry stressed, was different from the scale valid in Holland or elsewhere in Western Europe. Poland was a poor country, he insisted; "rich" or "well-to-do" there wasn't the same as for instance in London. The family business was the export of foodstuffs, especially Polish hams, which were a major producer of revenue for the country, and arts and crafts and decorators' wares like kilims. There were also investments in real estate in Krakow, where they lived. Mr. White had obtained a law degree and was about to begin the obligatory lawyer's apprenticeship when his father died. As the only son, he had to take over the business.

His choice of bride was conventional in the extreme. He married the daughter of the leading Jewish lawyer, also very well-to-do, and received a handsome dowry, including an apartment building on a good street within the walls of the old city. She had finished her own university studies, in Polish literature, and, when Mr. White sought her hand, was planning to obtain the higher degree required for teaching in state secondary schools. That project came to nothing, in part because eleven months after the marriage Henry was born. Running my father's household took up all her time, said Henry, even though she had a staff of four or five. The new family like the parents was too well placed, too respectable, and too Polish in speech and habit to have suffered in daily life from the campaign of insults and indignities directed at Jews beginning with the coming to power, after Marshal Piłsudski died, of a right-wing nationalistic and anti-Semitic regime. That had to wait for the arrival of the Germans.

Krakow became the seat of the German government of Poland, and there was no delay in requiring Jews to wear the yellow star, or in the establishment of the ghetto in the old Jewish quarter called Kazimierz. Before that happened, however, his mother's parents fled to Zakopane, in the Tatry Mountains, where it had been their custom to spend the summer months, always at the same hotel. The owner had agreed to hide them. Henry's parents never found out exactly where or how they were hidden; the general idea had been that they would be out of sight and earshot—therefore out of danger—in a cottage outside Zakopane belonging to that man. Did he eventually tire of harboring Jews? Did he sell them to the Polish police or directly to the Gestapo? Did a neighbor denounce them? None of his father's inquiries after the war elicited answers he could trust. He did hear that a Jewish couple that could well have been his in-laws was taken to the Gestapo building in Zakopane before Christmas of 1942 never to be seen again. The hotel keeper himself died in 1943, apparently of pneumonia; his family had moved away. The father found it troubling that the man should have died of a natural cause; it suggested treachery on his part. If he had been denounced for harboring Jews, in all probability he would have been shot.

The road to safety followed by Henry's parents was similar, but it did not end in disaster. His mother's old Latin teacher at the *gimnazjum*—he explained that this was Polish high school—one Pani Maria, a remarkable woman who during her youth had been involved in the Polish socialist independence movement, spontaneously offered to take Henry and his mother into her house on the outskirts of Krakow and hide them until the end of the war, which she didn't doubt would end in Germany's defeat. No less impressive than her courage and generosity were Pani Maria's scholarship and literary attainments. She was the author of the best Polish translation of Horace's Odes and Epodes. What she proposed seemed practical: she was widowed, living alone, with no relatives near Krakow. There was no need to fear the interference or indiscretion of visitors, and the house had a room that had always been shuttered. She would block it off. Pani Maria thought that if they were very careful the thing could be done. But she would not agree to take in Mr. White as well. She freely admitted that her decision was not rational. Quite simply, she believed that her nerves couldn't bear the presence of a second adult in that room behind a concealed door. Henry's parents didn't think they could get her to go back on that position. It was better to find another hiding place for Mr. White. He had a manager who had worked in his firm for many years, with whom he had always had excellent relations. The man hesitated, his wife had to be convinced, but finally he agreed to take in Mr. White. Mr. White didn't wait to be asked: as soon as the man said yes, he signed over to him the ownership of the firm, the buildings he and Mrs. White owned, and every other asset to which title could be transferred. The manager said, Don't worry, if we survive, we will sort this out fairly. They shook hands on it. The real difference between the hiding places was that Mr. White had to live in the cellar. The manager had small children as well as the wife; it was impossible to stop strangers from coming into the house.

Anyway, Henry said, we did make it through the war, and when the Russians chased the Germans out of Krakow, we staggered into the street like people who had been trapped in a mine. Out of all our family we alone had survived.

I was shaken by the story, and by the manner in which he told it: matter-of-fact and somehow dismissive.

What happened next? I asked.

When? After the war? We lived in Krakow for a while, in our old apartment, which had been taken over by Germans who had left in a hurry. It wasn't necessary to evict any Poles, and the Germans had left our furniture in place. The man who saved my father's life agreed to give him enough money to live on and to back him in some deals on the black market. They split the profits. It was a good arrangement. After a while, my father was doing so well that he was sorry to leave the business. Pani Maria—I loved her more than anybody—died of the flu followed by pneumonia. Then the summer was over and it was time for me to enter the *gimnazjum*. All I knew was Polish literature that I read with my mother, and Polish composition, and the Latin and German that I did with Pani Maria. I crammed and passed. There was a chance to buy some kind of visa that allowed us to get out of Poland and into Belgium. My father jumped at it. From Belgium we went to New York. There was one thing my father hadn't signed over. That was the firm's bank account at the Morgan Bank in New York, and, by reason of some prewar Polish tax requirements, it was in his own name. So we had a little money, after all, and in the end we were able to settle in Brooklyn.

I hesitated, but because the experience was unimaginable I let myself ask what it had been like to live hidden in a blocked-off room for three years.

What do you suppose? he asked. Do you want to know whether we used a chamber pot and who took it out and when? Or how we washed? Or how we quarreled? I won't tell you.

I apologized for the question and returned to how he had caught up with his studies. I said I understood about the Latin and the German. But the rest? The English?

I've told you, he said, I crammed. What I don't know, I fake. I have a good memory. Anything I can read in a book stays with me. But, he said, not everything is in books. As you've observed, I can't throw a ball. I don't know how to climb trees either. Chances are that I never will.

I continued to insist—in retrospect beyond the point of obtuseness—

that nothing he had told me should be a barrier between him and Margot. The war robbed you and your parents of lots of things, I said, and you have suffered a lot. The Hornungs should understand that better than anyone.

True enough, he allowed, in the abstract. But practically speaking, none of this is about what we were before the war, or what happened during the war. It's about what we are now. We have become a different species. What is my father's business? He has a little factory in East Brooklyn making curtains, upholstery, and stuff like that. He invests in little rental buildings. He learned some English before the war. You've heard him on the telephone. My mother is just the same. You can only get so far from where you start. Our starting line is in East Brooklyn. Have you ever been there? I don't recommend it. Until last year, we lived in an apartment there that was a real hole. Two small bedrooms—no bigger than my room here—a dark ugly living room, and an ugly kitchen. With a nice view of the air shaft. Now we have a big house that's all right, in Flatbush, a quiet part of Brooklyn full of orderly middle-class Jews. My parents' friends are like us. They're all former this or former that. What distinguishes most of them from us is that they got here before the war and so didn't have to hide in a cellar or behind someone's armoire. Some have more money than my father, some in fact have a lot, but what does it all add up to in relation to people like the Hornungs? Zero. You made a face when I said Margot's family and my parents are different species. All right: I give up that metaphor. Have another one. Right now Margot and Margot's parents are way up at the top of a tree. We're way down at the roots. But that's the one tree I will learn to climb. Otherwise, there is no point in my being here.

I wish I could say that after that exchange I stopped debating with him. But I didn't. I explained how where you lived and how much money you made were much less important than who you really were, inside. That, I said, was the difference between America and Europe. As I pontificated I was dimly aware that I was making an argument that I could not have sustained if the subject had been my own situation. Certainly, my parents were, on the scale of the Berkshires, of a very good family, and at the time I had more respect for Lenox and Stockbridge gentry than experience has shown they deserved. Therefore, except for the small issue of my not being my parents' biological child, it shouldn't matter that their reputation was stained and that their spendthrift ways and those of their parents before them had ensured that they would be dismally poor in comparison with my father's very rich first cousin and employer. That cousin with his spotless name and all the good a good name brings. Yes, there was the all-important country club to which his family and mine both belonged, where we came into frequent, uneasy contact. The cousins, however, belonged to other clubs, to which my parents couldn't aspire, and lived altogether differently. Could anyone in his right mind in Berkshire County consider my father and my father's cousin social equals? I knew that the answer was no, but the answer hurt. I wanted to have my cake and eat it, to be judged on my own merit and also get all the help I could get from my name, even though it was a name that, for all the legal adoption procedures, I couldn't convince myself was legitimately my own. All the same, in Berkshire County and, perhaps, beyond, it was nicer to be called Standish than Nowak or Mahoney.

In the end, it made no difference what I said. Henry laughed and laughed.

VI

I NOW REALIZE that all three of us—Henry, Archie, and I—used the word "Jew" with restraint, holding it gingerly with two fingers far away from the body, as though it gave off a bad smell. It was an embarrassing word to utter in polite company, especially if a Jew was present—unless, like old Gummy, you were telling jokes about Weisberg, Goldberg, and the like. In that respect it was not unlike "homosexual," or some of the less antiseptic variants in use at Harvard: queer, fairy, queen, pervert, faggot, fruit, and pederast. Nevertheless, I was certain that Henry had told Archie he was a Jew or else had otherwise brought it out into the open. I was far from sure that they had ever spoken about the war. One reason would have been Archie's dislike of what he called heavy conversations. His first instinct when he saw one coming was to run or hide. When that was impractical, he would assume an expression of great seriousness, cock his right ear as if not to miss a word, and, in a couple of minutes, bring the audience to a close by some more or less British injunction to buck up coupled with an offer to have another serious chat very soon. A brisk slap on the back or a squeeze of the arm just above the elbow might follow. It wasn't that Archie lacked compassion; on the contrary, I believe that he shrank from hearing other people's troubles because they affected him so very acutely. Very little by way of verbal communication was needed for Archie to take measure of anyone. I was sure that after two months of living with Henry at close quarters he doubtless knew all he wanted to know about him; the mechanics of the White family's survival and immigration to Brooklyn would have fallen into the category of matters better left alone. He would have heard Henry out if that had been what Henry wanted, but he wouldn't inquire. I had not forgotten that it was he, not I, who first realized that Henry was a Jew, and a Jew who didn't much care to be recognized as such. The interest he expressed hearing Henry's story someday had been, I now understood, nothing more than a polite formula. I had also moved toward the view that Archie's take on Henry's Jewism was fundamentally correct: the stuff about always being ready to admit that he was Jewish, if someone asked, and to volunteer the information in appropriate cases added up to little more than the determination not to be caught in a humiliating lie.

Occasionally I thought that I should tell Henry the best policy would be to make clear that he was a Jew as soon as he saw the question coming. I never did. Everything concerning Jews—a subject to which I had devoted little thought before—was too complicated, and Henry's responses were unpredictable. Perhaps it would be more accurate to say that I was no good at predicting. For instance, not long after he told me that he was Jewish, I asked whether he had seen *Gentleman's Agreement*. He nodded. When I asked what he had thought of it, he said that he had liked Gregory Peck and his clothes, the fine apartments, the house in Connecticut, and the restaurants. I replied there was a lot more to the film than the props. The message it sent was important. He shook his head and said, It's a bottle of aspirin for you and others like you. I protested again. His answer was that Gregory Peck is a Boy Scout on a camping trip. The business of his pretending to be a Jew was like sleeping out in the woods and getting bitten by mosquitoes. On Sunday evening he gets to go home to a hot shower and pancakes with maple syrup. It's Gregory Peck's friend, the John Garfield character, he continued, who has to go on being a Jew and dealing with Jew haters. What's that like? If you want to know what it's really like to be a Jew, let Shylock tell you. Listen to him while he spews out his rancor and hatred. That, Henry said, is a genuine statement of the Jewish condition. Let Shylock tell you.

By the way, he added, did you happen to notice that there is no mention in the movie about the murder of however many million Jews in Europe? Five? Six? Seven? Shouldn't that have come up one way or another? For instance, when one of the rednecks calls the John Garfield character, a decorated veteran in full army uniform, a dirty kike. Total silence. What does that say about Mr. Garfield, whose name at one time was Jacob Julius Garfinkle, and everyone else involved with the production? For instance, Moss Hart, who wrote the screenplay?

I told him I had no answer.

There is no decent answer. That's one of the reasons why I prefer to stay off this subject. Archie and I don't talk about it.

In fact, I couldn't imagine Archie letting himself in for that sort of harangue. He was, on the other hand, certainly up to date on the subject of Margot. When I told him that I'd been called to Sanders to identify her, he said that Henry had asked him to come as well, though for a different kind of opinion.

But I'm not doing it, he said. I'm sure I've already met that lollipop at Mario's party last week. She's a bit of all right.

Mario was a senior, an Argentinean polo player who had made time in his schedule for rugby.

I'll get Mario to invite her again, and you and I will bring Henry, Archie continued. It's the only way he'll ever meet her. But don't say a word about it to him. He won't come if he knows what we're up to.

That was the efficient and agreeable side of Archie, which matched his freckled good looks, neatness of person, and effortless manners. If a friend needed a hand with a practical problem, he was the man for it. The other side was his drinking. I had watched my parents hit the bottle for as long as I could remember. I couldn't fail to recognize someone for whom liquor meant something quite different from getting silly after a few drinks too many. Drunks marked for destruction like my father scared me; there's no other way to put it, even when, as in my father's case, they gave no hint of inclination to violence. That Archie was one of those drunks I didn't doubt, although he fooled most of his friends by holding his liquor so well. I thought he held it far too well. The huge quantities of booze I had seen consumed at the couple of parties given by Archie's friends I had attended, to say nothing of what he drank, put me off coming again. This occasion was different. If Henry was going to be introduced to Margot, I wouldn't fail to be present.

I had no doubt that Archie understood my disapproval. That his feelings were hurt was plain in his adjustment of attitude toward me. He had become watchful. Our camaraderie revived only when we met on the squash court. We played often. He was fast and nimble, and I had to work hard to give him a decent game. For my part, once it was clear where we stood with each other, I began to understand that neither my disapproval, which he surely considered another symptom of my prissiness, nor, so far as I could tell, anyone else's, mattered to Archie. He had talked himself into believing that to drink hard was a romantic gesture, an act of gallant defiance, one that he could pull off because of the total control he exercised over himself, if he chose to, as well as the strength of his constitution. Squash, incidentally, was another game to which Archie was taking care to introduce Henry, and Henry was eager to learn, rightly associating the sport with boarding schools. Why Archie took such pains with Henry, and had become so attached to him, was something of an enigma. Perhaps it was, at least initially, the attraction of the exotic. Henry was for Archie, just as for me, a strange and heretofore unknown type; Archie's previous contacts with Jews must have been even more limited than mine, but they had left him open-minded, as he was about most things except brands of gin and cigarettes and other paraphernalia required for a gentleman's comfort and pleasure. But it wasn't only Henry's Jewism or Henry's war experiences, which he may or may not have investigated, or the ambiguities of Henry's attitude that so engaged Archie's interest. What really hooked him, I believe, was that Henry, more intellectual and bookish than anyone Archie had ever known, should be so accommodating, so keen to be deeply involved with him. He was in awe of Henry's brains and would have understood it if in their dealings Henry had been aloof, perhaps even patronizing. Instead, Henry proved himself an eager pupil, learning the tricks Archie had to teach, and participating, without condescension, in the pastimes that were Archie's principal occupation—pastimes that Archie himself surely knew were silly. Such acceptance must have seemed to Archie little short of miraculous. It convinced him of Henry's true affection, and both Archie and Henry, each in his own way, had a huge need to please and to be liked. A price had to be paid, and they both paid it. It is probable that, beyond his mistaken impression that Henry's successes were effortless, Archie found in Henry's friendship a validation of his conduct, proof he was all right and could safely dismiss what he perceived as my disapproval. Perhaps the disapproval and carping of others as well. Henry could not have been unconscious of the role he played. What was, in that case, the measure of his responsibility for Archie's behavior? Did he feel relieved of any by a conclusion, similar to mine, that trying to reform Archie was a waste of time? I wondered whether Archie would eventually come to blame Henry for his complicity; perhaps on occasion he already did, during the awful hours when a hangover slowly recedes, making place for bleak lucidity. That seemed improbable, but then he was more opaque to me than was Henry, although one might have supposed that Archie and I would have understood each other better. His being particularly closemouthed about himself and his family contributed to the opacity, as did the fact that I was less intensely curious about him.

The party at Mario's was to take place after the Yale game, the last game of the season, at the house where we intended to live as sophomores. Archie and Henry were going to the game without dates. As I had not gotten a ticket and said I didn't want one, Archie instructed me to meet them at the house, at the porter's lodge, so that I could corral Henry if he tried to defect at the last minute. The afternoon had turned nasty, the wind blasting through the covered passage between the street and the courtyard where I waited. Harvard's ignominious loss to Yale had been expected, and perhaps for that reason it had not dispirited the undergraduates and girls hurrying inside from Dunster Street. I took in the red cheeks and noses, the long crimson or blue scarves wound around girls' necks, the occasional raccoon coat. Such a coat, dating back to my father's college days, hung in the hall closet at home. He offered it to me, very nicely, the evening before my mother drove me down to Cambridge. My refusal was a surly reflex, and I knew that I hurt him, even though he had his martini pacifier in hand and limited his response to the habitual "Fine and dandy."

Finally, Archie and Henry arrived. We crossed the courtyard and climbed two flights of stairs. The living room was crowded and noisy. Several people greeted Archie, and Henry prudently remained at his side. Not seeing anyone I knew, I drifted to the window overlooking the Charles, which glistened beyond Memorial Drive like a slick vein of anthracite. There was a stack of records on the phonograph. I identified the music being played as a tango. It was followed by passionate chanting in Spanish. The woman's deep voice would rise to a vertiginous height and then fall abruptly. It was accompanied by a guitar and rhythmic pounding of heels and clapping of hands. I was drawn to this strange music. The next record was similar and again I listened attentively. A wiry man with very black hair approached me and said, It's flamenco, Gypsy songs from the south of Spain. I collect flamenco records. You're welcome to come to listen whenever you like. By the way, I'm Mario Delgado. You must be one of Archie's roommates, the one who isn't from Poland. Mario's accent was as elegant as his navy-blue blazer, and quite unlike the intonations of Archie's other Latino friends.

I told him that I wouldn't have guessed he was from Argentina. The provincial stupidity of my remark was clear to me as soon as I had made it. I mumbled an apology.

Don't worry, he replied, nobody can place me, and everyone asks. It comes from my having been sent to school in England, but a couple of years too late. Come, you should have a drink.

He led me to the table that served as a bar and deftly left me. I saw Henry and Archie still near the door in a group of people shouting so as to be heard over the noise. I didn't want to shoulder my way in. Instead, I went back to my post at the window. On the way I examined first the contents of the bookcases, which proved unremarkable, and then the posters pinned to the walls advertising Dubonnet, the casino in Biarritz, French movies, and, inevitably, the Moulin Rouge. At the same time, I took inventory of the guests. The girls were all very tall. Perhaps that was the criterion that determined who was invited. Some I recognized, probably because I had stared at them in the library. The others might have been imported for this important weekend from Wellesley, Smith, Vassar, or Sarah Lawrence, or even more distant sources of supply. Among the men, foreigners seemed to be in the majority. They wore tweed jackets or blazers too beautiful, like Mario's, not to be noticed. Americans, all manifestly upperclassmen, sported neckties of the three or four best final clubs. Blond and serene, they were to a man products of the boarding schools that acted as principal feeders for Harvard College, a species not unfamiliar to me, except that its representatives assembled at Mario's were, on the scale of perfection, right at the high end. I glanced again at Archie and Henry. Their group was all foreigners, and therefore rugby players. It was impossible not to notice that both my roommates were out of place in this setting; to put it more brutally, they looked odd. This was so not only by reason of how they were dressed, or, in Henry's case, also his haircut, which was too short, exposing white skin over his ears. It was more their facial expressions. They had neither the clubmen's blandness and satisfaction with the place they occupied by divine right nor the foreigners' good-natured bonhomie. There was something too keen and too eager to please about Archie; Henry was nervous and uncomfortable, and couldn't hide it.

A good half hour had passed since Mario propelled me toward my martini, and I hadn't exchanged a word with anyone else. I wondered how much longer I could decently continue this way without asking for another drink or taking some other action to make myself a less conspicuous wallflower. I also wondered whether Margot would really appear and, if she did, how Archie was going to manage the introduction. I didn't think he had actually met her; more likely he had only observed her and found out her name. I had just decided I would give her another fifteen minutes and was making my way to the bar when Margot entered the room on the arm of my cousin George. To meet him this way for the first time since coming to Cambridge wasn't exactly what I would have wished, but it solved the problem I had been pondering: I would say hello to him, and the rest would follow. I checked on my roommates. They hadn't moved; standing with their backs to the door, neither could have seen Margot.

Fresh martini in hand, I threaded my way toward George. It took him a moment to see me. As soon as he did, he exclaimed with a look of pleasant surprise—I hoped it was in some part genuine—over the remarkable coincidence of finding me at this party given by people he didn't know and introduced me to Margot as his cousin. She mumbled some greeting, not particularly friendly. Without paying further attention to her, George told me that he had wanted us to get together right away, at the beginning of the term, but, with one thing and another and particularly crew practice, he hadn't gotten around to looking me up. I responded with assurances that he had been much on my mind and that, having made the freshman wrestling team, I understood the demands the crew made on him. Then Mario joined us. This was a good opportunity to bring Henry over. My two roommates are here, I told George. I'd like you to meet them.

In fact, I brought only Henry. As soon as she saw him, Margot came to life. She held out her arms crying out, At last, here is the boy in the window! This is too funny. I made a spectacle of myself trying to pick him up and he paid no attention! It was very humiliating, she concluded.

I couldn't tell whether her greeting embarrassed Henry or encouraged him. In either event, he didn't need me. Planning to remain at the party only a few more minutes before going to dinner, just to make sure that Henry was really all right, I moved back to the window. George disengaged his arm from Margot's and followed me.

You know, he said, when I told you that I wanted to look you up I meant it. We should be friends. I have only one Standish cousin, and that's you.

Strictly speaking that wasn't quite right. He had two older first cousins, daughters of his father's sister. I was only a second cousin. Their name wasn't Standish, but they were closer relations. Still, it would have been churlish to contradict him.

Pittsfield is a funny place, he continued, referring to the town where the bank had its head office. So are Stockbridge and Lenox. Knowing Father, I'm sure he wouldn't want people at the bank to think that he was treating your old man differently from everybody else, so I bet he makes sure he's all business with him. But that has nothing to do with you and me. We should be friends.

My astonishment was considerable. All through my childhood, I had thought that such a thing was impossible. When we were at the same day school, I went to his birthday parties because his mother invited the whole class. The invitations naturally stopped when we went to different boarding schools. Now he was taking the first step. I couldn't imagine what lay behind this overture. Remarkable discretion on the part of the Standish parents about mine, as well as about the adoption? It was, of course, possible that Mr. Hibble had told the truth, and no one really knew, except for my parents and him. And the Standish grandfather who was my benefactor. What could George possibly like about me? I could think of nothing. Perhaps some well-disposed person had said something favorable that caught his imagination. Or was he acting out of a sense of noblesse oblige? It occurred to me that, if a true friendship developed, I would need to tell him I had been adopted. It would be wrong to conceal it from someone who cared so much about family ties. But that could wait. I said that I would like nothing better than to be friends. Then I added Margot seems nice.

I like her a lot, he told me. If I can get her up to Stockbridge for the New Year's dance, you'll have to come too.

After we said goodbye, I found Mario and thanked him. I couldn't find Archie. Margot and Henry were still where I had left them. I thought I wouldn't disturb them. With luck, I could still get something to eat at the Freshman Union. I walked fast toward Quincy Street.

VII

A BIG WINTER STORM hit after Christmas, knocking down power lines in western Massachusetts and parts of Connecticut and New York, and blowing snowdrifts across many roads. In some places it took several days to dig out, and crews worked around the clock to restore electricity and telephone service. Like everyone brought up in the Berkshires, George thought nothing of driving in the worst of winter conditions and was determined to go down to New York in the family station wagon. He would spend the night with his aunt and bring Margot and Henry to Stockbridge. Far from objecting, his parents thought this was a splendid plan, his father counseling him only to throw a spare set of chains in the back of the station wagon, just in case. Mrs. Hornung, however, vetoed the project. She decreed that if Margot really had to go to a dance in the Berkshires, she would go by train, the more sensible idea being for George to come to the party she and her husband gave every New Year's Eve at their apartment in New York. There would be dancing, and George was welcome to bring friends. Her decision put an end to Henry's row with his parents over the prospect of his driving off with George into the storm. In the plan finally adopted, the Berkshire dance prevailed over the Hornungs' entertainment. Margot and Henry would take the train due in Stockbridge at three in the afternoon on New Year's Eve and, at Margot's insistence, Henry would stay at George's house, rather than with me as I had proposed. Not being very confident about my parents in the role of hosts during that particular holiday, I had been glad to yield. All the same, I went to the station with George to discharge at least some of my duties as roommate. There was no attendant on duty; there hadn't been one in Stockbridge for a long time. We waited some fifteen minutes, and then, the pay phone being broken, I remained on the platform, so that I would be on hand to greet Henry and Margot if the train suddenly appeared while George drove to a nearby gas station on Route 7 and called down the line to stations in the state of New York where there was a chance that someone might be on duty. It was as we had expected. Switches kept on freezing up. It might be an hour or more before Henry and Margot arrived or it could be less. As they would be unable to call, we stayed at the station.

Since Mario's party, I had run across Margot only in the Yard and in the street. We would wave and say hello, but in spite of my growing curiosity about her, we didn't stop to talk. Henry came back to the dormitory late the night of that party. He said he was frozen stiff. Archie was still out and I had just about finished my reading. As Henry hadn't eaten, I suggested that we go out for a hamburger. He refused, protesting that he was tired and too cold to go out again, but in the end he agreed. The wind had turned into a gale and, for a Saturday night of the Yale game weekend, the Yard and the streets abutting on Harvard Square were surprisingly empty. There wasn't even the usual gang of townies waiting outside Elsie's on Mount Auburn Street to bait unwary undergraduates. I let Henry eat in silence. We were having a second cup of coffee when I asked what had happened at the party after I left. Nothing, he replied. Margot introduced George and him to Mario. George drifted off to greet some other people, leaving him and Margot. They got to have a long talk. At some point, George came over and said, Let's go and eat, and he and Margot left for a restaurant in the North End. George had been very polite, asking Henry to join them. He declined, not wanting to impose. By then the dining room at the Union would have closed, and he didn't feel like dinner anyway. So he walked along the Charles on the Cambridge side all the way to Harvard Bridge. There he crossed over to Boston, wandering around for a while in Back Bay. He followed the Storrow Drive to Cambridge, went back to Harvard Square, and poked around Brattle Street and Spark Street. Beautiful houses, he said. I wouldn't mind living in one of them.

I was right not to go to the restaurant, he added. Your cousin George was nice enough to leave me alone with Margot the better part of an hour. He didn't need my presence at dinner. She was his date, right? The evening was his. Anyway, that will be the pattern. I might as well get used to it.

I must have looked puzzled. It's simple, Henry said, she's exactly the sort of girl they all want to take out, those men at the party, and George is exactly the sort of man she thinks should take her out. Maybe she even expects someone even fancier. I don't qualify. On the other hand, she told me that she hasn't got much to say to them, not that they would necessarily want to listen. So we can talk to each other. That's my role—she made it very clear.

I wouldn't have predicted for Henry a role as Margot's confidant. In all other respects, that was also my assessment. It led me to think that he should stop wasting time on his Jazz Age Penthesilea and also on the dogs he had been consoling himself with. There were lots of attractive girls at Radcliffe who would be happy to have him. Some might even be Jewish. Of course, I didn't tell him any of that. Instead I complimented him on his realism and willingness to accept the situation with good cheer.

Good cheer? he answered. Don't be ridiculous. I've been dealt a lousy hand. I know it, and I don't find anything in it to be cheerful about. Don't misunderstand me. I'm not giving up on Margot. This is a tactical retreat in a long campaign. For now, my plan is to be her friend. Whatever happens and whatever she does with the others, I'll bide my time.

That statement didn't reassure me. I had taken a good look at Margot and the other girls at Mario's. If he really thought that in time he would be able to get Margot away from the Georges and Marios of this world, he was only setting himself up for more disappointments. I knew I was changing my tune, but that couldn't be helped. In fact, I was beginning to think that perhaps Archie and I had made a mistake arranging the chance encounter at Mario's as though it were just another undergraduate lark. At the same time, something made me go on; I couldn't stop meddling. I asked whether he shouldn't put the matter to a test by asking her for a date.

She'd send me packing, he said. That would spoil everything.

Why? Do you think that she is an anti-Semite? I asked him point-blank. Is that the problem? Because if she is, what would make her change?

Isn't everybody? he fired back.

I don't think so, I replied. I'm not, Archie isn't, there are lots of people who don't care whether you're Jewish.

I'm not so sure, Henry said. Anyway, you haven't been put to any test. Sure, you and Archie don't seem to mind having had a Jew foisted on you. But in other contexts, who is to say? You seem positively fixated on the Jewish question. In changed circumstances it might turn out that you care a lot. Anyway, I do know that there are Jews and Jews, and that some Jews are acceptable for most purposes, except to real nuts, and others aren't. Margot's father and Margot are class A Jews. I'm class B—for the time being. I want to move to A.

Though a bit put off by his hostility, I wished him luck.

In the meantime, I watched him go about being Margot's best friend and must say I admired his eerie efficiency. I doubt that a single day went by without their meeting for coffee or tea at Hayes-Bickford between morning classes as well as in the afternoon, after leaving the library. He avoided Leavitt & Pierce's because there you had to sit at the counter, so that real privacy was excluded. Besides, it was where "they" hung out, the golden lads and lassies. Most days, Margot and he read side by side at the Widener. When she had to use the Radcliffe library, needing a book on reserve there, he would wait outside and walk her back to her dormitory. Occasionally, they went to the movies. George wasn't much of a cinema buff and, what with crew training and homework—he was a diligent student who read slowly, took careful notes on what he read, and fretted about deadlines for handing in papers—he was usually pressed for time. Margot, I gathered, worked quickly but without much application. According to Henry, she had been so well prepared by her school in New York that she found no need to take much trouble over her courses. I would have liked to know what Henry and Margot actually talked about. Books and coursework? Was he more open with her about Poland and the war? He gave no hint of that, but I did learn that George was not the only man who took Margot out on what Henry called real dates. There was also a Belgian at the business school, a rich fellow given to rushing to New York whenever Margot went home. He is an international playboy, Henry explained, manifestly parroting Margot's words, not a typical busi-

ness school grind. George was aware of the Belgian and bore his atten-
tions to Margot stoically. Tolerant equanimity seemed, indeed, to be
George's hallmark in his relationship with Margot. Henry told me, with
needless indiscretion, that Margot had explained the strict limits on liber-
ties George could take with her person, and that George had placidly
accepted them. Perhaps crew's rigorous training regime and the saltpeter
which, according to rumor, was added to the special diet fed to top ath-
letes facilitated his acceptance. Henry seemed to know that the Belgian
pressed his suit with greater fire. George was also notably easygoing about
Henry and, at least according to Margot, it was George who had come up
with the idea of inviting him to the New Year's party at the Lenox
Driving Club. Your invitation, Henry assured me, was also something
George had thought of on his own. I had no reason to doubt the accuracy
of the latter statement, since he had spoken about inviting me already at
Mario's party. And yet that harmless comment provoked in me an ugly
movement of jealousy—I considered that Henry belonged to me as did
also the connection with George and the Berkshires, and momentarily I
disliked the alliance that had sprung up between those two without my
active participation. I wondered how much Margot's influence had had to
do with the invitation to Henry. A lot, I was inclined to think, although
George had spoken to me favorably about Henry soon after they met at
Mario's. That roommate of yours with the funny accent is all right, he
said. Margot thinks he's remarkable. I acquiesced in both judgments. You
know, I think he may be a Jew, George pursued. Seeing no reason to feign
ignorance, I said he was. So he's a Jew, George repeated pensively. I didn't
take that as an indication that he was taken aback by the information. It
just took a moment to make sense of the new fact. The parents won't
mind, he continued. He's very polite, and he can talk to Mother about
books. Thinking of my father's strictures about Jews at our own country
club and old Gummy's views, I asked George how he thought Henry
would go over with the seniors at the very grand Driving Club. It was not
by choice that my parents weren't members there. I don't care what those
mummies think, he replied. The parents don't either. I absorbed George's
statement in silence. Once again he showed himself to be a far more

decent fellow than I had imagined. There was another aspect of his reply that was worthy of note: clearly setting yourself against the opinions of others was easier if you were rich and occupied an impregnable social position.

Like Henry, I had unexpectedly every reason to think well of George. He followed up on what I had feared might have been perfunctory party talk and invited me the very next day to lunch at the Chinese restaurant on Oxford Street. We began to see each other regularly, especially as we were taking the same English literature course, and he had trouble with the required weekly essay. Often, he wanted to see me to ask for my help with what he had written. Otherwise, we gossiped about the Berkshires. We knew the same people, although sometimes from different perspectives. I decided I had better tell him what Mr. Hibble had said about my adoption. George shook his head and said, Hibble is a lunatic. I mean senile. That's what Father thinks, and he should know. Hibble does all the legal work for the family.

I told George that my father would be glad to hear about Mr. Standish's opinion of Mr. Hibble, but my parents had confirmed the story. It had to be true. George fell silent. I am trying to think this out, he said after a while. There is something fishy about it, my grandfather stepping in like that. And setting up a trust! I think I see it. My sisters are older than I am and you are a year younger. That makes it simple: by the time you were born, Mother and Father had been married for six or seven years. Grandfather wasn't more than sixty-five, maybe younger, and he was in fine health. Hey, you might be my uncle! My sisters' and my uncle! Unless you're our half brother. Mother always says that Father was wild before they got married. Perhaps he hadn't stopped. How about that?

I told George that for a while after the meeting with Mr. Hibble I had thought of very little except the adoption, and the conclusion I'd come to was that there was no reason to believe anything of that sort. Abortions were easy to arrange, I said, if you had money. That's what would have been done in your family. More than likely some young woman your grandfather knew—perhaps an employee at the bank, perhaps the daughter of an employee, perhaps a servant, perhaps the daughter of a friend—

anyway, some girl he knew got into trouble and it was too late to fix it. So your grandfather stepped in generously and solved the girl's problem. At the same time he did his nephew and the nephew's wife a great big favor.

Could be, said George. But the family resemblance?

I replied that it extended to half of the Anglo-Scottish population of the Berkshires, there being nothing especially distinctive about the Standish looks. In any case, he could be sure of one thing: it wasn't his father. He had never paid attention to me, one way or the other, and although he seemed to know who I was, I would bet he couldn't remember my name.

We agreed that we wouldn't be solving the riddle. When I suggested that it might be better not to know the answer, he said that was all right with him, but he might start thinking of me as a kid brother anyway—it seemed more natural than uncle. We also agreed on a point of practical importance: we would not mention our conversation to anyone, his parents and sisters and my parents included. He was very solemn about it, which was a relief, and not only because I had given my word to Mr. Hibble. Speaking to George was justified; it was only fair if we were to be friends. But neither of us wanted to make trouble with his parents—if they really didn't know—or mine, or get the Berkshire gossip mill started.

THE SUN HAD SET by the time the train finally pulled into the station. Only one door opened. We ran toward it to help Margot down the steps and take her bags. Yes, she was very beautiful, even if her nose was too big for her face, and she was doing her best to be pleasant. During the few minutes it took us to get to the Standish house, she managed to pet George, who was driving, to wink encouragingly at Henry, and to distinguish me as a special friend, all the while commenting lazily on the Norman Rockwell winter landscape. I concluded that the air of boredom I had found so off-putting at Mario's party might have been only her cocktail party pose.

The Standish parents welcomed us at the door. I refused Mrs. Standish's offer of tea: if I was to make it home to Lenox to change and back in time for a drink before the party, I had better leave at once. My, my, she replied, perhaps you're right; the roads are so very slippery. Do give Jack's and my greetings to your dear parents. We did so like their Christmas card!

I couldn't have cared less about the road conditions and in truth didn't need very much time to get into my dinner jacket, but I felt I had to get away and clear my head before facing Mrs. Standish, Mr. Standish, George's two married sisters, and the sisters' husbands, a New York banker and a New York lawyer. Like everyone in the county my age or younger, I had always found Mr. Standish overbearing and threatening. According to George, that was only self-defense. In reality, his father was gentle and very shy; the real tiger was his mother. That could well be, but in my present situation appearances were more important than some hidden reality. I preferred Mrs. Standish's quiet eighteenth-century face and its expression of profound fatigue mixed with sympathy. Moreover, she didn't just remember my name. She actually seemed to notice me. In fact, the last time I saw her, at the final afternoon concert of the Tanglewood season after my return from France, she had amazed me by asking that I call her May, which was something I couldn't bring myself to do, any more than to call her Cousin May, which my mother had recommended as a suitable alternative when I reported the incident to her.

I had been worrying about what George's parents might say when he told them about our having become close friends and the high opinion of me that he appeared to have; I hoped they would not have found it necessary to say that the friendship was inappropriate. There was some comfort in the thought that they might find it awkward to explain their objections, whether or not they knew that I was a child of sin: What difference should my illegitimate birth make when Lucy Butler in Tyringham, who was invited everywhere, was widely known to have been adopted by old Dr. Butler and his wife? Of course, their feelings might be very strong if I was a skeleton in the family closet. But would they risk taking that skeleton out just to put an end to my palling around with George? There was nothing I knew of that they could say against me personally, other than that some of my contemporaries considered me stuck-up, by which I hoped they meant that I was too literary. They couldn't say I was a sissy; nobody could call me that. So it would have to be that I was disqualified simply as the son of my parents. But even if Mr. and Mrs. Standish thought that my parents' reputation was as bad as I feared, I somehow doubted that they would want to say so to George, or that being told, he wouldn't say that what my parents did was none of his business. In fact, I was coming to think that my vision of my standing in the Berkshires was tinged with hysteria only aggravated by Mr. Hibble's declaration. I had to sort out these thoughts, especially since, if the less pessimistic view was borne out, the gates of the Standish estate—their property deserved that appellation—would no longer be closed to me literally or figuratively and I might be permitted to swim in Mr. Standish's august pool, a privilege, I had been told all too often, granted only to the most favored children and teenagers. In the summer I might even be invited to the Standishes' Sunday lunches. Those gates would not open for my parents, but it didn't seem to me that duty or pride compelled me to refuse such invitations if they came, any more than they dictated rejecting George's friendship.

My parents were at home, still dressing to go out. I changed rapidly and waited for them in the living room. My father brought down a tray with their glasses and the shaker and got busy making another batch of martinis. He asked whether I wanted one. I told them I was to have a drink at George's house and added something about wanting to have my head clear on the road. That focused my mother's mind. She said, Whatever you do, don't crack up my car. And then, to my father, Maybe I'll drive. Maybe you won't, he replied. I won't have any of that stuff.

I looked at them. Their faces were puffy, but overall they were a handsome couple. Being very thin and dressed just right helped, as did table lamps with pink bulbs. My mother wore a silver strapless sheath. She had no breasts to speak of, and her posture in profile was peculiar, something like a sexy question mark. Her legs were exceptional, long and shapely. She had no use for girlfriends and liked men, perhaps even my father, and indeed men swarmed around her. Perfectly respectable men, as well as those about whom people talked. I asked myself whether knowing that she was not my real mother had enabled me to see her more nearly the way other men did, but I couldn't say that there had been a real change.

Are you going to bring your roommate over tomorrow? she asked. Not too early, please. My father interjected, You had better make it late brunch at the club. I said I would have to invite Margot and George as well. The news that George would be his guest caused my father to perk up. He reminded me to give his and Mother's New Year's wishes to the Standish parents, whom for this occasion he called Jack and May, and renewed his offer of a martini. I kissed my mother, shook my father's hand, and prepared to go out into the cold. The thermometer at the door had sunk to nine degrees. My father followed me to the threshold and peeked at the thermometer himself. Take the old raccoon, he said, go on, it won't bite you. I thanked him and put it on.

I hesitated about how far from the Standishes' front door I should park in the circular driveway, and whether my car belonged in the driveway at all. Three were already there: the station wagon George had driven and two other station wagons. I supposed that was the only kind of automobile the family used. A couple of other cars were in the parking space in front of the huge garage that must have once been a stable. It seemed prudent to put my raccoon in the backseat and leave the car right there. The snow had been meticulously cleared and swept. It squeaked cheerfully under my feet. At the door a manservant met me with a tray of drinks. I took a glass of champagne. Champagne was not the standard beverage in the Berkshires, any more than was a man in white gloves or any male servant except the club bartender helping out on his night off. For that matter, waitresses in black satin dresses and lace aprons and headpieces that made them look like chambermaids in a French movie weren't either. I thought of Henry's feeling when he took possession of the dormitory bedroom with a view that he had entered a new world. What could be his impression now? Probably he was concluding, quite correctly, happy and a little frightened, that this was another, wider vista of that same world. Such were my own feelings too, although I was in a territory where, in theory, my feet should be squarely planted, visiting my nearest cousins. These grand relatives were but a few steps away, Mrs. Standish smiling wanly and Mr. Standish, splendid in his white tie and tails, positively beaming. Welcome, welcome, dear boy, he boomed, without waiting for Mrs. Standish to whisper my name to him, I see you have a glass of bubbly, have some more—without pausing for breath he beckoned to the manservant—and meet your girl cousins and their lords and masters. You were still in short pants when they flew the coop! I approached as bidden, pecked Mrs. Standish's cheek when it was offered, took another glass—apparently glasses were exchanged, not refilled—and relayed my parents' greetings. Yes, yes, yes, boomed Mr. Standish again, now come along.

Joanie and Millie took after their father. In consequence they shared with him, George, my father, and, it must be admitted, with me as well, the dirty-blond hair with curls that resisted both comb and brush, the wiry frame, no-nonsense legs, and a facial bone structure that made Mr. Standish and my father indisputably lantern jawed. Perhaps that was a deformation accentuated by age. They were nice women and, like their husbands, briskly polite and full of chatter. In rapid succession, they told me the ages and sexes of their five children, ranging from six to thirteen, as well as their summer arrangements. One set of in-laws had a house on the North Shore of Long Island, the other on the North Shore of Massachusetts. This enabled Millie to spend the last couple of weeks of June and all of July in Beverly, during which time Joanie had the use of the cottage on the Standish property. During the first week of August, Millie, her husband, and their children squeezed into the big house with the Standish parents, so that the whole family could be together. Then Joanie took over the cottage until it was time for the kids to go back to school, while Millie and her gang moved on to Syosset. Having duly mastered and admired these arrangements, I said I should find George and his house-guests, and moved on.

They were in the library, Margot with her back to the fire. She said she was freezing; the hot bath hadn't gotten the cold out of her bones. She wore a long velvet dress of vivid red and red silk shoes. I supposed Mrs. Standish must be pleased by her chic. Henry's appearance impressed me. Archie had talked him into exchanging the double-breasted dinner jacket that had been his mother's purchase at Altman's for an ancient Brooks Brothers model from Keezer's with peaked lapels of exaggerated width, rather like the one my father wore. It had evidently been treated by the original owner with loving care. They had also acquired a silk dress shirt that had turned dark ivory with age. As a final touch, Archie taught him how to tie his bow tie loosely, so that it drooped like a Confederate officer's mustache. The jacket was slightly too big for Henry, enhancing the devil-may-care effect. His face was flushed—I supposed from champagne and excitement—and he gestured as he talked, making Margot and George laugh. I knew how conscious he was of the anomaly of his presence. Was that awareness contributing to his high spirits? Or was that how he overcame his anxiety? In either case he was managing just fine.

I DID NOT OBSERVE Henry's progress during dinner at the club. He and George and Margot were at Mrs. Standish's table, and I was with Mr. Standish. As soon as the tables had been cleared, a stag line formed, and Henry and I and most of the other young men drifted into it. Older men remained with their wives and daughters or, if they too drifted away, it was in the direction of the bar. Mr. Standish was in the latter group. As soon as Henry realized that Mrs. Standish had been left alone—her daughters were on the dance floor with their husbands, and George was busy introducing Margot around—he hurried to her side. A moment later, they were on the dance floor. I would not have thought ballroom dancing had figured in Henry's curriculum in Poland or Brooklyn, but Mrs. Standish's face left no doubt that she thought he was a fine partner. His example inspired me not to wait until the set was over. I cut in as soon as the band had worked its way through "Tea for Two." Unfortunately, the next dance was a rumba. My knowledge of the box step was too theoretical for spontaneity, let alone fun, and at first Mrs. Standish made an effort to lead that only confused me the more. We carried on grimly until she said she was thirsty and asked whether I would mind returning to the table and getting her something to drink. She longed to have a chat. Humiliated but grateful, I pushed my way to the bar. When I returned to the table with two glasses of champagne, I found that she and I were alone.

She gave me a thin-lipped smile and said, How nice, now we can really talk.

I had supposed that our subject would be Margot and perhaps some banalities about my parents. It wasn't that at all. Her voice as light as a dragonfly skimming over water, she murmured, Your roommate is so charming. How interesting that you and George and he should be friends. I suppose you have known Henry for a long time.

I said that we met for the first time in our dormitory room, the day my mother dropped me off in Cambridge. Our other roommate was someone I had also never seen before, the son of an army officer who had moved around a good deal because of his father's transfers to new posts.

Oh, said Mrs. Standish, how very interesting. You chose each other without ever having met!

Now I knew what she was driving at. Stalling, I laughed and said we hadn't done any such thing. The university housing office had played God and made all the choices. The marvel of it was that the three of us got along exceedingly well.

Oh, said Mrs. Standish once again, more pensively. What an odd system! Come to think of it, perhaps it isn't. I don't suppose that Henry knew anybody at Harvard. Or am I wrong? Perhaps he already had a large group of friends from New York. He is from New York, isn't he? I think that's what he told me. Or was it George who said so?

I didn't want to correct her by pointing out that Henry lived in Brooklyn, so I said that she was quite right. Hoping to move the conversation into a broader channel, I said that the university in fact matched many more roommates than one would think. For instance, I was the only member of my graduating class at school to be going to Harvard, and I knew no one else except George who was going to be in the freshman class. As it turned out I had assumed correctly that he was already spoken for.

He would have liked to room with you ever so much, Mrs. Standish assured me. You should have proposed it just as soon as you found out you were going. Or he should have thought of it. All of you are so brilliant and so completely scatterbrained! Jack and I are very pleased to see that you have become such good friends. We've always thought you should be, but of course one doesn't want to interfere.

I wasn't entirely sure whether I should believe her but found it easy to say that I was very pleased too. That was, after all, the truth.

It was Henry, however, who was on Mrs. Standish's mind. How well that boy dances, she exclaimed. I haven't waltzed in years. He made me quite dizzy. I believe that he told me he was Polish and came here with his parents after the war. That must account for the waltz and for that lovely little accent. I meant to ask him about it. Where did he prepare?

The extraordinary thing, I said, was that for all practical purposes he didn't. There had been one year in Poland, and two years in a high school in New York. It was all the fault of the war.

How perfectly remarkable. Three years of schooling and then Harvard College. Those schools he attended must be very good. But yes, he is, of course, exceptional.

Although this wasn't a question, I answered, Yes, he is!

She was clearly going to ask more questions, but Mr. and Mrs. Livingston, a couple no less exalted than the Standishes, sat down at our table, and I hurried off to get an eggnog for Mrs. Livingston. When we were alone again, Mrs. Standish asked whether White was a Polish name; the Poles who settled in Berkshire County all seemed to be called Kowak or Nowak. There are so many of them, she pointed out, in West Stockbridge they even have a Polish social club of their own. They are good workers, some of them, and serious churchgoers.

The parents changed the name, I said, shortly after they arrived. They have adopted the English translation of Weiss.

Weiss? she said. Jack guessed right away it was something of the sort, she continued. Oh dear, he thinks that Henry must be Jewish.

It was impossible to play dumb. Accordingly, I nodded cheerfully and said that Mr. Standish had guessed right.

Oh dear, she said. Of course it can't be helped. He is a very nice young man.

And very gifted, I interjected.

She smiled gently and continued. There are a good many of them at Harvard now. That's what Jack says. They're even at Groton. That has made some alumni upset, for instance that dreadful man, Cousin Hoyt. How lucky we are that he has decided to live in Tucson. We never have to see him. Oh dear! Henry's family must be very nice too. He seems so very well brought up.

Further discussion of this subject had to be suspended. Henry returned from the dance floor, bringing Margot.

VIII

SHORTLY BEFORE MIDNIGHT, the president of the club had the band play a fanfare to get the crowd's attention and proposed a toast to our fighting men holding their own against Chinese human waves and their leader, General MacArthur, under whom he had himself had the honor to serve. Someone called for a minute of silence, after which the band struck up "The Star-Spangled Banner" and we all sang. Some people were crying. The band segued into "Some Enchanted Evening," and dancing continued until it was time for whistles and other noisemakers, wishes, and embraces. All the while the band played first "Auld Lang Syne" and then "Greensleeves" over and over. Mr. and Mrs. Standish began to say their goodnights. As I was thanking them, Mrs. Standish invited me to lunch. One o'clock, as always on New Year's Day, she said. Oh my, we will have to soldier on even in this awful time for the nation, she said. It would be too depressing to cancel. And then she added, You really must stop calling me Mrs. Standish. It's May. You may call Jack Cousin Jack, if you like, but he would prefer Jack, *tout court*. He has told me so. She offered me her cheek to kiss. Mr. Standish held out his hand and said, Quite right. You've just heard *la patronne*. Call me Jack! Best to the parents. Tell your old man about the toast. He'll be happy to know a glass was raised to our boys in uniform.

The dance floor was still crowded. Henry was dancing with Margot, and George with a girl I didn't know. She wasn't a Berkshire person. Feeling suddenly very sleepy, and not wanting to wait until they had finished, I caught George's eye, waved farewell, and drove home. My parents were still out when I went to bed, and they were still in their room when I came downstairs in the morning. There was ample evidence, however, of their being at home. Odd pieces of clothing were scattered on the floor of the front hall and in the living room; my mother's panties hung over the banister. On the kitchen table, I found the remnants of a meal they must have eaten after getting in late at night. It was my father's firm belief that cheese and sausage consumed just before bed palliated the next day's hangover. Seeing and smelling the stuff discouraged me from making breakfast, but I scraped their plates and put the leftovers in the fridge. My father's Oldsmobile was in the driveway. He had not bothered to put it into the garage, but at least he hadn't cracked it up. The key was in the ignition. Despite the bitter cold, the engine turned over on the third or fourth try. I let it idle for about ten minutes and backed into the garage. This would be my second good deed for the day. I scribbled a note reminding my mother that I was taking her station wagon and, unable to think of any other place that would be open, drove to the drugstore in West Lee for coffee and toast. I didn't want to arrive at the Standishes' too early or with an empty stomach.

ONE LOOK AROUND the Standishes' living room sufficed to confirm that this event was reserved for the crème de la crème of Stockbridge, Tyringham, and Lenox. I knew many of the faces, even if I couldn't pretend to greater familiarity. No one but George, Margot, and Henry was roughly in my age group. Perhaps families were not necessarily invited as units, a circumstance that should have made me less queasy about being without my parents, who as the regulars would immediately realize upon seeing me, if they bothered to think about it, had always been excluded. But I remained uneasy, although I was grateful to be spared the embarrassment of greeting contemporaries and had no cause to complain about any lack of cordiality on the part of my hosts, or about the number of hands that reached out for my own as I crossed the living room. I found Margot in the library, on a window seat, face turned toward the Standishes' back lawn, which was blindingly white under drifts of virgin snow. Beyond were lines of black pine, and farther beyond the white bulk of Monument Mountain. She seemed lost in thought and didn't notice my approach. Perhaps because she wasn't wearing lipstick, her face seemed smaller, less outrageous, and oddly sad. I said I hoped she had slept well and asked about George and Henry.

Oh, she answered, just check the Ping-Pong table on the glassed-in porch over there. She gestured vaguely toward the side of the house. George is trouncing Henry. It's sickening to watch. Why does Henry want to play with him?

I said I could think of at least two reasons: to be polite to his host, who could never sit still, and to get good enough at the game to be able to beat him eventually.

She shrugged and asked me to get her a drink. Not this ghastly stuff, she specified, pointing at my cup of eggnog, I'd like a bourbon.

The previous evening's manservant was again on duty and brought the drink on a small silver tray. As soon as he was out of earshot, I asked Margot whether she thought that he was the Standishes' butler or someone hired for the occasion. You and Henry ask the same questions, she replied. Who cares? Judging by his clothes, I'd say he works here.

We clinked glasses, she said chin-chin, and unexpectedly gave me a big smile, like the one I saw that first day in the Yard, though without lipstick. Then, without another word having been said, the smile vanished, and she went back to looking at Monument Mountain. I was going to ask whether something was the matter, but the manservant—I wondered what it was she saw in his clothes that marked him as the Standishes' permanent employee—announced that lunch was served. Mrs. Standish, or May, as I was trying to think of her, directed us to our table. George and Henry were already there, as were the sisters Appleton, the elder of whom, Ellen, was the headmistress of a girls' school in Brookline. I had a dim recollection that the other one, Susie, wrote children's books that regularly won prizes. They were Mr. Standish's cousins on his mother's side and lived together in Boston, in a house on Beacon Hill. They also shared in Tyringham a Shaker house of great beauty that had belonged to their parents, where they spent summers and, out of season, long weekends and holidays. By putting the sisters with us, Mrs. Standish had achieved a balanced table without resorting to an equivalent of a children's table or seating George and Margot away from Henry and me. But at what cost? The sisters had the reputation of being ferocious and unapproachable blue-stockings, especially Ellen. Perhaps they would only speak to each other, and to George, because he was a relative. But I needn't have worried. As soon as George had named the girls' school in New York that Margot had attended, Ellen put to her a series of questions about the former head-mistress and the programs in modern foreign languages and music. Margot hardly bothered to answer, speaking in negligent monosyllables. I wondered why she was sulking. Perhaps it was in order to bait George, but so far as I could tell he had been very attentive at the dance and was trying to be a good host at this table. I kept my eye on Ellen. It seemed impossible that she would tolerate disrespectful behavior from a girl who could have easily been one of her own charges. There was going to be an explosion, but what form would it take, the usual punishments, such as keeping Margot after school or sending her home with an unpleasant note, not being available? George should have been coming to the rescue, but he didn't seem to notice anything amiss. Fortunately Henry was creating a distraction so surprising that I thought it might preserve Margot from the headmistress's wrath. He had told me that he really liked the Standishes' eggnog. Perhaps he had had one too many. That was, in any event, my explanation for the rather loud and peculiar conversation in which he engaged Susie. He wanted to know to what extent her stories had been inspired by the bodies of work of such writers as the Brothers Grimm and Hans Christian Andersen. He expressed at length his surprise at her dislike of these authors and asked more questions, the result of which was that Susie acknowledged one influence, Louisa May Alcott. Henry confessed that he had never read *Little Women*—for a moment I had feared that he would try to fake familiarity with it—and declared that he would now put it on his reading list. Then, as though determined not to yield the floor, he began, without transition, a discourse on the subject of a Polish fairy tale about a certain Pan Twardowski, the nobleman who sold his soul to the devil, lived like a king while the devil did his bidding, and in the end cheated the devil out of his due by fleeing to the moon. The figure of the man in the moon that you can see when the moon is full, he concluded, is none other than Pan Twardowski. He's laughing his head off.

A primitive retelling of the German Faust legend, observed Ellen.

Henry blushed. Yes, of course, he answered, I should have said so right away.

It was obvious to me and perhaps to everyone else as well that he had never considered the connection, and I wished he had simply said so. Susie decided to be merciful. But Ellen, dear, she said to the headmistress, isn't it true that Faust-like figures exist in most cultures? Perhaps it isn't a retelling at all.

Most may be an overstatement, was the somewhat grumpy reply. How is one to know whether there is a Zulu Faust?

With that, the headmistress turned her attention to Henry and inquired whether he was by any chance of Polish origin. She thought she was hearing a slight and very pretty Slavic accent, and added to that was his knowledge of a Polish fairy tale.

It is a Polish accent, answered Henry.

Really! And how did that come about?

I was born there, in Poland.

But you must have been very little when you left.

That depends on how little I seem now. We left Poland three years ago.

Really, the headmistress said again. And where did you go after you left Poland?

We came here, Henry answered.

Where is here? she pursued. Not the Berkshires, I imagine.

Oh no, we went to New York.

When you say we, do you mean you and your family?

Henry nodded. Yes, my parents and I. I'm an only child.

And you prepared for college in New York?

Yes, said Henry. And before that, for one year I attended a Polish secondary school in Krakow. That was right after the war.

The headmistress became very pensive and said she supposed that the high school in New York was St. Ignatius Loyola, well known for its high standards. She had seen the rector in October, at a philological society meeting.

No, no, replied Henry, and named his high school.

How extraordinary! the headmistress exclaimed. I've never heard of it.

Hasn't May told me that you and George are classmates? Is it possible that you went to Harvard College directly from there?

And on a full scholarship, Cousin Ellen, interjected George.

To my surprise, Margot gave him an unequivocally dirty look. Perhaps she thought that he was patronizing Henry. I doubted that George noticed, the response of Cousin Ellen being so striking that it must have diverted attention from Margot. That formidable lady stretched out her hand over the table, patted, and then squeezed Henry's hand, and said that she was going to tell May Standish how especially grateful she was for having been given the opportunity to meet such a remarkable young man. Would he come to dinner at her and Susie's house in Boston? she asked. Oh yes, she added, of course I will want you to bring this lovely young woman, your charming roommate, and dear George.

There was a large handbag on the floor next to her chair. She brought it onto her lap and, having extracted a notepad and a fat fountain pen, asked Henry to write his name, address, and telephone number, and Margot's too. After he had handed the pad back to her, she examined it, and with an air of puzzlement read aloud: Henry White. Henry White.

How odd, she said at last, I wouldn't have thought that White was a Polish surname.

It isn't. My parents changed our name when we arrived here. It had been Weiss. The name isn't necessarily Jewish, but in this case it was.

Remembering how Archie had been obliged to pull this information out of him, I was astonished. The setting then had been in a sense private: three roommates chatting as they walked through the Yard on the way to dinner. Here, Henry could be justified in thinking that he was on public display, and in enemy territory. Dragged along behind a victor's chariot, was the way he might have put it. Had he gotten into the habit of revealing himself? I doubted it; in fact, I wondered whether he had ever told Margot or George what his name had been. I couldn't be sure about Margot, but George would never have asked, and I didn't believe Henry would have volunteered. It occurred to me that if Henry had not said anything to those two, that might be a strong reason to get the disclosures over with quickly, the headmistress being most unlikely to relent until her questions had been answered. He was killing two birds with one stone:

forestalling the continuation of questions that I was sure humiliated him and clearing up an ambiguity in his relations with Margot and George.

You poor boy, said the headmistress, once again reaching for his hand. You and your parents must have suffered greatly. Were you in a concentration camp?

Henry told her that they hadn't been. We all saw that he wanted to leave it at that, but the headmistress's long habit of sounding the depths of her girls' souls prevailed over her sympathy—sympathy vivid enough to require her to dab at her eyes with a little handkerchief. She went on prodding him, very gently to be sure, and at last I heard Henry speak of the grubby indignities endured during the years at Pani Maria's, which he had told me so firmly he wouldn't discuss. He showed no emotion. At first I admired his composure, which in a way seemed well suited to the comfortable room and the refinement of the lunch table. Then I saw that it wasn't composure at all. He was absent. He talked as if in a trance, not entirely aware of those around him or his own presence in their midst. Perhaps he had learned to abstract himself from his own past. Perhaps the faculty through which we feel outrage and self-pity had been cauterized in him.

When the story had been told, Susie asked Henry whether he had read John Hersey's new novel, *The Wall*.

What is it about, Cousin Susie? interrupted George.

She said it was about the destruction of the Warsaw Ghetto during the Jewish uprising. What the Germans did to the Jews: a dreadful, almost unbelievable story but entirely true.

My mother has given it to me, he replied. I haven't read it yet, but I intend to.

You'll love it, Susie assured him. Mr. Weeks gave it the most brilliant review in the *Atlantic*. I would so much like to know what you think.

Henry smiled and said nothing.

Under the butler's supervision, the waitresses were passing green and gold demitasses of coffee in the adjoining room. As we were rising from the table, the headmistress said that the story Henry had told was of the highest importance. Would he be willing to tell it again, she asked, at her and Susie's home, to a small gathering of friends, some of whom would be her colleagues? This was not to be in place of the much more jolly dinner to which she hoped he would come with his young friends; indeed the many dinners she hoped they would have together.

Henry shook his head. I told it to you because you made me feel that you really wanted to know, and that you really wanted to understand an experience that I'm no longer sure I understand. That was an exception. I really don't want to talk about the war to a group after dinner.

She didn't seem offended.

Almost at once, Margot declared she had a headache and went to her room. I thought I'd go home, but George suggested that Henry and I take turns at Ping-Pong against him. I agreed, and saw that Margot was right: had I been Henry, I wouldn't have kept coming for more. But I wasn't him. The implications of that simple fact were too numerous; I felt crowded by them. After a few games, I did capitulate. Paddle in hand, George was an insufferable bully. Since Mrs. Standish had also gone upstairs, I asked him to thank his mother for me and say that I would write from Cambridge.

Henry caught up with me at the door.

You know, he told me, I really don't like people who ask personal questions. Aren't they willing to figure out anything for themselves?

They're nice ladies, I replied, though pretty tough sledding. They didn't mean any harm. They've just never met anyone like you. They think you're great.

He mulled that over, and said, Yes, they're nice ladies. Then he added, I didn't know you were so thick with all these people, the rich gentry. You know every one of them, and they all know you!

These are small New England towns, I told him. Full of small-time scandal and curiosity. Summer people come and go, but the locals all know one another. That's all it is.

The following day, Henry and Margot took the train back to New York, and the day after, before dawn, George and I went up to Stowe. We planned to ski and get back in the evening. Driving three hours over those icy roads twice in one day was a crazy thing to do, but by nine-thirty we were on the slopes. Except for the bitter cold, the conditions were perfect, and, by the time we finished, we were exhausted and also famished. From a grocery store still open we bought a loaf of Wonder Bread, a jar of peanut butter, grape jelly, and a quart of milk. I made sandwiches, and we passed the milk bottle back and forth while George drove. This being his father's new car, he was reluctant to let me take the wheel. I was about to doze off when George began to speak about Henry and Margot's visit.

She's a hard nut to crack. I think I've really gummed it up with her. Did you notice how she'd hardly talk to me at lunch?

I said I had. She had seemed gloomy.

You mean pissed off!

Should she be?

I don't know. We've been necking, but it's never gone far. After the dance, when everyone had gone to bed, I decided I'd make my move. I guess it wasn't appreciated.

I made no comment.

She's sexy as hell, and she isn't exactly the Virgin Mary. She talks a great game, but when it comes down to it, you'd swear nobody had ever touched her. It's true. I kind of forced the issue, and that really pissed her off.

I asked what he was going to do about it.

You tell me. When I said let's get together as soon as we get back to Cambridge, she said she wouldn't have time. Full stop. I think I'll ask Henry to talk to her. She really likes him, and he's a really good guy. You saw how he made a hit with the parents and with those two old birds? They've never said more than two words to me before. I'm glad I invited him. Mother said I should get him to come back in the summer.

We drove in silence for a while and then he said, Do you know what Bunny Rollins told me about her? I wasn't going to repeat it, but I'm pissed too. According to Bunny, Margot is the only girl in her class who has a diaphragm. Now I ask you, why does she have it if she doesn't want to get laid?

Bunny Rollins was a girl from Tyringham with quite a reputation for round heels herself.

How does Bunny know? I asked.

Damned if I know, he replied. That sort of thing gets around.

IX

I GOT BACK TO CAMBRIDGE late in the afternoon on the day before the start of the reading period. George and his mother gave me a ride, and May invited both of us to dinner at her club in the Back Bay where she was staying. We were to be there at seven. In the meantime, I went to the dormitory to drop off my bag and freshen up. I saw no sign of Archie's or Henry's having returned. The telephone rang as I was leaving. The caller introduced himself as Colonel Palmer. We had never spoken before; my previous conversations had been with Mrs. Palmer. The colonel said he had distressing news: Archie had been in a car accident on Christmas Day. His leg was in a full-length cast. The doctors thought that in a week or ten days he would be able to take the plane to New York and from there another one to Boston, but the cast wouldn't come off for some weeks after that. Archie would need a wheelchair at the airport and certainly wouldn't be able to cope with his luggage. Would Henry or I meet him? I explained that Henry was still away and assured the colonel that one or both of us would be there. Splendid, he said, in that case he or Mrs. Palmer would be in touch again, as soon as the travel plans had been finalized. I asked whether I could say hello to Archie. Not this afternoon, replied the colonel. He is full of painkillers and in and out of sleep.

As it turned out, I went alone to pick up Archie at Logan. Henry had a class that met during the reading period which he couldn't miss. Neither my first phone conversation with the colonel, nor the second when he called with the flight information, nor even the one with Archie when at last I got him on the telephone had prepared me for how badly banged up he was.

You're a real mess, I said to him, once I had collected his luggage with the stewardess's help and we were propelling him in his wheelchair toward the taxi line.

He said it could have been much worse. The broken nose, entirely taped over, and the cuts on his forehead and left cheek were from having been thrown against the windshield. How the leg had gotten broken in two places was a mystery. He didn't know, having passed out cold.

A fuller description of the crash came during the ride to Cambridge. He had stayed late at a reception at the officers' club on the base, talking to a second lieutenant's wife whom he described as a bit of all right, and afterward drove his mother's Simca to a party given by locals at a hacienda some thirty miles away over a straight and reasonably well-paved highway. It was a moonless night, with the sky full of stars, and he was having fun. The Simca was a piece of junk, and he floored the gas pedal to see how fast she would go. In fact, it held the road better than he had expected, and the speedometer went up to one fifty. Kilometers, of course, he explained. Everything was fine, he was tooling along pleasantly, when a pickup truck full of peons pulled in from a feeder road. They had no business there; he was on the main road and had the right-of-way. In fact, he didn't even realize that they were there before he had rammed them. Later he found out that the hombre riding in the passenger seat of the cab was dead and another, who had been thrown from the truck bed, wasn't going to make it. The rest were no worse off than he. Someone in a car that stopped to look at the wreck noticed his mother's Canal Zone license plates and when he got to a phone called the base so that the MPs got there first, ahead of the local gendarmes.

That was pure luck, he added. I was taken right away to the American hospital, and we didn't have to deal with the natives. That is something you definitely want to avoid. Not that anyone could have tried to make me walk a straight line with my leg looking like a corkscrew! I don't know whether anyone cared about my breath, but I had the brains to gargle before I left the club. One good thing is that Father now wants Mither to get a real car to replace the Simca. The other good news is that she has decided to give me wheels of my own, as soon as I get rid of this—he tapped his cast—and finish rehabilitation.

The wheels turned out to be the Nash in which I would take Clara to her prom.

Archie told me about another pleasant change in the Palmer family's circumstances. For years, his maternal grandfather had bought oil and gas rights in the Texas Panhandle. Few people paid much attention to these properties, but it was the old boy's custom to make investments—small bets on real long shots. When he died, Archie's mother, being the only child, inherited them. Now on one location a wildcatter working in partnership with his mother had hit a gusher. A couple of other sites seemed promising as well. More gas than oil, he added, and not enough to make them rich, though it would make it easier for his father to retire.

Several days passed before I had a chance to ask Henry about his impressions of the Berkshires and the Standishes, and the other autochthons he had observed. He was very pleased and made no attempt to appear nonchalant. When he said he wished he had been able to meet my parents, I told him that they had particularly asked me to bring him over to the house for lunch, but the Standishes' lunch had made that impossible. In reality, I had made an alternate plan to invite him to tea on New Year's Day, but thought that I should hold off until I had returned home from the Standishes' and checked my parents' condition. My prudence proved justified. They were too sick to make it downstairs, let alone receive a guest. I made a pot of coffee, carried it upstairs, and put it outside their bedroom door. At about six, I scrambled some eggs and ate them at the kitchen table. *The Asphalt Jungle* was playing in Great Barrington. For a change, I took my father's Oldsmobile instead of my mother's Chevy and went to see it.

We talked afterward about George and the day's skiing at Stowe, and I asked whether he understood what was eating him and Margot. Henry hesitated before admitting that he did. I believe that he would have preferred to hold his tongue. We had, however, by then gotten into a habit of speaking to each other frankly, without sufficient regard for discretion.

It's an odd business, he told me, and you mustn't ever repeat what I'll tell you.

I laughed, because the warning that whatever he was telling me in confidence must remain between us was the invariable preface to such disclosures, and I regularly teased him about it.

All right, he said, this time I'm serious. Margot and I went for a walk up the road from the Standishes' toward Monument Mountain. This was before the New Year's Day lunch. After a while, she took my arm and said she wanted to speak to me about something rotten that had happened to her. Here is the story: When they got back to the house after the dance, and everybody was milling about saying goodnight, George asked whether he could come to her room after everybody had gone to bed. She said that was all right, but he couldn't stay long. They had been making out in Cambridge, of course, mostly when he walked her home in the evening, but they'd never gone very far. So she waited for him, reading in bed, in her pajamas. She would have stayed in her party dress if it hadn't been so uncomfortable, and anyway she hadn't taken off her bra or her panties. Just between you and me, I'm sure she thought that was more sexy and she wasn't opposed to some heavy necking. Anyway, about half an hour later, George tiptoes in and they go through their usual routine, or a little more, only this time George doesn't want to stop; he says they have to go all the way. She said no, they argued a little; she let him do something that wasn't part of the routine; at some point she thought the pressure was off because he got all subdued, as though he'd lost interest. Anyway, he kissed her once more very nicely and left. She took off her underclothes, got back into bed, and was out like a light. Probably it was the champagne at the club and the nightcap back at the house. Anyway she woke up to find George wasn't just in her bed. He was inside her. She didn't scream or anything; she let him finish. She'd just had her period, so no problem there. When he started to tell her how he loved her and how happy she had made him, she told him he was a shit and they were through. She wasn't going to tell Mrs. Standish or go home by the first train, but she warned him he had better stay away from her.

George picked a great way to start the year, I said.

Henry nodded. So the following night—that's the night before Margot and I left for New York—the whole house went to bed early. Everybody was bushed. I don't know whether you have been upstairs at the Standishes'. The parents' bedroom, the children's bedrooms, and the best guest room, where Margot was, are on the second floor, on two sides of a wide corridor that is more like a hall. The smaller guest rooms are one flight up.

They put me in one of the guest rooms on the third floor. It was cold up there, much colder than the rest of the house, but I had three blankets and was very snug. Sometime in the middle of the night I realized that my door was being opened. Guess what—it was Margot. She said, It's me, will you let me stay with you? Before I had a chance to answer, she slipped in under the covers and put her arms around me. I can't sleep, she said, I'm too afraid that he is going to try something again. My heart was beating like crazy. She was wearing a nightgown and I could feel that she had nothing under it. She said her feet were blocks of ice, and she warmed them on top of mine. But when I tried to touch her, she said, Please, please don't, it can't be like that, I want you to be my brother. I asked her, Don't you know I love you? She told me that was silly, because I didn't understand anything about her, and if I did I wouldn't feel that way. Please, let's sleep, she said finally. I'll be gone before daylight. She turned on her side and asked me to put my arms around her. We stayed like that until she left. She did sleep; I don't think I slept at all.

Why do you think she wouldn't do it?

He shrugged and said, I suppose it's for all the reasons we've talked about so many times. It doesn't matter whether she is fond of me. She knows I'm not right for her. There may be one other reason that occurred to me during that night. It could be that she doesn't want me to realize how much she knows about sex. Probably that's nonsense, one of those literary notions. How would I be able to tell, and why would I care?

So what happens now? I asked.

Nothing. I do love her. That won't change. For the time being, I have my term papers to worry about. By the way, he added, I've been to her house; I've actually met those parents.

Really?

During the train ride to New York she asked when I was going back to Cambridge. She was going the same afternoon, so she asked me to dinner at their apartment the evening before. You wouldn't believe this place. It's on Park Avenue, and it takes up a whole floor of the building. You step out of the elevator, and you're in their apartment, there isn't even a doorbell, not even a door, just a man, like the Standishes' butler, waiting to lead you into the living room. I only saw the living room, the dining room, and the library, and that already was like being in a museum, no joke. Mr. Hornung collects Dutch drawings and paintings. He also seems to like Dutch furniture. The only other guest was a very tall old man who had been the U.S. ambassador to Romania or Hungary before the war, or maybe both at one time or another. Mr. Hornung and the ambassador were in tuxedos, sorry, I mean dinner jackets, and Mrs. Hornung wore a long dress. Margot had warned me about that. She said her parents dress for dinner every night, but I didn't have to and she wasn't going to put on a long skirt. By the way, she told me to say dinner jacket or black tie and use the word "tuxedo" only if I'm talking about Tuxedo Park. Did you know that? If you did you should have mentioned it to me.

I answered that there were lots of rules like that, but I didn't take them very seriously. In fact, I said, many people break them on purpose. Then I asked whether the evening had been a success.

It was weird, he said, but on the whole all right. Practically the first thing the father did was to ask me when, in my opinion, did the Renaissance end. The silence in the living room was complete, except for the butler saying, Sir, here is your martini. I was petrified and thought I would spill my drink, but I took my time before answering. Finally, I said I couldn't give a specific date, but it seemed to me that the Renaissance began to end when the Counter-Reformation took hold. Sometime after the last Council of Trent. As soon as I got this out, I began to feel faint. I was wondering whether he would order me to leave his house at once and never darken his doorway again or just call me a pretentious ass. Instead, he looked at me very thoughtfully and said, Quite plausible, quite plausible, though of course there would be local variations. After that, he launched into a discussion of Rubens and Rembrandt that I couldn't really follow, so I only kept nodding. Then dinner was served, and as soon as we sat down he began to grill me about Poland. That wasn't too bad. After the workout I got with those old ladies in Stockbridge, I could handle it and concentrated on finishing the crabmeat salad, which was very good. Just as veal with morel mushrooms in a cream sauce was being passed, Mr. Hornung asked whether there was some novel I had read when my mother and I were in hiding that was my absolute favorite.

I thought it would be lowbrow to say *Ivanhoe,* so I said *Jean Christophe.*

This got him very excited. Romain Rolland, he said, really. How did you come upon him? I told him that all my books during the war years came from Pani Maria, and she had especially recommended that one. Probably it was because she loved Beethoven and played his sonatas on the piano. Ah, Mr. Hornung cried, when I was young *Jean Christophe* was my bible! I too played Beethoven! Have you read this great work in its entirety? I answered that certainly I hadn't read all ten volumes—if that is the right number. The book I read was quite thick, but it might have been some sort of abridgment. He gave me this big smile and said that it would be worth my while to read the entire work someday in French, if possible, because it's so very beautiful. Perhaps during the summer vacation.

Where did you get the Counter-Reformation idea? I asked.

I bet you think I was shooting from the hip, as usual. It's something I've been thinking about for some time. I don't know whether I'm right or even whether it's a respectable theory, but it makes sense to me. The repression of disagreement and new ideas—with the Inquisition and the way the Church clamped down on science. Protestants weren't the only target. Humanistic ideals that had propelled the Renaissance were also repressed. Anyway, after the Romain Rolland incident I once again thought I was out of the woods. But right away the ambassador returned to the subject of Poland, and it wasn't to discuss personal experiences. Far from it. He wanted my views on the problem of Jews who wouldn't or couldn't assimilate, not just the very religious Orthodox or Hasidic Jews, but also the ignorant lower class that spoke Yiddish and wouldn't learn the national language. An intractable problem, he said, very tough for the governments in Poland and Romania. Maybe he mentioned Hungary too. And for the nationalist Christian populations of those countries. I didn't answer, so he asked me whether I had been brought up speaking Yiddish. No, I said. But you speak it? he said in this very thin voice with an accent like May Standish's. You get the feeling that he picks each word up with tweezers and examines it before actually opening his mouth. No, I said again.

Ah, he says, you were brought up in a Polish-speaking culturally Polish family.

I nodded.

That confirmed, believe it or not, he asked whether, in view of my secular education, I agreed with his assessment that these unassimilated hordes—I'm not making it up, he said unassimilated hordes—were a problem that, like it or not, called for a solution.

By this time I was furious, and I no longer cared about the Hornungs and their Dutch art, and whether they would throw me out of their house. So I asked him why in his opinion the wise people who didn't like unassimilated Jews had locked them up in ghettos—before they figured out it was even more efficient to kill them. Didn't ghettos stand in the way of assimilation?

That didn't get the sort of rise out of him that I had expected. He said that obviously, at my age, with my secular Polish family, I couldn't have acquired much direct familiarity with the problem. Then he began to ask me whether my family had been friends with a whole series of Polish nobles who had been great friends of his, at whose estates he had hunted the wild boar. Count Potocki and Count Zamoyski and Prince Radziwill and on and on. I said I didn't think we'd known them, with one exception. I had heard that one of my paternal great-uncles used to sell manure to Prince Sapieha.

This is when Mrs. Hornung said, Really the world is so sad and so dangerous, and Mr. Hornung—perhaps taking the hint that the conversation had to be moved into another channel—began a long speech about Truman and how it may be necessary to drop an atom bomb or two on the Chinese. That launched Margot into the stratosphere. She said that dropping the bomb on the Japanese had been a crime that America would never live down and how could he even think of perpetrating such a monstrosity on another nation in Asia. They got into a real fight, with the ambassador explaining how national self-interest has to come ahead of any sentimental considerations. Nobody asked my opinion.

I congratulated Henry on how he had handled himself.

Actually, he said, if I had it to do over, I'd really let that old fart have it.

After coffee, Henry continued, when her father and the ambassador had quieted down and begun discussing investments, Margot asked whether I would take her to hear a black singer, Mabel Mercer. I could see that Margot and her parents were enthusiastic about her; suddenly I remembered that Margot's mother had been in the business herself. Probably this singer was someone I should have known about and perhaps even seen. I don't have to tell you that I would have taken Margot to hear anything—including "Baby It's Cold Outside"—if she only asked. So we went to a little nightclub twenty blocks down from her parents' place, on East Fifty-fourth Street. I thought they might not let us in when they asked whether we had a reservation, but they did. They even gave us a good table. Mabel Mercer is fat but in a kind of sexy way. Surprisingly, she has an English accent. Margot loved the performance, and I must say I liked it quite a lot too. When we asked for two Scotch and sodas they brought them without asking about our age. Two whiskeys seemed plenty, but when I saw that there was a minimum I said, Let's have two more. To make a long story short, after the check, including the waiter's tip, and the taxi fare to Margot's house, I found I had spent literally my last nickel. I didn't even have the subway fare to get home. At least she let me kiss her, not in the door of her apartment building, because of the doorman, but sort of in the middle of the block. She even opened her mouth.

And you didn't ask her to lend you the subway fare?

How could I? It would have made her feel bad about having gone through all my money. I figured I'd walk home, but by the time I got down to the Bowery it was three in the morning. The thought that I still had to cross Manhattan Bridge and then keep going all the way to Flatbush, which would have taken at least an hour and a half, was very discouraging. That's when I noticed a nice-looking young cop standing in front of a shuttered pawnshop. I went up to him, told him exactly what happened, and said that if he lent me a dime and gave me his name I'd send him back a paper dollar. Or leave it at the precinct. He said, Here take a quarter and get a good night's sleep. The truth is that when I got home I did sleep like a baby, although I was so excited that I didn't think I'd be able to close my eyes.

I said that the chances of his becoming Mr. Hornung's son-in-law were improving.

Henry smiled. I'd be satisfied with much less.

X

SOON AFTER THE START of the new semester, Henry went to dinner with the Appleton sisters at their Louisburg Square house. The invitation came by letter and said nothing about George or me. Henry asked what I thought he should do. I told him he should go. It was bound to be amusing to see how the sisters live, and they would probably invite us together some other time. We'll see, said Henry. Margot certainly won't come if she knows that George is going to be there. But he agreed that he would accept the invitation.

I went to the movies the evening of the party. When I got back to the dormitory, Archie was still out, but Henry was there, reading. I asked him whether he had enjoyed himself. He shook his head and told me it was awful. That *Atlantic Monthly* man Weeks who'd reviewed *The Wall*—Susie mentioned him at lunch in Stockbridge—was there, and the idea seemed to be that we would talk about the novel and I guess more generally about the war in Poland. That was just what I told them I didn't want to do: have dinner discussions on that subject. So I had to lie again. I hated it.

What do you mean? I asked.

I mean that I lied when I told Susie and Ellen that I hadn't read the goddamn novel. Of course I had read it. And I have just lied to them again. I said I'd still not read it.

I would think these were harmless fibs, I said, but why tell them? Did you hate the book and didn't want to contradict Susie and Mr. Weeks? I asked.

Henry groaned. Of course I didn't want to contradict her or Mr. Weeks. But that's not it. You heard her describe the book: it's a novel about the

Warsaw Ghetto and what Germans did to Jews in Poland. That's the stuff of my nightmares. They're bad nightmares. When I wake up from them I am scared. Sometimes I can't go back to sleep and sometimes I don't even want to for fear that I'll start seeing the same newsreel. There is no place to run and no place to hide. In the end, they always find you. Why would I want to discuss such stuff at lunch with two ladies I'd never seen before, especially in front of you, Margot, and George? Or with a literary critic? It's unpleasant and unseemly. Besides, whether *The Wall* in its way is a good book or not, and whatever Mr. Weeks may think about it, I resent it. I resent Hersey's inventions—for instance all those conversations, even though I'm sure they are based on careful research, and Hersey is very respectful of the suffering, and obviously admires the courage of the Jewish fighters and all that. I suppose that if someone absolutely wants to write a historical novel about the Warsaw Ghetto, rather than a straight historical account, there is probably no way that's better than Hersey's. But that doesn't mean that it's a good idea. Or that anyone should expect me to read such a book. Or that I could "enjoy" it, whatever that means. Should I read it in order to learn more about what happened in Poland during the war? I don't want to learn more. In fact I think I know enough. And if for some reason I can't imagine I wanted to learn more, I'd rather read real history. Or is it to make sure that I don't forget? If that's the idea, it happens there is nothing I would like better than to forget, if only I could.

I mumbled some form of apology. But Henry waved it aside and said that it was he who should apologize for having made a speech. I suppose I should apologize to the Misses Appleton as well, he said. I have a feeling I ruined their dinner party.

A couple of days later he told me that there was yet another reason for his tirade against Hersey's book: the fight he had with his mother when she gave it to him. As soon as he opened it, he saw her inscription in the upper-right-hand corner of the title page. She had written, in English, "For my beloved Son, so that he will remember from what I saved him" and signed "Mommy." How could she? he asked. "Son" with a capital *S*. Herself as Mommy? Has she no ear for language? Couldn't she have at least used the Polish word? That means something to me. The English is a travesty.

I was not surprised. He had told me months ago, not long after we met, that in English he always addressed his parents as Mother and Father. He couldn't bring himself to say Mommy or Daddy. All three of them, his parents and he, had come to English too late. The diminutives refused to take form in his mouth. But Mrs. White took the usage he had adopted as an insult. She claimed it humiliated her in anyone else's presence by denying her the term of endearment that corresponded to the word that Henry or any other normally affectionate child would naturally use in Polish. The compromise he offered, to call his parents Mom and Dad, was also rejected. She found there was something unacceptably breezy about those words, a quality that made them even worse than the stiff and cold form on which he had first settled. His anger grew, Henry said, once he had absorbed the message of the inscription itself and the connotations of the present. Never mind, he said, the sickening sentimentality. Wasn't his graduation precisely the right moment to give him respite from the war, the unending epic of his mother's heroism, and the rest of the debris that his mother and his father both knew he hoped at last to put behind him? Wasn't that liberation exactly what they, as good parents, as his loving mommy and daddy, should have wished for him?

The long and the short of it, he told me, is that for once it was I who made a scene, and not my mother. I actually yelled at her. It was a new experience, and at first it made me feel good. After I had cooled off, I apologized. Not because they had made me. My father had not bothered with the usual routine about how if I don't say that I am really very sorry and get my mother to forgive me she will do something to herself and then he will have a heart attack. My vehemence had put them in shock. They just sat there. No, I apologized with complete sincerity, of my own free will, in part because suddenly I realized how they might have come to think, in all honesty, that there was no more suitable way to mark my small triumph than with a reminder of what had come before. I wished they had chosen some other gesture, but when I had calmed down I was able to see that there hadn't been any intention to bait me. Of course, they interpreted my contrition as a victory for them, a sign that I had been brought to heel. Perhaps for that reason the rest of the summer went by without major explosions.

.　.　.

EARLY IN FEBRUARY Archie told us that his parents were coming to visit. His leg was still in a cast, and the understanding had been that they would wait until it was off and he had begun physical therapy. But the colonel had received orders to report to General Ridgeway's headquarters, and he wanted to see Archie before shipping out.

This is a big deal for Pater, Archie told us. It may mean that the curse is off him, especially if he gets to command a regiment. Even to serve on Ridgeway's staff will be a step forward. Anyway, they expect you both at dinner.

The nature of the curse was unclear, although Archie had dropped a hint or two about how the colonel's personal closeness to General Patton had put him in the doghouse with practically every senior general. Then Archie announced a change in the drill. His father's departure had been advanced; he was leaving immediately. Mrs. Palmer would be coming alone. The other change was in the venue of the dinner. Gas royalties notwithstanding, she considered dinner at the Ritz a wasteful extravagance. Instead, we were going to Cronin's. Count your blessings, said Archie. If I had let her have her own way, she'd be having dinner with us at the Union. The drill was changed once more, and the visit postponed to an as-yet-unspecified date around Easter, to coincide with the delivery of the Sex Boat, Archie's appellation for the Nash that Mrs. Palmer had bought for him, now that his rehabilitation was complete. According to Archie, Mrs. Palmer didn't like the expense of traveling to Cambridge, especially if the colonel wasn't there to pay, but was determined to go for a spin with Archie on Route 128, where he had told her he would be able to floor the gas pedal. Besides, she was busy preparing to have the Palmer household goods moved to Houston, a location that put her close to the oil and gas and yet not too far away from sources of the pre-Columbian artifacts in which she traded. A cousin with whom she had remained in contact was a member of the River Oaks Country Club and she intended to buy a house in the vicinity. The colonel liked the idea of a stateside home, particularly one that would give him a fairly decent place to play golf all year-round if he decided to retire from the army after Korea.

As though to fill the breach that had been opened in our calendar,

Henry announced that his parents were arriving the following weekend to celebrate his birthday. It would be their first view of the college and, for that matter, Cambridge and Boston. The travel agent who had booked their reservations for the trip to Maine the previous summer recommended a hotel that was a short walk from the Yard across the Common. He had also given them the names of museums to visit with Henry. The open question was where and how they should entertain Henry's roommates, which they were determined to do. They also wanted to invite George, in order to return his parents' hospitality. Henry did not mention Margot. I guessed that he hadn't told them enough, if anything, about her to arouse their curiosity or to make them think they had a duty to acknowledge her existence. Since they were to leave Brooklyn by car on Friday morning, Henry expected them at the hotel in the late afternoon on Friday. They would start for home on Sunday, after breakfast. But Margot, although she didn't figure in his parents' questions and instructions, rapidly became Henry's biggest worry. When he told her about the impending visit—a big mistake he later thought—she expressed the categorical wish to meet them. If Henry had misgivings about exhibiting his parents to Archie and me, and, even more likely, to George, he kept them to himself but made no attempt to hide some of them from us in the case of Margot. As he considered the available solutions, one he thought he dreaded most was the prospect of a family dinner with Margot as the only guest. At the same time, the way things stood between her and George, inviting her to dinner with him there was out of the question. There was also the more fundamental issue: Should his parents meet Margot under any circumstances? On one hand, he had become very proud of Margot, or anyway of their odd friendship, and would have liked nothing more than to show her off. On the other, there was the risk that they—to be specific, his mother—would afterward make unpleasant comments about her, for instance singling out Margot's brash curtness or, if his mother guessed that he was in love with her, about her not being Jewish. The mere idea that his mother might refer to Margot as that Gentile girlfriend was intolerable. We did not discuss the effect Mr. and Mrs. White would have on Margot, and how that entered into his calculations. However, he did explain that Margot's being half Jewish might weigh against her. That surprised me.

It's simple, he said. Even if Margot can't be a real Jew because of her Gentile mother, she is Jewish enough to give my mother a reason to apply with full force the code of Krakow to her, the way she dresses, and her demeanor, and anything else you care to name. There were no bigger snobs than prewar Jewish bourgeoisie in Galicia. Forget the Berkshires and your cousins. They've no standards at all. The only person I met there who would pass muster in Krakow is George's mother. She's dressed just right and has the right combination of sweetness and venom. If Margot were just another shiksa, my mother might say that how she behaves is her own business. But a girl who might be mistaken for a Jewess, one that happens to be the object of the attention of my mother's only son—everything about her is my mother's business and subject to the severest censure.

Archie examined the underlying logistical problems and came up with a solution. Three of us—George, he, and I—would have dinner with Henry and his mother and father the evening of their arrival at the hotel, since they were likely to be tired from the drive. Because of their fatigue, the meal wouldn't drag on, and that would be all to the good. On Saturday afternoon, following a museum trip or some other cultural expedition Henry might devise, there would be drinks in our suite. Sherry, he specified. Margot and three or four of our dormitory neighbors should be invited, as well as perhaps Jerry, our proctor. That number of guests should make it possible to have Margot in the same room with George.

I overheard Henry announce this program by telephone, first to his mother and then again to his father. Henry was speaking English. The language he used in addressing them varied with circumstances. It seemed to me that he used Polish when he didn't want Archie or me to understand, and also when the subject matter didn't require a vocabulary that he hadn't learned before leaving Poland. I had no doubt, however, that his Polish was equal to communicating about dinner and drinks. From Henry's long silences and the way he repeated certain sentences, it became clear that Archie's proposals weren't being received with complete enthusiasm. There came a moment when I felt particularly embarrassed (since by that time I was eavesdropping, and not merely happening to hear, as was most often the case) when he gave his estimate of the cost of dinner for five at the hotel, and of the gathering at our room on Saturday. I could imagine that Mr. and Mrs. White's experience with buying sherry and pretzels or peanuts for an undergraduate cocktail party was limited, but surely they had paid for meals in a restaurant. Never mind, I heard him saying, never mind. None of this is necessary at all. Let's just skip it. Having heard more than one discussion about money between Henry and his parents, I was surprised that he didn't reassure them right away, as was his custom, that the expense they were facing was small, and I began to wonder whether he hadn't decided that it would be just as well if his parents canceled the entertainments. It was a possible outcome that would spare him a good deal of anguish. He would, of course, have to announce the cancellation to Archie and me, and I supposed to Margot as well, but that awkwardness would be as nothing to the one he dreaded. In fact, all he had to say was that his overly possessive parents had decided that they would prefer to savor the company of their only son on this birthday weekend in strict family intimacy and without any dilution. Or something more or less like that. The ground for that sort of thing was prepared; he had bad-mouthed his parents so relentlessly.

As it turned out, the parents didn't veto either the dinner or the party, but the party became unnecessary, and Margot was invited to dinner along with Archie and me. George said that he had to be away, at Mount Snow, with his parents, sisters, and the sisters' husbands, on the Standishes' annual ski weekend. Another change, for which Margot was responsible, was that the dinner would take place on Saturday, at the Henri IV. She explained to Henry that hotel food and hotel restaurants were fatally *triste;* she couldn't abide them. Besides, she added, won't your parents be thrilled to celebrate your birthday in a restaurant named for you?

HAVE YOU EVER HEARD of such a thing? You, his roommate and best friend: Can you imagine what kind of son I have? Mrs. White asked as soon as we reached the table Archie had reserved. Margot and Archie had been waiting for us. She put me on her right and Archie on her left. In accordance with her instructions, Mr. White was next to me and Margot between him and Henry. Archie's standing at the Henri IV was lofty; that was why we had been directed to the corner table, and had been spared, even though it was a Saturday evening, the wait at the bar upstairs.

When we arrived at the hotel yesterday, Mrs. White continued without releasing her hold on my arm, we found your roommate spread out in an armchair in the lobby—asleep with his mouth open. Thank God, he wasn't snoring! I spoke to him, and nothing. Then his father called him by his name. Still nothing. Finally, when I kissed him, he decided to wake up. I said, So this is how you greet your parents: you get drunk. And do you know what? Right away, he got so mad I thought he would kill me. Look at him. He had to be drunk. Only drunks and eighty-year-old men can't stay awake in the afternoon. And he isn't even ashamed.

This was the second time I was hearing this anecdote. She had told it to me on the way to the restaurant, so that I could only guess that she was repeating it not for my benefit but for the edification of the rest of the party. Since Margot had offered to bring Archie in a taxi, I had gone with Henry to get his parents at the hotel. I had supposed that we too would take a taxi to the restaurant, but Mr. and Mrs. White said they preferred to walk. We split into two pairs. I accompanied Mrs. White, who took my arm before I remembered to offer it. Mr. White and Henry followed.

Rysiek is a very lucky boy, she said. He doesn't know how lucky he is.

Who is that? I asked.

Who is Rysiek? she replied. Rysiek is Rysiek.

Then, having realized how obtuse I was, she laughed, gave my arm a squeeze, and told me she was referring to Henry by his little name. What was the English word for such a little name? Diminutive, I suggested. She repeated diminutive after me, and cast about for the Latin root, which she found.

Henry is Henryk in Polish, she explained, like Henryk Sienkiewicz, the author of *Quo Vadis*. From Henryk you get Henrysiek, and you shorten Henrysiek to Rysiek. That's the way it is in Polish. We use diminutives. For example, my father's name was Jacob, but his family and friends called him Kuba.

I was going to ask her about Mr. White's name and her own, but she cut me off to express the hope that my parents were well. I assured her that they were, whereupon she inquired whether they came to see me often. Not waiting for my answer, she said once again that Rysiek was a very lucky boy, but why did he have to drink so much? Neither his father nor she drank alcohol, except perhaps a glass of wine with dinner, if they went out or had guests at home. I said that I didn't think that Henry drank, but she insisted I was wrong. That is when she first related the scene of coming upon his comatose body in the lobby. Had she been in his place, she would have been worried sick about her parents' being late and asking herself whether the car had broken down or, the way his father drives, whether they had had an accident.

The idea that Henry had conked out in the hotel lobby struck me as no less strange than Mrs. White's suspicion that he was drunk at that hour of the afternoon until I remembered that he had not slept at all the preceding night, writing a paper on Pericles' funeral oration and swallowing one Nodoz pill after another until, as he told me that morning, he found himself at dawn unable to stop chewing the pages he had pulled from his typewriter, crumpled, and thrown on the floor. I proffered the explanation of a deadline to be met, without any mention of the pills.

Why should he be writing a paper at night instead of sleeping? she countered. Normal people work during the day and sleep at night.

Again, I came to Henry's defense. He was working very hard, I said, harder than anybody I knew, what with difficult Latin and Greek courses and intensive French. Although I knew that she was aware of the grade he received on every quiz, exam, and paper, I added that he was a remarkably good student.

And you, Mr. Roommate, she said, are you also at college to learn Latin and Greek?

I replied that I was convinced I had learned all the Latin I wanted to know at school. I was going to major in English.

English. She laughed. And here I thought that you already spoke the language perfectly.

I laughed with her.

The subject of my intellectual development having been for the moment exhausted, she returned to what I could see was her bête noire. Why does Rysiek think he should study classics? she asked. She went on to speak about how they had lost everything in Poland, how hard she and her husband were working to give Henry a good home and a good education, and how he should be thinking about his future instead of throwing away his opportunities.

Not having a ready answer, I remained silent and concentrated on her. She was good-looking—no, in reality she was beautiful and sexy. It was odd to have that impression of the mother of my roommate, but I certainly did. She made me think of a Lana Turner with jet-black hair. Henry's flaming top had come from his father. I had observed her wool suit of a lighter brown than the voluptuously ample beaver coat with which Mr. White helped her as we were leaving the hotel. May Standish might well have worn such a suit and such a fur, but, on a night as cold as this, with patches of ice on the sidewalk, she would have had her feet in some sort of booties. Mrs. White wore burgundy pumps with high heels. I thought of my own mother, who was no less good-looking or well turned out if the occasion called for it. There was a big difference. In my mother's case, it always seemed as though she had thrown on her clothes at the last minute, improvising the entire effect to include just a hint of slatternliness. Mrs. White exercised her charms differently. Mr. White's grooming also left nothing to chance. I liked his gray herringbone tweed jacket, crisp Oxford gray flannels, beautifully shined black wingtips, white-on-white shirt, blue necktie of heavy silk with a darker blue stripe, black overcoat, and black fedora with a little red feather in the hatband. A white handkerchief, neatly folded to make two triangles, peeked out from the breast pocket of his jacket. Black calfskin leather gloves, looking new and expensive, completed the picture. Once I had examined Mr. White, the secret of the garments Mrs. White had bought for Henry so that he would be appropriately equipped for college was revealed. She had quite simply gotten him the clothes she was in the habit of choosing for Mr. White, only larger, because Henry, though small boned, was taller, and needed room to grow. How could she know that those of Henry's classmates he had chosen to emulate affected quite a different style?

To return to the Henri IV, Mrs. White's opening salvo had put the king's namesake in a state of mute rage she must have foreseen. I began to wonder whether the quarrel between son and mother would explode right then and there, and I believe that it would have if Archie had not headed it off. It wasn't likely that Henry had told his parents what he knew of Archie's accident. To do so would have heightened the suspicion with which they were inclined to regard both Archie and me. Perhaps the parents didn't even know how badly he had been banged up. Normally, he made light of his injuries, but this time he made use of them. His crutches were leaning against the wall behind his chair where Henry had put them. Therefore, I was well placed to see him perform the maneuver that sent them crashing to the floor. Once the clatter had stopped the conversation, Archie slowly recounted the story of the car accident omitting none of the details other than the drinking at the officers' club that had preceded it. The Whites listened to him as though mesmerized, presumably calculating the risks to which Henry's friendship with this strange and charming young man exposed him.

There is a silver lining, Archie added. I am getting my own set of wheels. I mean a car.

At that, Mrs. White drew a deep breath and said she had never heard anything like it. She felt very sorry for his parents, especially his mother.

Archie shook his head.

Actually, he replied, Mother is tough, tougher than my father even though he is the soldier.

Then he told us that the colonel thought a Chinese attack across the Yalu River was imminent, in which case Russia would get involved as well as China, so that the U.S. would have to use tactical nuclear weapons.

Absolutely, said Mr. White.

As he talked about the designs of the Russians and the Chinese on the rest of the world it occurred to me that the one person I knew who would agree with him all the way down the line was old Gummy, at our country club. Except that Gummy also thought that we should have limited our involvement in World War II to the defeat of Japan, and let the Germans and the Russians finish off each other, a notion that Mr. White, if he thought of his family's likely fate in such an event, would not have approved.

It fell to me to take Archie back to the dormitory that evening. While we waited for the taxi the owner of the restaurant had called, I told him that I had rather liked Mr. and Mrs. White.

They're not half bad, he replied, but they'll get in Henry's way.

XI

IN THE END, there was to be no dinner at all with Mrs. Palmer. She told Archie that the coffee shop at the Commodore where she was staying—across the street from the hotel the Whites had chosen—was perfect for her needs. A bite there alone was all the evening entertainment she needed in Cambridge. Archie laughed about it and said we weren't missing much, and Mater was having a blast pinching pennies. She did, however, consent to come to our rooms for a drink. This time there was no talk of sherry; Mrs. Palmer favored S.S. Pierce bourbon, which had managed to make its way to the far-flung officers' clubs she and the colonel had frequented. Having studied her photograph on the dresser in Archie's room, where she appeared at the side of a young officer resplendent in dress blues, I was disappointed. Instead of the more mature version of Hedy Lamarr I had expected, the little old lady I was introduced to evoked a missionary nun or the housekeeper of a bedridden old codger living in a house too large for him at the end of a hillside village in a black-and-white French film. Either the photograph had been heavily touched up or time had been particularly cruel to her. As I might have surmised, Mrs. Palmer's dress—black crepe-soled shoes, black stockings, a dark gray skirt of harsh flannel, and a black cardigan worn over a gray shirt with a small round collar—had a purpose. The point was to be comfortable on the Greyhound from Houston to Cambridge and back. In fact, Mrs. Palmer liked travel by bus and discoursed cheerfully on the courtesy of her fellow passengers and the cleanliness of toilets wherever Greyhound made them available. But most of our conversation was about the many virtues of the Nash, which Archie had taken us to inspect after his mother and he returned from the inaugural ride on Route 128 earlier that day. I thought that the most striking of them—the reclining front seats that turned the car into a double bed—would not be mentioned, being the stuff of so many off-color jokes. I was wrong. Mrs. Palmer brought up the savings Archie could realize forgoing motels, if only he learned to travel with a sleeping bag. She seemed even more pleased by the power of the engine—or perhaps it was some ratio to the weight of the body. They had taken her up to ninety-five, miles I mean, Archie said, and he thought there was still some muscle to be flexed before the car reached its limit. And she's solid, Mrs. Palmer added with a smile. If you'd been driving her in Panama, you wouldn't have wound up on crutches, with a face like a scarecrow.

For some reason the reference to the Christmas events led Henry to ask how the colonel was adjusting—that is, I believe, the way he put it—to his duties in Korea.

He hates the place, said Mrs. Palmer, who wouldn't? But he has his command, and that's what matters to him.

Good for Pater, Archie exclaimed. Doesn't that mean he'll get his star?

They had better give it to him, Mrs. Palmer replied. They've made a fool of him long enough.

Colonel Palmer's regiment was to suffer atrocious losses some weeks later, and the colonel himself was wounded. The promotion did come through, however, after he had been discharged from a stateside hospital and reassigned to Fort Benning. Military etiquette, or perhaps something more specific, compelled him to serve out a year in that post before retiring with his new rank. There was no need to hurry, as it turned out; the quantity of shrapnel that the surgeons were obliged to leave in his right leg made it quite impossible to play golf with the assiduity he had anticipated.

Clearly, Archie had not known that his father's dream of commanding a regiment in combat had just come true. I supposed that, even without Henry's polite inquiry, Mrs. Palmer would have eventually told him before she left Cambridge. But momentarily her not having said anything sooner—for instance while they were putting the Nash through its paces but before they hit ninety-five mph—took me aback. When I thought about it later I understood that it was the result of her single-minded concentration on Archie, in its way perhaps as obsessive as Mrs. White's on

Henry, although it manifested itself differently in most respects. Mrs. White was certainly interested in how Henry spent his time and with whom. She was downright nosy. I couldn't detect in Mrs. Palmer any curiosity about Henry or me or any of the other friends who took up so much of Archie's time; certainly none was revealed during the couple of hours she spent in our living room. She did, on the other hand, ask to see his martini shaker and tumblers—which he hadn't taken out, as they were, in his opinion, not right for the bourbon on the rocks we were drinking—and his cigarette case. Perhaps she feared that he had hocked them, I thought at first, but it became clear when they were produced that she wanted to touch them because they were love offerings, tangible signs of her tenderness. Given her miserliness, about which Archie couldn't stop talking, the emotional cost of those expensive objects must have been painfully high. Perhaps it made other forms of involvement with her son less urgent.

A NUMBER OF THINGS did not go well for Henry at the end of the spring semester. He took the rejection by the house hard, much harder than Archie, in part because he was convinced that Archie would have been admitted had he applied alone. I'm the Jewish monkey on his back, he said. I was convinced that the master's class snobbery was more virulent than his anti-Semitism, but I didn't say so to Henry. I believed that he'd rather be turned down as a Jew. Archie claimed that he couldn't care less; the rooms at the Mount Auburn Street hall were larger and more agreeable than anything they could have gotten in the river house. Henry agreed but said that for the first time since having come to the United States he had been treated unfairly and had been left behind undeservedly.

Also, Henry was beginning to think that people he was drawn to—Archie and I, George and Margot, and a few others excepted—didn't like him. The classics and other literature courses he was taking were full of preppies. He had assumed that shared academic interests would lead naturally to friendships, but nothing of the sort happened. I'm not one of them, he told me; they make it very clear. People taking the same course as he, whom he knew by name, would among themselves say, Let's go for coffee. But the invitation never seemed to extend to him—or if it did it was without the clarity he thought he would have needed in order to accept comfortably. No one knocked on his door on the way to the movies, and no one tried to catch his eye as he looked for a table at which to sit down when he came to lunch or dinner at the Union. He had his meals with Archie or me or else alone, wherever a vacant seat could be found. In the way his instructors treated him when he approached the podium after class, there was none of the ease and cheerful give-and-take that other bright undergraduates of his caliber enjoyed. I wasn't surprised. His instructors were, to a man, old preppies or wished they had been and were attracted instinctively, no less than Henry, to the style of their preppy students, only in Henry's case without reciprocal feelings. If Henry had listened to his parents and taken premed courses, he would have been one more eager beaver surrounded by others, all just as brainy as he and no more socially acceptable. They would have liked him because he worked hard and was a nice guy. As for being friends with professors, it was a safe bet that no one expected or wanted to have a personal relationship with his organic or inorganic chemistry instructor.

Most painful was the change in his relationship with Margot. Ever since the evening on which they had gone to listen to Mabel Mercer, she had been letting him kiss her and fondle her breasts. He told me that he had made no attempt to do more. I want her to trust me, he said, I don't want her to think that I am forcing her hand. The way we are now is better than anything I had expected, and I am still her best friend. If it was true what Bunny Rollins had told George about Margot, and George in turn related to me during our drive home from Stowe, perhaps Henry was wrong. Margot might have wished him to be more enterprising. I decided against telling him that. His feelings were too intense, and the risk too great of his turning on me if he thought that I lacked respect for Margot. At some point, perhaps in early April, Henry told me that Margot had put a stop to any physical contact between them; she had become too involved with someone else. Someone else turned out to be Etienne van Damme, the Belgian business school student. According to Henry, she had all but told him that she and the Belgian were having a real affair, conducted principally in New York, where van Damme would stay in a fancy hotel, and, when he or she had too much work to dash off to New York for the weekend, across the river, at his business school dormitory or at the Ritz in Boston. Henry claimed that he wasn't jealous; she was still his long-term project and he had implicitly recognized that he would have successful rivals. He wondered, though, what had happened to their friendship. The Belgian had become her only topic of conversation.

Suddenly, the spring reading period was upon us. Right after exams, Henry was leaving for Grenoble and the French-language summer program. To Archie's astonishment and mine, he mentioned casually that Margot would be staying at a big property the van Damme parents owned in the Ardennes, and that she and Etienne had invited him to spend a week with them. Archie planned to divide his summer between a coffee plantation in Brazil, in the state of São Paulo, and a couple of haciendas in Argentina, visiting rugby friends. George and I had decided to drive out west and then return to the Berkshires via the Southwest and South.

XII

WE MADE A SHORT FORAY into Baja California and would have liked to continue there, but time was growing short. After two days, one spent at the beach, we began to make our way home following a route that took us through Arizona and New Mexico to Houston. Our next stop was to be New Orleans, where a certain Walter Trowbridge, who had been at school with George's father, maintained an apartment on Toulouse Street in the French Quarter for the use of guests, most of them fellow oilmen. May and Cousin Jack had stayed there, and May described it as sinfully luxurious. August not being a month when the apartment was in demand, it was offered to us for as long as we liked. Urged by May, we signed up for five days, thinking we would use it for exploring the Quarter, the Garden District, and the bayou country. We were also tempted by the Mississippi delta, if a boat trip could be arranged. By the time we were leaving Houston, we felt we urgently needed to be pampered. The heat had been brutal, and ever since we had stopped camping we had shared rooms in very modest motels and hostels, most recently in the Houston YMCA. George had in his possession a lordly letter of credit issued by the Morgan Bank, and I had a suitable amount in traveler's checks I had bought with the sum advanced by Mr. Hibble. We could have afforded better accommodations. The Standish code of conduct, however, called for young men to travel on the cheap. I wanted to be as good a Standish as George at least in this respect, and the idea of transgressing against the code didn't cross his mind. The code did permit occasional intentionally extravagant gestures, if they were justified by the occasion. We had read Frances Parkinson Keyes's novel, *Dinner at Antoine's,* and perused the section on New Orleans in our guidebook. It seemed clear that the fabled pleasures of New

Orleans were justification enough. We would dine at Antoine's and Brennan's and visit the best jazz joints on Bourbon Street.

We had passed Shreveport when George advanced another idea. Once we got settled in Toulouse Street—which was just an apartment with a cleaning lady who came in during the day but no concierge or anyone like that to watch our comings and goings—we would pick up a couple of girls and bring them home. Not the first night, but perhaps after the dinner at Antoine's. The prospect filled me with disquiet, but I thought I had better be a good sport about it.

The apartment was reached from a cobbled courtyard along the walls of which various potted tropical plants were disposed in great profusion. May had not exaggerated. Everything in the apartment was huge and agreeable: the four-poster beds, the oversize bathtubs, the soft leather sofas and armchairs in the living room. Next to the telephone directory we found a volume bound in leather entitled *Information for Use of Toulouse Street Guests*. George went through it quickly in the hope that it would contain a hint about where to look for girls. Either there wasn't one or the reference to that activity was phrased too subtly. He learned, however, that in order to get a good table and be treated right at Antoine's one should ask to speak to Michel, a waiter mysteriously attached to the person of Mr. Trowbridge. George called at once and made a reservation for the following evening. We spent most of the day brushing off mosquitoes aboard a boat that toured the bayous and were late getting to Antoine's. It didn't seem to matter. Michel greeted us like celebrities traveling incognito but known to him, and we ate our way through crayfish, Gulf fish, and shrimp. When George called for the check it turned out that we were Mr. Trowbridge's guests. He had also left strict instructions to have us taste the Cognac kept in his private locker. We did more than taste. The snifters were very large, and Michel filled them generously.

Henry must be at the van Damme château by now, said George.

I said that was right. The course at Grenoble ended in early August. I suppose it's pretty fancy, George observed. The parents say that no one eats like the Belgians. All the same, I'd be surprised if he was eating any better than this.

I nodded, thinking I had just eaten the best meal of my life.

I still can't get over Margot, he continued. Why is she sleeping with that Belgian? What has he got over me? Or over Henry? Or you? Why did she make such a fuss just because I got a little pushy? Lord knows she had asked for it.

I said I wasn't a contender and speculated that van Damme had snowed her. He is older, drives a fast car, and has that family château up his sleeve.

We drank the last of the Cognac and went out into the night.

There were approved Bourbon Street addresses in Mr. Trowbridge's book. We tried them all. In truth, the music was no better than what one could hear most nights on Tremont Street in Boston, perhaps not as good. We'd have a weak Scotch and soda and move on.

I'm sick of these joints, said George.

I said, Amen! Let's go home.

George shook his head. Thinking about Margot had made him horny. We've got to find some action.

The question was where. According to the conception I had of such things, garishly dressed women should have been leaning against lampposts or sauntering down the street, swinging large handbags. They should have been sidling up to us and asking in their dripping southern drawl, Hey honey, lookin' for company? But no streetwalker or pimp, white or black, approached us. In fact, there was no one in the streets other than loud groups of men milling outside bars, couples strolling arm in arm or holding hands, and solitary figures hurrying somewhere. Accountants, I thought, going home after a long day.

I told George that in New Orleans people probably went to brothels. You had to know the address of the house and, since we didn't, we might as well give up. We were wasting our time. George disagreed. He thought we had to check out the seedier bars that hadn't made it onto Mr. Trowbridge's list. That's where the broads would be. We went up and down Bourbon again and then started walking into bars on side streets. Finally, off Chartres Street, we came upon Sonny Boy, which seemed deserted except for some men who could have been garage mechanics grouped at the bar and two busty women with vacant faces sitting alone at a corner table in the back.

George said, This is it.

The table next to the women's was empty. As we were sitting down, they made a show of staring at us and whispering to each other. George stared back and said hi. They didn't seem to mind; in fact, they giggled. When the waiter came over, George told him Scotch and soda for us and for those ladies anything they like. They didn't mind that either, and what they liked was rum and Coke. By the time the drinks had arrived, we had moved over to their table. I sat next to Jonelle; George was next to Debbie. They were hospital ward nurses at Tulane, on a two-day break between shifts. Jonelle was from Baton Rouge and Debbie from Lake Charles. They had met in nursing school and were roommates at the hospital dormitory.

Are boys allowed in your dorm? asked George.

Now don't get fresh, Debbie told him.

George amazed me by lying. He explained that we had just graduated from Harvard and were working in New York, on Wall Street. We were in New Orleans on a little vacation. A friend had lent us his apartment in the Quarter and said we could invite girls—nice girls like them.

Outbursts of Isn't he fresh? followed, and we had another round. I knew that I had passed my limit, but I didn't want George to think I was a wet blanket. Besides, the whiskey was helping me deal with a new sensation. Jonelle had put her plump forearm over mine and said, Hey, pleased to meet you. I was going to hold her hand as a gesture of appreciation, but it was no longer there. It had slipped off the table onto my lap where it busied itself. At the same time she was talking a blue streak into my ear, which apparently made it necessary to press her breast against my arm. I limited myself to neutral rejoinders such as You're right, or Isn't that amazing. The truth was that I didn't understand most of what she was saying. George meanwhile had finished describing our apartment and said it was about time all four of us got going.

Going where? asked Debbie.

To Toulouse Street, George explained a little petulantly.

You mean you want us to come to your place, asked Debbie. You crazy or something? We don't know you guys. Did you hear that jerk, Jonelle?

Yeah, I heard him, she replied. She didn't take her hand away, but its activities ceased.

Come on, said George. It won't take any time to get to know us. We're nice guys. We like girls like you.

Oh yeah? Just because you've bought us a couple of lousy drinks? You're real cheapskates. You could've asked us to dinner.

Wait a minute, George replied, don't be like that. It's too late for dinner tonight. We'll take you out tomorrow.

Yeah, and what about tonight? We don't even get a present?

Sure you do, said George.

I'm bushed, Jonelle interjected suddenly. I need to get back to the dorm.

Come on, George said, you'll get to sleep in at our place.

Wait a minute! Let me just get this straight. You guys want to fuck? Jonelle asked, giving me a squeeze. It wasn't clear whether the squeeze meant she was for it or against. What kind of gift you talking about?

How about fifty, if you stay the night? George answered.

Hey, said Debbie, you hear that? This guy thinks we're cheap whores!

Then she got up on her feet and screamed: Did I hear that right? This creep thinks we're whores! Joe, get over here and straighten him out.

The bartender sauntered over, a crowbar in his right hand. The men at the bar didn't move but stopped talking and were following the action.

Get out, Joe said very calmly. Pay up and get out of here. I don't want any college fuckups in my place.

We both got up. George looked in his wallet, hesitated, and put a ten down, saying keep the change.

It's twice that, motherfucker.

George threw down another bill.

Get these guys out of here, said Debbie.

We're going, I told her, and stupidly added, Take care!

We had just reached the door when George turned, faced the room, and at the top of his voice shouted, Fuck you, you redneck crackers!

I grabbed him by the arm and shoved him out the door. We started in the direction of Toulouse Street, not as fast as I would have liked because the liquor had gone to his head. Every few steps he'd stop and say, I want to go back there and talk to them. I just don't get it. What are they sore about?

Nothing, I told him. Just keep walking.

We had covered several blocks when presentiment or the sound of footsteps that weren't ours caused me to look back. Three big guys in jeans and T-shirts were gaining on us. They were some of the guys who had been standing at the bar.

We've got company, I told George, step on it. Maybe they had heard me. Right away there was a yell: Wait up. We want to talk to you.

Don't stop, I told George, and don't turn around. It's a delegation from the Sonny Boy.

We might have tried to make a run for it, but a couple of others, just like the ones following us, appeared at the next intersection. They closed in on us. They had tattoos on their arms. I glanced down and saw that they were all wearing heavy army-surplus engineer's boots. One of the men who had been following us pointed at George and said, That's him.

Hey you there, boy, said another one, giving George a shove in the chest, did I hear you say you want to fuck my sister? I think I'm going to beat your head in.

Shit, Bill, give him a chance to say he's sorry, said another one. Come on you son of a bitch, get on your knees and say you're sorry.

Yeah, on your knees and kiss my hand.

George said, Look, we didn't mean any harm. They're nice girls. We were just kidding around. Anyway, I am sorry.

Are you deaf, shithead? yelled the one called Bill. I told you to get down on your fucking knees and kiss my fucking hand.

He followed up by hitting George in the mouth. George sat down on the sidewalk and didn't move. The blow must have confused him.

I had wrestled for my school, and had done well on the Harvard freshman team, where the coach had judo ranking and taught it to me and a couple of others informally, judo not being a varsity sport. I was only a little taller than George but a good bit heavier and not as drunk as he, though drunk enough, I suppose, to think I could take care of myself. I stepped in between George and the man called Bill, saying, Lay off, he had too much to drink but he didn't mean any harm. Bill's response was to swing at me. I ducked, and grabbing his arm threw him at the plate-glass storefront window. There was the sound of breaking glass, a moment of silence, and then Bill began to moan. I saw that his face was in shreds.

According to the coach, in martial arts if you stand alone against several adversaries you get to take them on one by one. I didn't expect that this was the custom in New Orleans. Looking down at the army engineer's boots, I realized that I'd had it. Sure enough, almost at once, someone slugged me hard on the ear, and someone else rammed me in the stomach. I went down and was trying to curl up like a fetus and cover my face with my arms before they began to kick.

There were dimly lit stations along the road of my return to consciousness. One was someone telling me to take it easy, I would be given something for the pain, another was a distant voice asking my name and the names of my parents and the president of the United States, and at last George's voice telling me I was in recovery and not to worry. I tried to turn toward George, but I couldn't and instead his face swam into my field of vision. For some reason it was hidden behind a thick textured veil. Then it was George's voice again, telling me I had been moved into a regular room where I would stay until I was all better. I tried to say something but what came out of my mouth was a gurgle.

You've got a tube up your nose, George told me. The doctor says you can speak with it, but it takes getting used to. Then he said, You saved my life, you big ape. You goddamn saved my life.

I think I fell asleep almost immediately, but he was there when I woke up. It's a private room, he explained, and he was going to be with me most of the time. Our mothers were on the way. At some point he told me about the beating. It was lucky you threw that guy into the store window, he said. When the glass broke an alarm went off at the precinct. It's the sirens that made those guys stop, and then the cops were all over the place.

Some days later, with my mother, Cousin May, and George present, the surgeon reviewed my condition. I had a broken nose that he had set and a broken jaw that he had wired. I had lost three front teeth. That was something the dentist could fix by giving me a bridge, and the nose and the jaw would be all right once the swelling went down and the hematomas had dissolved. Fortunately, a plastic surgeon happened to be on hand and worked on my face. That was the straightforward part of the job. The complicating factor had been serious internal bleeding. He removed my spleen as part of the repairs. All in all, he said I should consider myself lucky to be alive. The police and the ambulance got there in the nick of time. In due course, I would be almost as good as new. Hearing that, I asked whether I'd be able to go back to college in the fall. He tittered and said that patients must be patient; we'd discuss that when I was well enough to be released. Then, growing serious, he said that I shouldn't count on being able to take the plane for Boston before at least two or three weeks. After that a surgeon there could look me over, and, if I felt up to it, I would be free to resume my studies.

George remained with me in New Orleans until I was discharged and insisted on taking me home, over the objections of his mother and mine, each of whom thought it was her duty—duty that my new reputation for heroism had turned into something like privilege. As it turned out, George missed only some early crew practice; he was back in Cambridge in time for the start of classes. I was delayed by the need for a second surgical checkup at the hospital in Pittsfield. Finally, both my parents drove me down to Cambridge more than two weeks after registration, my father coming along in order to carry my meager possessions from the car to my suite. This shouldn't have been too much to ask of him, especially as my suite was on the ground floor and could be reached directly from the street without passing through the porter's lodge to get into the courtyard. Even so, the expedition was distasteful to my father. He didn't like his work at the bank but hated taking days off even more and loathed anything that smacked of doing family chores. His mood lightened, however, when he saw George waiting on the sidewalk to help me move in. Here was further living proof of my new status. Knowing that both of my parents, for respective personal reasons, couldn't wait to get back to Lenox, I begged them to leave at once. But George's presence, though rendering my father's presence superfluous, had awakened his sense of propriety and the regard due to the son of the head of the family, precluding my parents' speedy exit. He insisted on taking us for a steak lunch at Cronin's. Mother cut up my meat for me.

Afterward, my mother and George made up my bed, a task that I realized I would have difficulty in performing in their absence. As soon as they left, I collapsed on it and slept until I heard voices in the living room. I rose to find Henry and Archie, Henry holding with both hands a large potted chrysanthemum.

My mother's idea, Henry explained, she called twice today to make sure I didn't forget.

When George appeared a while later, we all went into the dining room together and lingered at table, the conversation shifting between Archie's tales of Carioca high life and polo ponies at the hacienda of Mario's parents, and George's description of our drive on Route 1 into Baja, which he considered the high point of our trip. I deflected all attempts to talk about the Sonny Boy and asked Henry, who had said nothing about his summer, whether Grenoble had lived up to expectations. Surpassed them, he said, best idea I ever had.

He really wants you to ask him about Margot and Etienne, broke in Archie. George's face turned somber. Although he claimed to have given up on Margot, Etienne had remained on his shit list.

There isn't much to say, Henry answered, he drives too fast over mountain roads and she claims not to be scared. Why she isn't, I can't figure out. Etienne took me to a town twenty kilometers away to buy a ribbon for my typewriter, and I came back sick to my stomach. And that's never happened to me on shipboard during a storm. The property is magnificent and the parents are very civilized. But Etienne is like a wild man and I don't understand it at all.

We said goodbye at the steps leading to my entryway. George went back to his house. To my surprise, Henry didn't follow Archie to their dormitory and asked whether he could come in for a moment.

I had become used to the privileges conferred by reason of my infirmity and told him I was good at most for another fifteen minutes.

Don't worry, I'll be out of here before then, he said. I just wanted to say very quickly how glad I am that you're all right, and also something that you may perhaps find strange: I think that you're especially lucky. I envy you.

I said I assumed he meant I was lucky to be alive and not to have lost an eye or some other important organ.

That too, he said, but I meant something else. You have actually been through it, the ultimate violation. You got the hell beaten out of you but now know that you can take it. You've survived and now you can go on with that knowledge. I can only wonder how I would have come out of it. I envy you.

You're nuts, I said. Do you also want to know what it's like to be hit by a truck?

No. He laughed. But you're right. I am nuts.

XIII

As George had been driving first through the empty spaces of the Midwest, there were long hours of silence in the car during which I reviewed the events of past months. One of my actions before the summer began troubled me: Wouldn't it have been better—or anyway more elegant—to turn down the suite in the river house that had been offered and join Henry and Archie in their Mount Auburn Street exile? Wasn't that what George Standish would have done in my place? To be sure, he had never uttered a word of reproach or criticism to me, although he knew the entire story, including my decision to live alone, which had coalesced about the time that applications to houses were made; from his silence I couldn't necessarily infer approval. He had never told me that I had done the right thing. Certainly, our situations were very different. His father was an overseer of the university and had something to do with the investment of its endowment. Had George turned down the invitation to live in a house because he thought his roommates had been badly treated, someone would have made a fuss, and some dean or perhaps even the president would have had a word with the master. The master would think long and hard before pulling such a stunt again. It was also not out of the question that he would miraculously discover he had a place in the house for the slighted roommates after all. My own refusal to move into the house, on the other hand, would have been no more than a quixotic gesture to which no one in a position of power would have paid attention. There was another difference as well: my need to live alone, which I felt more acutely than ever, a need that was alien to George. Even if I had gone to Mount Auburn Street with Henry and Archie, it wouldn't have been to share rooms with them again. I would have insisted on a single accommodation.

All the same, I had resolved over the summer to be particularly attentive to my friendships with Henry and Archie, now that the intimacy of close quarters was ended. It seemed to me, for example, that I must call them as soon as I got to Cambridge and suggest that we go to the house dining room together, as opposed to meeting them there by chance. Knowing them, I was certain that they would feel like interlopers, even though, as affiliates of the house, they were supposed to take their meals there. The same would be true of the common room and the library. I was also worried about asking them over to my suite. There were no better rooms to be found in any of the houses, and I didn't want to appear to flaunt my good fortune. And they might not think it was good fortune; they might suspect favoritism, the senior tutor pulling strings for someone called Standish. I needn't have worried. Their unannounced visit took matters out of my hands.

Tom Peabody, the senior tutor, had advised me in my convalescence to sign up for no more than two courses instead of the usual load of four. He was right. Everything I undertook seemed to require twice the time I would have considered normal. Each weekly visit to the surgeon at Mass General consumed a whole morning. The Pittsfield dentist who had always cared for our family had equipped me with temporary front teeth of which I had to be very careful when I chewed. For the permanent work, he referred me to Dr. Fine, a colleague on Newbury Street in Boston, whose crack about giving me the best smile in the country club infuriated me. It didn't help matters that the two bridges I needed required seven visits in the space of three weeks. The Novocain put me in a foul mood, as did the cost of the work, none of which was covered by the Harvard medical plan or, so far as I knew, the bank's, but the latter point was moot since my father had canceled my insurance under the bank policy in favor of what the university offered. Perhaps there were cheaper dentists, but Dr. Jacobs had told me not even to think of economizing on those front teeth, and I did believe that he put my welfare ahead of the pleasure of directing the honorarium to his friend. I supposed that my parents would pay, if necessary, although a sum greater than the price of a new Buick was needed, but I had grown to prefer dealing with Mr. Hibble about money. He agreed at once to send the required sum. As we talked I learned that he had already covered whatever part Harvard wouldn't of the cost of the surgeon and the hospital in New Orleans as well as my airfare. When I told him that I was sorry about these unexpected expenses, he made a ho! ho! ho! sound, and said that those were things for him to worry about. I began to wonder whether the trust wasn't bigger than he had led me to believe. Another hypothesis was that he had been softened up by my defense of the Standish heir. Mr. Hibble's mellowness notwithstanding, there was a change in my attitude toward money. When I still believed that my school bills and allowance were paid by my parents, I didn't think about them, my principal concern being to escape as quickly as possible from the lecture that attended my every attempt to extract cash from my father. It never amounted to much anyway: I had no interest in ski boots or skis or in clothes of any sort. But, once I realized that there was a trust worth a fixed though unknown sum that was mine—or anyway reserved for my benefit—and that each outflow of cash and each investment loss diminished it, I became reluctant to spend money. It was my anchor to windward; I didn't expect any other, my mother having drummed it into my head that when my father died there wouldn't be anything left other than debts and the mortgage.

To HIS OWN SURPRISE, Archie was taken into a final club that was not at the very bottom of the social pecking order, and very quickly club activities—festive alumni dinners and bouts of drinking—absorbed most of his time. One of the oddities of his club was that no one seemed to know its members. In fact, at first I didn't believe that a club so named existed. Only after Archie joined, and I learned to recognize the club tie, which he wore every day, did I realize that I could actually identify another member of the club in the house dining room. Perhaps on account of some past dark misdeed, perhaps simply because the members had no link to Boston society, having joined the club didn't work all of the magic he had hoped for. Members were not invited to coming-out parties as a matter of course. You had to fend for yourself. Nor was admission to the Hasty Pudding or the eating establishment favored by artsy students guaranteed. Archie would have liked to join the former, because of the weekly dances, but wasn't elected. And to my dismay, the artsy club did not ask Henry to join. In fact, someone took the trouble to tell him that an upperclassman had boasted of blackballing his candidacy with a promise to block any future attempt. It was Henry's second rejection and, like the first, he took it hard, to the point of not wanting to walk by the club's building at lunchtime or if a tea or cocktail party was in progress. As a result, he took strange detours on his way to the house dining room. I didn't blame him. Except for his Brooklyn address and Brooklyn high school diploma, he conformed so well to the stereotype of a member that people routinely assumed that he was one or asked why he wasn't, in either case making Henry cringe. He would answer—and sometimes announce preemptively—that it was out of the question for him to join such an organization. His parents couldn't afford the dues or the cost of meals on top of meals at the house that had to be paid for in any event. I did receive an invitation but never answered. For one thing, it arrived at a time when I had begun to find it extremely difficult to take any action. I may also have wanted to stand by Henry at least once, as though that could have made up for my passing through the door that the master of my house had slammed in his face.

Mr. Peabody, the senior tutor, or Tom as he had asked me to call him, continued to show marked approval of me, consistent with his well-known weakness for undergraduates who fit a certain conception of Carolingian knights. I no longer attributed his regard to the term paper I had written in the spring semester of my freshman year, which he had given an A plus. That paper, I now realized, had at most shown him that I wasn't an imbecile. Tom almost always lunched in the house dining room, and I knew I was most welcome at his table. I brought Henry along as often as I could without creating the impression that we were tiresomely inseparable or that I was foisting his presence on Tom. It seemed to me after several such lunches that Henry and Tom got along well. Therefore, one day when Tom and I were alone at table I asked him why Henry hadn't been taken into the house. Tom raised an eyebrow and said that mistakes do happen. I might want to tell Henry not to worry about next year. Then he inquired about Archie, Henry's strange roommate. I told him that Archie was harmless. Oh well, he said, in that case . . . The sentence remained unfinished. You do realize, I said, that the reassurance isn't any use unless it includes Archie. Henry will never leave him behind. Tom nodded. Of course, he told me, that's exactly as it should be.

That evening Henry and I went to see a rerun of *The Third Man.* He walked me home afterward, and on the way we argued about the nihilism of Lime and whether Orson Welles or Trevor Howard was the finer actor. The chase through the sewers had made me jittery, and although it was late, I didn't think I could go to sleep right away. I offered to make some coffee in the electric coffeemaker George had given me for my birthday. We each had a cup. I thought Henry was about to leave when he said he had a question. I didn't have to answer if it would upset me, he said. Did I think that what happened in New Orleans had changed me?

What do you think? I said. I lost my spleen, I had broken ribs, my nose will never be the same, and they knocked out my front teeth. Doesn't that answer your question?

He protested, claiming that I was playing a game with him. Had I not understood that he was asking whether I had become afraid of people?

I was genuinely taken aback and told him so. After a moment of thought, I said I didn't think so. I might be more careful to avoid townies prowling the streets at night spoiling for a fight. The big mistake in New Orleans was that somehow we had gotten the idea that, as harmless tourists, George and I had some sort of diplomatic immunity. I would never make that mistake again anywhere because if anything the contrary was more true.

Henry thanked me for the coffee and said goodnight.

I didn't sleep that night, and the one benefit of lying in bed wide awake was that eventually I grasped this was a follow-up on the question he had asked the day I got back: that he had been groping for some sort of similarity between my experience of brutality in New Orleans and his terror at being subjected to something of that sort during the war. My obtuseness, I realized, must have been like a slap in the face. Normally, first thing in the morning I would have looked for an opportunity to apologize and ask him to come back for a talk, but something bad was happening to me. I found it difficult at the time to describe just what it was without bathos, and I am not sure that I can do it any better now. My reluctance to take the simplest everyday actions and to make decisions increased to the point of not doing anything and deciding nothing. For instance, more often than not I didn't answer the telephone when it rang. I could not bring myself to make calls, even those that I ordinarily would have thought routine and necessary. I did not get out of bed when the biddy came in to do my room. I was crushed by fatigue. I stopped going to classes and taking meals in the house dining room. When hunger forced me, I dressed perfunctorily and went to get something at Elsie's, two blocks away. Attendance at classes wasn't compulsory, but in addition to cutting them and not doing any reading, I failed to show up for the midterm exams. It's possible that I actually didn't know when or where they were scheduled to take place. I no longer listened to the radio or to records, although being able to play my Bach undisturbed had been one of my reasons for insisting on private quarters, and I had brought from home both my record collection and the record player that had been my Christmas present. Most frightening, it seemed to me that I no longer knew how to sleep or even fall asleep, except for sudden catnaps that were more like a loss of consciousness. At night, I lay under the covers quite helpless, my eyes open or shut—it didn't matter which—condemned to work out arithmetical problems that surged up like dreams and perhaps were dreams. I would get near to the solution and find that an element was missing or else I would lose some necessary thread of my reasoning. I knew that the problems were absurd and that I couldn't possibly work them out in my head, but that didn't stop my trying or make me get up, turn on the light, and attempt to solve them on paper. Of course, they would have vanished at once. I even lost the will to masturbate, although I had learned at school to make it the regular prelude to sleep. When I went at it anyway, hoping for the usual release, I couldn't even get a hard-on. Another nocturnal torment was an itch that afflicted every part of my body. I scratched and tossed in my bed; my skin was loathsome to me; I thought that my bones would burn with heat.

I didn't want to see Henry or George. When one of them called saying we should get together, I was evasive or said I was too tired. I doubt that being with them would have made a difference: they coddled me and at the same time took it for granted that I would go on looking and feeling awful for many months. Since we weren't taking the same courses, there was no reason for them to know that I hadn't bothered to go to class or that I hadn't taken the midterms. Tom Peabody may have noticed my absence from the dining room and drawn his own conclusions. Possibly there had been some sort of official notice sent to him about the midterms. Whatever the reason, a few days later, unannounced, he stopped by after lunch. I was in bed and had left my trousers and shirt on the desk chair. He took in the scene, sat down on the edge of my bed, and said that he hadn't been seeing me in the dining room. Without additional preliminaries, he told me he had had the impression that I was going to pieces, which was now confirmed. He made a gesture with his hand that took in my unshaved and uncombed condition and the mess all around me.

What's going on? he asked.

I told him as much as I knew how. I had been waiting for that question to be asked by the right person.

XIV

FEAR AND DESPAIR FOLLOWED. Sent by Tom to the university health services, I found myself several days later once again in a room decorated with execrable Harvardiana—on the walls two class banners, '37 and '42, assorted pennants, a group photograph of the football team, and engraved views of Sever, Emerson Hall, and Sanders in thick black frames, Harvard chairs, and Harvard ashtrays—talking to the pipe-smoking university psychiatrist, Dr. Winters. He had reviewed the tests, he told me, and the notes of two previous interviews. There was no doubt about my condition: I had hit a bad bump and was still in an uncontrolled skid. I didn't reply. After a couple of puffs, he spoke again, and said that I was a sick young man. I was, however, far from the scrap yard. My ailment, while serious, was closer to a mild than to a severe depression. With intensive treatment I should be able to get back on the road. I asked whether this meant I had to be in a hospital. Not necessarily, he answered. Let's talk about the treatment after you've seen the dean. At University Hall, the dean in charge of my case, a nice man who also smoked a pipe, told me that I had been placed on medical leave. Suddenly, I felt bereft. What was to become of me? I didn't protest but asked whether I would be allowed to return and how long it would be. I was hoping that he hadn't noticed that I trembled.

Mr. Standish, he told me, you have to be realistic. You aren't up to doing the work. You're not taking care of yourself. There's no point in your being here while you're in this condition. Come back when you are well. He added that he would be in touch with the senior tutor of my house. Though crushed, I couldn't help thinking that he was right.

It turned out that the dean didn't stop at notifying Tom Peabody. Without any warning he called my parents, a betrayal that rankled, although when Tom, whose patience I thought might be wearing thin, observed that I couldn't have imagined that they would be left in the dark, I had no answer other than to repeat querulously that he should have spoken to me first. So they came down to Cambridge and joined in the debate about where to put me away. What to do about the crazy son? My father's presence was particularly loathsome. I disliked his long fingers, pale and freckled just like mine, drumming on the table, his polite and pedantic diction, and his eyes, pale blue like mine, that tried to smile but were to me the eyes of a drunk in which I could always discern the little blood vessels no matter how much Murine had washed across them. The rage he put me in was a distraction from my mother and, although I did not then realize it, from the void Dr. Winters was opening before me. He too was not to be trusted. To hear him, now that he'd gotten an audience, and all three of them had me by the balls, the only choice I had was among hospitals. I suspected that he had a list a yard long, but there were three he favored: McLean, in Belmont, just outside of Cambridge, Silver Hill in Connecticut, and, of all places, Austen Riggs Center, in Stockbridge. I said I wouldn't go to any of them. McLean was a place of straitjackets and electric shock therapy; the name alone filled me with dread. I had scorn for the other two, Silver Hill because of tales I had heard of alcoholics sent there to dry out who returned after long sojourns only to hit the bottle—in fact, at one time, my mother had badgered my father to check in there—and Riggs because, in Berkshires folklore, it was a place for rich crackpots and wastrels hiding from husbands, wives, children, and other sundry obligations. I didn't want to be known as a Riggs patient, and I didn't budge when Dr. Winters changed tack and began to tell me that perhaps I could be an outpatient there. My parents hadn't much to say about any of this, and they shut up altogether when Riggs was named. I saw through them. It wouldn't have been at all convenient to have me there. In any other loony bin, I would be out of sight and, as they might hope, out of mind. George's parents would know, because of George, but they wouldn't carry tales about their son's rescuer. Especially since they might think it was all his fault. So we were at an impasse, because neither the doctor nor my parents seemed to have any stomach for having me locked up against my will. Perhaps it couldn't be done and they knew it. Tom, whom I had begun once more to consider the only person I could trust, came up with a solution. I would remain in Cambridge and live off campus under the care of a local psychiatrist. He got both the dean and Dr. Winters to agree to the principle, and then came up with the psychiatrist and the lodging. By the end of the week after Thanksgiving, I had become a paying boarder at the house of Madame Shouvaloff in De Wolfe Street and a patient of Dr. Jacob Reiner. As my parents were leaving, I told them I wouldn't be home for Christmas.

A long time into my analysis, Tom Peabody, whose store of gossip was inexhaustible, told me something of my analyst's personal history. He had preceded his mentor, Dr. Freud, into exile and was living in London at the time of the *Anschluss*. With Freud dead and the war likely to spread, he decided that New York would be a better refuge. Dr. Brill and other influential friends at the New York Psychoanalytic Institute pulled strings enabling him to obtain a visa for himself and his wife and, in 1940, he was already taking licensing examinations and conducting training analyses at the Institute. Around that time, Frau Dr. Reiner decided to go her separate way with a widowed Viennese art dealer. It was just as well, since Dr. Reiner was about to acquire an interesting patient: Grace Leffingwell, a young and ethereal descendant of Henry Clay Frick. It might have been more seemly not to personalize the relationship until Grace's analysis had been brought to completion. The end, however, wasn't in sight, and Dr. Reiner made his move, winning Grace's heart and hand to the horror of her family and the New York psychoanalytical establishment. The new Mrs. Reiner, married to a Jew, was promptly thrown out of the Junior League and dropped from the Social Register, the latter indignity being, in Tom's opinion, comical, since the New York Social Register was only slightly more exclusive than the telephone directory. The trusts and the money, however, couldn't be snatched away from Grace by the irate Leffingwells and Fricks. More to the point, those millions, and the family connections even if they were strained, had an intimidating effect on Dr. Reiner's colleagues: there was no move to sever his connection with the Institute. Even so, he no longer found the New York professional scene congenial. An affiliation with the Harvard Medical School became available, and a psychiatrist, who had trained in Vienna and was practicing in Cambridge, had an opening for Grace as a patient. The move to new quarters on Sparks Street was completed with the kind of dispatch that only the possession of a great fortune makes possible.

The brick house at the corner of Highland and Sparks Streets, where I went every morning at ten Monday through Friday, was remarkable only for its gleaming black shutters. The waiting room was reached by a separate side entrance. From there, a leather-padded door led to the office. Dr. Reiner required absolute punctuality. One arrived on the hour; the session began immediately and was over in fifty minutes flat. The point was to pick up one's coat and any other belongings from the waiting room and leave before the next patient arrived. In my case the system failed only once. Arriving a minute or two early I met in the waiting room the wife of my odious housemaster. She was just leaving. I bowed and said hello. She returned my greeting absently. I didn't mention the contretemps to Dr. Reiner.

I wonder whether psychoanalysis has ever helped one become like the people one envies and admires, who have power to hurt and will do none, husbanding nature's riches from expense, secure in their knowledge of what life owes them. For instance, George Standish. Dr. Reiner did not turn me into a more intellectual George, and gradually I came to understand that such was not his ambition. During two weeks or so I sat in a straight chair, his desk between us, and gave rambling confused answers to questions about my family. I have always had a tendency to ramble; for once I wasn't obliged to keep it in check. Then the drill changed: I lay on a couch like the one in Freud's study in Vienna, a large framed photograph of which hung above me, Dr. Reiner off to the side where I couldn't see him, and tried to connect words to dreams I was teaching myself to remember. Dr. Reiner had warned me that he would speak only "to get me into the right lane on the highway." Except for the occasional "this needs more work" and the few times when I asked to speak to him as though we were two normal human beings, that turned out to be all. He wasn't silent, however: he whistled nonstop, almost noiselessly, what I thought was invariably the same tune. One day, while I lay still, my head empty, unable to speak, I recognized it: "When Johnny Comes Marching Home." A feeling of outrage overcame me. I sat up and yelled, For Christ's sake, stop whistling. Oh, he answered, you have noticed. I will stop.

Had he been goading me? I came to think it must be so; the whistling had to be voluntary. If it were a real tic, beyond his control, I reasoned, he wouldn't have replied as he had. Finally, I asked him. The question was futile. He threw it back at me with What do you think? Equally futile was a question I put to him later, at a time of mounting frustration with my utter lack of progress: What makes you think, I said, that you can understand me? You can't. You weren't brought up here; you learned your English at school; you're a Jew. I sat up and stared him in the face. He didn't smile or frown. That's all beside the point, he told me. Getting to the bottom of your problems is your job; I'm only directing traffic. Then he tittered. I yelled at him a second time: I hope I never hear a shrink use another goddamn automobile metaphor so long as I live. Why don't you apes learn how to talk! He said nothing. I got up from the sofa and left without saying goodbye, a good twenty-five minutes of my hour remaining. Hayes-Bickford, where I went for coffee, was deserted. There wasn't a soul I knew left in Cambridge. Everybody, Tom Peabody included, had left for the spring break. It was too early to go to the movies. Instead, I walked for hours, retracing the itinerary Henry had followed after he had met Margot at Mario's party, although I avoided Sparks Street. The next morning I was back in Dr. Reiner's consultation room. He didn't reprove me, and I didn't say I was sorry; we resumed whatever it was we were doing. In obedience to him I hadn't gone near *The Interpretation of Dreams* or any other work on psychoanalysis. The previous day, however, during my walk, it occurred to me that perhaps the question I had put to Dr. Reiner about his undertaking to analyze a fine flower of New England like me was stupid. Wasn't it likely that from his point of view the development of neuroses was governed by quasi-mechanical rules that applied generally, so that cultural differences between him and me, although interesting, didn't matter very much? I tried this insight on him some sessions later. He told me we weren't there to discuss theories.

At the end of July, Dr. Reiner left for his usual summer vacation on the Cape. I didn't even think to ask him whether we had finished. Some weeks earlier, I had reminded him that the deadline for letting the college know whether I would be returning in the fall was upon us and asked his opinion. The question, he replied, was whether I would like to return. I said I would. But was he able to give me the sort of document about my health that would satisfy the dean's office?

Back to college in September, he mused. That's soon, Mr. Standish. All the same, if you want to do it, I think you should.

I said that I was getting better.

Everything is relative, he replied. I'd rather say that your approach to your problems has been changing in a positive direction. You need to keep up the momentum. I recommend that you remain in treatment, certainly so long as you are at the college. Perhaps later as well.

I asked whether it would be five times a week.

He nodded. Yes, with me or another qualified therapist.

And when will it be over? I asked again.

I can't tell you, he answered. Most likely, you will be the first to know.

A part of the answer was what I had hoped for: it meant that I wouldn't be set adrift. Although by this time I knew that Dr. Reiner was more expensive than the two other psychiatrists on the university's referral list, I decided to remain with him. Mr. Hibble didn't seem to mind, and I was glad to think that was all I really needed to worry about.

I spent the month of August at Madame Shouvaloff's reading French novels and listening to stories she told in French of her late husband, a favorite in the tsar's corps of pages, who escaped from Russia in the course of some movement of a White division across Siberia. Further improbable adventures brought him to Harvard, where he coached the fencing team. Her own family, she told me, was no less grand than the late prince's. She was a Karouguine. I might have liked to remain her lodger, but Tom Peabody's wiles secured for me again the single suite in O entry. During my absence he had used it to lodge visiting lecturers attached to the house. Those two rooms of my own tipped the scale against reminiscences told over glasses of tea with raspberry preserves redolent of Russia.

XV

It is time I brought Henry back onstage.

Tom Peabody's promise—in the end I interpreted it as such—was made good; in the fall of their junior year Henry and Archie moved into the house. I was back in my old quarters, as a sophomore, readjusting to college life. It wasn't long before the old intimacy between Henry and me was reestablished. We saw each other at meals and often late in the evening in my room. Henry liked to stop by. If I had finished my work and wasn't asleep, we talked, sometimes past midnight. On one such evening soon after the beginning of the semester he asked me, out of the blue—unless it was apropos of the course in Jacobean drama I was taking—whether I had ever heard of a fin de siècle French playwright called Alfred Jarry or his play *Ubu Roi,* both of which he said were very famous. He spelled Jarry and Ubu. I shook my head.

That's too bad, he said, Jarry and *Ubu* are the great discoveries I made at Bayencourt.

Seeing that I was puzzled, he reminded me that he had spoken as long ago as April of the job that Etienne van Damme's parents had offered him at Bayencourt, the name of their château and of the Ardennes village above which it perched. He was to teach English to their nephews and nieces starting on the first of July until early September, when he would have to leave to register for classes. I confessed that I had forgotten. It turned out, he continued, that also staying at Bayencourt was Mr. van Damme's much younger brother Denis, the director of the national theater in Brussels. One evening, after his pupils had gone to bed, he was in the library of the château, a room he had been encouraged to use. He had before him on the table a volume of plays by Plautus and a Latin dictionary he was consulting. Seeing that I was smiling, Henry quickly assured me that he wasn't doing it for show; he was really trying to get a head start on a seminar he knew he would be taking. Denis had looked over his shoulder and said he had a distinct recollection of *Menaechmi,* the play to which Henry's book was open. They began to talk about the theater generally, and Denis asked what he thought of Jarry. When Henry replied that he had never heard of him, Denis said this was a lacuna that should be filled; he was sure Jarry's works were on the bookshelf with other *J*s, his brother being a stickler for strict alphabetical order by author. Indeed, in no time at all he had handed Henry the volume containing *Ubu Roi,* saying it was Jarry's masterpiece. They would talk after Henry had read it.

Henry put Plautus away and plunged into *Ubu.* He read in bed. The French gave him no trouble except for the strings of epithets, many of them obscene, the meaning of which he had to guess, not having in his room an adequate dictionary, and the puns, some of which he realized were plain beyond him. The next day, Denis asked what he thought. Henry replied without hesitation that he had been dazzled. That's as I had hoped, Denis told him. I'm glad to have introduced you to Jarry. He's the point of departure for everything important in avant-garde twentieth-century theater that followed *Ubu,* including the work of Brecht. The point Jarry put across definitively is that to pretend that what happens on the stage is real is not the best way to evoke reality. It can be done more convincingly if you make manifest to the audience that they are looking at a performance—at actors who are performers presenting personages in the play and not those personages themselves, and that the space in which the action takes place is a stage, and not the castle at Elsinore or some bourgeois drawing room.

There is a need for distance between the actor and the role, Denis told me. No one in the audience can possibly believe a performance of *Ubu* replicates the way in which events actually unfolded. Its analogue is the "Mousetrap," the play within a play in *Hamlet:* "the image of a murder done in Vienna." No one in the audience—neither in the theater's seats nor in the crucial audience on the stage, King Claudius and Queen Gertrude—believes for a moment that the players are the Duke Gonzago, his murderous brother, or his unfaithful queen, but for that very reason the point is gotten across all the more powerfully.

True, I said, but what about the play *Hamlet* in which it's lodged, *Hamlet* itself?

It's the same thing, he answered impatiently. You don't suppose for a minute that the audience in the real theater's seats believe that the man in a black Renaissance costume wearing a blond wig and declaiming gorgeous lines, much of the time to himself, is the prince of Denmark!

As you can imagine, Henry continued, what Denis said then and on several other occasions made quite an impression on me. I went on to read Brecht plays in a French translation that Denis had his assistant send from Brussels, as well as the plays of Apollinaire and Cocteau, which were in Mr. van Damme's library. Denis was right. Jarry was some sort of flash-in-the-pan genius. All the same, I'm not sure that I would have paid so much attention to him or what Denis had to say about the theater—however interesting—if I hadn't been hooked by *le père* Ubu, this Falstaff without charm, obese, gluttonous, cowardly, and totally cruel. Naturally cruel. He is a mercenary soldier in the service of Wenceslas, the king of Poland. By the way, I don't know whether Jarry knew the Christmas carol, though he surely knew Czech history, and Jarry's Wenceslas is that kind of king, a good Saint Wenceslas. Ubu seizes power and kills him, crowning himself king. Then he slaughters Polish nobles and tax collectors, as well as his own chief coconspirator, and bleeds the country dry. He applies to Poland pataphynancial principles—that's one of Jarry's inventions—hilarious and fraudulent nonsense that you wouldn't be surprised to see written up on the front page of the *Times*. Then it's Ubu's turn to be overthrown. You can see that the plot is all nonsense and I won't say any more about it. The odd thing is that somehow all the Polish business struck me as wonderfully apt—inspired. It was my Poland and my Poles. A jolly gang. And that was the hook.

Would you like to read *Ubu?* he asked me. If you would, I have it right in my book bag, in the original and in English. I did a translation in Bayencourt. Denis thinks it's publishable—if ever I find someone interested in Jarry.

I said that of course I'd read the play.

He rummaged in the bag and extracted from it a beautiful little volume in a leather binding, which he said was Denis' own copy given to him as a parting gift, and the typescript of the translation.

You'll have fun, he said. I have decided to stage *Ubu*. When you read it, you will see why and you will also think that I'll need a cast and sets on the order of *Birth of a Nation*. But that's not true. The first performance by real actors—real professionals—was at the Théâtre de l'Oeuvre in 1896, with W. B. Yeats of all people in the audience. When the curtain went down, there was a big brawl; many in the audience found the play and the performance utterly outrageous and shocking. What's interesting from my point of view is that *Ubu* had been successfully performed prior to that time by amateurs using marionettes, and there have been marionette performances since, in regular theaters. I want to do it in the patio of the Fogg. It's the perfect setting; not too big and not too small, and I love the irony of the Renaissance setting for this pseudo-medieval farce. I don't see why undergraduates can't do as well as marionettes, provided the right puppeteer pulls the strings. That will be my job. I'll direct and I suppose I'll produce, unless someone else on the same wavelength and frequency volunteers.

I asked Henry whether he'd gone off his rocker.

By way of an answer, he pulled out of his book bag a notebook full of production notes, sketches, and stage directions, and talked about his plans so convincingly that I began to think that this might just be yet another seemingly impossible undertaking that he would somehow pull off.

I wished him luck and asked whether Margot had also been at Bayencourt. I had not seen her since our freshman year, and whatever Henry had told me about her during the winter and spring of my illness I had forgotten.

He hesitated and said that he wanted to make it very clear that the van Dammes had hired him because of the impression he had made on them during his short previous visit as someone who could get their gang of six- to eleven-year-olds to become interested in speaking English and actually doing it—a crazy idea, since the result might be a gang of little Belgians speaking with a Polish accent, but nevertheless it was their idea—and neither Etienne nor Margot had intervened. A couple of times Etienne had come to the château from Brussels, where he was working for the utility holding company controlled by the family. Margot hadn't appeared at all. He thought she had spent the summer with her parents in London and the south of France. He didn't know whether Etienne had gone to visit her.

In that case, I observed, they must have broken up. Henry answered that he didn't know; neither Margot nor Etienne had told him anything.

I NEEDN'T HAVE WORRIED that Henry would feel himself an interloper in the house dining room and perhaps be treated as such. Over the course of his sophomore year, although he and Archie were still living in exile on Mount Auburn Street, he had climbed the house social ladder, reaching one of the higher rungs to which an intellectual or an aesthete who hadn't gone to the right school could aspire. He was on easy terms with Tom Peabody and the other younger tutors and didn't hesitate to sit down beside them at lunch or dinner. It was more surprising to see him at a table Tom called the Parnassus, the fiefdom of a coterie consisting mostly of juniors with heavy pretensions to culture whose conversation was a potpourri of anecdotes concerning the Lunts, Cole Porter, Wystan Auden, Thornton Wilder, General Marshall, Ruth Draper, and various other luminaries, all of them—General Marshall excepted—referred to by first name. They had been friends since kindergarten and had all been to the right schools or, in any event, to schools that were acceptable. I had gone with Tom Peabody to see Jerome Robbins's ballet *The Cage* in New York. The attractiveness, cohesion, and fundamental hostility toward outsiders of Parnassus made me think of Robbins's endogamic insects; a foppish junior by the name of Ralph Wilmerding, to whom I took an instant dislike that I hoped was not induced by envy, was clearly their carnivorous insect queen.

I was friends with another member of the coterie, a senior called Jack Merton, who was in my small creative writing class. A rich orphan from San Francisco, he was probably the only undergraduate to wear day in and day out gray worsted suits and brown brogues, in preference to the standard ratty tweed jacket, chinos, and loafers. His Chevy convertible was parked and kept spotlessly clean at Mrs. McCartney's garage right off Harvard Square; one of his two leggy girlfriends was at Sarah Lawrence, the other at Vassar. He gave them equal time, spending alternate weekends with one in New York and with the other at his house on Narragansett

Bay. The poetry he wrote was convoluted and sometimes precious, but I liked it better than anything else that was written in our class, and I liked him. I sat down occasionally at the Parnassian table when Merton had an empty chair beside him. This initiative let Henry off the hook; he didn't have to decide whether he was in good enough standing to introduce me. In fact Tom Peabody's frequent presence at the table, especially at lunch, would have given me sufficient entrée, had I wished it.

Henry's apparent friendship with these men, none of whom he had known when we were freshmen, mystified me. I asked Henry whether they could possibly be friends of Archie's. He laughed and assured me that they weren't. Then he told me rather airily that it was quite simple: he had found them attractive, more attractive than anyone else in the house, and had taken advantage of an occasion when Tom was at their table and there was room for one more. Then one thing led to another, and he was thinking that a couple of them—he named Wilmerding and his acolyte, Scott Allen—might want to be involved in his production of *Ubu*. There was no way he could do it all alone. I was surprised, but not much later I attended, in Wilmerding's living room, what Wilmerding called an organizational meeting for Henry's and his *Ubu* project.

SHORTLY BEFORE that afternoon, Henry was putting up notices in all the houses announcing the audition for *Ubu*—to run an ad in the *Crimson* was in his opinion a waste of money. There was an oversize sophomore with a stentorian voice and a tendency to pontificate whom he had been observing here and there with an eye to casting him as Ubu, and he had ideas about the two other principal male characters, Capitaine Bordure, Ubu's adjutant whose name Henry translated as Gagarbage, and the young son of the king of Poland, Bougrelas, or Buggerson in Henry's version. Wilmerding had not yet told him whether he liked those choices, but Henry saw no reason why he shouldn't, and anyway wasn't going to waste time talking to him about it. It took an eternity for Wilmerding to make up his mind about anything. Perhaps he was preternaturally careful. The other role still to be cast was *la mère* Ubu, a gross personage, as fat and repulsive as her husband. There were enough girls at Radcliffe, he remarked, who fit that description, but, as he was not after method actors, he wondered whether a beautiful girl who could act might not be more effective if she could convey obesity and grossness notwithstanding her real appearance. It was worth a try.

Margot, for instance? I asked.

We were walking back to the house from the Widener. Henry stopped to retie the laces of his tennis shoes and asked me to wait. When he straightened up he said that he wasn't sure where he stood with Margot. It was a complicated business. I suggested we talk about it over a cup of tea at Hayes-Bickford. We took a table in the back, Henry wanting to be sure that we weren't overheard. He drank his tea in a couple of gulps and looking away from me said he was sure it was wrong to say what he was about to tell me, but, at the same time, he had to talk to someone. Archie was out of the question so it came down to me. Jarry and *Ubu Roi* were not his only once-in-a-lifetime experiences at Bayencourt, he said. There was something much more grave and extraordinary. Something between Madame van Damme and him.

Did you get into some sort of trouble? I asked. I hadn't gotten the impression that you left there under a cloud.

He laughed, and said that wasn't the problem—or perhaps there was no problem at all, in any event not yet. He had slept with Madame van Damme. I mean Madeleine.

Such was my astonishment that I asked him to repeat what he had said, and when he had done so, I asked how such a thing was possible. He said it had been very simple, weirdly simple. Monsieur van Damme was at Bayencourt only on weekends, and not necessarily every weekend, and Denis had already left. He was spending the last three weeks of August with friends near Biarritz. There was no one at the château during the week except the children, the servants, Madeleine, and himself. From the start, Henry had gotten along very well with the husband and wife. As he had already mentioned when telling me about Denis van Damme, he had been told to make himself at home in the library. Usually he went there after dinner. He would sit on a sofa near the windows, which were left open to let in cool evening air. When Madeleine came to the library, she almost always sat in one of the huge tapestry-covered armchairs on either side of the fireplace. Monsieur van Damme would sit in the other.

Here Henry broke off the story in order to get another cup of tea. I asked him to get one for me as well.

I should tell you, he continued, that Madeleine is very attractive—as an objective fact, without thinking that there could be something between us. It would have been preposterous. She is tall, big boned, and athletic looking, with an incredible head of blond hair barely touched by gray. She can't be more than fifty, and I have no idea whether she seems younger or older. Anyway, that evening I was absorbed in my book—by a weird coincidence *Le rouge et le noir*—when she sat down at the other end of my sofa and began to ask me a series of personal questions, first about college, then about Margot, whom she said she didn't really understand, and then about the war. She knew something about my past but not much, or perhaps she was simply pretending not to know. That, as you can imagine, put me on edge, and I answered her questions with real difficulty because I felt that my back was against the wall, more so than at the Standishes' lunch. I couldn't disregard the fact that she was my employer and in a sense my hostess. At the same time, no doubt about it, I found her interest and sympathy flattering, perhaps even exciting. So I answered but as briefly as possible. Then she told me that during the war her parents had helped a number of Jews to hide. That hadn't been as difficult in Belgium as in Poland—or so she thought. Although her husband personally had absolutely nothing against Jews, the rest of his family was all Flemish rightists and anti-Semites. That made a lot of trouble during the war and put her parents in danger. Her too because she was involved in the Resistance. The Resistance was also anathema to her in-laws. The tables were turned right after the war, when it was the in-laws who faced various difficulties. I'm not sure whether it was the way she told this story or that the air had gotten colder, but I shivered. She noticed it, asked me to close the windows, and, when I had done so, asked me to sit down beside her. I did as she said, whereupon she took my hand, held it against her face, and said, Aren't you going to ask me to come to bed with you?

My response, Henry continued, was to put my arm around her and kiss her. I was very awkward, but she let me, just once. Then she pushed me away very gently and said, Turn out the lights here and go to your room. I won't be long. My room at Bayencourt was a little bigger than your bedroom here: an armoire and a chest of drawers, a worktable at the window, a straight-back chair, and one armchair. I quickly stuffed the underwear and shirt that I had left on the bed into the armoire, took off my jacket and tie, and waited. The time before she appeared moved very slowly or very fast, I'm not sure which; my heart was beating so hard that I could hardly bear it. Then the door opened. She wore a long red velvet bathrobe. Her feet were bare. I stood up and held my arms out to her, and when she did the same the bathrobe opened. She was naked. It was like seeing Dürer's Eve except that her hair was pinned up in a bun behind her head. She helped me undress and we lay down on the bed. She spoke before I did. Is this your first time? she asked. I nodded, without daring to touch her. Then just lie on your back, she said, and be very quiet. She bent over me and let down that amazing hair, which fell like a tent over her shoulders and me. When it was over she said, Now you can be patient and tender. She stayed with me until dawn. From then on she came to me every night, twice even when Monsieur van Damme was there. They sleep in separate bedrooms so that after he had gone to his room all she had to do was to wait ten minutes to be sure he was asleep. I can hardly describe what it was like.

I nodded. The truth is that I was shaken by his story.

Anyway, to go back to Margot, he said, which is how I got started telling you all this, you can imagine how uneasy I am about Margot and Etienne. It's not that I am afraid they know; that's not possible. But I can't help feeling terribly anxious, as if I had wronged them, betrayed our friendship.

And how do you feel about her, I asked, about Madame van Damme?

Madeleine? It's all so preposterous. Just saying her name fills me with happiness and gratitude, but I can't really think that I love her. Surely she doesn't love me. If I didn't know that it had happened, I wouldn't believe that it had. Why did she choose me? Do you realize that she must be four or five years older than my mother? She never told me her age, but I am pretty sure that's right given what she was doing during the war. She will be in Boston at the end of the month, staying at a hotel. She's coming alone, for some Wellesley alumnae business. Can you imagine it? A whole week.

XVI

Some time later, Henry told me gravely that Madeleine had arrived in Boston. For several days he was not to be seen in the dining room at dinner, and he didn't stop by my room as was his custom.

An unpleasant incident occurred more or less at that time involving Margot. Rehearsals of *Ubu* were in progress and whenever we spoke Henry said he was pleased with the cast, especially the pompous sophomore, who had turned out to be a friend of Ralph Wilmerding's. Henry thought he was "quintessentially ubuesque." There was a good deal of interest in the production, and while the other roles were never easy to fill, he had many candidates to choose from. A big problem he faced was Margot's determination to play *la mère* Ubu. Remembering our earlier conversation, and the suggestion I had made, I said that was splendid, for once proof that telepathy can work.

Yes, Henry said, I also thought it was a great idea at first, but she doesn't know how to project her voice and can't be heard. The acoustics at the Fogg are terrible, because of all that stone. I don't know whether she can overcome it.

A week or so passed before we talked again about the play. Henry came to my room after a rehearsal. He threw himself into an armchair and told me that he had bad news about Margot. After he had gotten the actor playing Ubu to work with her on her breathing, he told me they had a special rehearsal at the Fogg, just the three of them, and it was no better. That was, he thought in retrospect, the time to tell her nicely that he would have to replace her, but he didn't; the prospect of directing her was irresistible. He let matters more or less slide until this afternoon's important full rehearsal when, in the presence of the entire cast and Bob Chapman, the tutor helping him with technical aspects of the production, and with Wilmerding and Scott Allen watching from the side, he suddenly blew up. He was standing where the last row of seats would be, Margot was in the midst of one of her big speeches, and he mostly couldn't hear and when he did hear he couldn't understand, although he knew the lines by heart. Suddenly, without any forethought, he found himself yelling at her: You sound like a debutante at a freshman smoker! Stop speaking through your goddamn nose! Even as he yelled, he heard Wilmerding and Allen snickering. Then Wilmerding stood up to applaud—you couldn't tell whether he was applauding him or Margot. The situation was so ghastly that Henry didn't even notice Margot stride across the space that was cordoned off as the stage until she stood before him shouting—this time projecting so well that no one present could fail to hear—I've had it with you, you bastard. Then she slapped him hard across the face, first one cheek and then the other. He just stood there, silent, while she stomped off.

How could I have let things slide so badly, how did I lose control? he asked over and over, shaking his head in disbelief. I know I've been tense, I know that I'm behind in my work, I know that I've spent too much time with Madeleine, and I know that Margot's been frustrating, but how I let such a thing happen is beyond me. I guess it was saying that she spoke through her nose that got her, he said. She's very sensitive about it. Still, it wasn't the end of the world.

I replied that Margot evidently thought otherwise.

He nodded and pointed to the red marks on his cheeks. Somehow, they got through the rehearsal, with him reading Margot's part. Afterward, Bob Chapman and he walked back to the house. On the way, Chapman told him not to take what happened too hard. You'll both get over it, he said, and the play might be improved because Margot isn't right as *mère* Ubu, unlike Jackson as Ubu—that role was made for Wilmerding's blowhard friend, it fits him like a glove. At the same time, Chapman said I should learn a lesson: one should look for ways to turn a liability into a strength. I might have taken advantage of Margot's snobby elocution and made it into another incongruous facet of Mrs. Ubu's grotesque personality. At least I might have tried to. This advice, given so calmly and discreetly, really hurt more than the slap and made me feel boorish and stupid, but I was grateful for it.

He looked utterly wretched and asked whether I had any liquor in the room. In fact, there was some sherry left in the bottle George had given me for my birthday. I poured a drink for each of us. Henry finished his, looked at his watch, and asked to use the phone. I supposed he was going to call his mother so I went to wash my hands and afterward, to give him more time, stayed in the bedroom putting away the shirts that had just come back from the laundry. I was surprised to hear, instead of a Polish conversation, Henry saying that he would like to speak to Margot. A moment of silence followed. The girl on bells at Margot's dormitory must have been looking for her. Then Henry spoke again, saying a rather cheerful Hello, Margot. The bang of the receiver being slammed down on the other end was so loud that I heard it from the bedroom. Henry hung up too, very gently, and addressing me said, I don't know what to do now, she won't speak to me. I've got to fill that role. That can't wait and I'll have to manage it one way or another. But that she should be so angry, that I should have lost her, is more than I can bear.

It was seven. I said we should go to dinner. Most people had already eaten, and we were able to have a table to ourselves. I told him I couldn't understand how he had those feelings for Margot and could continue whatever he was doing with Madame van Damme. He told me he didn't have an answer; he was utterly confused.

IT WAS A MYSTERY to me what made Henry think he could stage and direct a play. His experience consisted of nothing more than being taken to Broadway shows by his parents, an imposition he complained about as yet another effort to infantilize him. Nonetheless, if I hadn't known him well, I wouldn't have suspected that every step he took was improvised. His self-assurance was impregnable. He replaced Margot as *la mère* Ubu with a Radcliffe freshman, a Walküre with a voice to match. A week later, after the dress rehearsal, Chapman gave the cast the victory sign. The enthusiasm of the audience at the premiere was such that the director of the Fogg agreed on the spot to two more performances to take place the following week.

There was a party afterward given by Mr. Ryan, an economics tutor affiliated with the house, and his wife, who had painted the play's only backdrop, a curtain held aloft on two poles at each end. The cast and everyone connected with the production, as well as their friends, were invited. The Ryans lived at the corner of Brattle and Fayerweather streets. It was a beautiful night in March. Although it wasn't especially cold, George had gotten his car so that as soon as Henry was ready, we could drive him there. Archie came with us. Practically everyone must have already arrived. One could hear the roar of the guests from the street. We were quickly separated, and I didn't see George again until Bob Chapman's toast, for which someone managed to quiet the crowd. As soon as he had finished, Henry made a toast and offered his thanks without, it seemed to me, omitting anyone. We got back to the house very late, and I was surprised when Henry followed me to my room. He sat down and asked: Did you notice Wilmerding and Allen? What about them? I answered. Neither came to the party, he said, although they were both at the play. I don't understand those two.

XVII

Success, observed Tom Peabody, having made sure that Wilmerding and his two sidekicks with whom we had just had lunch were out of earshot, ah success. It's hard to earn and harder to wear gracefully. *Inde ira et lacrimae.*

We were lingering over coffee in the house dining room. Henry had been at lunch with us as well, but had left abruptly in the middle of the meal. I asked Tom what he meant by the English part of his aphorism; I understood the Latin.

It's simple, he answered, I would have thought you could figure it out. Henry's sudden blaze of success doesn't suit Wilmerding. Ergo, it doesn't suit Wilmerding's disciples. Henry should have pleaded with Wilmerding to take ample credit for *Ubu;* in fact, he should have forced it on him. Now the harm is done. Are you ready for another old saw, *ira furor brevis?* Not this time. Hell will freeze over before Wilmerding relents.

I protested, telling Tom that I knew for a fact that Wilmerding had done nothing to help out with the production, although he had been given every opportunity. The same was true of his pals, Thatcher and Burlingham. Hot air: that was all.

Tom waved that aside. I don't doubt it, he said, but it doesn't matter. Never ask someone to help unless you really want him to help and you think he will. Otherwise, you're asking for trouble. And if you fall into that trap and you happen to be dealing with someone like Ralph, you had better pretend that he has been immensely helpful. Better yet, indispensable. As it is, Wilmerding feels slighted and will make your friend Henry pay for the insult. Of course, he might have turned against Henry whatever he did. They all think he's too big for his britches.

I asked whether, as a practical matter, there was anything Henry could still do to repair the damage.

Do now? Probably nothing. He can hope for the best and not expect much. It wasn't very smart to try to worm his way into Wilmerding's circle. He did that, you know. I observed it with interest because I was in a way an accessory to the crime. He'd see me at Ralph's table and ask whether he could join me. After a while, he began to act as though he were entitled to be there and didn't need my presence as a pretext. That's when Wilmerding began his cat-and-mouse game with him, a game designed only to humiliate, because Wilmerding is a house cat and doesn't eat mice. If you know him well enough, you will realize that if Ralph chooses the game, he wins. It doesn't matter whether it's chess or checkers or who remembers more dates of famous battles or how many rounds Joe Louis went with Tommy Farr. I don't know whether Wilmerding and Henry have actually played, but if they have I'm sure Wilmerding won. Then Henry came up with a game of his own: putting on a play no one had ever heard of with no opportunity for Wilmerding to beat him. That left only one solution. The banishment of Henry! For the sake of the established social order.

Having said this, Tom folded his napkin and got up. I followed him to his entryway. Before he went in, I said, I want to ask a question: What do you really think of Wilmerding and company?

Tom raised his eyebrows. Not much. But as undergraduates go, they're decent company: good-looking, well dressed, reasonably civilized.

But in relation to this case, I insisted, to what they've done.

They've been rough with him, he replied. But don't worry too much about Henry. I suspect that he's very resilient.

After lunch I recalled incidents that Tom's remarks illuminated for me in retrospect. It was a fact that only one Parnassian—Jack Merton—as well as Tom Peabody, of course, had come to the Ryans' party for *Ubu*, although all were invited and I had heard Henry repeat the invitation the day before the premiere. Also, very recently I had noticed on several occasions at lunch and dinner that it was difficult for Henry to get a word in edgewise: whatever he said, Wilmerding or Allen would break in and, speaking more loudly than he, take the conversation in some other direction. This was to some extent how they normally behaved. They were enamored of clipped private jokes and anecdotes that were sometimes difficult to decipher. But at this last lunch they had been openly brutal. Wilmerding had ignored questions Henry addressed to him—rather than answer he turned away and spoke to Thatcher or Burlingham—and Allen had once or twice imitated Henry's accent in answering something he had said.

I didn't doubt that Henry knew what was happening, and in the days that followed my talk with Tom I took to waiting for him at the door of the dining room so that we could sit together, or, if he had arrived before me, I joined him at whatever table he happened to have chosen. I didn't think that he would again attempt to scale Parnassus, though I was reluctant to be the first to mention the change in his and Wilmerding's relations. It wasn't long, however, before Henry asked whether I could explain what he had done to Ralph and the rest of that crew.

I seem to have become public enemy number one, he said, and I don't know what crime I have committed.

Although I had come to believe that Tom was right in everything he had said, I didn't have the heart to repeat his words to Henry. I avoided the question partially, telling him that with the exception of Merton, they were pretentious second-raters unable to accept the success of anyone who wasn't a charter member of their club but came into daily contact with them. I added that I had become tired of seeing them at lunch and dinner. That at least was absolutely true.

Nothing more was said at the time. A couple of days later, he asked me out of the blue whether I had imagined that *Ubu* could turn into such an albatross.

I shook my head.

It has, he said, most probably because it has been such a success. If it had fizzled some might have snickered but no one would have really cared. Instead it has made trouble. Not just between Wilmerding and me—by the way there may be more to it than my success, but I can't put my finger on it. But the classics department too has its nose out of joint. A couple of old fogies claim that my having staged such a play is a sign that

I'm not serious. A self-respecting classicist, they say, if he were to do any such thing at all, would have chosen a Greek or Latin text instead of some French drivel. They wouldn't have even noticed that there had been a production of *Ubu* if there had been less talk about it.

The following week he reported that he was pretty sure of having placated both the department chairman and the professor with whom he was reading Greek tragedies. He told them about the coincidence of his reading Plautus in the library of a château in the Ardennes awakening the interest of the director of the national theater of Brussels, and the rapprochement the director had made between Plautus and Jarry.

Name-dropping clinched it, he added, brazen name-dropping. Denis van Damme, Ardennes, a French château, a Belgian industrial fortune. They began to regard me with a certain new respect. Unfortunately, I made them a foolish promise that I will live to regret. I told them that if work on my thesis permits, I'll stage a Greek or Latin play next spring.

In all likelihood, he could have skipped that commitment. A few days later he learned that the election to the national honor society had taken place and that he was one of the handful of juniors chosen. Over dinner at Henri IV, where Archie and I took him to celebrate, Henry refused to be congratulated. For one thing, when he told his parents his mother said, That's all you have to tell me? What's so good about being one out of eight? You aren't at the head of your class?

Besides, he said, this election is based on arithmetic; they take the juniors with the highest grades. Nobody needed to vote for me because he liked me. It would be fun to be elected to something just once because everyone thinks I'm such a nice guy.

DR. REINER AND I were going through another crisis at just that time. I had begun a novel for my creative writing course and it was going no better than my analysis. There were days when I could manage at most a few lines. And I was spending more time with George, not only because I liked him but also because he did not try to involve me in problems that couldn't be solved. We would have a meal, drink a beer, chuckle over Berkshires gossip, and say goodbye. I had spent only one week in Lenox during the past summer, most of it playing tennis on the Standishes' court. I hadn't gone home for Christmas, and I wasn't planning to go at Easter. George was my source of news. I had no doubt that I hurt my parents' feelings by staying away. But their silence—my mother had stopped writing to me—and my Christmas present, three pairs of thick wool socks and a pair of red flannel pajamas out of the L. L. Bean catalog, left no doubt in my mind that they considered me damaged goods. Which was more to blame: the beating I had received in New Orleans or my subsequent nervous breakdown? I also thought it possible that, after all those years of bringing up somebody else's kid, and putting a more or less good face on it, they'd had enough. A Standish trust was paying my way. I was off their hands and out the door. Good riddance to a bad job. Dr. Reiner showed no interest in these speculations; he said, We're not here to discuss current events.

Had I been less absorbed by these personal worries I might have realized how isolated the collapse of the relationship with Wilmerding had left Henry. If you crossed off Wilmerding and his companions, he had no friends apart from Archie, George, and me—an odd situation for an undergraduate so accomplished to find himself in just in the second half of his junior year. I should have once again made an effort to have meals with him regularly. But I was skipping more dinners and lunches than I ate, and almost never went to breakfast. The hours kept by the muse and the house dining room staff did not overlap. So it happened that I wouldn't spend an evening with Henry until after the Easter break. We went to an early show at the University Theater and then sat up talking in my room.

I saw Madeleine in New York, he told me. She timed her trip so that I could be there.

Is it possible that I said something as stupid as, Did you have a good time? It didn't matter; he could hardly wait to tell me. She is fabulous, he said, I am beginning to believe that she may be in love with me. Anyway she really wants to be with me. Just think—we had three nights together. Then she went back to Brussels and I took the subway to Brooklyn.

I was intrigued and asked whether he had actually slept at her hotel. He laughed and said, Yes, at a very big hotel she had chosen on purpose, the Waldorf-Astoria. It was so big that even if someone she knew happened to be in the lobby there was little likelihood of that person's realizing that he was with her unless she took his arm, which she was careful not to do. They were together all the time, even when she went shopping, except for two lunches, when she had to meet the wives of her husband's business friends. That Mr. and Mrs. White could have survived the news that their only son was staying at the Waldorf with a woman more than thirty years older didn't seem likely. I asked him how he had managed to get that past his parents.

I told a huge lie, he answered. I said I was staying with George. Naturally they were furious, and I had to agree to call them every morning so that they'd know I hadn't been hit by a car. Of course, I couldn't have those conversations in front of Madeleine. They were too embarrassing. I had to wait until she was in the bathroom. The risk of their calling me at the Standishes' was very small because they wouldn't want to disturb such grand people, but just in case there was an emergency and they got up their nerve to dial the number, George was ready to back up my story and get hold of me right away.

You've told him about Madeleine!

I had to, he replied. Besides, I trust him. I've told you about it because I tell you everything. I haven't told Archie.

He paused, but I didn't say anything, and he asked whether I thought he had made a mistake confiding in George. I assured him that he hadn't. Henry looked relieved.

There is something else, he said. Madeleine knows about the business with Wilmerding, he said, I told her in a letter. She thinks that my friends let me down. They didn't stand up for me. That's what she wrote, and she said it again in New York. I think I've convinced her that there was nothing that you could have done. Perhaps Peabody could have brought them to heel, but that sort of thing is not for the senior tutor to concern himself with. Anyway, what would my relationship with Ralph have been if he'd had a talking-to? Worse than nothing, and that's all it is now.

A nothing that rankles, I said, hoping that Madeleine had not hit the nail on the head.

Either he really thought we hadn't let him down or he was determined to put a good face on our conduct. He gave me his other big news.

Madeleine had told him that she had allowed her husband to talk her into engaging Henry again for July and August as the resident English tutor in Bayencourt. He was even going to get a raise. But first he would go to London, where she would meet him. They would spend a few days together, and then she would go home so as to be there on the first of July, when he was scheduled to arrive. This, he said, would be the amusing part of the vacation. In order to pacify his parents about his being away all summer, and also because he felt somewhat guilty about the Easter break, he promised that right after his last exam he would go with them to a resort they liked in the Catskills, a short distance from Woodstock, run by a Polish couple, a former lieutenant in the army of General Anders who had survived his campaigns and the lieutenant's wife. The clientele was all Polish Jews, including some who'd come to New York as refugees after the war ended. The scenery was truly beautiful, and there were good walks in the nearby woods, but the great attraction was the Polish cuisine. Even during a heat wave at lunch the guests would tuck away huge helpings of stuffed cabbage followed by a cucumber salad and a nice cheesecake. For dinner they might have *zrazy* with kasha and more cucumber salad. After that strawberries and whipped cream and a different cake, possibly one made with poppy seeds, which was a great favorite, except, of course, for guests like his father, who lived in the shadow of a heart attack and ate nothing but cottage cheese and watermelon. His father had already announced that they had reserved a bungalow on the grounds, which meant that Henry would have to sleep on a pullout sofa in the living room and listen to him snore. He made an attempt to persuade them to get a bedroom for him in the hotel itself. His father refused. There was no extra charge for a third person in the bungalow, so he would be throwing good money out the window if he paid for a bed in the hotel. Henry said that in the end he didn't care all that much. The walls in the main building were thin too and, if the choice was between listening to his father's snoring and that of strangers, he came out in favor of his old man.

My own plans for the summer were neither so grand nor so piquant as Henry's. I knew that, after the semester ended, I would stay in Cambridge, at Madame Shouvaloff's, in a room one of her graduate student boarders was vacating, until the first of August, when Dr. Reiner started his vacation, and if I went away from Cambridge I would have to return in time for my first appointment, two days after Labor Day. I wasn't sure that my parents wanted me in Lenox. Even if it turned out that they did, I didn't think I could endure them for more than ten days. George was planning to travel in Europe and, promising that he wouldn't get into brawls, proposed that I join him for the last part of his trip, which would be in France. He would have a car, he said; we would have fun. I told him I was tempted, but didn't dare to make yet another application for money to Mr. Hibble, and clearly I couldn't expect any from my parents. That's all right, said George. His parents had told him to invite me and they fully expected to take charge of everything. They had even picked two sailings, from New York to Cherbourg and back, that would get me to Cambridge on schedule.

Please don't say no, he said. My father even asked me to tell you that he will take the blame if there is trouble at home about your not getting to Lenox.

I didn't want to refuse. We decided to meet in Paris, which I would reach by the boat train.

It must have been just before the reading period that Henry told me of another development. Margot had called to tell him that she wanted to see him in his room. He asked her to meet him at the porter's lodge, signed her in, and took her upstairs. Once they were in the living room, she said here, read it, and handed him an envelope with his name on it. Inside was a two-page letter of apology.

Are we friends again? she asked after he had read it.

He said, Of course we are.

Archie was out, he continued, and I didn't expect him to return until late. Can you imagine it, first she kissed me and then we necked. Really necked, although I was very careful to let her lead and not get ahead of what she wanted. She stayed until seven, when I had to push her out the door. And she has been back.

I said that was wonderful; he must have learned a great deal from Madeleine that he could show her.

XVIII

GEORGE'S APPETITE for mercenary sex had not diminished. Even in a small city as sober as Reims, where we spent one night, he insisted, with the stubbornness of a little boy determined to play with another kid's toy, on prowling neighborhoods he thought were promising, usually near the railroad station, in search of a bar or corner where the magical contact might be made. I would tag along up to the moment when he seemed poised to conclude the transaction and then return to the hotel room alone. Most often I was asleep by the time he got back, or pretended I was. Otherwise, he would sit down on my bed and describe in minute detail what he had gotten for however much he had paid. Playing dead, however, only postponed the report until the following morning. The one exception to my abstinence occurred in Paris. A cousin of May Standish's and her husband invited us to dinner at the restaurant of the great hotel on Place Vendôme. Later, George and I had a nightcap at the bar. George's cousin was the political officer at the embassy, and we discussed the gossip and propaganda—or so it seemed to me—that he had used to monopolize the conversation at dinner. He was convinced that the Communist insurgents in Indochina had to be stopped. Since the French were incapable of doing the job alone, it was our duty to support their effort with money and supplies. I asked whether that meant putting in our troops. If absolutely necessary, he told me, yes, but every effort should be made to limit it to special situations. We were lucky in that we had them in there doing the heavy lifting. George and I were both Francophiles and so instinctively enthusiastic about helping the French. But we believed in decolonization and had both read *Man's Fate*. We wondered whether whoever the French and, indirectly, we were backing could be the equal of Ho Chi Minh. Were we betting on the right horse? It was difficult to debate these questions with George's cousin. He knew too much, and his mind was made up. Our nightcap turned into a couple of drinks. A bit on an edge, we left the hotel by the rue Cambon entrance. Almost immediately we were propositioned. The specific service offered made me feel faint. I took hold of George's arm for support and said, Let's do it. We didn't have far to walk. The maid's room they called their studio was on the rue du Faubourg St. Honoré, up five flights and at the end of a long corridor painted battleship gray. In it was a double bed, a washstand, and a bidet. They were transvestites. When George said that we should go another round, changing partners, I agreed. We didn't leave until early morning.

WE WERE IN REIMS for the cathedral and because it seemed a good place to spend the night before visiting Verdun and the adjoining battlefields. From there we intended to go directly to Dijon but didn't know whether we could make it in time for a late dinner if we did justice to Verdun. Over breakfast, George had been less exuberant than usual about how his evening had ended. I had more coffee while he studied the road map.

I have an idea, he said. What would you think if after Verdun we headed northwest instead of south and dropped in on Henry? The van Dammes might put us up for the night.

I looked at the map. Once we got to Verdun, it would be a short drive to Bayencourt. But could we do such a thing, both knowing about Henry and Madame van Damme? I thought I would be uncomfortable even if Henry hadn't told me that he had spoken to George. As beneficiaries of Henry's indiscretion, we would be looking at Henry and Madame van Damme through the prism of our guilty knowledge. And he would be aware of the low comedy being enacted.

Do you think we really should do it? I asked George. In view of the circumstances?

He turned red and said, I should have figured out that he would have told you. I nodded.

He thought about it and said, It was Henry's idea to tell us, nobody made him.

I could see that Bayencourt and perhaps the opportunity for voyeurism as well tempted him. Then he shrugged and said, I guess it would shake up old Henry to see us pull in the drive or roll across the drawbridge. I bet they have one at the château. Let's call ahead; he can always tell us not to come. Have you got their number?

I shook my head.

Too bad, George said. Sure would've liked to see her, but I think we had better concentrate on getting a good meal in Dijon.

HENRY ARRIVED IN CAMBRIDGE on the last day of registration. We saw each other that evening during dinner at the house. It was my first meal there; I had been living at Madame Shouvaloff's since returning from France, waiting for the dormitories and houses to open. In the meantime, I went my appointments with Dr. Reiner. We made little progress that I could discern, but I was able to function. Whether this was due to his ministrations I couldn't tell. I had managed to pick up the thread of the novel I had begun during the spring semester and had worked on it at Madame Shouvaloff's until I left for France. Although I had my Olivetti with me, while traveling with George I got little done beyond taking notes and mapping out a few scenes. Having been admitted to Archie MacLeish's writing class, a literary summit of sorts, I was relieved not to have bogged down just as the course was about to start. When I asked Henry how his summer had turned, he gave me a broad grin; he'd been given a regular day off each week, which he had used to go on long hikes, sometimes with his friend Denis, who was at Bayencourt for part of August. There couldn't be a place more beautiful than the van Dammes' part of the Ardennes, with its forests, fortified farms, and tiny villages where you could stop for a beer and a sandwich of fresh baguette and butter and local ham.

That's nice, I said, but what about your romantic life?

He was less nervous about Madeleine this time—certainly he no longer felt he had wronged Monsieur van Damme. During their hikes, Denis became very voluble, confiding the secret of the harmony in his brother's and Madeleine's marriage: the brother's mistress in Brussels. The mistress's husband, an important politician, and Madeleine were au courant; in fact the two couples were on the best of terms, the affair being conducted with great discretion and dignity. As a result, Denis continued, his brother made few demands on Madeleine. At most, from time to time he exercised his conjugal rights; otherwise, she had her total freedom.

Hearing this, Henry said, made me nervous. I wondered whether he was trying to tell me that he knew about me and his sister-in-law. To smoke him out, I asked whether Madeleine also had affairs. He replied that she is the most secretive of women. There must be other men, he said, because she surely isn't a lesbian, but there are no traces.

And Margot? I asked.

She hadn't been to Bayencourt, Henry told me, although Etienne, who was now working for the family business in Paris, had come twice for the weekend. According to Madeleine, Margot was staying at her parents' place in Cap Ferrat, where Etienne would spend his August vacation with her. This was not welcome news to Madeleine, who hoped that her son would find someone more suitable through the new connections he was making in Paris. Henry said nothing about where he stood with Margot. I supposed that he hardly knew; they wouldn't have had the chance since the summer to see each other.

Henry's being a senior, absorbed by his courses and beginning to work on his honors thesis, led to our spending less time together. George wasn't an honors candidate, but he was going out with Edie Bowditch, a Radcliffe freshman, and what with Edie, the crew, and classes, he too was short of time. I liked Edie. Without repeating herself, she talked a mile a minute, saying whatever came into her mind on her great subject, the milieu of old New York families—her parents' milieu—about which I knew nothing that I hadn't read in Edith Wharton. But she was deadly serious about her work and not losing George's attention. Those twin occupations at best allowed us to have coffee together after our respective eleven o'clock classes. That left Tom Peabody, Jack Merton, and Archie as people I saw most frequently. As soon as the surgeon gave me permission, Archie and I resumed our squash games, Archie showing remarkable patience about letting me get back in form. I had the feeling that he was more relaxed when we were together than in the past, probably taking my breakdown as proof that I wasn't quite right in the head. That must have taken some of the sting out of the air of disapproval I had worn during our freshman year. I too had relaxed, though my new attitude toward him was closer to tolerance than to approval. We went to the movies, and in the course of one of those evenings he told me that he couldn't use his room during parietal hours. Margot's visits had become a daily occurrence, and Henry was much happier if he could have the suite to himself.

Soon after Thanksgiving, the *Atlantic Monthly* accepted for publication an excerpt from my unfinished novel. It ran in the February issue. I would never have dared to submit it; Professor MacLeish all but ordered me to put it in the mail together with his letter of recommendation. At first the news of the acceptance, and then the actual appearance of the excerpt, had a variety of consequences some of which I found comical. For instance, Dr. Reiner told me at the end of a session that his wife, who read the *Atlantic* and was a connoisseur of fiction, had found my writing accomplished. This was the first time he had ever alluded to her existence or had any conversation with me other than in the line of business, usually to rebuff my questions or to prod me to work harder on themes we were developing. He never indicated whether he himself had read my piece, but I thought that I detected in his manner a new interest in me that wasn't exclusively professional. I wondered whether he had told his wife that I was his patient. Also, Henry extended, on behalf of his parents, an invitation to visit them at Christmas. He said, My mother is determined to have Mr. Roommate, the future famous author, as her guest. As an added attraction, he told me Margot would surely organize a dinner or cocktails with her parents.

I had not seen Mr. and Mrs. White since the dinner at Henri IV, when we had celebrated Henry's birthday, but I had been thinking about them, occasionally feeling nostalgic about the telephone conversations with Mrs. White and even my role as an answering service and buffer between mother and son. I had also asked myself whether, given her combative nature, she held it against me that I decided not to room with Henry and Archie after our freshman year. Apparently she didn't, or had forgiven me, perhaps realizing that subsequent events, New Orleans and my breakdown, would have in any case upset any arrangement we had made to live together. Of course, there was no telling what Mrs. White knew; it was a good bet that New Orleans and my depression both fell into the category of information that Henry did not reveal to his parents or had heavily censored. I had no plans for the holidays, except that I didn't intend to spend Christmas Eve or Christmas at home. This was a cruel decision; I realized that my absence at the few parties we had normally attended as a family would embarrass my parents and perhaps wound them as well, but I was going to stick to it, and offer as a salve a few days at home after Christmas. I accepted the Whites' invitation and burned my bridges. Archie was going home to Houston and offered to lend Henry his car. It was no longer the Nash. After a debutante party, he had driven it into the stone gatepost of a North Shore estate. It was a freak accident: the engine block cracked, but, miraculously, neither he nor the Argentine beauty who was his date was hurt. By way of an ex voto, Mrs. Palmer gave him a Chevrolet convertible, which, Archie said, she believed had better pickup. How that would prevent future collisions, or might have prevented the one in Beverly, was left unexplained.

On the way to New York I discovered that Henry too was a dangerous driver, crossing the solid line to pass on two-lane highways and coming into tollbooths at full tilt as though he intended to crash through a barrier. I knew that any remarks about slowing down, keeping his eyes on the road when he talked to me, staying in his lane, or the like would only make matters worse; he would feel challenged and set about showing me what he was really capable of. It was best to find a neutral subject for conversation. He had told me to pack a dinner jacket for the evening at the Hornungs. This gave me an opening to find out about him and Margot, and I asked why we needed to be in black tie if he hadn't had to dress for his first dinner at Margot's parents'. He said that was right; he had forgotten to tell me that we were going to the Hornungs' annual New Year's Eve party. They hadn't been sure that the party could be given this time. One of their oldest friends was sick, and they had felt obliged to wait to see whether she would take a turn for the worse. A few days ago the doctors assured them that she was getting better, and they didn't have to risk having music in the house as she lay dying or dead.

I remarked that there was something ghoulish about this sort of calculation. Henry laughed and told me he had said just that to Margot, who got huffy and, speaking through her nose, assured him that it was done all the time: when people have sick relatives and they are planning a wedding or a coming-out party. Apropos of wedding plans, I asked whether any were likely for Margot and Etienne. He didn't answer at first and then confessed that he really didn't know. He understood Margot less and less, although they saw each other all the time, practically every day.

To be very specific, he continued, we haven't done it yet, but it's almost as though we had. I still let her lead—wherever that takes us. She's satisfied, there is no question about it. As for me, it's paradise.

As good as with Madame van Damme?

He gave me a dirty look and veered into the middle lane to pass the car ahead of us with not a moment to spare.

Yes, he said, as good as with Madeleine. It's different, that's all. What I've just told you about is part of the reason I don't understand Margot. She and Etienne still write to each other all the time. He's coming to Boston right after exams to speak at some kind of seminar about European banking at the business school, and she's already told me that while he is here she won't be seeing me. Perhaps I am some sort of avocation for her.

Have you asked her to explain?

Not really. She knows there is this big question in the room with us, and she disregards it. To put the question would surely provoke a fight. I don't want to fight with her. And I'm not in a very good position to say, How do you expect me to share you with Etienne?

Do you mean that she knows?

Absolutely not, he said. Madeleine is very careful. I should tell you that she's going to be here again, on Wellesley alumnae business. I don't know the dates.

He added, with a giggle, I hope it's not at the same time as Etienne.

I thought for a moment and decided to ask, Do you understand yourself?

In a bleak sort of way, I do. I know that I mustn't get caught. That seems to be my only concern. Obviously, I am immoral, but I can't believe it of Margot.

And Madame van Damme?

Oh, he said, with her it's habit, the example set by her husband, the manners of the country.

XIX

HAVING BEEN STUCK in rush-hour traffic, first on the West Side Highway and then in the tunnel, we arrived at the Whites' after six, a good hour later than Henry had told his mother to expect us. He had repeated so many times—immediately when he transmitted his parents' invitation, after I had accepted it, before we left Cambridge, and again as we inched forward in the Battery Tunnel—that Brooklyn wasn't at all like Lenox or Stockbridge or any other place I was used to, and he hoped I wouldn't be shocked, that I began to expect to find his parents living in some version of a slum, perhaps on the order of the rundown part of Pittsfield we avoided. As it happened, we came to a stop on a tree-lined one-way street, in front of a substantial stucco house with a minute front lawn covered by patches of snow. This is it, Henry said. I'll pull into the alley after we've taken our stuff out of the trunk. The alley, he explained, led to a garage where his father parked his car. The parents had bought this house sixteen months ago. Mr. or Mrs. White must have heard our voices or the slamming of car doors. They came out on the front porch just as we were walking up the steps that led to it.

Oh my God, said Mrs. White, pressing her right hand against her heart, where have you been? Thank you for worrying so much about Daddy and me. Where have you been driving? In some country where they haven't invented telephones? Or maybe you've forgotten our telephone number.

Anticipating Henry's snarl, I stepped between him and his mother in what later struck me as a replay of my Sonny Boy role and said, Mrs. White, please don't blame Henry, it's my fault that he didn't call, I don't know how many times he wanted to get to a pay phone, and every time I stopped him. I kept telling him that with traffic so heavy, and people not willing to let you back on the highway at exits, we'd be here much sooner if he just kept driving. I beg your pardon if what I did was wrong.

Mrs. White didn't look very forgiving, but she said, OK, never mind. Taking that for absolution, I walked around her to face Mr. White and pressed my house present into his hand. The expression on his face was exactly as I remembered it from Cambridge: preoccupied but mildly cheerful. He said it wasn't necessary; I shouldn't have spent money on a present. His wife and he were happy to see me again and hoped I'd have a pleasant stay with my friend Henry. Thereupon, Mrs. White said that the dinner was already ruined but unless we wanted to ruin it even more we had better sit down and eat. Mother, protested Henry, who had remained silent up to this point, Mother, can we be allowed to wash our hands? Go wash, she replied, do anything you want. What difference does it make? We took our things upstairs. I was in a narrow room next to Henry's. To my relief, there was a bathroom for our use; we did not have to share with the parents.

Henry and his parents normally took their meals at a table in the kitchen. Mr. Roommate Author, however, was too important, Mrs. White told me, actually smiling, for that kind of informality. I understood that we were to go to the dining room. It turned out to be a large front room. On the two credenzas were displayed porcelain animals, shepherds and shepherdesses, and little silver objects, some of which might have been bar utensils. Impressionist-influenced still lifes and nudes hung on the walls, rather more of them than I would have thought could fit. The table was covered by a starched white tablecloth and set with floral pattern china and a lot of silver coasters, boxes, and baskets, some of which held mints. Candles burned in two silver candelabra. Mrs. White placed herself at the head of the table and put Mr. White on her left and me on her right. Henry was to be next to me. It being Friday, Mrs. White explained, she had lit the candles at sundown. That was when dinner should have begun, if only Henry remembered how people behaved.

It doesn't matter, she added. Anyway, it's nothing like my parents' house. My husband doesn't care, and he hasn't bothered to teach my son. I'm doing it for myself, to remind myself how things were once. This is how it is now.

Mr. White opened his mouth as though to say something and quickly shut it.

Henry mumbled, For God's sake, Mother.

That's right, said Mrs. White, go ahead and swear. Do anything you want. So long as your father doesn't care.

She brought the meal to the table herself: mushroom soup, roast chicken with gravy, braised carrots and creamed spinach, a salad of iceberg lettuce and cucumber with blue-cheese dressing, cheesecake, and cookies. Henry made several attempts to help, but Mrs. White told him to sit down, she didn't need food and broken dishes on the rug. She carved the chicken and put huge helpings of food on our plates. I told her that the soup was the best I had eaten. She agreed it was good; she had been able to make it out of real Polish dried mushrooms. However, she disagreed when I praised the chicken. It's ruined, she said. I should have taken it out of the oven, but how was I supposed to know you were going to be an hour and a half late? The chicken is ruined. You can thank your friend Henry for that.

Henry's face had darkened. The effort he was making to control himself was so obvious that I asked myself whether its purpose was to intimidate his mother. I held my compliments until I had tasted the cheesecake. It was really very good, and I asked for more.

You see, he knows how to eat, Mrs. White told Henry, giving me a slice twice as big as the first one.

Then she told him to refill our wineglasses, if possible without spilling on the tablecloth. We will drink to Mr. Author who brought us such good wine.

It was a Pommard I had bought at the Mount Auburn Street liquor store and had the salesman wrap as a gift. After two visits to the Coop, I had given up on the idea of an art book. This wine I knew to be respectable, but I had begun to worry that Mrs. White or perhaps both of them would find that it was an inappropriate sort of thing for a young man to give to his hosts. If they held such a view, they didn't express it, not to me; I supposed that if there was to be criticism Henry would hear it. We ate most of the meal in silence. The hostilities between mother and son made me reluctant to speak unless spoken to or moved to praise the food, as when I extolled the cheesecake. That may have also been Mr. White's strategy; his one attempt at communication that didn't relate to passing the bread was to say that, whatever one thought of Senator McCarthy, the attacks in the press on Cohn and Schine were unfair. Henry immediately retorted that those two were contemptible scoundrels. His father raised his eyebrows and told him that one shouldn't believe everything that one read in the paper, whereupon Henry asked whether he knew where to get more reliable information.

I was curious to see how Mr. White would deal with Henry. Before Mr. White got a word out, however, Mrs. White said, I wonder why Rysiek always takes the side of anyone blaming Jews. Has a Jew ever been right? Addressing me, she asked whether, as a fair person, I didn't agree with her that Cohn and Schine were victims of anti-Semitism.

As a matter of fact, I was convinced that Cohn and Schine were providing plenty of grist for the anti-Semites' mill, but I didn't dare to say so to Mrs. White. Instead, I told her that I thought that pretty much everyone, except reactionary nuts mesmerized by McCarthy, agreed that those two were awful, and that I was of that view, but it had nothing to do with their being Jewish. I realized immediately that I had just insulted Mr. White and perhaps Mrs. White as well by seeming to suggest that they too were nuts, but I didn't know how to undo the damage, so I said nothing more. That may have been the right decision. Mrs. White said that many decent Gentiles had closed their eyes when Jews were abused or murdered and that she hoped I would keep my eyes open because she knew I was a decent man and had been a good friend to Rysiek. With that, she let the matter drop.

Having refused Henry's offers and mine to help clear the dishes, Mrs. White served us coffee at the dinner table along with a platter of cookies she had baked, unlike the cheesecake, bought at a pastry shop, and a box of cream chocolates. Having watched me help myself enthusiastically, she addressed me. Mr. Roommate Author, she said to me, what is your book about?

I had been waiting for that question. It was one always asked by people who knew that the *Atlantic* was a magazine and had heard that a part of the novel would appear in its pages. I felt particularly uncomfortable because I still didn't know whether Henry had told his parents about my breakdown or New Orleans. It was possible that Mrs. White was curious about the relationship between the novel and my illness, a subject I wasn't prepared to discuss. I should have had an answer ready, but I didn't, so I told her that since I hadn't finished the book and had miles to go, I wasn't entirely sure what it would be about in the end.

But you must know what you are writing about, said Mr. White, who seemed interested. Or do you sit down every day before your typewriter and wait for inspiration? By the way, do you type?

I said I did type. Since I could hardly deny having a general idea of what I was putting down on paper, I said that I was telling the story of a boy who grows up in a small town not far from where I live.

Then you are writing about yourself and your family, said Mrs. White.

Not really. In my book the boy has an older sister and a younger brother. I'm an only child. That's one difference. There are many others. The towns are similar, like all old New England towns.

I think your parents will recognize themselves in your novel, she replied. Will they like what you have done?

I told her the truth, that I was worried about it. Whether Mrs. White and her husband were satisfied by this or had realized that it was time for the television news, she wished me luck and said she hoped my parents would be proud of me. Meanwhile, Henry had been examining movie schedules. He had found a late show of *La Ronde* at the theater on Flatbush Avenue and asked whether I would like to go. Eager to get out of that dining room, I said yes. Mrs. White began to object on the ground that many side streets had not been cleared and ice made driving dangerous. You'll have an accident in your roommate's car, and then what will you do? Besides, she said, you should be tired and just for once you could rest. He told her we were going, but we would walk.

The next day was Christmas Eve, but Henry's dentist was keeping regular office hours, and Henry went to have four temporary fillings replaced. He suggested that I take Archie's car if I wanted to go to Manhattan. Otherwise, I could walk over to the Newkirk Avenue station and take the IRT. I toyed with the idea, because I had never been to the Metropolitan Museum, and then decided against it. I was tired and my grasp of New

York's geography and transportation system was almost nil. Instead, I went for a walk. When it began to rain, I returned to the Whites'. My intention had been to creep to my room and escape notice until Henry came home, but Mrs. White intercepted me at the foot of the stairs and said we would have lunch in half an hour, just the two of us, unless that would be too boring for me. I didn't have the courage to say that I wasn't hungry and preferred to skip lunch. When I came down to the kitchen I found that she had put on the table slices of ham and something she said was headcheese, which turned out to be better than it looked or sounded, sausage, rye bread, butter, and Swiss cheese, as well as a plate of radishes she had just finished cleaning. We drank a beverage that was new to me—buttermilk. At the end of the meal, Mrs. White served what was left of the cheesecake and coffee. I had grown so accustomed to university dining room food and hamburgers at Elsie's that everything she set before me was a treat. I told her so, and she encouraged me by exclamations such as, Eat, eat, it's good for you.

You need good food, she told me, you are so very tall like Henry, and went on to claim that she had forgotten how to cook. There was no one to cook for: her husband shouldn't eat meat or butter or cheese, Henry never came home, and when he did he made faces at what she prepared. When they invited guests—they did so rarely because the few friends they had lived on the Upper West Side, or in Riverdale, or Forest Hills—she gave them cold cuts for lunch and roast chicken for dinner. Everything else was too complicated and, anyway, no one cared anymore. She was wondering why she should care. The house didn't make any sense. It was too big for her and her husband, and anyway it was in the wrong place. Nobody lives in Brooklyn. Driving to where their friends lived in Westchester or even just to the city if they wanted to go out to dinner or see a play was too tiring for her husband. He wasn't like other men who know about cars and like to drive; he was like the very religious Jews in Poland who study the Talmud all day and leave everything to the wife. I am stuck, she concluded, trapped, and my husband and my son don't care.

She put her handkerchief to her eyes and told me to pay no attention. She was saying things I couldn't understand, because all day she had no one to talk to; we should talk about Henry instead. Did I think, she asked, that he was all right? I said that he seemed to me to look better than ever and that he was a brilliant success at college—right at the top of his class. Yes, she said, but the people he is with, his friends, are all so different from him. That Archie, that girl Margot, those Belgians, even you. I don't think he has one Jewish friend. Where will they be after he graduates? All these people will go back to their families and friends, and he will be alone. What's so special about Belgium and being a tutor? He could make more money working as a busboy in a resort. Anyway, he doesn't need money. His father would give it to him. He's such a good student, but he doesn't have a career before him. What can he do, teach Latin all his life? What's the use of loving him so much? He doesn't care. She sobbed and then, as she began to cry quite hard, she excused herself and left the room. She returned after a while, entirely composed; I saw that she had put on fresh makeup.

Do you think he's going to get one of those scholarships to study abroad he always talks about? she asked.

I answered that I didn't know what scholarship he had in mind, but that his record ought to entitle him to some grant.

She interrupted to say that he was so ambitious.

I agreed, adding that, since so far he had gotten everything he had set out to get at Harvard, she shouldn't feel anxious. The subject of the van Damme family was one I particularly wanted to avoid, but I assured her that Archie and George Standish and I were Henry's friends for life.

Although I had not said anything that I thought could impress her, she brightened and told me he was lucky to have me as his friend. She added, Are you more careful now?

I was puzzled, and I suppose she realized that I didn't understand, because she said several times, It's nothing, never mind.

Feeling suddenly sorry for her, I said, Please Mrs. White, I'll be glad to tell you whatever it is you want to know.

I mean, she said, those hooligans who attacked you. Are you more careful when you go out, at least for your parents' sake if not for yourself?

I assured her that I had always tried to stay out of trouble and was even more careful now.

When she held out her hand, I kissed it, remembering Henry's endless disquisitions about how in Poland women's hands are constantly kissed, even by taxi drivers when they open the door for them. In return, she squeezed my hand, saying, I love him so much, and I am so scared. He's all we have.

IT WAS VERY COLD on New Year's Eve, the temperature hovering in the low teens, and Henry had trouble finding a parking place. After a while we gave up and looked for a garage. The first few we saw were full; finally we got into one between Lexington Avenue and Third and, shivering in the glacial wind, walked west to Park Avenue, and then south on the avenue until we reached the Hornungs' building at the corner of Seventy-fourth Street. This is it, said Henry with a quietly satisfied proprietary air. It's an amazing place.

We left our overcoats in the lobby, in care of two somber white-haired ladies, and got into the elevator. Henry had prepared me for the phenomenon of its door opening directly into the foyer of their apartment, and the party at the Standishes' had familiarized me with the phenomenon of men serving in white gloves who offer a glass of champagne and exchange it for a full one as soon as it's empty. But nothing in Henry's description had led me to anticipate the brilliance of the chandeliers or the massed flowers—orchid plants of astonishing colors and shapes and cut flowers—or, for that matter, the number of guests, many of our age, children of family friends, I supposed. Margot led us to her parents, who had stationed themselves just beyond the entrance of the living room. Except for being in black velvet, Mrs. Hornung was as I remembered her. Her husband, tall, stooped, and black haired, with a tiny black mustache, reminded me of Harry Levin, a professor I admired, who taught the Jacobean drama and Shakespeare courses I had taken. I did not suppose that Mr. Hornung would be likely to pass, even if he had taken the trouble to change his name to Horne. It was clear to me from the smile with which he greeted Henry, and their animation when they talked, that Henry was in the Hornungs'—or anyway Mr. Hornung's—good graces, far more so than he had given me reason to think. An older couple was waiting their turn behind us; I got out of the way, and Henry and Margot followed. We looked at the paintings. Teniers the Younger's landscape of a village with an inn and peasants was, according to Margot, the best work they had on the wall. Her great-grandfather, who had been in the lumber trade in Russia, bought it at an auction, the sale of a Russian prince's collections. The great-grandfather's own collection, by the time he died, was also princely but he had four sons among whom to divide it, and her grandfather's share was divided on his death among her father and his brother and sister. The uncle and aunt and their children were killed by Germans, she added coolly, and their paintings and antiques were stolen. They were stupid not to listen to Father and leave when he did. Father did in the end get some of the family's art back and gave the best pieces to the museum in The Hague.

I could sense Henry's impatience as I listened attentively but in silence: he wanted a clear sign that I was impressed, as impressed as he on the first visit to the Hornungs.

Only in part to satisfy him, I said, Margot, these are magnificent paintings and magnificent furniture. You are lucky to have grown up with them around you.

Before she could answer, an old man, completely bald and wearing heavy black-rimmed glasses, came up. While she was introducing Henry to him I glanced in the direction of the piano, the pianist who had been playing Gershwin having just started a tune I didn't recognize. Leaning against the piano, I saw Wilmerding. He saw me too—perhaps he had been staring at us—and after a wink in my direction he gave a silent Bronx cheer. He then continued staring right through me, as though I weren't there. I had never paid attention to Wilmerding's appearance other than to note that his ears stuck out at almost right angles and that he wore clothes that looked as though they had been made by an English tailor. Now I saw a resemblance between him and a photograph I had seen of a young, smirking D. H. Lawrence with just a trace of a mustache, before he had grown his beard. A great anger welled up in me, making Wilmerding's presence in the room intolerable. I walked over to him and said very quietly, Fuck you, Wilmerding. Was that for Henry or me or for both of us?

He didn't answer and continued to stare into the distance, his expression unchanged. My champagne glass was full. I threw the wine in his face. He tensed, opened and closed his mouth, and then deliberately dried his face with a handkerchief he took from his breast pocket. I wanted a pretext, however slight, to beat him, and particularly to punch him hard in the mouth, those very white even teeth. But he remained completely still. It didn't seem that anyone had paid attention to us. I stomped hard on his foot with my heel and walked away.

Margot and Henry were in the library. She was laughing over something, and said something to him, at which he laughed too. I was glad to see them together. My anger had left me. I wondered whether Wilmerding had been so passive because people thought I was a brawler.

Margot said, Let's get something to eat. There was a buffet supper on the table in the dining room. She and I went ahead, with Henry following. You should perhaps get some champagne first, she whispered. I saw you emptying your glass.

XX

Mrs. White took to telephoning me after the Christmas visit. I told her it reminded me of my freshman year. The first call was to thank me for my thank-you letter, which I had written as soon as I got back to Cambridge. She wanted me to know that all mothers should have sons like me, so polite and so able to express themselves. Then she segued into questions about Henry. Was he working hard? Was he perhaps working too hard? Did I think he looked well? Was he getting enough sleep? Flippant answers on the order of "I am not Henry's keeper" no longer tempted me; I reassured her as best I could without overstating wildly my knowledge of Henry's day-to-day activities. I did, I believe, beg her to understand that for various reasons I too was working very hard and had little time for seeing even my closest friends. She wasn't discouraged and subsequently called without advancing any pretext: she would simply say that she wanted to talk about her only son. Was he really doing well? Occasionally, I was able to demonstrate knowledge of the basic facts. Thus I congratulated her on the news that one reader of Henry's senior thesis, John Younger, a distinguished Latinist, was submitting it, with a strong recommendation that it be published, to the *Journal of Roman Studies*. It was an unusual honor. The thesis was an analysis of Horace's use of Greek prosody; Henry referred to it when we spoke as an idiot savant's delight. Younger owed him one because in the end Henry made good on his promise and put Plautus on in the Lowell House dining room. But not all Mrs. White's uncertainties and fears had been unfounded, and I had to commiserate with her about her son's disappointments. Henry said it was too bad that he didn't get a Rhodes, though in truth he had given up on it: he wasn't an athlete, and he hadn't done well at the final interview in New

York. The harbor view from the law firm's reception room, the collection of Delft plates on the walls of the conference room, and the imperturbable sly elegance of the four men weighing his candidacy had cowed him. He felt incapable of speech. They bore in with questions about his name, Poland, where he and his family had been during the war, and so on, not out of sympathy but to be sure that nothing had remained concealed. He returned to Boston with two of his classmates who had also advanced to final interviews. It turned out that all three had been asked which is better, *The Marriage of Figaro* or *The Magic Flute,* and why. One of them said that it had to be *Le nozze* because of Cherubino, while the other claimed to prefer the *Flute* for two reasons, the Queen of the Night's arias and the men's ensembles. They laughed their heads off at their own cleverness. As for me, said Henry, all I could think of was that one could no more say that *Hamlet* is better than *The Tempest* or vice versa. The truth is I haven't been to either opera. All my father ever wants to go to is Puccini! Far more bitter were the successive announcements of the other grants for study in England or for travel. One after another, they were distributed, and Henry received nothing. He told me one evening that he had objectively considered the winners, all of whom he knew, and couldn't call them unworthy; they were all very good, but he was no less good, perhaps better. Apparently, something had tipped the scales against him every time. What was it? he wanted to know. I said I couldn't tell him. It was fabulous to have done so well. He had been running a race without having trained. Particularly in classics, for which he had almost no background.

Nonsense, he told me, I did plenty of Latin while we were hidden in Krakow. There's nothing wrong with my Latin or Greek or with any of my other subjects. When the measure is quantitative, I win. When the measure is who they like, I lose. They don't like me. I'm different. I don't look the way they look, I don't talk the way they talk, and I don't play the games they play. They'd rather not have me around. They win: I'll get out of their hair. Out of everybody's hair!

He told me his plan: first the army, then law school—at last a decision, he added snickering, that will make my parents happy, though maybe there will be a battle over not asking for a deferment so that he could finish law school before military service. That didn't matter; his mind was made up. Besides, he had already volunteered for the draft. His physical was scheduled for the week before Commencement, in South Boston. I asked whether he was sure about law school. He shrugged. There was also the question of the summer. If he could get his parents to pay, he would go to Spain and Italy, with Archie. You could join us, he said, for the Italian part in August. The Ardennes are not on the itinerary.

He said those last words calmly, but I sensed the bewilderment and hurt that lay behind them. Right after the spring break, late on a Friday evening, Margot's housemother, checking the register and then Margot's room, discovered that she had not signed in as having returned to the dormitory and indeed wasn't there. She reappeared only the following morning. The investigation wasn't arduous: Margot admitted that she had spent the night at a hotel in Boston with a man. Although she was due to graduate in two months, and had not lied to the housemother when questioned, the administrative retribution was swift and final. She was expelled. Henry said that she had told him already that Saturday evening that she was in trouble but didn't want to discuss its nature. After she had been notified of the administration's decision, she called asking whether she could come to talk to him at the house. She had once told him that she liked being naked in his room; this time too she let her clothes drop to the floor, keeping only her slip, but she bit her lower lip and shook her head violently when he asked her to come into the bedroom. She sat down instead in an armchair in the living room, wouldn't allow him to touch her, and, only when he was in the other chair, told him that a man called Ross, a business school friend of Etienne's from Hartford, had invited her to dinner at the Ritz. They drank martinis and then a bottle of wine. The meal ended. He paid, and without having made any sort of pass at her, not having even held her hand, he said, Come up to my room. I don't know what got into me, I did what he said. I should have known it wouldn't be worth it.

Then she asked me to get in bed, so we could say goodbye nicely, Henry continued, but she wouldn't go all the way. She said the time wasn't right. I know what got into her when she went with this guy Ross. She's a slut.

I remained silent.

You're surprised, said Henry. I was too. After she'd gotten dressed and I had signed her out she told me that this had to be the end, we couldn't go on as before. Why, I asked, and said that I would walk her to the dorm. She nodded but didn't answer. Neither of us spoke again until we had crossed the Common. My head was swimming. It occurred to me along the way that our accounts were nicely balanced so long as she had Etienne and I had Madeleine. This Ross fellow had thrown everything out of kilter. At the same time, why should an immoralist like me care? Who's to say that the day after she left for New York I wouldn't try to screw the first Radcliffe girl who would let me? The difference is that I knew about Etienne and now Ross, while she couldn't know about Madeleine. I was tempted to tell her, but something held me back. I asked her once again, Why? Are you going to break off with Etienne? She answered, Yes, I've already written to him about Ross. I put the letter in the mailbox on my way to see you. Good God, I cried, will you please explain yourself? She nodded and told me that everything around her had become impure. She was up to her armpits in mud with Etienne, with me, with everyone else. She was going out of business. But I didn't need to worry about Bayencourt. She hadn't said anything to Etienne about me, and wasn't going to. We stopped at her door. She gave me her cheek to kiss. There's been nothing since.

There was, however, more to come concerning Bayencourt during the reading period. Mr. van Damme's secretary wrote to confirm the date of Henry's arrival. But Henry now told me that he couldn't bring himself to go. It was all too tied up with Margot. Also, absurd though it was, he couldn't get out of his mind Margot's having called the relationships with Etienne and himself impure. What would she say about Madeleine? Two days later, he wrote to Mr. van Damme telling him that he was about to be called up by his draft board and couldn't make plans for the summer. That's stretching the truth a little, he told me, considering that I had volunteered and don't really have to report before October. But these are details, he said. I've also written to Madeleine. A nice letter, saying that I hoped I'd be sent to Europe after basic training.

So far as I was concerned, the academic year had ended. Most seniors, however, wouldn't be leaving until after Commencement in the first days of June. I found it odd not to be graduating with Henry and George and the other men with whom I had been a freshman. However, I was still in Cambridge, staying at Madame Shouvaloff's because my suite would be used by some alumnus returning for his reunion and later by summer school students. In fact, my plan was to remain until some time after Dr. Reiner's departure on his sacrosanct vacation. I hoped I could finish my book while I was still under Madame Shouvaloff's roof, so that in the fall I could show Archie MacLeish a completed draft. At Henry's request, Tom Peabody got me invited to the Commencement lunch for graduating seniors and their families in the house courtyard. We were an incongruous group at table: Henry and Archie and their parents, and Tom and I. The master joined us between the main course and dessert. Waving away Tom's offer to yield his own chair or to bring another one, he squatted beside Mrs. White and told her in a whisper loud enough for everyone at the table to hear that Henry was quite the brightest diamond in the diadem of his house, as well as a source of immense pride to him personally. The encomium the master delivered after dessert, when he handed Henry his diploma, was if anything more appallingly unctuous. When the applause subsided, Mrs. White, a luminous version of Scarlett O'Hara under her huge white hat, leaned over as far as her hat allowed and spoke into my ear. I am so upset, she said, about Mrs. Palmer and the general. I almost died when the master didn't say anything about their son. They must feel terribly humiliated. I glanced at Mrs. Palmer who looked more than ever like a visiting nurse. She had finished her chocolate parfait and was placidly eating Archie's. As for the general, he had his own view of things, including, I supposed, Archie. When I chatted with him over sherry before lunch he said that Harvard students looked to him like an effete lot, and Commencement seemed an anemic sort of event. You fellows haven't got the sort of spirit one takes for granted at the Academy; you don't measure up to our good cadets. Mark my words, Standish: Dien Bien Phu has fallen, the Frenchies are kaput. You know what is going to hit the fan.

There was a general movement to get up from the table. I pulled out Mrs. White's chair, told her once again that she looked beautiful, and assured her that she needn't worry about the Palmers. I have to, she replied, I worry about everything. Tell me the truth: Do I have a wonderful son?

Mrs. White upstaged her husband constantly. He didn't seem to mind, but the result was that I hadn't spoken to him. To make up for it, as we said goodbye I ventured that he must be very proud of Henry. Mr. White smiled happily and said, yes, he was, especially since Henry had finally decided to go to law school. You know, he added, I studied law and could have been a lawyer. I assured him that Henry had told me his story.

Then you know how it is, he said. Nothing has worked out for my wife and me the way we expected, the way our parents intended. Now we have one hope, that Henry will make something of himself, that he will be really successful and happy. I have worked hard to give him the opportunity.

I nodded. He took my hand, pressed it in both of his, and then, after a tiny delay, reached up and kissed me on both cheeks.

I spent the rest of the afternoon squiring Cousin May around the Fogg and showing her the glass flowers in the Peabody Glass Museum while George and his father attended a function at the final club to which they both belonged. Then George and I packed most of his belongings into Cousin Jack's station wagon and a few odds and ends into George's Mini and they drove off to Stockbridge. The next day, Friday, I had my session with Dr. Reiner to look forward to, and then another on Monday, and da capo. My portable Olivetti and my manuscript were waiting in the attic bedroom at Madame Shouvaloff's. I would get to them after dinner. Tom Peabody had invited me to dinner with him at Henri IV. He was spending the summer doing research at Oxford, and I wouldn't see him again until the fall.

George had taken a summer job at the bank but would live at home, in Stockbridge. His father didn't disapprove of his decision to become a lawyer but wanted him to know enough about the family business to be able to step in if necessary. Unlike Henry, George had already applied to Harvard Law School and been accepted. And he was not going into the army, having been classified 4-F. To our general amazement, the army physical detected a congenital defect in his heart valve that his family doctor—the same as ours—had missed. I was planning to be in Lenox for a part of August. My mother had written to let me know that my father wasn't well and came as close as her nature allowed to demanding that I come home.

XXI

THE DAY I ARRIVED in Lenox I called George at work and we agreed to go to Great Barrington that evening to see *Shane,* his favorite western. Since I was picking him up, I had to leave at six-thirty. At about quarter of six, I went downstairs, certain that my parents would already be having drinks. I found them on the back porch. The gin, vermouth, olives, and the shaker, as well as a bowl of peanuts and another one of Ritz crackers, were all on the wicker table at my father's side. As usual after work, he was dressed in khaki trousers and a fresh white Brooks Brothers shirt, the kind that doesn't button down, starched to his liking by the Seven Dwarfs laundry, and old tennis shoes that he wore without socks and never whitened, unlike those in which he appeared on the court, which had to be spotless. His picture is vivid in my mind, as is my mother's, in her light blue cotton dress the straps of which slipped whenever she stooped or let her shoulders slouch. My father offered me a martini. More ice was needed. I offered to get it, but my mother said no, she would do it, I could stay with my father. I thought this meant that he was going to tell me something while she was in the kitchen, but he just pointed to the crackers. When my mother returned, I caught her looking at him questioningly. He made no response, shook the gin and the vermouth, poured a drink for me, and refreshed my mother's and his own. Only after we had raised our glasses and had a sip, a large one in their case, he cleared his throat and spoke. This was not the sort of thing he had wanted to write to me about. The point was that he had a growth in his gut, and the doctors would be taking it out the following Wednesday. He didn't mind missing the tennis tournament this once, and Mother wouldn't have trouble finding another partner. Perhaps Chuck Riley. He was a real estate agent who belonged to the club whose wife had limped ever since a skiing accident.

I asked him whether it was bad. He made a face and said that, probably, he'd have to wear one of those funny bags under his trousers. At least he'd never again have to wait for some guy to decide to get out of the john. He laughed at his joke and drained his glass. I shouldn't be doing this, he said, but it's a little late to worry about my health.

He won't listen to the doctors, said my mother.

No, I won't, replied my father, it's quite enough that I let them work on me.

I turned to my mother and asked whether the surgery would be in Pittsfield. She nodded and said that Dr. Pierson would do it. They'd been to Boston for a second opinion, and the Boston doctor's advice had been the same: the operation shouldn't be postponed.

It hurt me to hear that they had come down to Boston without letting me know. I asked how they would manage.

Your father will be home from the hospital in ten days, she said, if there are no complications, and we'll have a nurse here for the first week. Anyway, Mrs. Heaney said she'd give me an extra day.

That was our cleaning lady, who lived in Housatonic and worked for my mother three days a week, besides helping in the kitchen and serving when people came to dinner.

I'll be in the office within a month, added my father, fixing another shaker of martinis. Seeing that, my mother threw up her hands.

That's all right, he said. Nobody wants to know what you think. Here, have another one yourself.

There was a telltale thickness in his voice, a signal for my mother to lay off. Expressionless, she passed the peanuts and the crackers.

I reminded her that I was supposed to be going to the movies with George and asked whether they would prefer that I call him and stay at home.

You run along, said my father, and take my car. By the by, I've told Jack and a couple of other people at the bank about this thing.

That meant I could speak to George about my father. Normally, my father didn't let my mother or me use his car, so this permission was a sign of momentary benevolence. I thanked him.

Don't be late for George, said my father, and pressing on the armrests of his chair pulled himself up to shake my hand. I thanked him again and kissed my mother. These gestures surprised me, perhaps all of us; they weren't the norm.

Three days after my mother, the nurse, and I brought him back home, I returned to Cambridge. It had been necessary to take out a greater length of intestine than Dr. Pierson had anticipated, but he told us that the recovery should be normal. He recommended only that the nurse stay longer than had been planned, perhaps two weeks, until my father had learned to take care of himself. Being very squeamish, Mother agreed readily. The nurse was another Irishwoman from Housatonic, a friend of Mrs. Heaney's. She assured my mother that between them they would handle everything. We let them settle my father down for the evening.

As soon as he dozed off, my mother said, There's nothing in the kitchen except baby food and what I got for the nurse. Let's go to the club.

We sat on the screened veranda overlooking the golf course while she drank three Tom Collinses, one after another, and smoked. It doesn't matter, she said, you're driving. We talked about the doctor and the nurses first. After that she told me local gossip, much of which I couldn't follow. It's natural, she said, you haven't been here in a long time. Then, I suppose because the various ostensible reasons for my not coming home during holidays and school vacation nagged at her, she asked whether I was all right.

Do you mean the injuries? I asked.

She said no, she really meant the other stuff. This was a subject to which neither she nor Father had alluded since the university had placed me on leave. She fished another Chesterfield out of a pack she had just opened. I lit it for her. She was a finicky and methodical smoker, every gesture being part of a ritual that had used to fascinate me.

I told her that I was fine; everything was under control.

That's good, she said. But you're still seeing this doctor.

I replied that in all likelihood seeing Dr. Reiner or someone like him would be my lifetime occupation.

I suppose it doesn't matter so long as you can afford it, she said. Mr. Hibble must be printing money.

She saw the waiter lounging nearby and told me to call him over and order another drink for her, to be brought to the table. With that, we went in to dinner.

I HAD TOLD GEORGE that I would stop by late, and after taking my mother home I drove to the Standishes'. He met me at the door and said, Come into the library; the parents are still up.

They must have had dinner at home. May wore a long skirt, and Cousin Jack one of his velvet smoking jackets. I thanked them for the flowers they had sent to the hospital. Oh yes, May said, your mother has already written. We drank our Scotch and sodas, and George and I worked out the plan for his driving me to Cambridge. He was going early, before law school started, to move into a house that he and a couple of Yalies who had been at school with him had rented on Garden Street. As I was about to leave, Cousin Jack said he wanted to have a word with me. I followed him to the back porch. He motioned for me to sit down, sat down himself, and offered me a cigar, which I declined. I had stopped smoking after New Orleans; besides, his were much larger and smelled stronger than anything to which I was accustomed.

Your father is a very sick man, he said, I've talked to Pete Pierson.

I replied that I was astonished. When we spoke with him, Dr. Pierson had been optimistic.

Jack examined the lit end of his cigar and drew on it deeply. Doctors have different stories, he told me, depending on who they're talking to. There was stuff that couldn't be gotten out. What they were able to do was, of course, necessary. He would have been in great discomfort without it.

I nodded.

No need to tell your mother, Jack added, all in good time. I thought one of you should know, and that it had better be you.

Again, I nodded wordlessly.

By the way, he continued, you don't need to worry about your mother. She'll be well provided for. The bank will see to it.

I thanked him, saying that this was a great relief, especially as I knew almost nothing about how my parents were fixed.

Never mind all that, he replied. Your father is my first cousin. I wish I had looked after him better.

DR. REINER did not initially resist my attempts to explain the turmoil of contradictory emotions awakened in me by the visit to Lenox. Even I could see, though, that I was going around in circles, and, after a week of listening he said that the subject should be put aside until I was better able to externalize it. That left me to brood alone over the mysteries of the Standish family, on which my sporadic trips to Lenox threw little light. Two weeks before Thanksgiving, Dr. Pierson told my parents that the cancer had metastasized. He did not advise additional surgery. The nurse from Housatonic returned and was relayed at night by yet another Irish-woman from West Stockbridge. I continued my visits and spent Christmas and New Year's and the week between the two holidays at home. It was plain that my mother was stir crazy. I took her to the movies several times; she didn't care what film she saw. When May Standish invited me to their New Year's lunch, she surprised me by saying that she hoped I would bring my mother. My mother thought about it and said she'd go.

My father had another six weeks left, the last two of which he spent in the hospital. I was in Cambridge when he died and came back to see him buried in the family plot in Stockbridge. Neither Henry nor Archie came to my father's funeral. Archie had already been posted to an army unit based in Pusan; Henry was in advanced infantry training.

Meanwhile, in early February, the New York publishing house to which, on Professor MacLeish's advice, I had sent my manuscript wrote to me. For some minutes after I had read and understood the editor's letter I was hardly able to breathe. He was agreeing to publish my book and would even pay me an advance for it. It wasn't much, but I had never had more than a couple hundred dollars in my account that wasn't in transit to Dr. Reiner. I called Professor MacLeish—the first time I had dared—and, after him, Tom Peabody. I didn't call my parents. I knew that what I had written would hurt my mother's feelings, and, if he lived long enough to read it, my father's too, probably even more. It would be better to give them the news very casually when I went home. As it turned out, when I made my next weekend visit, my father was too far gone to absorb what

I was talking about. I did call Mr. Hibble. When I saw him during the summer, he had asked how much longer I would be seeing a psychiatrist five times a week. It adds up to a tidy sum, he told me. I said I knew that, but couldn't tell him how much treatment I would need after Dr. Reiner, when I moved to New York. By then, I reminded him, there would be no more tuition and room-and-board bills, though, of course, there would be other expenses.

New York, he mused, so that's where you intend to be.

That's right, I told him, unless the army takes me, in which case there won't be any psychiatrist's bills until I'm discharged.

We'll see, he said, and asked what kind of work I planned to be doing in the city. When he heard that I was planning to write, he shook his head and told me that I was very fortunate indeed to have old Mr. Standish's trust to back me up; there was no money in scribbling. I wasn't stupid enough to think that my advance proved him wrong. All the same, I wanted him to know about it.

Even with the changes I had to make in the novel, as I wasn't writing an honors thesis my workload wasn't heavy. I went to see my mother twice after the funeral. Before my father died, she had chafed under the constraints imposed by his illness. Now she didn't seem to know which way to turn. Couples who used to have them to dinner hadn't begun to invite her as an extra woman; she didn't have girlfriends; the men who had been the subject of so much whispered gossip were lying low or had disappeared. Her telephone didn't ring. Material cares might have provided a distraction, but Cousin Jack had been true to his word: one of Mr. Hibble's associates put my father's affairs in order; the pension the bank agreed to pay her for life would let her go on living just as before, without trying to cut back. There was an insurance policy she hadn't known about or had forgotten that paid off the mortgage on the house. Another policy she was aware of paid her an amount that she had always thought might just suffice to provide for her basic needs. Now it was icing on the cake; Mr. Hibble advised her to go ahead and buy herself a treat that would help lift her spirits. The rest he would help her invest in sound securities.

She told me on my last day in Lenox that she wanted to get a job, perhaps at the office at Riggs, perhaps something connected with Tanglewood. What did I think? I said both were good ideas. Did I believe that my doctor could put in a word for her at Riggs? I told her I didn't think that was the sort of thing analysts did for the families of patients and offered to speak instead to Cousin May, unless she preferred to do so herself. It would have to be over the telephone from Cambridge if I was to catch the five o'clock bus to Boston. In the car she told me that she would speak to May; she really wanted the Riggs job. Then in a more urgent tone she said that what she wanted right then above all else was to get away from Lenox. These are the hateful months, she said. I want to be in the sun, away from the mud and the cold.

Will you go with me to Puerto Rico for a few days? she asked. We could leave from New York next Thursday and get you back to Cambridge on Monday or Tuesday. My treat.

Hold on, I told her, let me think.

Dr. Reiner would have to be paid for at least three missed sessions—Thursday, Friday, and Monday—if I was in Cambridge in time to see him on Tuesday, and four otherwise. That was a waste of a lot of money. But it was money that would be spent anyway, and it wasn't as though I got my money's worth for every fifty minutes on his couch. He would, of course, want to talk about it: What was the relation between not seeing him and going off to a warm place with my mother, the role of money in this, the trust money versus the money my mother had offered to spend, what kind of fantasies did my mother's proposal inspire, was this a case of a little wish fulfillment?

Up his! I said to myself, and told my mother she had a date.

We stayed at a monastery in old San Juan newly converted into a hotel. A little bus ferried guests to the beach where brown boys set up parasols and deck chairs. The same bus took you back to the hotel. Lunch was served in the restaurant that opened onto the monastery's cloister. You could also eat at the beach, at an installation, half glorified hot dog stand and half tropical bar, that offered sandwiches, daiquiris, and beer. Perhaps there were other drinks as well, but my mother liked daiquiris and after she had put one away it was difficult to get her to stop or even pause. She had made all the arrangements for this expedition and equipped herself at the cruise wear department of Kaufmann Brothers in Pittsfield. On the beach she wore a bright two-piece, hardly more than a bikini, over which was knotted a light Tahitian pareo, and white sandals with only a strap of leather over the big toe holding them in place. I noted that she had painted her toenails violet. This was a far cry from her pool costume at the club: a one-piece bathing suit that flared out in a tiny pleated skirt, white or pink oxford cloth Brooks Brothers button-down shirt, a hand-me-down from my father who favored them for the office, and white tennis shoes. The afternoon sun was ruthless. Being even fairer than I, after every swim my mother asked me to put suntan lotion on her back, shoulders, and the backs of her legs, and she insisted on rubbing it on me, although I tan easily and have never suffered from sunburn, even after a whole day on the water. We'd already had lunch at the beach, and I was drying myself after a long swim, when I realized that she was turning bright pink. I asked whether she wanted another parasol, so as to be completely out of the sun. She said no, she was dizzy, and was beginning to feel the burn. Would I mind going back to the hotel—if I wanted to stay she would take the bus alone. I said I'd go back with her; we'd been at the beach for hours.

The rooms all had screen doors that opened on the balcony circling the courtyard. They were cool, even in the heat. I took a shower and sat down at the desk in my pajamas to work on my manuscript. It was tough going, and I decided to close my eyes for a few minutes. Instead I fell into a sleep from which my mother, rapping on the screen door, awakened me. She was wearing a pink silk bathrobe that I had never seen before. I got up and let her in. She said she was feeling better and asked me to order a couple of daiquiris from room service. Then she stretched out on the other twin bed. She said her skin was burning; she'd tried to take a nap but it was no use. Anyway, she wanted to talk. I looked at her from my desk chair. She too must have taken a shower or a bath. Her hair was wet. When the waiter brought the drinks she asked me to tip him and asked him to bring another round in half an hour. I said, Please bring only one, but she laughed and said again she'd drink my daiquiri if I didn't. We sipped our drinks for a moment in silence. Then she said that taking this vacation was the best idea that she'd ever had; she could never have taken it while my father was alive. He refused to get away even during the dreariest winter months, when everyone with two nickels went somewhere—as far from the Berkshires as possible. All he ever wanted to do was play tennis and golf and sit around the locker room and drink. It was a struggle to get him to go skiing even when the golf course was under a foot of snow.

That was true. They had sent me to a sailing camp in Marion several summers in a row, but we had never gone on a holiday as a family. We had skied at Catamount when I was little, and later at Stowe or at Mount Snow, but hardly ever stayed overnight and never any longer. My father, like George Standish, thought nothing of driving six hours to get in six hours on the mountain, and if he drove in the dark he knew he wasn't wasting time that could have been spent on the slopes. When he went to bank trust officers' conventions in Florida, he could be counted on to complain about the clientele at the hotels and the boredom he had suffered. My mother must have been pursuing this same train of thought because, turning on her side, she told me that if he had only enjoyed his business trips like other men who took the opportunity to have a little fling on the side while they were out of town he might have been less mean.

The thirty minutes she had stipulated for the second round must have passed, because the waiter came back with the daiquiris, which he set down on their tray on the night table beside her. She told him that was perfect and started to say she wanted another round, but I interrupted and told him we'd call if we needed anything.

You can't imagine what it was like to live with him, she continued, or what he tried to make me do. Stuff you'd do when your sex life is dead. I won't go into it. Not with you. You've been away from home so much, and now you're a stranger, a tall dark stranger.

I didn't say anything. She laughed and said, I bet you don't even know what I'm talking about.

I answered that I realized that there had been difficult moments.

Oh that, she said, that wasn't what I meant, but that too. He insisted on believing the stuff about all the men I'd gone with. He'd keep hammering at it. I don't see why. There was always plenty there for him, for him and his weird ideas.

We sat for a while in silence. When there was nothing left in her glass she sat up, reached for the other daiquiri, and said, Here, sit down here with me and have a sip. It won't go to your head.

I told her I really didn't want it. All right, she said, come over here anyway.

When I did, she put her arm around me and in the same motion bit me on the ear.

Tasty, she said. She downed her drink, plumped up her pillows, and lay back.

I remained on the bed for a moment and then moved back to my desk chair.

You were right, she said, to tell me to call May Standish. There's an opening at Riggs for a receptionist-librarian. I told May I'd take it. Some of the doctors and patients seem very interesting.

I said I was very glad.

I thought I'd start two weeks after I return. That will give me time to clear out your father's clothes. I don't think you want any of them. You already have his raccoon, and everything else would just hang on you. I'll have the Salvation Army take them away. Once I've settled in at Riggs, I'll look around. None of the old crowd, don't worry, but I can't be alone all the time. You won't mind, tall dark stranger, will you?

I shook my head and said I understood. I had been looking at her carefully while she talked. She had one of those astonishing metabolisms: no matter what she ate and drank, she never gained a pound. Yet there seemed to be a slight new pudginess in her face.

It's really all right, I repeated, but you should watch the daiquiris and the martinis. They could spoil your looks.

Good advice, she answered. But I don't intend to waste time.

XXII

IN EXCHANGE FOR a small amount of key money, the super eased my way into a rent-controlled apartment on East Thirty-sixth Street between Lexington and Park. Three months in the sublet down the block, where I had been living since my move from Cambridge, had convinced me that I loathed Murray Hill. However, my rent for a large two-bedroom apartment was about one-third that of the furnished studio, and, based on the *Times* classifieds, I didn't think I could do as well anywhere in Manhattan unless I was willing to live in Harlem or on the Lower East Side. There was one incidental benefit to my location: Dr. Kalman, the New York colleague to whom Dr. Reiner had referred me, was only two blocks away, across the street from the Union League Club. It took me five minutes to get to my appointments. The publication of my book, scheduled for mid-November, was still a month away, but galleys had been sent to reviewers long since and, according to my editor, the first signs were favorable. He thought that I might be interviewed by the *Times* and the *Herald Tribune*. In the meantime, following his advice, I was trying to stay busy and keep my mind on other things. I began a new novel and bought furniture for my apartment. I was heading out the door one evening, on my way to the Indian restaurant around the corner, when the telephone rang. Before the man on the other end had finished asking for me, I recognized the voice. It was Henry's father. I said, Hello, Mr. White, is something the matter?

It must have required a huge effort for him to call me. He didn't allow himself to be interrupted and went through the business of introducing himself before he answered my question. Yes, there was something the matter: Mrs. White. Could I come over right away? He gave me the name and address of Kings County Hospital in Brooklyn and told me how to get there on the IRT. They were in the emergency room. On second thought, maybe I could take a taxi; it would be much quicker at this hour. He'd pay the fare. I hailed a taxi at the street corner. The driver didn't know Brooklyn, but in the end, after stopping at gas stations twice to ask directions, he found the hospital, which stood in a dilapidated neighborhood off some wide boulevard. The nurse at the emergency room desk told me that Mrs. White had been moved to intensive care. I could look for her husband in the corridor outside the unit. That's where I found him alone in a chair. The others there seemed to be in family groups.

He got up and put his arms around me. I realized that he was trembling and asked what had happened.

I don't know where Henry is, he said. I thought I could talk to you. She's killed herself.

I pulled up a chair next to his, and little by little, while we waited for news, he told me that some two weeks earlier, during one of Mrs. White's conversations with Henry—he called her twice a week, collect— she learned that he had applied for ten days' leave. Then you will come home for the holidays, she almost shouted. She told Mr. White later that she thought she'd faint at the thought she would have him at home for Rosh Hashanah or Yom Kippur. Henry replied that it was impossible. He had already made plans involving other people—some friends—he was going to Ghent, Amsterdam, and Delft. You know how mothers are, Mr. White continued, you know my wife, she argued with him, and he hung up. Hung up on his own mother! She even tried to call him back, but it was no use; he was calling from a pay phone. I didn't know what to do with her when I got home. She looked sick and kept saying that she would throw herself under the subway and asking me to call Henry.

That sort of threat when she was very upset was nothing new, but all the same he tried to reach his son perhaps four times in the next two days, to make him call his mother and tell her he was sorry. Show her a little affection. Each time the soldier who answered the telephone said that he wasn't there, and could he take a message. Not being able to get through to Henry was nothing new as well, and in any case he was supposed to call home in two more days. When he didn't, Mrs. White, without telling her husband, sent him a telegram saying: "Parents sick telephone immediately." He called the next day, late at night this time, when Mr. White was at home, so he heard her say that his father hadn't had a heart attack, but no, she couldn't tell him how his father was, and so on. Then they really fought, and Henry hung up on his mother again. The next day it was she who called Fontainebleau and asked for Henry, saying it was a medical emergency. She was put through to a sergeant who said he was sorry but Specialist White had gone on leave. He checked with someone while she waited and finally came back to tell her that no one in the orderly room knew how her son could be reached.

Somehow they got through Rosh Hashanah, and on the second night of the holiday even had to dinner two couples they had known in Krakow before the war. But the next day, when he came home from the factory, he found a note on the carpet in the front hall.

Here, he said, drawing out a folded sheet of paper from his coat pocket, which he smoothed and handed to me.

I looked at the writing and reminded Mr. White that it was in Polish.

Excuse me, he said. My wife says goodbye and asks me to remind Henry that this day is the anniversary of the day she last saw her parents, as they were leaving for Zakopane. Excuse me, he said again, and began to sob.

I hugged him again, patting his back. He calmed himself enough to continue his story and said that he rushed into the bedroom and found her on the bed in her nightgown, her mouth wide open, her legs splayed wide. When he touched her, she was cold. He couldn't feel a pulse. A doctor who has an office two blocks away came over at once, although they weren't his patients; he examined her and said he was very sorry; there was no heartbeat or any other vital sign. Then he pointed to Mrs. White's arm, which was hanging down to the floor, got down on his knees, and peered under the bed just where her hand touched the carpet.

Here it is, he said, straightening up. It's empty. Seconal. Do you know how many she had? When Mr. White said he didn't, the doctor shook his head and told him that he couldn't certify the cause of death since he had not had Mrs. White as a patient. Mr. White had better call the police. It took them more than twenty minutes to arrive, by which time the doctor had left. Two policemen and two medics. One of the cops looked around and said, Suicide. Did she leave a letter or anything like that? While Mr.

White was explaining that he had found the letter in Polish, he saw that one of the medics was pounding his wife's chest while the other one, having filled a syringe, was holding it up to clear the air out of it.

She isn't dead, he said. I'm going to give her Adrenalin. Let's get her out of here.

They told him they were going to Kings County Hospital, and he followed in his car. That was almost three hours ago. After they had pumped out her stomach in the emergency room, the doctor who was working on her said that she was in a deep coma but alive. That's when they took her to intensive care.

I didn't know what to say to comfort him, or what I should do next, so I asked whether he would like coffee and a sandwich or a doughnut from the hospital cafeteria. At first he insisted that he couldn't touch a thing; when I pointed out that he really had a duty to keep his strength up, he agreed to coffee with cream and a lot of sugar.

I returned with the food. Mr. White drank the coffee in a gulp, wolfed down a cheese sandwich, and fell asleep. He didn't lean his head on my shoulder or slump forward; he sat perfectly upright in the chair, eyes closed, and snored. An occasional especially raucous snort would wake him. He'd open his eyes, shiver uncontrollably, and go back to sleep, murmuring something in Polish. At last, at about half past ten, a nurse came out of intensive care, but it was only to announce that everybody in the corridor had to clear out by eleven. I got up and asked softly, so as not to wake Mr. White, how Mrs. White was doing. Are you the family? she inquired. That's the husband, I told her. Then just wait, the doctor will be out to speak with you. I'll say you're here. I shook Mr. White awake and told him the doctor was coming.

Your wife, the doctor said, has done quite a job on herself. We've got her breathing and hydrated. The question is whether she'll start coming out or slip back. I don't know yet. You and your son should go home now. Anyway, you can't stay here. We have your telephone number, and I'll call you if anything happens during the night. Otherwise you can check in by phone in the morning or, if you like, you can come over.

It wasn't easy to get Mr. White away from that corridor, but I finally did, explaining over and over that no one would bend the rules and let him see her in the intensive care unit, that there was nothing he could do for his wife except keep his head and stay well himself, and that it was very important to avoid antagonizing the hospital staff. That last argument hit home.

He had left his Chrysler in the hospital parking lot and asked whether I would mind driving. There was a place at Flatbush and Church where we could still get something hot to eat, he told me, if I cared to come. We ate some sort of meatloaf with gravy and mashed potatoes, followed by apple pie and coffee. I wouldn't have minded a beer, but the place didn't have a liquor license. He told me how Mrs. White had been through a lot and how her nerves had never recovered from worrying about him and her parents and, of course, from fear for Henry and herself. She's a good wife, he kept assuring me. Henry should be kinder when he speaks to her, less impatient. He should learn not to be so harsh. You understand what I mean? he asked. I nodded, although I wasn't completely sure with what I was agreeing: his assessment of Mrs. White's nervous condition or Henry's dark side? These didn't seem to me to be subjects I could discuss with him anyway—certainly not right then. Ten in the morning was the hour of my regular appointment with Dr. Kalman. I asked Mr. White whether he would like me to come to the hospital the next day, in which case I could be there by twelve. I could also come earlier if something happened. He didn't think so; it would be a waste of time that I should use to write. Were there friends he wanted me to notify? He snapped to attention when he heard that and said no; his wife wouldn't want anyone to know about this; she wouldn't forgive him if the word got out. But he would call me if he needed help again and, in any event, would call me regularly to tell me how his wife was doing. As soon as we finished the meal he said I should get some sleep and insisted on putting me into a taxi right outside the restaurant. This time it was I who hugged him. He pressed into my hand a twenty-dollar bill and wouldn't allow me to give it back.

Mr. White did telephone regularly in the following days. He had tried to reach Henry and had spoken to the company master sergeant only to be told that the best he could do was to give him the message when he returned from leave. For the better part of the week there was no change in Mrs. White's condition, or none that he could describe, and I began to wonder what he and Henry would do if she remained permanently comatose or emerged from the coma with some sort of mental or physical impairment. Dr. Kalman had told me that such an outcome was very possible if too much time had passed before the medics or the emergency room people were able to get her breathing.

Then she began to improve, quite rapidly, and Mr. White reported triumphantly that she would be as good as new. The final telephone call was to tell me that he had taken her home. They were both all right, he had gotten a nurse to help, and, of course, they had the cleaning lady, but he hoped that I would understand if he didn't invite me to visit. They weren't up to it. I told him I was relieved and happy for the whole family. The florist on Lexington Avenue having told me that he could deliver to Brooklyn via Interflor, I sent Mrs. White a dozen red roses. Some weeks later, I received a note of thanks for the roses and my kindness to her husband. She was too ashamed, she wrote, to say more.

Henry didn't telephone or write to me after his return to duty. I made no effort to reach him either, in part, no doubt, because the appearance of my novel in bookstores—sometimes in bookstore windows I passed—abruptly opened the door to a new and oddly engrossing social life. I was invited to cocktail parties and dinners by hosts I didn't know; older people with large reputations seemed to take it for granted that I could be found at their friends' houses and conversed with me as though we were on equal footing. I stopped feeling embarrassed when I was introduced to strangers as a novelist or when people showed something like respect for my opinions.

I had been very anxious about the way my book would be received in the Berkshires, not by my mother, from whom I expected hostile silence or worse, but by people I cared about who would also be able to decipher what lay behind the story I had told. George surprised me. He must have read the novel in one sitting, almost surely a first in his life as a reader. Less than a week after it had been mailed to him, he called, saying he had already bought copies for his girlfriend Edie and the Appleton cousins and wanted to know whether I'd be willing to come and talk about the book and the life of a writer to members of his law school eating club. Then May Standish wrote that she and Cousin Jack wanted to give a cocktail party in honor of their novelist, as she put it, either the day after

Christmas or the day before New Year's Eve, whichever suited me better, although she thought that people would be less frantic and more attentive the day after Christmas. Having discovered that Dr. Kalman would be in Canada skiing from Christmas Eve through New Year's Day, I chose the earlier date. My mother had been strangely insistent that I come for the holiday, and I had told her I would, thinking that, in the worst case, if she attacked me over the book, I would make my appearance at the Standishes' party, spend the night with them, and the next day take an early train to New York.

At last the letter from my mother arrived. It was brief. After thanking me for the book and the inscription, she wrote: "You must have worked very hard. I hope you do well with it. Mrs. Jennings [that was the Lenox bookstore owner] has told me that a lot of people seem to want to read this kind of novel." I felt relieved. She must have worked on those two sentences almost as hard as I had on my book, but at least there were no recriminations, nothing about what my father might have thought or said. I answered, confirming my arrival, and told her that I'd be driving. I vaguely recalled her telling me in San Juan that she intended to sell her car and drive my father's. I didn't want to depend on her as my chauffeur, and I certainly didn't want to oblige her to stay at home if I went out alone. I reserved a Hertz rental. As it turned out, I needn't have gone to the expense. Although she had indeed sold the Buick, she had at her disposal another car as well as a driver.

I knew that she had started at Riggs, but I hadn't heard that she had quit. And I didn't know until she told me, when I came down to the kitchen after dropping my bag in my old room, that she had found a boyfriend, in the person of Greg Richardson, a former Riggs patient. She meant former in the sense that he was no longer living in the Center; he was renting the apartment over the Jacksons' barn and seeing one of the Riggs analysts as an outpatient. For the holidays, however, he was staying with my mother, which was the reason it mattered so much that I had come home. My presence made it more like a real Christmas.

It's hard for him, she said. He has two daughters, eleven and nine, living with their mother in Darien. She's an unspeakable woman. He misses those girls terribly. You've heard of the Richardsons. It's old Connecticut money.

Has it trickled down to him? I asked.

Not yet, replied my mother. His father controls all the trusts. He keeps Greg and his younger brother on a very tight leash.

Then she added that Greg had had those girls late. He's a couple of years younger, but I'm not robbing any cradles.

She was clearly expecting me to say something, so I said it was too bad about the girls and the money. She nodded and told me that drinks would be at the usual time and dinner would be at seven-thirty. While my father was alive, that meant as soon as he came home from the office and had taken a leak. Dinner, so far as he was concerned, could always wait. I told her I'd be there. A beautiful afternoon was ending. I got into the Hertz car and drove over to Stockbridge. I first deposited my presents for the Standishes and Edie, who was spending the holidays with George. That accomplished, I made a tour of the village, which I had always liked better than Lenox. On Main Street, Riggs was lit up and festooned with wreaths and pine-branch garlands. Through the windows I could see that a large crowd was milling around in the rooms downstairs, presumably munching on sugar cookies, drinking eggnog (laced with bourbon for those who were allowed and plain for those who weren't), and singing carols. For all I knew, my mother and this Greg character were there getting into the Christmas spirit. There was no risk of my going to look for them. I turned up toward Snake Hill, parked when I got to property belonging to people I knew who were living in Europe, and walked to the terraced garden in the back from which there was a view in all directions. During the few minutes I remained, night fell and the snow that covered the valley turned from a delicate shade of violet to a color that was darker and menacing. It was time to go home.

I found a note for me on the table in the front hall. My mother and Greg were washing up and would be right down. I was as washed as I cared to be, so I went into the kitchen, put water on to boil, and checked the oven. Roast beef surrounded in the pan by potatoes—one of my mother's standbys. Having made myself a cup of tea, I sat down in the library and waited. It was a while before Greg and my mother came down, my mother's face flushed from the hot bath or contentment or perhaps both. She was wearing a long black skirt I had never seen before and a cheap white cardigan with red buttons in the form of hearts that I had given her for her birthday four or five years ago. Greg was in festive dark red corduroys, a yellow turtleneck, and a green blazer with some club's silver-stitched insignia over the breast pocket. Perhaps to show that he felt at home, he had donned black velvet slippers. He was easily as tall as my father but more solidly built. We shook hands pleasantly and I sat down with my mother while Greg went to the kitchen to get ice and then to the pantry to assemble the martini components. I wondered whether his would be as good as my father's and what troubles or vices had brought this fine carefree-looking fellow to Riggs, away from those daughters he loved and their unspeakable mother.

Isn't he nice? my mother whispered. It's such a help that he's of good family. Just before you came in, May Standish telephoned. She asked me to bring him to the party they're giving for you, and she invited us both to their New Year's Day lunch. Can you imagine? She has never once invited me with your father.

I REMEMBER THE DAY and time of Henry's call with the precision usually reserved for nightmares: St. Valentine's Day, seven in the evening. I had gotten a late start that morning, having returned only the previous evening from San Francisco, where I had been for two weeks, leading a seminar at Berkeley. The florist's delivery boy awakened me, bringing my mother's present, a large white azalea. I called to thank her, did the usual morning chores, and went to the Forty-second Street library, where I spent the rest of the day, with one interruption for a hamburger at the Harvard Club. The key was still in the front door of my apartment when I heard the phone ring. I realized at once that something was horribly wrong: it was Henry, and his voice was cracking as if he were out of saliva and breath. Between gasps, he kept repeating, Please come right away, for God's sake, come over. I asked where he was. At home, he said, please hurry. Within minutes I was in a taxi on my way to Dorchester Road. He was waiting for me on the front stoop. This time she's done it, he told me, she's really gone. He led me upstairs to his parents' bedroom. Mr. White was there, crying.

She's in here, said Henry and opened the door to the bathroom.

Mrs. White, dressed in a nightgown, lay in a shallow pool of blood. Her head was twisted to the side as though in an immense final effort to see something over her shoulder.

She slit her wrists, Henry said. An open straight razor lay in the fold of the nightgown between her legs.

How long has she been like this? I asked. Have you called the police?

No, we haven't, he said. He wouldn't let me get near a telephone. I had to beg him to let me call you. He's out of his mind. Will you talk to him?

Mr. White, I called out, I am terribly sorry. We have to get the police. Please understand.

He made no reply and didn't move. I turned to Henry and said, Do it. Please make the call. You must do it.

As I pieced it together in conversations that night with Henry first at the morgue, then over the meal Henry and I had alone toward the early morning—Mr. White was unable to hold down any food—at the same restaurant at Flatbush and Church to which Mr. White had taken me, and later at the funeral parlor where Henry and I had gone to make arrangements for the burial, the story was a jumble of the old family misery and specific new horrors. Father and son meanwhile seemed unable to take any action beyond insisting that Mrs. White had to be buried; they wouldn't allow her to be cremated. Otherwise, all I could get out of them were gestures I interpreted to mean I can't answer, you do it. In the end I did the things I imagined had to be done, although I had no experience with death or the care of the dead other than the burial of my father, every detail of which had been arranged by my mother. Thus I found myself going through the Whites' address book and calling people who seemed initially suspicious of my unaccented American speech and then became unnaturally polite when I explained my business, addressing me in careful stilted phrases about conventions I didn't understand.

Henry had come home on five days' hardship leave. As soon as he arrived he telephoned me, and had tried my number many times in the days that followed, getting no answer. I had no service that could have told him I was away and how I could be reached. The reason for the leave was a series of frantic appeals from his father, begging him to do whatever it took to spend a few days with his mother. She had taken sleeping pills again, although in a smaller quantity this time. The same doctor who had pronounced her dead the last time had come to examine her. In his opinion, it wasn't necessary to empty her stomach. Let her sleep it off, he said. And get her some help, I mean real help, in a clinic with a psychiatrist who knows what he's doing.

Did they? I asked.

She wouldn't hear of it, Henry told me. To tell you the truth, my father didn't want it either. It was too humiliating, he said; he didn't want to treat her like a crazy woman; she didn't deserve it. I knew, Henry said, what my father meant: if one of their friends found out that she had to be in a mental hospital he would die of shame. Instead, he bought her a Persian lamb coat and booked passage on a cruise ship going to Bermuda in April. At first this seemed to cheer her up; she had been after him to get her this fur coat and to go on a nice spring vacation but, some two or three weeks ago, everything turned black again; she told Mr. White and Henry as well on the telephone that this was the end. Conversations with her from a phone booth in Fontainebleau had become unbearable and more surreal than ever. Either she got angry and hung up on him, or she berated and insulted him to the point where he'd hang up on her even though he remembered vividly where that could lead. Finally, he applied for leave and, when he got it, caught a flight to New York and showed up in Brooklyn. It didn't take more than one meal at which he did something or didn't do something quite right before she put on what Henry called her "Why are you here?" act. She wanted to know where he had learned to exaggerate everything and throw money out the window, wasn't the army in Fontainebleau going to think that he was taking advantage, shouldn't he go back and make up the work he had missed, and so on. There hadn't been one pleasant moment. She killed herself on his last day in New York; he was scheduled to fly to Paris that evening. They were meant to have a farewell dinner the evening before at a restaurant his parents particularly liked in Sheepshead Bay, which served good broiled lobsters and steamed clams. However, when his father came home from work—Henry had in the meantime gone to the Brooklyn Museum but had already returned—his mother said she didn't feel like going out. There was nothing to celebrate: Henry had better go to bed and get a good night's sleep since he was spending the following night on a plane. There was a scene after that. He wasn't sure how it started, but she ran up to the bedroom and slammed the door, and his father went into his office and wouldn't talk to him although Henry pleaded with him, saying that it would be a long time before they saw each other again. Mr. White kept saying, You want everything your way, you make trouble and then leave the trouble to me. In the end, Henry decided he was in an absurd situation and saw no point in staying home. He hadn't told Margot he would be in New York. On the off chance that she was at her apartment, he called and found her free. They had dinner and he spent the night at her place. That had not been his plan; he had fully intended to come home but didn't; nor did he call to say that he'd be out until the morning. To call would have only led to one more scene on the telephone.

You spent the night with Margot? I asked.

Yes, he said, she's working at the Metropolitan Museum. Never mind all that now.

He came home at about ten in the morning. His father was there; he hadn't gone to the factory. Both he and his mother had these blank and stony faces, and, when he addressed them, they didn't simply remain silent: they made a show of looking past him. That form of punishment wasn't new to him. His mother reserved it for major transgressions. But his father's joining in represented a novelty. After a while, he gave up and went upstairs to take a bath and change his clothes. When he came down, his father was gone, and his mother sat at the window, staring out at nothing. He spoke to her; in fact he implored her. He wanted to be forgiven. Nothing. He went for a walk, saw about half of a movie matinee, and was home by two-thirty. His father had come home by then and greeted him with, Where have you been, your mother had to call me at the factory because you'd disappeared. What was I supposed to do? Henry answered, You wouldn't speak to me, Mother wouldn't speak to me, so I went out. Now I'm back. That was followed by some shouting, but by then he was on automatic pilot preparing himself to go to the airport. He went upstairs, threw the stuff he was taking to France into his duffel bag, got into uniform, and went downstairs carrying the bag. They were right there, waiting. I'm leaving, he said in their direction. Thanks for a great visit.

His father barred the door and told him, You can't go away like that. You have to apologize to your mother. All right, he answered, I apologize, I am sorry, I regret everything, and now goodbye. With that he tried to kiss her. She pushed him away and said, If you leave now, this is the last time you will see me alive. No it isn't, he replied, and said goodbye again and kissed his father, who let him. Meanwhile his mother was screaming, You can't let him leave, you can't let him leave, I know I am going to die. At this point, Henry said, he was so confused he didn't know anymore whether he was speaking English or Polish and when he did try to speak Polish he found he couldn't. The words weren't there. He faced them and very self-consciously told them in English that there was no use arguing, he had to go to the airport at once and get on the plane or he would be AWOL. It was a while before a taxi passed by the corner of Flatbush Avenue where he was waiting. He got in and slept all the way to the airport. When his turn came to check in, the man behind the counter told him there was an emergency message for him to call home at once. Although he was convinced that this was another one of his mother's stunts, he went to the telephone and found out what had happened.

The rest he got from his father. His mother said that she was exhausted and needed a sleeping pill. All right, he said, I'll get you one. After the first suicide, he had put their store of barbiturates in a drawer in a bedroom desk to which only he had the key. He went upstairs without realizing that she was right behind him. The thick carpet had muffled her steps. When he opened the drawer, he saw her hand suddenly appear to swoop up the vial of Nembutal. She dashed into the bathroom. He opened the door before she could lock it, forced her fist open, and flushed the pills down the toilet. She became hysterical, screaming, Get out of my bathroom, leave me alone, and trying to scratch his face. He backed out of the bathroom keeping her at arm's length. The moment he was through the door, she slammed it shut. Assuming that the door was locked, he wondered whether he should call a locksmith to force it, but he didn't want to break the door or aggravate the situation. In the end he lay down on the bed planning to wait for her to calm down. Of course, he fell asleep. When he awakened, he saw that more than an hour had passed. The house was absolutely silent. He tried the bathroom door. It opened at once.

XXIII

It was a race to the grave. It had taken less than a year for Mrs. White to follow my father, the clear winner. Then it was Mr. White's turn. He died, as he had feared, of a stroke, in the first days of January 1957. The funeral was held later than Jewish custom prescribed in order to give Henry time to get back from Fontainebleau. Meanwhile, Mr. White's executor and business lawyer took charge of all the arrangements. George later told me that this was fortunate, because Henry seemed completely disoriented. I received the cable notification a week after the funeral. No one seemed to have my correct address in Rome, where I was living in a pensione near the Piazza del Popolo, busy revising my second novel.

The revisions done and reworked, I dispatched the manuscript to my agent, toured Tuscany and Umbria with Tom Peabody, who was on sabbatical in Florence, and finally made my way alone to Athens, Istanbul, and Vienna. I had submitted to a magazine a proposal for a very personal account of my first visits to these capitals of fallen empires. It was accepted; a photographer met me at each location. I was able to travel in style without worries about paying rent on my New York apartment, which I hadn't been efficient enough to sublet. Away all summer, I sailed home from Southampton. By the time I landed in New York, Henry had already gone up to Cambridge to start his life as a law student, and I didn't see him or George until one Saturday in October, at the engagement party Edie's parents gave for her and George. When I moved to New York I resolved not to be impressed by the glamorous ways of the rich. As May Standish was fond of saying, there were too many of them in New York. The Bowditches' double brownstone on East Eighty-first Street, and the walls of its two drawing rooms, dining room, and library covered with

Renoirs, Manets, and Monets, put my resolution to a severe test. It would be hard hereafter to treat Edie as just another nice Radcliffe girl without reflecting on her robber baron ancestors or the extraordinary collector of impressionist art and benefactress of the Metropolitan Museum, who I now realized, having put two and two together, must be her grandmother.

My newborn small celebrity, pleasant enough in itself, was useful in certain practical ways: for example, I couldn't believe that Dr. Kalman would have otherwise acquiesced without fuss in my long absence, and without the payment of some sort of retainer fee, or found for me a slot in the early morning when I returned. At large parties such as the Bowditches', even if I knew only the host and hostess and a handful of their guests, I could make my way through the crowd confident that when I introduced myself my name would elicit a response along the lines of You must be the novelist, I am so glad to meet you, I haven't read your book, but I've read the reviews, and what are you working on now. I would answer such questions more or less pleasantly, depending on the degree of inanity and the attractiveness of the person putting them, and then move on. That is how, after a few words exchanged with Edie and her parents and George's, I slowly reached Henry. He had just come in from the garden, and asked whether I would be having dinner with George and Edie and the two sets of parents, in my role of cousin, friend, and bodyguard. I laughed and said that I hadn't been invited; in fact, I hoped to spend the evening with him if he was free. There was someone he needed to see first, but we agreed to meet at nine at a restaurant in Irving Place that served late.

This gave me time to talk briefly to George. He had spent the past summer—crucial for law school students because firms decide during that summer between the second and third year of law school on the students they want to hire upon graduation, and students look firms over—working at Wiggins & O'Reilly, a firm that, in spite of the Irish name of one of the founding partners and the world of small-time courthouse politics it evoked, was at the summit of New York's legal establishment. He had been offered a position as a regular associate, and, having had a fine experience during the summer, he was going to accept it.

It didn't hurt, he told me, that Lee Sears & Bowditch sends most of its work to Wiggins, which makes it the most important client of the firm.

One of the most important, he corrected himself; they keep that kind of specific information very secret. It shouldn't hurt in the future either, when they decide who is going to make partner.

Lee Sears, I knew, was the investment bank of which Edie's father was the senior partner and essentially the owner. The Wiggins hiring partner must have rubbed his hands in glee when he roped in the future Bowditch son-in-law.

I asked George whether he had lived at the Bowditches' over the summer. He laughed and said that had been the idea, since Edie had decided she'd be in the city as well, but the parents on both sides nixed it. They're dead set against making the course of young love run too smooth. He was forced to share a sublet with one of his Yalie roommates from law school. On weekends, however, either he went out to the Bowditches' place in Syosset or else Edie and he drove up to Stockbridge. He'd brought his car to the city just for that purpose.

He put his hand on my shoulder and said, I trust that as my younger brother you'll be my best man. Of course, you'll have to make sure you're around next June. I'm giving you so much notice so you don't fly the coop and so you can get your tailor started on building that cutaway you've always wanted.

At a loss for words, I embraced him. He had gotten to know me as well as anyone, in his way as well as Henry or better, and our friendship, which for so many years had seemed impossible, now astonished me by its solidity. It was a great reassurance, for though I was as devoted to him and to Henry as ever, I knew that I was drifting away from them and would have to count on their forbearance and willingness to accept me on my new terms. Inevitably, the characters I was inventing laid the strongest claim to my attention; I gave them more thought, certainly more intensive thought, than I did to any real person.

Realizing how I was moved and the need to change the subject, George asked about my mother. I said that he probably knew more than I did. I had been in New York only for a week and had no plan yet to go up to Lenox.

I saw something of her during the summer, he said, at the club. She and this fellow Richardson played doubles a lot. He's got an amazing serve.

They've given him a summer membership so he could be in the Labor Day tournament with your mother. They came in first, and were the Lelands pissed! The word is that your mother and Richardson are going to get married. Isn't that a bit of good luck?

I told him that if true it surely was for her. My own feelings were another matter; I would have to sort them out.

HENRY WAS ALREADY at the restaurant when I got there, brooding over a bottle of Chianti. He perked up when he saw me. When I said that he seemed terrifically absorbed in his thoughts, he said it was nothing. Then he said, No, it is something important. He had been worrying about his study group at the law school. There were five first-year students in it, including him, and while the others were intelligent, and were certainly up on all the business vocabulary that he was only beginning to learn, speaking frankly they were creeps. In general, he said, law school students were a terrible lot, real turkeys, if you compared them with undergraduates at the college, but this group was as bad as they get. Their redeeming quality was their brains—which he didn't think were any better than his. He wondered whether people would assume that since he'd chosen to be with these characters he must be like them. I asked why he had, in fact, hooked up with them.

He said, All five of us were always volunteering to answer questions in civil procedure and property, or else we were called on by the professor, and we didn't make asses of ourselves. These two professors are really tough. After a class one of them came up with the idea that we be a study group and everybody agreed.

I said that sounded reasonable, although I would have supposed that he would be in a study group with his roommates.

I have no roommates, he answered, I live alone at Harkness. I didn't know if anyone from our class was going to law school like me, after the army. Now I see that there are a few but none I know well. Anyway, there is no one to whom I could have suggested rooming together. All the people I knew and liked at college are in their last year—like George. He, by the way, is going out of his way introducing me to people. He's a great guy.

Harkness was a dreary modernist dormitory for law school and graduate students designed by Walter Gropius, who had founded the Bauhaus and really should have done better. Its only advantage was being right next to the Langdell Library. No one socially desirable lived there, only the dreariest graduate students condemned to be snubbed by faculty members in their departments. Poor Henry had started off on the wrong foot.

Then the food came, and when we spoke again it was about his parents. Henry's head was full of practical problems connected to his father's business. There were apartment buildings his father had owned with mortgage payments to be made, repairs for which the landlord was responsible, ordinary upkeep, and rents to be collected to pay for it all. Vacancies were rare enough that he was spared at least the headache of replacing tenants. The manager looking after the buildings was doing a good job, according to Mr. Berger, his father's lawyer, but Henry remembered his father's saying that you had to keep after that manager, and this was something Henry hadn't the time or inclination to do. Everything relating to the factory was even more complicated. Fortunately, his father had taken in his best salesman as a fifteen percent partner. Again according to Mr. Berger, this man was competent and honest enough to run the business until it was sold.

I can't let the factory go belly up, said Henry. It's not only the money; there are about forty employees. Either the business continues or I have to close it down very carefully so that everybody gets well taken care of, at least those employees who were already there when my father took over.

He hadn't even tried to go through the house on Dorchester Road to empty it of stuff he didn't want—ninety-five percent of the contents, he estimated—or to decide what to do with his parents' personal papers. Mr. Berger had organized the business papers; there would be money from his father's life insurance to pay estate taxes. For the time being, Dorchester Road would remain as it was, with the cleaning lady continuing to come in twice a week until his summer vacation. Then he would move in for however many weeks it took and to clear out the house for sale. How he was going to keep his sanity while he camped out there he hadn't been able to figure out. One ray of hope was Mr. Berger's belief that the factory might be sold before the summer. He advised Henry to keep the apartment buildings; according to him they were a great investment and Henry could afford to hold on to them.

I'll take his advice, he said, because I trust him, but only if he is the one to keep after the manager and whoever we get to replace him.

He fell silent, though clearly struggling to say something. I waited and in the end he spoke first.

I can't get away, he told me, from the double vision—that bathroom, of course, and also my father, his face clean shaved and green with just a little foam in the corners of the mouth. He had shaved, as always, a second time in the evening to please my mother, never mind that she was gone. In the morning two lathers and two passes with the razor, in the evening only one. That was his rule. I know that is how it had to be, I could tell just from the way he looked when I saw him wrapped in a shroud at the funeral parlor. You'll tell me that I'm making this up, since he died alone, with his son overseas. Indeed, at the hour when the coroner said he probably died, a bunch of us who had gone to Paris for the evening were sitting down to a late meal at the Coupole. I don't think I'll ever be able to touch choucroute again. You want to know something else? They'd refrigerated him while they waited for me to arrive. He was like a block of ice when I kissed him.

There is something you don't know, he continued. When my mother died, the army would have given me a compassionate reassignment to some place like Governor's Island so I could be near my father. All I had to do was ask. But I didn't ask. I think that if the company commander had offered to send me home I would have said thank you sir, but no sir; I believe my duty is to remain right here, in Headquarters Company. Why? I didn't want my father to glom on to me. I didn't want to be there with his grief, his fear of dying, his stubborn incompetence in everything that wasn't running his business. If I let him, he would have swallowed me alive, like a python. That's what I thought. So instead I helped kill him.

I pointed out that ever since I met him I had heard about his father's weak heart and the threat of a heart attack or a stroke.

Yes, Henry answered, I know, that's why I said I only helped to kill him. He would have died of his heart anyway sooner or later, but I almost surely made it happen sooner and I certainly made it sadder and harder.

What happened was exactly what he feared: dying alone, found by a stranger. The cleaning woman, when she came in the morning. You'll tell me that even if I had stayed I wouldn't have been with him twenty-four hours a day—not while I was pushing papers on Governor's Island or anytime later, and that is the pragmatic truth. The symbolic truth is different: it says that I willfully and unequivocally abandoned my father. I didn't want to be around Daddy any more than I had wanted to be around Mommy!

He paused while the waiter cleared for dessert.

A napoleon, he exclaimed. That's what I'll have.

When the pastry was brought he examined it with great care and said, It was my mother's favorite pastry. A Krakow specialty that she missed here. Quite honestly, can you believe that anyone else could have made such a hash out of his one and only visit—emergency leave, no less—to see his mother who was clearly bonkers? Show me another monster like that, if you can. He's my missing brother. A fellow mother killer: I wonder why that isn't the all-purpose GI epithet. It says it all so much more clearly than the one we use. I arrive and she tells me, Why are you here, go back to your barracks. What do I do? I get on my high horse. I can't help it. I do it every time she says something that wounds me, and I make a point of being wounded. I do it like a fool, as though I didn't understand the mechanism of what we do to each other so thoroughly that I could take it apart and put it together blindfolded. She was faint with the happiness of having me near, but for her to acknowledge happiness was to invite the thunderbolt that would destroy it. Far better to end it herself, design the set and direct the drama. Add to this her pride and her fear that I would rebuff her, and her craving for tension and excitement and risk—how long can she goad me before I turn on her?—isn't that a better game than baccarat and roulette, which she never played? After four years in Pani Maria's room behind a locked door, waiting for the evening so she can emerge for an hour or two, in each hand a chamber pot covered up so very carefully to contain the stench—what better games can you suggest for her to play? Why couldn't I, why wouldn't I, since this was certainly within my power, why wouldn't I say, It's all right, Mommy, I'm here because I love you and Daddy, and I'll be back as soon as the wicked,

wicked army lets me. Wasn't that my ordinary and simple duty? Why did I have to be such a prick?

He stared at me as though expecting a reply. Only the most obvious occurred to me: in the long time we had known each other, I had never doubted his love for his mother and father, or doubted that they knew he loved them. And I knew that their love for him was the central fact of their lives.

That's what makes it so much worse, he said. I did it to them and I did it to myself. As though I had been sleepwalking.

Although it was late, I couldn't simply leave him, not with that masque of murder playing itself out in his head. If he didn't have to go back all the way to Brooklyn, I'd propose a nightcap. I asked where he was staying.

At Margot's, he said.

I contained my astonishment and asked whether, in that case, we might have a drink at some bar near the restaurant or at my apartment. He consulted his watch and shook his head.

I'd better get back. Margot said she'd be out late, but she should be getting home just about now.

All right, I replied, I'll see you in Cambridge sometime before Christmas, unless you get to the city earlier.

We shook hands, and just as we were each about to turn, he east to the subway station and I west toward Park Avenue, he called out, Wait, I have an idea, why don't you have a drink with Margot and me?

I asked, Are you sure that she won't mind?

She'll be thrilled.

In the taxi going uptown I reminded him that when we saw each other last—I took care not to refer to the circumstances—he had said that he would explain next time where he stood with Margot.

Ah yes, he said, I remember. She wrote right after Commencement, very affectionately, congratulating me on the summa and so forth. At the end she suggested that I call her at her parents' apartment. Fortunately, the letter caught me just before I sailed for Europe so I called immediately and she said, Come over. The doorman told me to go up. It turned out that Mr. and Mrs. Hornung were away for the week, but the butler was there and he served us a cold dinner with wine—and drinks before that.

The full treatment. Then we went to Eddie Condon's to listen to jazz. I forget who was playing. I was too excited to pay attention. We couldn't really talk over the music so we went back to her house. She kicked off her shoes and we both sat on the sofa in the library. She told me she'd go to Sarah Lawrence in the fall and wouldn't even try to return to Radcliffe. Then she said she was sorry about the way she left me, that it was all her fault, a crazy period of too many things happening in her life all at once, and only one thing was certain, that she and Etienne were through. He was a major part of the craziness, he and his friends, and all the running around in New York hotels and in Europe, as though in some novel F. Scott Fitzgerald hadn't written. So could we go back to the way we were? She held out her face for me to kiss. I thought I was in a trance. She told me that meant we would be the tenderest and closest of friends; she might even sleep with me, though not that evening. But I would have to recognize the way she was, which for the time being didn't include being faithful and pretending we were married when we weren't. I said yes. Can you imagine my saying no? She's a curatorial assistant at the Met now, in the drawings department. Mr. Hornung is a big donor. She has a little apartment near the parents. Have I already told you that? I know that I've told you—I think the day we met—that Margot would be my long-term project. Well, I was right.

THE TINY APARTMENT was of the sort devised, she said, in certain Park and Fifth Avenue buildings as a dwelling for widows, old maids, and confirmed bachelors, so that at absurd expense they could live in four exiguous rooms and benefit from all the services and security that people like her parents considered appropriate. Two sofas faced each other in the living room. A long and narrow coffee table had been placed before one on which she and Henry sat after she had served us whiskey and sodas. I sat on the other, facing them. I had to hand it to Henry. She was superb, changed not only from that first vision of her in the Yard but from wherever I had seen her last, at some cocktail party or in the Square. She was wearing her hair longer, so that her face seemed softer; the lipstick was subdued; her dress was straighter and shorter and had a softer line than what I was accustomed to think of as the New Look. Her incredibly long legs shimmered in iridescent white stockings. Leaning back against the cushions, she told me how glad she was to see me. We talked about her plans, Sarah Lawrence, and the Met. After next summer she'd study in Europe, at the Courtauld or the École du Louvre, perhaps both. She'd be in New York during Henry's summer vacation, while he was settling his father's estate. She'd try to get him out of the city on weekends. Her parents might rent a house in East Hampton, instead of going to Cap Ferrat as usual. It depended on whether her father could arrange to join the Maidstone Club. She laughed as the words left her mouth. It's absurd, she said, neither he nor Mother plays tennis or golf, but he would be unhappy if he couldn't pick up the telephone and reserve a court.

I said that some people who came to the Berkshires apparently felt the same way about our club, which wasn't much, and then asked why the Maidstone would be a problem for her parents.

She laughed again and said, Jews and Negroes aren't welcome. Irish Catholics aren't either, or Italians, unless they have what the admissions committee thinks is a real title.

And your parents? I said, thinking, perhaps wrongly, that I shouldn't let on that Henry had gossiped.

Don't you know they're Jewish? she asked. My mother too, although it's a big secret and she'd be furious if she knew I'd told you. My father's different. He doesn't hide being Jewish; he just doesn't push it.

I had finished my drink and Henry offered to refill my glass. It was very late. I told them that I had been very happy to have dinner with Henry, perhaps even happier to see them together.

She said she had meant to thank me for all I had done to help Henry.

Help him? I inquired, genuinely puzzled.

Yes, she answered, from the beginning, when you told him to stop being so shy with me. We're not self-hating anti-Semitic Jews. We're only snobs.

I asked whether that was better.

Certainly, she said, so far as we're concerned everyone gets a second and third chance.

To do what?

Don't be so dense, Henry said, to remake himself.

XXIV

ARCHIE STARTED AT WHARTON right after the army, but he didn't like Philadelphia, and after the first year he quit and went to work for a Wall Street investment bank. The idea was that with his perfect Spanish, elegant manners, and local contacts he would help invigorate its business in Central and South America. I began playing squash with him again. My game was once more in shambles, and Archie was exactly what I needed to force me to play with some energy and will to win. After a while I managed occasionally to beat him. He was all cunning and speed, which I preferred to cannonball serves one can't possibly return and the like. So long as Archie worked downtown, we played at the end of the afternoon, which suited me very well. At some point, he changed jobs. His new firm was midtown, and we began to play almost always during the lunch hour, which at first seemed less convenient for me, but as I was learning to get up early and get right to work, a midday break in reality wasn't too disruptive. We'd play at the Harvard Club and then have a hamburger in the grillroom downstairs. Some time later, Archie joined a much grander uptown club, with squash facilities of regal splendor, and began inviting me to play there after work. I accepted once in a while, with considerable reluctance. I didn't like having him pay for me, and he refused all my offers to contribute toward the court fee and drinks that followed. It was the custom of the place to have the waiter bring cocktails or whatever else you ordered to the large room adjoining the locker room. The custom also called for conversation to be general so that you were more or less forced to talk to the members and occasional guests who happened to be there. I didn't care for the type to which they ran; they reminded me of certain friends of George's at college who, to a man, wore their club ties pushed forward like battering rams by the gold pins that squeezed together the wings of the collar. Or their conversation. When they spoke, they honked like geese. A hot subject just then was the number of girls they or their female cousins knew whom Jack Kennedy had raped, as though well-brought-up girls wouldn't jump into bed with the president just because he happened to be a Mick.

Neither these appalling clubman friends nor the amount of booze Archie consumed had so far discouraged his new girlfriend, Phoebe Jones. Behind the various facades he erected, she sensed lying hidden the nagging insecurity. With that discovery, the road to her grand objective—building up his self-esteem—was clear, and the distance from there to falling in love was quickly covered. For a twenty-four-year-old graduate of a small liberal arts college in Ohio working as an assistant editor at a magazine for teens, she was very maternal, notwithstanding her own facade of all-business gray or brown suits like those in the windows of Peck & Peck, crisp striped shirts, and brown pumps with high heels that made her half a head taller than Archie. Unlike him, she was a reader, with a taste for nineteenth-century novels. She was well into Dostoyevsky. Stendhal was next on her list. I supposed that someday she would reach Henry James and recognize herself as an updated and milder Henrietta Stackpole.

Archie sought me out regularly to make a threesome for drinks after our evening games. The reason was obvious: as a novelist I was the kind of New Yorker Phoebe wanted to know, and I was living proof that being Archie's girl didn't condemn her to the exclusive company of his Voorhis, Schermerhorn, van Gelder, and Phipps stockbroker and lawyer club mates and their more staid conversation, once they were out of the locker room, about Squadron A reunions, Blue Hill Troupe performances, summer rentals in Amagansett and Newport, and, of course, the importation of Irish and British nannies. Although Henry, like Voorhis, was a lawyer, and Phoebe found lawyers as dull as stockbrokers, she liked him as a fellow lover of books. However, his usefulness to Archie was even more limited than mine, because he spent most evenings and many weekends at the office.

Even the hard drinkers I knew among classmates who had come to live in New York had reduced their intake of booze to a modest if steady trickle. Archie was a notable exception, as I discovered anew every time he maneuvered me into going out to dinner with him and Phoebe. If anything, he was drinking more than at college, and, I gathered from Phoebe's occasional sarcasm and stories he told on himself in his old self-deprecating way, he was still getting drunk. Not just at weekend parties but pretty much every day of the week. The first martini or two would convince him that the occasion was festive; the rest was a familiar, drearily routine process. Countless infallible remedies, the recipes of which he had acquired from the most seasoned of bartenders, accounted for his being able to report for work the next day at almost the normal hour and got him through the morning until a little hair of the dog and lunch were at hand. There was also a secret weapon: a tank of oxygen he kept at his bedside. He assured me that a couple of whiffs cleared the head and most if not all other symptoms. I disliked watching him drink, and having Phoebe as another witness only made it worse; I thought it was unseemly.

The news that they were going to get married—given over the phone by Archie—came as a surprise. I would have thought she had more sense. The engagement was confirmed in the next morning's *Times* and, a few days later, by an invitation to a party for the couple hosted by two brothers who were pillars of Archie's grandest club. I was unable to attend and instead invited Archie and Phoebe to have a drink with me a couple of weeks later at the Plaza. I asked Henry as well, but he was in Washington, making a presentation to the Treasury about the impact of some newly introduced tax on the business of a client. From remarks made by each, and from a conversation with Archie, which must have taken place around the time of the engagement, in the course of which he said that Henry didn't have much of a social life, I knew that Archie and Henry were seeing each other. Archie wished he could help by getting him into some of his clubs. The Harvard Club, to which Henry did belong, was all right for squash, which Henry had in fact given up because he had too much work, but not much use for anything else. The situation would be entirely different if Henry were in the Union or the Racquet, but that was out of the question. They don't let them in, he told me.

Not long afterward I received an invitation from Archie that was more like a plea to have drinks again at the Plaza. It caught me in a moment of weakness, and I agreed although I had pretty much decided to limit our

encounters to the squash court. I was late to the Oak Room and saw immediately that he and Phoebe were close to finishing a round of martinis. Archie made some good-natured noise in response to my apologies and got the waiter to take my order and bring another round for them. She told him not to bother; she'd be leaving in a moment. I told you, she said, that I can't face another one of these evenings. Besides I have a terrible headache. In a gesture of discouragement, she took off her glasses and looked away. There were tears in her eyes.

Don't get cross with me today of all days, replied Archie, you know I have a lot on my mind. This will be different. Come on, if you stay, Sam will stay too, and he'll make sure I behave. Right? He squeezed my forearm and then patted it.

I nodded, thinking that since my tardiness had given Archie a head start on the gin I bore some responsibility for this unpleasantness. My whiskey and soda came, and I drank it slowly. This turned out to be a mistake because Archie used the time to ingest two more martinis before we walked over to one of his favorite hangouts, on Lexington Avenue and 60th, just a few blocks away. It was I who suggested it, wanting to be spared the taxi ride to the Mafia restaurant on East 114th Street that Archie also favored, but that too was a mistake, because as usual we had to wait at the bar for a table, and it was not an establishment where one waited empty-handed. In fact, we all three had a drink. I was relieved that the liquor didn't seem to be affecting Archie. His face was red; that was all. Perhaps the cold air during our short walk had given him the equivalent of a hit from his oxygen tank. It was only when the waiter finally brought the main course that I noticed the change. Archie was droning on pedantically, repeating himself, brooking no interruption by Phoebe. First it was all about how the securities firm for which he worked had decided that he would have to spend at least half of his time in Mexico, Salvador, and Venezuela where his contacts were concentrated. He would also have to develop clients in Argentina and Peru. Peru, said Archie, was a cinch. He had a perfect point of contact: one of his rugby pals, whose Spanish mother had vast properties there and a house in Lima where he would meet everybody who counted. Argentina was tricky. Phoebe would definitely have to travel with him, job or no job, particularly her current job, which she should quit anyway as too time-consuming for Mrs. Archibald P. Palmer III. She didn't have time to answer, and perhaps wouldn't have answered anyway, because Archie suddenly got up and headed in the direction of the toilets. His gait was unsteady, as if on the rolling deck of a boat before having got his sea legs. I followed his progress, hoping that he wouldn't collide with the waiters rushing from the kitchen with steaming plates of spaghetti.

After he returned, Phoebe and I watched in silence while he picked at his food. Archie was an irritatingly slow eater under the best of circumstances. Having vomited, as I surmised from his pallor, he seemed determined to make up for what he had expelled, at least in drink. Over Phoebe's protest, he ordered a second bottle of wine, had the waiter fill our glasses, and, having emptied his own, launched without any sort of transition into a series of anecdotes about the proceedings of the admissions committee of his grandest club. He had gone on the committee only recently, and his stories all concerned the cunning with which committee members would ferret out, reading between the lines of letters of support and canvassing their own acquaintances, the guilty secrets that the candidate, and sometimes even his sponsor or second, had hoped would pass undetected. Typically, it was Jewish relatives whom the candidate had kept at a long arm's length, although all his money came from the Jewish family's fortune. It was much the same with Irish Catholics, and there was, he said, the case of an Italian about whom it was claimed that his family were all landed gentry in Tuscany, whereas in fact his mother, father, and cousins all lived in northern New Jersey and prospered dealing in scrap iron. As he rambled on the waiter arrived to take orders for dessert. I saw in this an opportunity, and said I had to go home to do a little work before turning in.

AT THE BEGINNING of the summer I left for Paris. During my stay I received a phone call from Phoebe. She too was in Paris, as a reporter attached to the Paris bureau of *Time*. We had dinner, and during the course of the meal she confirmed what I had already deduced: her breakup with Archie. She was bitter and upset. The drinking, she felt, had become an instrument of aggression; Archie was signaling that he didn't want to be married. In any event, that he didn't want to be married to her. She knew that I was an old friend of his and wasn't asking me to agree or disagree.

I returned to New York in late September, moved into an apartment in a converted carriage house in the East Seventies, and invited Henry to a housewarming dinner at which he was the only guest. I told him about Phoebe's tale of woe. He nodded and said that Archie was off his rocker. There was more to it, he added mysteriously, but he would let Archie clue me in. It was Henry's third year in practice. He told me he was working as hard as ever, perhaps harder. There was much to talk about, but the next day he was again going out of town and had to rush back to the office to prepare. We agreed to have dinner when he got back, in two weeks' time. It was his turn, he said, he would take me to a restaurant.

In the meantime, to get my game in shape, I played squash at midday with the Harvard Club pro. I didn't make lunch dates, preferring to have a bite alone or to go home and eat something out of the fridge. After one of those games, I was walking out of the club when the hall porter stopped me, saying the chef has his radio on in the kitchen and has just heard that the president has been shot. I stopped and, in my colossal stupidity, asked, The president? President Pusey?

No, he answered, the president of the United States.

I WENT INTO THE STREET, and for some reason started running. Running where? At first, I didn't know, but it turned out to be home. By the time I reached Park Avenue, flags were being lowered and limousines stopped at the curb with the door on the driver's side open. The radios turned on full blast repeated the news. He had been shot and he was dead.

But I was alive. A week later I was about to call Archie to ask for a game when he rang me. I must have made good progress with the club pro or perhaps Archie was out of shape. I beat him. He waited until after the game to tell me his news, over a beer at the bar. His engagement to Phoebe was off. I let on that she had called me in Paris. Without giving me time to mumble about being sorry, he said, Now here is the good news, I'm getting married. He produced a picture of the bride-to-be he had in his wallet. She was very blond, blue eyed, slightly on the plump side. German? I asked. I was clever to guess, Archie said, German on both sides, her parents living in Buenos Aires since the end of the war. The father had held a high rank in the German navy and had built a big food export-import business. The wedding would be in six months, in New York. The parents were happy about the location; they knew a lot of people in the city and it would be more convenient for their family and friends in Germany. Then he and Alma would go on a little wedding trip out west. After their return, the parents would have a big reception in BA. It'll be a perfect wedding, he said, if you agree to be an usher. Henry has already said he will be the best man. It's a good match, and Alma's a very special woman, he said with great seriousness. She's a wonderful influence on me.

So may I count on you? he asked as we parted. I said I would be delighted.

That is how I found myself under the command of Henry in a strange platoon of assorted Verplancks, Phippses, and Voorhises greeting Admiral and Frau von Holberg's guests at St. Ignatius Loyola, and later dancing with Alma's oversexed Latino maids of honor, every one of them, I had been told, a certified virgin. It had fallen to me to escort Archie's mother to her pew. Desiccated and hunched over, the general's wife had aged less well than he. She no longer had the optimistic bounce of a registered nurse; now she looked more like an old lady waiting for a bus in some small town terminal, clasping a huge black pocketbook from which no force on earth could separate her. At the Colony Club the last guests had just made their way through the receiving line when we were called to attention by a roll of the drums, and the bandleader's cry of Olé! Olé! We all turned toward the dance floor and saw Mrs. Palmer make her way to the bandstand. She said something in Spanish to the bandleader that caused him to give her a handheld portable microphone. The drums were heard once again as she searched in that pocketbook. Finally, she found the sheet of paper she had been looking for, settled a different pair of glasses on her nose, and began to read. I was expecting a toast, although it was not the usual time for the mother of the groom to speak. In fact Mrs. Palmer was saying that if we would look through the windows on Park Avenue, we would be able to admire the automobile she had given Archie as a wedding present. She hoped he and Alma would have fun in it on their honeymoon road trip. Appearances are misleading, she continued. This baby may look like your ordinary Mercedes convertible, but she's got an engine with twice as many horses champing at the bits. That is why I also offered Archie, when he last visited his old mother in Texas, a week of car racing instruction. Happy flying!

The band struck up "La Cucaracha," and Archie did the box step with his mother, who turned out to be very nimble, while all the Latinos—men, women, and virgins—spontaneously formed a circle around them and clapped hands in time with the music. I followed Mrs. Palmer's precept and took a peek at her offering. It was fire-engine red and very beautiful. When it came to presents, she certainly had style.

Some time passed after the wedding without any word from Archie. Probably I didn't notice; I don't recall discussing his silence with Henry. Then one day after a lunchtime game with the club pro, I ran into one of the other ushers, Bill Voorhis, whom I knew vaguely from college.

Perfectly horrible, he said to me, when I think of that wedding, and how much fun we all had.

What can you mean? I asked.

Don't you know? he replied.

He went on to tell me that Archie and Alma got to Denver by plane and were reunited with the Mercedes, which had been shipped by train. Someone brought it to their hotel right before lunch. They went out to inspect it and afterward, as Voorhis put it, had one of those Archie lunches. When they finished, he took Alma for a spin. Fifty miles on, they were both dead, crushed against a beer truck on a blind turn.

I told Voorhis that I felt sick.

We all did after the general's call, he replied, but what else could you expect? The general reached Phipps first, and then Phipps called the rest. A couple of us went out there to help with taking the bodies to Buenos Aires. That's what the Holbergs wanted, and the general agreed. That's right, he added, I guess there's no way you could have known. Poor Archie didn't rate an obituary.

I had lunch alone in the grillroom. Afterward, I stepped into the telephone booth in the front hall of the club, shut the door behind me, and dialed Henry's number. He was on the phone, but I told the receptionist that I would wait. Finally he came on and I told him. There was a long silence. That was, I realized, how Henry grieved until such time as some dam inside him would break.

So there it was. Henry didn't know the Union Club gang, and no one—not even General or Mrs. Palmer—had bothered to call him any more than me, so completely had Archie's life changed. It wasn't as though Archie himself had come to feel less close to Henry. He had asked him to be his best man, and not Voorhis or Phipps. But to the general and the pillars of Archie's backgammon set, Henry was as good as invisible, some misfit poor old Archie had been stuck with at college. After I got home I thought of Phoebe. It was more or less the hour when she would be leaving for work. I got her right away but couldn't bring myself to get to the reason for my call. We chatted. She was with an English journalist who refused to get a divorce, but most of the time the wife stayed in London and let him live as he pleased in Paris. Did I know any single men, she asked, who weren't queer and wanted to get married? I said they had discontinued that model, and then, without more beating about the bush, I gave her the news.

XXV

ARCHIE HAD BEEN RIGHT about one thing: Henry's social life. Perhaps getting into the Union or the Racquet Club or one of the smaller and even more exclusive institutions that Archie himself had not yet managed to join would have been a big help. He would have been able, when lonely, to seek shelter and company at the club bar and the members' dinner table. Perhaps he would have acquired a taste for the ambient conversation and by and by become a desirable extra, a man in demand among the wives to whose husbands he lost at backgammon. Except that he would have found it hard not to win.

Certainly, he had the cultural riches of New York at his disposal. But the peonage in which New York law firms like his held associates—at partners' beck and call at any hour of the day or night, weekends and holidays included—made going to a movie, play, or concert frustratingly difficult, unless one went alone or someone was always available, resigned to last-minute cancellations and good-natured about them. That was usually a long-suffering wife. Many of Henry's colleagues had them as well as children in various stages of teething and toilet training, and those with money of their own also had nannies to push the prams, change the diapers, give the bottle, and otherwise keep the little angels out of their parents' hair. That did not mean, however, that they were apt to rush off to see a Broadway show and say to themselves, Wouldn't old Henry like to come along. Much more likely, as part of a round-robin of invitations exchanged within the inbred and hermetically closed world of posh law firms and investment banks, they would be giving or attending a refined little dinner at the apartment of some other young couple on the Upper East Side or possibly the Upper West Side. The table would be aglow with wedding-present linen, silver, crystal, and china, a display of which poor Mrs. White herself would have approved. The martini glasses having been twice filled and twice emptied, the hostess and the most enterprising of the other husbands would serve the meal: six times out of ten, it consisted of stuffed quail, wild rice, Brie (small slices of which had already appeared on Norwegian flat bread as hors d'oeuvres), and, for dessert, perhaps a fruit tart purchased at Dumas on Lexington Avenue, all washed down with more Beaujolais than was good for anyone. Scotch and soda and Cognac followed. It didn't matter all that much if one of the husbands—even the host!—had found himself stuck at the office or, having gone to the printer to proofread changes in some registration statement, missed the party and didn't appear at home until dawn, just in time to shave, change his shirt, and head back to the office. The good-sport supergirl he had married would cope, just as she coped with everything that stood in the way of living like Mommy and Daddy. Meanwhile, the men lucky enough to have a night away from the office would exchange tall stories about deals they were on, the billable hours they had racked up the previous week or month and since the beginning of the year, the eccentricities of partners they worked for, and, if all other similar subjects had been exhausted, the finer points of opinions rendered to lenders in secured financings. They took stock of one another, as it was a close and unsettling question which form of chic was higher: to have come directly from downtown, bearing a Peal's attaché case heavy with documents to be studied and marked up before the sun rose (as though any such thing could be accomplished after the second after-dinner whiskey or Cognac) or to have stopped at home and slipped into a pretty Jermyn Street shirt and blue blazer from Anderson & Sheppard.

Of course, Henry could count on George and Edie to invite him to their little dinners. They invariably did, George explained to me, because Edie was so fond of him, fully as much as he. It was she, in fact, who had first thought of asking him to be an usher at their wedding. Otherwise, he wouldn't push her to have him over, that sort of thing being really better left to women, particularly if someone is as hard to place as Henry.

I expressed some surprise that he didn't think Henry an easy fit.

It's a bunch of factors, he said. Edie likes the table to be balanced, which is fair enough, and Henry never seems able to bring a date. I don't understand it. I can't believe that he doesn't know any girls, or that he's ashamed to show us the ones he's seeing. We've tried to fix him up with Edie's cousin Mary and a couple of the girls Edie went to school with, including the Adams girl who was in the wedding, but it didn't work. We were really counting on Mary. She's always been a great reader, so they should have hit it off. He took her out once or twice after we placed them next to each other at dinner, but that was all. Edie suspects he came on too strong too soon. I don't believe he even called those other girls.

I asked how Henry got along at the office, and why, in a firm as large as Wiggins & O'Reilly, there wasn't some sort of social life for him to plunge into.

One thing you don't need to worry about is how Henry's doing at the firm, George answered very seriously. Mr. Allen uses him all the time. That alone means a lot because he is a real taskmaster. And he's very powerful. Henry does work for Jim Hershey too. That is, when Hershey happens to be around. He travels all the time for his international clients. People say that in his wily way Hershey keeps an eye on Henry, and he's very powerful too. But this is all outside of my little department so I'm only repeating what I've heard.

George was in trusts and estates, while Henry did fancy corporate work. The two worlds hardly met. Nonetheless, I renewed my question: Even if all this is true, why should Henry be lonely after work?

That's a different question, George said. We don't have much organized social life at Wiggins, no monthly cocktail parties the way they do it at other firms. All we have is one dinner for all lawyers in the winter and one in June. People organize their own lives. Partners hardly ever invite associates. I'm sure that the Allens have him to dinner when they need an extra man, he's practically Mr. Allen's slave. Perhaps Hershey takes him to dinner at his club. Mrs. Hershey had polio after they were married, and she's in a wheelchair. I don't think they ever entertain at home. As for associates, I don't know that he's all that close to anyone. Maybe that's because he's just too busy or maybe the other two guys we hired from his law school class, Forrester and Lovett, and he have never been especially friendly. To be honest, I never knew who his friends were. I only happen to know those two fellows because we were at school together.

As I pondered this, I recalled George's attempt to get Henry into his law school eating club, an embarrassing initiative for George that miscarried.

What happens usually at the firm, George explained, is that unmarried associates from the same class, or in the same small group like trusts and estates, hang out together, have parties at their apartments, and so on. Some are good cooks. They have roommates, which makes entertaining easier. I don't know why Henry doesn't at least have a roommate. His apartment's all right. He had us to drinks soon after he moved in, with Margot of all people. That could have been hairy, but I think she and I both handled it well. I'm probably talking through my hat, but I've heard it said that Henry was brought in because Jim Hershey went to the hiring partner and said hire him. Why he'd do that, I don't know, but the rumor doesn't do Henry any good. The fact is that I don't even remember his being interviewed. I know Edie asked her old man to arrange it, but he said he'd tried and found out there was nothing he could do. If Henry had been interviewed, the guy in charge of his schedule would ask whether he had friends among associates at the firm and take him around to visit them. Wouldn't I have been one of them? So there might be something to the theory that he came in over the transom. That's in addition to what you and I know, which is that even with all his brains and energy and law review he isn't exactly the sort of fellow you think of as Wiggins & O'Reilly material.

I knew that. I also knew—and perhaps George as well—the larger history of Henry's job search, which was hardly typical of someone who graduated close to the top of his law school class. The summer between his first and second years was spent winding up his father's affairs, as he had predicted the evening we went to Margot's apartment. Any free time he had he spent with Margot. But it was the following summer that was crucial. Henry applied to five or six of the leading New York firms, basing his views of excellence on scuttlebutt and comments posted at the law review. That meant that he was going against the opinion shared by every Jew he knew at the law school, including his classmates on the review, that these were the firms that didn't take Jews except in the rarest cases, usually involving sons of the highest German Jewish bourgeoisie. But even these special Jews, once hired, were denied partnership, with one known exception. That was the case of Augustus Stern, an Albright & Kinsolving partner, brilliant and universally known as the least Jewish of Jews, who was the cousin by marriage of the family that owned the grandest of the Jewish investment banks and grew up, as Mr. Bowditch liked to put it, to be the master of hounds at one of the South Jersey hunts. Henry insisted that with a part of his brain he knew that all this was true. But something in him rebelled against worldly wisdom: This is a free country, he said to himself, I won't be like those fatalistic American primitives in basic training at Fort Dix with their motto: "Fuck me, I'll never smile again." You, George, Archie, and Margot, you've all sold me on the American dream, he told me at Henri IV, where I had taken him to lunch in the fall of his third year at the law school. I was in Cambridge, visiting Tom Peabody.

I remarked that I wouldn't have expected to find Margot on that list.

What do you mean, he answered, she let me through the door I most wanted to enter!

I asked him to go on with his saga.

Oddly enough, he said, of the five firms that had interviewed him in New York only one wanted to hire him, the one he liked least, full of Irishmen dressed up like lawyers, probably all firemen or policemen in real life. They must have made a mistake; mixed him up with O'Boyle or Sweeney. Anyway, he'd be damned if he was going to accept their offer. Not when there were Jewish firms in New York full of partners and associates with better academic records than anyone in the firms he had set his heart on, any one of which would be thrilled to have him. But the heart has its reasons: he thought that if he took that route he would be diminished in our eyes. What would I, Archie, George, or Margot think if he, a free spirit, with zero interest in being Jewish, bowed his head and moved into the ghetto? Mr. Hornung came to the rescue and rendered the question moot by inviting him to spend the summer at the bank as his assistant. He even made a trip to Boston to put this proposition to me personally, Henry said, although his bank doesn't recruit lawyers and he certainly doesn't travel to recruit a glorified office boy. Just picking up the telephone would have sealed the deal.

Both the proposal and Mr. Hornung's interest in his career surprised Henry; a third surprise was that he hadn't heard a word about it from Margot. She had enrolled at the École du Louvre and was living in Paris, and her father hadn't told her. When Henry got over the shock, he concluded he must have found favor with this powerful rich man who had so terrified him and almost certainly did not know anything of the nature of his relations with Margot. Grasping at the golden straw, he took the job. At the end of the summer came another surprise: Mr. Hornung took him to lunch at La Côte Basque and advised him to get his law degree, take a long vacation, and then return to the bank. He assured Henry that he had a far better head for business than he might think and would be making the mistake of his life if he didn't put it to work. Henry thanked him with all the warmth he dared show. Then he explained that, contrary to his expectations, it had turned out that he liked the law and was able to do well at law school. He was determined to give practice a try. Mr. Hornung nodded and said he was disappointed. Margot would probably be disappointed as well—it was the first time he had mentioned her to Henry. But in his own case, disappointed or not, he wouldn't be discouraged; the offer would remain open. Unless, he added, he sold the bank. Henry permitted himself to ask what would happen to his prospects in such an event. Mr. Hornung chuckled and said that solutions might be found.

I too found this denouement startling. What will you do now? I asked, remembering from George's case that there soon would be another round of recruiting for permanent positions in law firms.

Actually, I have my eye on two Supreme Court clerkships, he said, with Frankfurter or Harlan. The trouble is that they don't take clerks straight out of law school. You have to clerk on a court of appeals first, and very few court of appeals judges interest me. Really there is only one, Henry Friendly in New York. If that doesn't work out, I guess I'll apply to the same five law firms. Just to see whether the Irish still want me.

Our lunch had taken more time than I had expected. I was to have dinner with Tom Peabody, which meant dinner on the early side, and hoped to get some work done in the remaining hours of the afternoon. I called for the check, and while we waited for it Henry asked whether I would be in New York at Christmastime. I told him that probably I would be away, skiing, but whether or not I was there he was welcome to use my apartment. That was what he had hoped to hear. The house on Dorchester Road had been sold—not that he would have wanted to stay there anyway—and Margot had given up her apartment.

As it happened, I postponed my ski vacation in order to accompany my mother and Greg Richardson to the Pittsfield Town Hall for the civil marriage ceremony that took place, inconveniently, two days after Christmas. Spending Christmas Eve and Christmas Day with them was more than I thought my nerves would bear. The Standishes took me in, and, as soon as I had given my mother away and sat through a lunch at the club—Greg being now a full member—at which there were also no fewer than three Riggs patients, their clinical status as uncertain as Greg's, I left for New York and the quiet of my apartment. Feeling quite distraught, I was afraid that I would not be glad to see Henry. I was wrong. He understood what I meant when I told him that I wasn't at the top of my form and stayed clear during the day.

His near-term future seemed decided, he told me at dinner my first night back: he would take that vacation Mr. Hornung had suggested, perhaps with Margot, if her own situation became less puzzling. Then he'd go to work as an associate at George's firm, Wiggins & O'Reilly.

I said that congratulations were clearly in order. It was a surprise to everyone, he told me, especially George. Archie—he had then four years to live—had been very funny about it. What next? he said. Jews in the DAR? George told me in confidence, Henry continued, that knowing how anxious I had been about the job situation, Edie had asked her father to approach Nick Allen, who pretty much runs Wiggins, but her father said that could only backfire, because they've made a shibboleth of not letting even the biggest clients interfere with hiring and partnership decisions. Edie thought that her father had been absolutely straight with her and would have made the call if he had thought it could help. According to her, he remembered me from the wedding and had said nothing that indicated that he knew that I'm a Jew. So that couldn't have been the reason.

And Margot, I asked, what does she think?

That's really quite unexpected. She told me in November that I was a fool not to go to one of the Jewish firms, where they would welcome me with open arms and I would have a normal life. I said I wouldn't. So of course I called her as soon as I heard from Wiggins & O'Reilly.

What an unusual girl, I said.

She is strange, he agreed, and very intelligent. But there I think she was wrong.

He was more confused about her than ever and no less convinced that they were destined to be together. At the same time, although he understood her insistence on sexual freedom, he couldn't imagine accepting it if they were to marry, not that he thought she would marry him. Or the strange game she was playing with him. For instance, in November, when he came to New York to see her, he got a room at the Waldorf so that they could be together.

The Waldorf? I interrupted again.

I see that you remember Madeleine's visit, he replied, I do too. I didn't decide to go there on account of that memory. It was just that I thought that if Madeleine picked that hotel it had to be all right. I know nothing about New York hotels.

Am I to think that you and Margot do it now? I asked.

He shook his head and said, No, not exactly. In November, she would get in bed with me. It was all right if I was naked, and all that I wanted to do was all right except the thing itself. She said it was again a matter of purity and coherence. I grew faint when I heard this and asked whether Etienne had come back. That wasn't it, she told me, although she had dinner with him occasionally in Paris. He's more or less getting married to a French heiress. No, now it's someone else she's met in Europe. An American lawyer. Apparently he's in Europe all the time and tells fascinating stories about his cases. I wonder whether he is a spy.

So that's how she has become so knowledgeable about lawyers, I said. And how about the clerkships?

He let my crack go and replied that he would go to Wiggins only if the clerkship with Judge Friendly didn't come through. He wouldn't know that until the spring. If he had to bet, he added, he would give odds against himself. He was silent for a moment and then said, You know, I am beginning to have second thoughts about the Jews. Perhaps I should call one of those firms and say here I am, will you take me, and, if they say yes, let Wiggins know what they can do with their racial purity. Don't you think I'm nuts—worse, plain wrong—to go where I'm not wanted?

I pointed out the fallacy: if they hadn't wanted him at Wiggins, he wouldn't have been asked to work there.

He nodded and said that was logical.

Tom Peabody arrived the next day. He was spending the reading period at my place, justifying his absence from Cambridge to me and perhaps his conscience by the availability at the Forty-second Street Library of manuscripts he wanted to consult. Henry cut short his stay. He had remained on good terms with Tom, but I suppose he thought three might be a crowd.

XXVI

SLEEPLESSNESS, fatigue, and heartbreaking sadness—a state of being all too familiar—once more descended on me like a lead cloak as we won and lost in the valley of Ia Drang and our B-52s went into action to support the First Cavalry on the ground. I did not attempt to flatter myself by thinking that my sickness and those events were connected; I did not yet understand that the country was lurching into madness. Dr. Kalman changed my sleeping pill prescription and suggested adding one of the new antidepressants for which claims were made, paradoxically in my opinion, that it also helped with sleep and anxiety. I refused to take it on the grounds that my work depended on my being myself, such as I was with all my sorrows, not only when I sat down at my desk but also when I puttered about without any apparent purpose. Dr. Kalman raised his eyebrows and said it seemed to him that my first objective should be to feel better. I suggested that he didn't know what he was talking about. On that footing, we continued our explorations. They did no good. Kalman and I were stuck, unable to progress or find an exit.

Meanwhile, my career was perking along. My third novel, which, unlike the second, I wrote in a sustained élan of creativity, was published. The publishing house called me on the promise I had made to be available for a book tour and interviews. The general view in the house was that the sales of my second novel would have been less anemic if I had been willing to cooperate. Kalman once again proposed the antidepressant. This time I listened to him and muddled through readings and book signings in an interminable series of cities I hoped never to revisit. When I returned to New York, however, the sessions with Dr. Kalman seemed no better than before. I screwed up my courage and asked whether he could recommend someone in Paris, if I went to live there. Not permanently; I had no intention of becoming an expatriate.

Aha, he replied, you find that we've gone cold. You may be right. I can think of one or two people in Paris, but I would prefer to speak to Jake Reiner first.

Shaken suddenly by the enormity of what I had done, I tried to assure him of my affection and respect, but all I could get out of him was a vague nod. Manifestly, he thought I was a parricide. Nevertheless, a few sessions later he told me that Dr. Reiner and he agreed that if I did move to Paris I could call Madame Bernard. He had already taken the liberty of speaking to her over the telephone, and it appeared that she had a place for me in her schedule. I asked whether she was a medical doctor.

Oh no, he replied, that's hardly necessary. She's a Freudian analyst, and a member of the Paris psychoanalytical society.

I told him I sensed that he was throwing me into the arms of Lacan. No no, he said, nothing like that. Anyway, you're not committed to her. There are other possibilities.

Thus began the season of my daily treks to the rue de la Faisanderie, so inconvenient to reach by public transportation from rue de Tournon— where I had taken an apartment with a view of a large garden behind the building—that I bought a Peugeot 404 principally to go back and forth between the Sixth and the Sixteenth Arrondissements.

Fortunately, I had a parking space in the rue de Tournon courtyard. The money spent on the car—indeed, the whole cost of my Parisian installation—did not seem unreasonable given my earnings. Also, Mr. Hibble, preparing to retire and hand over his duties as trustee to a trust company in Boston, had submitted to me the accounts of my trust. My respect for the old geezer shot up into outer space. He had invested heavily in IBM almost from the start, when I was still at school, taking a big risk, he told me, considering the rule that trust assets should be diversified. Unable to restrain my curiosity, I asked whether this was his own personal strategy or one that Jack Standish had also followed. For the first time in our acquaintance, he smiled, then put his finger to his lips and whispered, Shhh.

The habit of August vacations, so peculiar to American analysts, was also the norm in France, but it applied to the entire population. Not only Madame Bernard, but seemingly all of Paris was on the road. Wondering whether members of the psychoanalytical society had a particular roosting place of their own, I asked where she planned to spend the month. Unlike Dr. Reiner, she eschewed cutting rejoinders. She simply left my question unanswered. In fact, I was going away as well. When Tom Peabody wrote that he was coming to Europe without fixed plans other than to be at the Bodleian in the first three weeks of July, I proposed that when he finished we drive from Paris to Montreux and spend August at the hotel overlooking the lake. I wouldn't be the first novelist to have tried working there.

Before our departure, I received a telephone call from Margot. Henry had told her that I was in Paris. For a moment I considered proposing a dinner at my apartment, but that would have been the first meal I had served to a guest, and I wasn't sure that my very nice *femme de ménage* was up to preparing a summer meal of which Margot would approve. I invited her instead to a restaurant in the rue Marbeuf, around the corner from her parents' pied-à-terre, where she was staying. I hadn't seen her since the late evening when Henry took me to her apartment for a drink. She had changed some more; the quintessential Radcliffe girl had turned into a woman. I asked whether she was in Paris on a visit, Henry having told me about her attending the Courtauld or perhaps working in London. She said it was up in the air where she would live; it depended on news she was about to tell me—if I promised to remember that nothing is settled, nothing is guaranteed to happen. Then she said: I may be getting married!

I offered the customary congratulations, even while imagining how hard a blow this must have been for Henry.

She told me rapidly her intended was a Frenchman living in Paris, so that London might be out of the question. He was Jean du Roc, a novelist some fifteen years older than she.

To her visible relief, I assured her that I knew his name and reputation, that we had the same publisher, and that I had read one of his novels—probably the second one—with great interest.

I'm so glad, she exclaimed. Did you like it?

Very entertaining, I told her. In truth, I recalled being surprised that this tale of a young man infatuated with a married countess and fast automobiles, which could have been a joint venture between Louise de Vilmorin and Françoise Sagan, had been written by a man.

Margot went on to tell me that du Roc's real name was Lebon, that his parents lived in Chatellerault, where his father owned a pharmacy, that Jean began by studying political science and then, out of boredom, decided to try journalism and happened to write a novel. Of all people, she said, you understand how such things happen.

I nodded and asked about the wedding plans.

There's a complication, she said. Jean is married, and we're waiting for the divorce to come through. The wife is dragging her feet. It's malice or refusal to face facts or both. By the way, my parents don't know anything about Jean; they haven't even met him. The age difference will be a problem and, of course, money. He doesn't have a cent. The wife he is divorcing is his second. He'll have to pay her something, and he's already paying some sort of alimony and child support to the first. I guess Mommy will like him because he's so polite. They'll be in Cap Ferrat in August. That's when I'll spring him on them.

And Henry?

I told him last week.

That must have been tough to tell and tough to hear.

Her eyes filled with tears. Then she collected herself and said it hadn't gone so badly. Henry had made a real effort to be nice.

Utter callousness on my part? Inveterate meddling? As though there would never be a better moment, I asked point-blank why she was marrying Jean du Roc instead of Henry White, who'd been in love with her for seventeen years, was single, and had never married. I thought it was the strangest story.

It is, she said, but do you realize that he has never asked me?

I told her that, in fact, I hadn't known, but she and I both knew it was a technicality. If he hadn't asked it was for only one reason: he was sure she'd say no, and he didn't want to lose what little he had.

She lowered her eyes and whispered that even her father wanted her to marry Henry. He had offered to propose to him on her behalf.

I said I was renewing my question.

It's very personal, she answered. You know that I sleep with him.

I nodded.

From time to time, she corrected herself. I'm never sure that it will happen. And you know that I've had others, and that he's had others too.

I told her I knew he loved her and that their relationship took various forms. I knew nothing beyond that.

She reached out to pat my hand and said, You're talking nonsense. I know that he gives you at least the highlights of everything. You know it's tawdry on both sides. It doesn't matter anymore: Jean makes me do what he wants. Henry doesn't and never will. He got down on his hands and knees before me right at the beginning, and he has never known how to get up. Etienne—remember him?—knew how to make me get down on my hands and knees and crawl. I made a terrible mistake letting him go.

What's become of him? I asked.

Just what you'd expect. Since his father's retirement, he's been running the family businesses, he has married a blond Frenchwoman from the best French society, and any day now the king will make him a baron in his own right, so he won't have to wait for his old man to die. Oh, and he has three children, little boys, she added. Probably they're all blond and beautiful too. Then there was a lawyer: yes, another lawyer. I've been with him for years, literally for years, if you can be with someone whom you see so little. Someone who shows up without warning and leaves a message: Come to the hotel. As if I were a call girl. It doesn't matter. He's married and works so hard and travels so much that even when he's supposed to be in Europe it's as if he weren't here. He'll never leave his wife. I've even begun to think that he's tired of being unfaithful to her.

I remained silent while she carefully finished her grilled sole.

Apropos of lawyers, why haven't you asked me about Henry?

Haven't we been talking about him? I protested.

I don't mean Henry and me, she said, I meant how he is doing in his career, at the firm, all those things. You know, the way law firms deal with associates the coming year will be the fatal moment for Henry. Either he'll be made partner or he's out in the street. Of course he will get another job—there's always my father. As soon as she said that she giggled.

I said that didn't sound right. George had gone to Wiggins two years earlier than Henry and was still an associate and seemed very calm about it.

That's different, she told me. Lawyers who do estates are made partners more slowly—because they don't work as hard and don't bring in as much money.

I protested again. George worked very long hours.

That's not how they see it, she said. George will have to wait until Henry's law school class is up, perhaps longer. Of course he isn't worried. They love him at Wiggins, and they certainly won't do anything to tick off Mr. Bowditch.

And Henry? I asked.

You really haven't kept up with him, have you? They've asked him to come to their Paris office because they really need someone here who can do very big international deals with tax complications. Right now, no firm has anyone like that in Paris. Henry could give Wiggins a real competitive advantage—if it all works out. But he's very worried, because being sent to a foreign office as senior associate can be the kiss of death: out of sight, out of mind. You'll be passed over when your group is considered. At the same time, he realizes that they may be saying to him in their wonderfully subtle way, Go to Paris, Henry, or you won't be a partner.

That's rough, I said. You certainly know a lot about law firms. That thought had occurred to me, I remembered, the last time we had met.

One picks up these things here and there.

Won't Monsieur du Roc make coming to Paris that much harder for Henry? I asked.

She admitted that was true, but not becoming a partner might be harder.

But what if he comes here and doesn't make it? Isn't that the worst case? Isn't there some senior person at the firm he can ask for advice? I seem to remember that there was an important partner for whom he did international deals. What does he say?

Jim, she said, you mean Jim Hershey.

She blushed and I quickly averted my eyes.

This time I told her the truth: I couldn't remember the name.

He did speak to Hershey, she said. He told him to trust the firm.

What about you, Margot, won't this be hard on you? I asked.

I don't know, she said very slowly. It depends on Henry, on what he is willing to accept.

XXVII

Madame Bernard and her illustrious teacher, Dr. Otto Abend, believed in imposing a time limit on analysis; she announced early on that we would finish within eighteen months. Having spent many inconclusive, though I sometimes thought indispensable, years with Drs. Reiner and Kalman, I took this at first to be another example of the appalling psychoanalyst sense of humor, an unpleasant joke intended to jolt the patient into heightened self-awareness and fuller cooperation. It turned out that she was dead serious. Shortly before we reached the deadline she had set, she announced that we had gone as far as she considered appropriate. The analyses of her other patients were ending as well. She had accepted a teaching position at the University of Geneva and was moving there.

You are leaving me in the lurch, I told her. You knew about this university appointment when you took me and decided on the length of my treatment to fit your personal plans. I think that you've behaved unprofessionally.

I should have known by then that I wasn't capable of ruffling even one of her blond feathers.

You have it wrong, she said. I assessed your case and came to the conclusion that you could be treated within the available time. Otherwise, I wouldn't have accepted you.

Before I was thus cast adrift, with only an untested lifeline to Madame Bernard's own training analyst, a man with a white goatee who received patients at his apartment near the metro station Gobelins, a destination marginally easier for me to reach than rue de la Faisanderie, I attended Margot's wedding, which had been postponed for a month by reason of

the events of May 1968. The first part, the civil marriage, took place at
the *mairie* of the Eighth Arrondissement, within the jurisdiction of
which lay the Hornungs' pied-à-terre. Du Roc apparently could claim no
domicile. Ever since leaving his wife he had been squatting in apartments
lent to him by friends going on vacation and in temporarily vacant maids'
rooms. I suspected that his sleek Lancia, the backseat of which was clut-
tered with disparate objects one would have hardly looked for in a car, had
also been his occasional shelter. There was no church ceremony. Later in
the day, however, the Hornungs gave a reception at the Ritz, where they
were staying. They had abandoned their apartment to Margot until such
time as she and Jean moved into a place of their own. That won't be anytime soon, Mr. Hornung told me. Monsieur Jean has strong opinions
about how things should be. He missed his true calling. He should have
been a contractor. No matter what kind of place they decide I should buy
for them he will want to tear out every wall and move every piece of
plumbing. It will take years; I guarantee it.

Mr. Hornung may not have taken his son-in-law into his heart. However, the reception made me think of the peaceable kingdom, the lamb
lying down with the wolf, the leopard with the kid, and the child leading
forth the young lion and the fatling. As there was no custom dictating
that witnesses for the bride in the civil marriage must be women, Margot
had asked Henry and me to fill the role. I was perhaps the more startling
choice, and I wondered whether I owed my place to the connection with
Henry—with Archie dead, I was surely his closest friend—or to my
renown as a novelist, thus a counterweight to du Roc and the two sexage-
narian academicians, of the French and Goncourt Academies respectively,
who stood up for him. I suggested Etienne for my place or added as the
third witness. She gave me a glacial stare, leading me to think that perhaps she had considered such a move and decided against it, fearing that
Henry, whose sense of humor was unreliable, would take it hard. Etienne,
however, was present at the *mairie* and at the Ritz, with his glamorous
wife and his mother, to both of whom he introduced me. I supposed that
I would be able to identify Jean's pharmacist father, Monsieur Lebon, and
his mother, if not at the *mairie,* then in the cream-and-gold salons of the
Ritz, but there was no one there who fit the description I had invented.

Taking advantage of a brief conversation with my publisher, who was there with the editor who looked after du Roc's books, I asked whether he could introduce me. His parents aren't here, he told me. They're *insortables*. Jean doesn't show them off. He just puts them in his novels.

We had a late dinner afterward, Henry and I, at a brasserie in the Halles. How bizarre, he said. Why didn't that idiot girl want me? Tell me why she took him and not me.

She's peculiar, I replied.

And tell me why he hasn't knocked her up yet, to get a chokehold on the money. I've made inquiries about him. He has one kid from his first marriage and two from the second, so we know that he can do it. It's non-sense that he hasn't any money because he spends it on them. He doesn't contribute a cent, never mind paying any attention to them, so having a fourth kid with Margot would hardly cramp his style. What's going on? Don't tell me it's a matter of principle, the struggle against overpopulation.

The Pill, I told him. Not available to the previous Mesdames du Roc, so they took their chances and got unlucky.

He didn't laugh. I'd gotten used to his not laughing at much of any-thing. He had come to Paris because the graybeards at Wiggins & O'Reilly in the end made their wishes sufficiently clear, and at every moment he knew that the clock in the mahogany-paneled office down on Wall Street was ticking. So many months, days, and hours until the dreaded date, when the decision about him and some other poor bastards—George Standish probably included—would be made. No doubt there was a clock in the place de la Concorde office as well, and local bosses watching it too. How much of my suspicion about Jim Hershey was right? If I was right, how much had Henry figured out? These were imponderables. Certainly, I couldn't ask him. But when he said that Hershey had told him to trust the firm he obviously took it as important advice that he should follow. How clear an idea he had of his own worth to the firm was uncertain as well; he could swing wildly between pride verging on conceit and excessive self-deprecation. George had told me often enough that partners at Wig-gins who really counted thought Henry walked on water, and I supposed he would have also said it to Henry. But Henry had seen other prizes snatched from him, and the prospect of being beached in Paris, while nearby the one prize he wanted above all others was possessed and enjoyed by another, was insufferable and terrifying.

I had told him my analyst's plan to move to Geneva by the summer, and that, consequently, I would have less reason to remain in Paris, though I didn't know what I would do next if indeed I left. Tom Peabody was urging me to consider Rome. As Henry and I talked, I was forced to realize the extent to which he had counted on my continued presence in Paris, imagining a resumption of our old intimacy, with daily unscheduled contacts built into it subject only to unavoidable obstacles. Now that had proved to be a mirage. He did not attempt to conceal his disappointment. There wasn't much I could do to buck him up beyond saying once again that I had not yet made a decision to leave and certainly would return to celebrate when his partnership was announced.

Oh that, he said, it's a crapshoot with loaded dice. I'd rather not think about it, but I do.

It was very late, even for this restaurant that claimed to remain open until four in the morning. I paid the check. The radio taxi arrived. I told the driver to go first to Trinité, where Henry was living in an apartment he had not wanted to show me, claiming that the owner had furnished it to look like a concierge's loge, down to a large radio covered with a lace doily that was the chief ornament of the living room. If I stay in Paris, he said, I will stop living like a clerk, but so long as I am a clerk and I'm paid like a clerk, I don't see why I should put on airs. This was a new development in Henry's outlook. Perhaps it betokened a decision to devote less time and energy to trying to be first in everything—without regard to whether he needed to win.

MADAME BERNARD left for Geneva. The bouquet of flaming-red roses I had brought to our last session had probably been deposited in a trash can or given to her concierge. She had seemed pleased to receive them, thanked me without sticking in the interpretative knife, and asked whether I ever went to Geneva. If you do come, she continued, my husband and I would be pleased to have you at our home for dinner. She gave me her card. I thanked her in turn and, emboldened by her initiative, asked whether her husband would also be teaching at the university. Oh no, she said, he is a poet—rather well known but his name is not the same as mine.

An onset of shyness prevented me from asking his name, and some similar emotion probably impelled Madame Bernard to explain that in Geneva she intended to do only training analyses. She wouldn't treat patients. I sensed that the existence of the line separating the analyst and patient had been drawn anew, and that if I made my visit I wouldn't be crossing it.

My curiosity had been aroused, and I might have found a reason to pass through Geneva in the fall, if a letter from my mother had not caused me to go instead to Lenox. She wrote that she and Greg had grown tired both of Berkshire winters—the ski slopes were more and more crowded, and neither of them cared for skiing all that much—and Berkshire summers with their hordes of Tanglewood tourists. That left the spring mud, about which the less said the better, and the fall, which was glorious if you could disregard the busloads of old ladies in search of foliage and maple syrup, but that was impossible. She was also tired of the cattiness of her friends. They had decided to move to Hawaii—not Oahu, which Greg found too commercial and too American, but to Maui, which was as Hawaii used to be. I would no doubt see that keeping the house in Lenox, a big financial drain despite its excellent condition, didn't make sense for her and Greg. She thought that I should buy it. The house had been in the family since it was built—while Cousin Jack's house in Stockbridge had only been given to him and May as a wedding present from May's father. I wouldn't regret it, she assured me. Values in the Berkshires were rising; a historic house owned by a famous writer would command a premium.

I answered that I would think about her proposal, and if it seemed that I could go along with it I would come to the Berkshires in early October. I'd stay with George and Edie, in the stable that the Standish parents had turned into an independent cottage for them to use. Then I telephoned Mr. Hibble, to sound him out about the transaction. It was a steal, he told me, with or without the family furniture, but he couldn't understand why my mother wouldn't just give the house to me. With the pension the bank paid her, plus the Richardson money, she shouldn't need the cash. Of course the cash by all rights should go to you anyway on her death.

But can I afford it? I asked. Yes, he said, even if you never earn another dollar. Besides, she's right about Berkshire real estate; there are few better bets.

Dealing with my mother had always been pleasant if she was getting her way in every detail. I went over to the house the day after I arrived at George's and found out that she meant to let me have all the pieces that had come from the Standish side except a desk I considered too small to be useful. In that case, I said, it's a deal, subject only to inspection for termites. I can assure you that we have no termites, she informed me haughtily. I replied that I was sure she was right, but I wanted to check anyway. Someone in Mr. Hibble's office would have my power of attorney so that the closing could go ahead after I had returned to Europe. It's all right, honey, Greg said, it's what's always done. All right, she replied, I'll go along, but I think my own son ought to be able to trust me.

I RETURNED TO PARIS at the end of November, having shown my editor an early draft of a long study of Hawthorne. He encouraged me to work on it, but suggested some changes in approach. Thinking them through and revising the manuscript accordingly would be time-consuming. In early December, Wiggins & O'Reilly announced its decisions. Henry and George had both become partners. When Henry called with the news, I invited him to dinner at Maxim's that night. To my surprise, he arrived with Margot.

Jean is in Marseille, she told me, at a book signing. Isn't it nice, having just the three of us?

She and Henry seemed to be on the floor each time the band played a fox-trot, and I couldn't help noticing the way she clung to him. By midnight we'd become very sentimental. Henry said he wished we could call Archie. Instead we went down to the telephone cabin and placed a call to George. He was at a meeting from which he was going directly to the theater to meet Edie. We gave up. Since I had not brought my car and Margot had hers, they drove me home.

Henry also invited Margot, this time with Jean, to the ponderous official celebration of his partnership. It too was held at Maxim's. The Wiggins resident senior partner, Derek de Rham, a spidery man, all thin arms and thin legs, in an ancient dinner jacket that miraculously fit his strange frame, had taken over the narrow section of the restaurant known, because of its shape, as the omnibus, the only place where an habitué would agree to be seated at lunch, but less desirable in the evening because of the distance from the dancing. To be away from the band, however, made it particularly suitable for toasts, of which there would be a considerable number. George and Edie had come from New York, he in his double capacity of Henry's best friend at the firm and representative of the class of new partners, as had old Mr. Allen, Henry's mentor and the strong man of Wiggins & O'Reilly, as well as a couple of other partners and their wives and a platoon of clients. De Rham's little brother and one of his cousins had been at school with me. After I mentioned that to him, and Edie had explained who I was, he found it was worth his while to speak to me. In fact he beckoned to his wife, a stern bony woman, to join us. I asked how Henry had adapted to practice in the French outpost of the firm.

Adapted? exclaimed de Rham. He's taken over. If we didn't want as a matter of policy to have a couple of seniors here to keep an eye on the kiddies, both Warner—he indicated a solidly built man patiently listening to Mrs. Allen—and I could pack up and go home. He has excellent relations with all the *avocats* and *notaires* we deal with and has already reeled in some big fishes. Do you see this man over there—I don't want to point—the one talking with Henry and the young woman who's married to a Frenchman?

I nodded.

That's one of them. A Belgian, Count de Sainte-Terre. Immensely rich and in control of a very aggressive holding company making strategic investments one after another. He's fallen in love with Henry, or rather the structures Henry's been inventing for him. A man worth meeting.

XXVIII

THE NEXT DAY Edie went shopping with Margot, Henry was at his office, and I had lunch with George. He showed me new photos of the children and gave me one of my goddaughter, dressed as a Halloween witch, in a Tiffany silver frame engraved with my initials. It was my Christmas present. At some point, I asked about Henry's new Belgian client.

You mean Goldfinger? George asked. Henry says that's what they call him behind his back. He knows about it, of course, but doesn't seem to mind.

I told him I meant the very muscular blond man with ears that stuck out to whom de Rham had referred as the count of something or other.

Right, he said, Hubert de Sainte-Terre. Did you see his wife? She was there too, looking like the lady leading the unicorn. Hubert's supposed to be the richest man in Belgium, one of the most powerful too. Henry has him eating out of his hand. Last July he got him to ask our group to do his estate plan. The partners in the group now think he can do no wrong. Just to prove my point, I'll tell you what Billy Rhinelander told me. He was taken in two years ago so he participated in this election. Anyway, Billy said that this time there was only one partner who got one hundred percent of the vote. Guess who!

You, I said.

No, Billy specifically told me it was Henry, though to be honest I have to tell you I can't believe that anyone voted against me. Or maybe I can—one of those self-appointed censors who are always inveighing against nepotism.

I raised my eyebrows and asked since when did he have uncles or even cousins among the partners.

Of course I don't. I couldn't have gotten in the door, they're so strict about it. But I am Hugh Bowditch's son-in-law. That's not nothing, but believe me it's a double-edged sword. Sure, all the partners know that as a practical matter they can't turn down a guy whose father-in-law controls thirty percent of the firm's business unless they have a damn good reason. I'd have to be a real bonehead or really lazy or screw up in a major way. On the other hand, a case like mine sets off all kinds of alarm bells, because Hugh has so much influence. They start to worry about the firm's depending too much on a single client, the other associates' perception of unfairness, and on and on. Thank God, nobody can say that I don't do a good job or don't pull my weight. My hours are way up there, on a par with the corporate guys.

Henry managed to find time to have dinner with me before I left for Malta, where Tom and I were going to spend the Christmas and New Year's holidays together. Afterward, he would return to Cambridge. If the island turned out to be as attractive as I had heard, and the climate as mild, I thought I'd stay on, perhaps until summer, if it took that long to finish my book.

Henry had told me to pick him up, and I found him waiting in what would soon be his old office, a nice room with a window on rue Royale. He showed me the one he was moving into as soon as the paper hangers had finished with the wallpaper, which wasn't paper but silk, and the cabinetmaker had installed the mahogany bookshelves. The new office had two windows overlooking place de la Concorde, was almost as large as old de Rham's corner office and equal in size to that of the other corporate law partner, Dick Garland, who on the night of the party at Maxim's was in Amsterdam at the closing of a bond issue. Henry introduced me to this sturdy-looking fellow, perhaps ten years our senior. After I'd shaken his hand I looked at Henry and then again at Garland and suppressed the urge to crack up. On the surface, Henry had come to resemble him and George and, I was certain, all the other bright Wiggins partners more or less his age. How deep did the likeness go? I supposed that among these future grandees of New York, he still saw himself as a Moses—a Moses who had slain no Egyptian for smiting a Hebrew and wasn't likely to and would neither lead his kinsmen into the wilderness to feast unto the Lord nor go forth into it himself.

This time Henry was the host. He took me to one of his favorite flesh-pots in Paris and as soon as we had ordered told me about his holiday plans. He was in high spirits. The de Rhams had an annual Christmas Eve party for lawyers and staff. In the new circumstances, he thought it was his duty to attend and would be glad to do so. They were all nice people. On Christmas Day he was invited to dinner at the Garlands. Two days later he would be picked up at Le Bourget by Hubert de Sainte-Terre's private plane and taken to St. Moritz for a week of skiing with him and Gilberte—Gilberte, he explained, was Hubert's wife. He'd stay at their chalet. They would all come back together around January 5. There was an argument for treating most of this time as client development; otherwise it would be charged as vacation days. He wasn't sure which he'd do; he didn't really care.

Since when do you ski? I asked.

I don't, he said. Hubert has told me I must learn, so that I can go with them on their vacations. They're both passionate about it. He says the teacher he has on retainer in St. Moritz could turn an elephant into an Olympic skier.

In that case, I told him, perhaps you do have a chance. Babar was pretty regal on skis, so why not you?

Why indeed, he replied, though it does seem to me that Babar started younger.

I didn't remember whether this was so, and I didn't ask where he had come across Babar, my own acquaintance with him being from books I had bought in Paris for the Standish twins. Instead, I asked by what magic he had conjured up such an important client and become so close to him and his wife.

No magic at all, said Henry, blushing. Pure luck. You remember the van Dammes?

How could I forget Madeleine? I asked. Besides, don't you remember that she and Etienne were at Margot's wedding?

Of course, he said, that's all ancient history. It slipped my mind. Actually, Etienne and I have been seeing each other in New York, pretty much every time he has come through. He'd ask me to dinner to get some free legal advice.

It occurred to me that this would be news to Margot.

The Sainte-Terres, he continued, have been family friends of the van Dammes for generations. Hubert is only a few years older than Etienne, and they are very close. In fact, Madeleine is a cousin of Hubert's mother-in-law, whose husband—the father-in-law—is a member of the French family at the head of which stands Duc de Grandlieu. Gilberte's being a Grandlieu is a source of considerable satisfaction for Hubert. Anyway, unlike Etienne, who is a very good businessman but not very ambitious, Hubert is a bird of prey, what the French call *un rapace*. About ten years ago he inherited from his father a profitable but relatively small Belgian bank—Banque de Sainte-Terre.

Palestine! I interjected.

Shut up, said Henry. As the only child, he inherited all his father's shares and became by far the largest shareholder, with something like sixty-five percent of the capital, the rest being held by some of Belgium's best-known companies. Belgium, in case you don't know, is the land of holding companies. Companies invest in each other's shares and then scratch each other's backs. A few years ago, when Hubert set out on a buying spree of companies, Belgian, French, and Dutch, he was able to get his shareholders to join forces with him. Usually, he and those shareholders as a group take control. In Europe that doesn't necessarily mean buying a majority of the capital. Bearer shares rarely vote, so a much smaller position can give you control, or at least a veto over any important corporate move. Take Banque Industrielle d'Occident. Occident is worth perhaps twice, some people say three times, as much as Hubert's bank, Banque de Sainte-Terre, and has most of its value in businesses outside of France. Banque de Sainte-Terre has control over that bank although it owns only about forty percent of the capital and the vote. It was one hell of an investment. Of course, when I say that Sainte-Terre owns all those shares, I don't mean that it acquired them directly. For tax and bank regulatory reasons, it's often done through intermediate holding companies located in countries with a particularly favorable tax regime. The Netherlands and Luxembourg are used a lot. In some cases Switzerland may be better, but it has lots of problems. Using holding companies, by the way, makes financing this sort of acquisition easier because third parties can be brought in as equity investors all the way up the line, so that you take effective control with minimum capital outlay.

I raised my hand to stop the rush of words while the waiter refilled my wineglass. Henry's enthusiasm for this esoterica took me right back, I thought, to the evening so many years ago when he first spoke to me about *Ubu Roi*. There was something zanily wonderful about it.

Apparently having judged the pause long enough, Henry went on. You can imagine that such operations, especially if they involve more than one country, as Hubert's almost always do, eventually result in complex legal structures and very tricky tax problems. Believe me, even if the basic business is sound, the real profits depend on structure. In order to realize tax savings in each country that's involved, you have to make these transactions sing under company laws and currency control and banking regulations. Otherwise, you've bungled it.

All right, I interrupted, that's very interesting, but how does that put you and Hubert together?

Excuse me, he said. I do get carried away. Who would have thought that this stuff would become my passion? To answer your question, the van Dammes put us together; it's that simple. Hubert and Gilberte were at Bayencourt. Etienne was there as well. They talked about business, and Hubert said that he'd been looking without success for a suitable American lawyer who could act as his general adviser. He wanted someone based in Europe but American trained, with the resources of a first-class American firm behind him, ready to jump in when the right opportunity presents itself and he tries to enter the American market. Etienne mentioned some senior lawyers doing international work in Paris and London. Hubert had already seen them all and was unimpressed. In some cases it was a lack of personal chemistry; in a couple of others he wasn't sure that the particular lawyer would be willing—or even able, given his other commitments—to give him full-time attention. Between him and his bank, he said, he had enough work to keep a partner and a team of associates going full tilt. He had come to think he needed someone younger. As soon as they heard this, Madeleine said that she and Etienne knew the right lawyer for him. Between you and me, Henry said, blushing, I don't know how she could have any idea of my legal skills or talent or why anyone would trust her on that subject. But Etienne, who does know these things, chimed in and said all sorts of extravagantly flattering things about me. I gathered that he had been making inquiries about my reputation for his own purposes. Perhaps he was trying to decide whether one day he would hire me and pay for my time. Anyway, this conversation was in early June. Hubert came to Paris shortly afterward and invited me to his office to discuss a possible project. He grilled me for about two hours about my studies, the work I had been doing at the firm, and how I would solve various hypothetical problems and, believe it or not, about Latin and Greek poets. He's something of a classicist himself. I sensed that the session was coming to an end, when he asked, as if it were an afterthought, By the way, why aren't you listed in Martindale & Hubbell as a partner in your firm? I said, It's simple; I'm not a partner. I wanted desperately to say I wasn't a partner yet, but I didn't dare. I see, he said, you've been passed over. I pulled myself together and explained that my turn hadn't come yet. He shook his head saying, Etienne might have told me. I thought that was that; he'd thank me for having taken the trouble to see him. Instead, he looked at me very intently and said he was willing to bet I'd make it. And I was hired!

Quite a story, I said.

He's quite a fellow. It's the most exciting work I can imagine. Besides, we've become friends. If I didn't know that he likes women a lot, in fact too much, I'd wonder whether I should be on my guard.

Don't worry, I don't think you're much as queer bait, I told him.

Of course not, he answered, excuse me. But, speaking very seriously, I would like you to meet Hubert and Gilberte. You'd hit it off. I've talked a lot about you.

I told Henry that would have to wait until late spring or early fall, depending on how long I remained in Malta and what I did in the summer.

Whenever you can will be fine, he answered. In the meantime I'll get them your books.

By the way, I asked, how did you manage to remain on such good terms with Madeleine even though I gather the more intense part of the friendship is over?

A rare diplomatic triumph of mine, he said. I remained available in theory but more and more busy in practice, and then a year passed and soon the other thing was no longer there. It had evaporated.

TOM CAME DOWN WITH PNEUMONIA within hours of his arrival. We thought it was treated skillfully by the Italian doctor recommended by the hotel. All the same, it cast a pall over the holidays, and I was relieved to be able to put him on the plane for Rome. He planned to spend a few days at the American Academy before the long flight to New York and then Boston. I stayed on in Malta. The old-fashioned hotel and its mostly empty restaurant suited me so well that after I sent off my corrected manuscript I got to work immediately on some short stories that I hoped could be published together in book form. It was late June before I returned to Paris, in the midst of a heat wave. Henry was in Brussels attending meetings at the Banque de Sainte-Terre headquarters, and his secretary told me that he wasn't likely to be back for another week or ten days. Over the intervening weekend he would stay with the count and countess. She discouraged me from acting on the idea, which had immediately crossed my mind, that I could go to Brussels for the night and have dinner with him.

He will be much too busy, she said. They work very late and have food brought into the conference room.

She gave me his telephone number, however, and asked whether the photos of Henry on skis during his second trip with the Sainte-Terres, which he had directed her to send to my hotel, had reached me. Indeed, they had, and I apologized for not having acknowledged their arrival. They showed Henry in a black snowsuit, poles tucked under his arms, his knees bent, executing a turn on a steep-looking slope. I called at the end of the afternoon and told him I was in Paris for just a few days and would like to see him. He confirmed what the secretary had told me: even if he could get away for a meal, it wouldn't be fun. He was too wrapped up in what he was doing.

Practically everybody else I would have liked to see was also out of town, but I did have a drink with my publisher who told me that Jean and Margot du Roc were in Paris. Seeing Margot was as good an opportunity as any to check up on Henry. I dialed her number, fully expecting an answering machine, but it was she who came to the telephone and invited me to lunch the next day at her parents' pied-à-terre, where they were still living.

As I had hoped, we were alone. I declined the offer of a preliminary drink and we went directly to lunch, which was served by a somber elderly man in a black suit. When he was out of the room, she explained that he was the houseman who like the cook came with the apartment. It wasn't a disagreeable arrangement. In fact, Jean had come to like it and now expected her to reproduce the same level of service at the apartment in rue Barbet de Jouy where they would move in the fall as soon as the renovation was done. Before I could stop her, she launched into a description of the changes they were making and of the neglected garden with great potential to which they would have exclusive access. Then she confessed that all the ideas were Jean's and it was he who had planned everything with the architect and then the contractor.

I complimented her on moving to such a charming street and said I hoped she was happy in her new life; it seemed that she had every reason to be.

Yes, so it seems, she said, but it's a rather odd life. Jean works in his study. She pointed vaguely away from the door through which we had come into the dining room. When he needs a break, he goes for a walk in the Cours Albert 1er. Always alone; he needs to think. For entertainment, we go to parties and dinners. I don't know anybody there, and worse yet I never understand what they're talking about. It's not because they're speaking French. My French is fine. It's who and what they're so worked up about. When I ask Jean he says, *Ah, c'est très compliqué,* and changes the subject or else he tries to explain and gives me a headache. Henry is the only person here who cheers me up. But he is almost always working on something superimportant and superurgent, usually for that Sainte-Terre. He's like a child with a new toy.

Her face lit up when she spoke of Henry.

I told her I was sorry I would miss seeing him.

It's a pity, she said. It's fun to watch him grow into his new position. He's moving too—an apartment on the rue de Rivoli, just a few blocks from his office. It's the entire top floor of the building, with a fabulous view of the Tuileries. His *travaux* will actually be finished by the end of the summer. The contractor has agreed to all sorts of penalties for being late.

Won't the noise of the traffic be unbearable? I asked.

That's what I was worried about too, she said, but Hubert has recommended a firm that puts in windows that cut out the noise completely. They're the people who did Hubert's apartment on the Quai Conti, where he had the same problem. You wouldn't believe how Hubert manages Henry's life.

Have you met this new best friend? What's he really like?

Oh yes, she said, at dinner at his house and at the opera; he takes quite an interest in Henry's old pals. He wants to meet you; I've heard him say so. What's he like? He's an oaf with a title. When I told Henry that, he almost strangled me, but the primordial Hubert, the ur-Hubert, is exactly that. What else? He's very intelligent—perhaps not as brilliant as Henry but intelligent enough to understand what Henry's about. He's stupendously rich, of course, and very conscious of his position. I don't mean only in business. The family is very ancient and very distinguished. I don't think he ever forgets that or lets you forget. But he really likes Henry and relies on him. Do you want to hear something funny?

I nodded.

Henry told me—I guess I knew it anyway—that there's a lot of anti-Semitism in Belgium. Hubert's business successes aren't to everybody's liking, and a rumor has spread that the Sainte-Terres are Jewish, which would explain his rapacity. You can see the train of thought—de Sainte-Terre, therefore from the Holy Land, therefore Israelite. That is, of course, nonsense, as Hubert explained to him. The first member of the family to bear that name was a knight who was given the name and title of Count de Sainte-Terre by Louis VII during the second crusade. It just happens to be the one in which by far the most Jews were slaughtered. Perhaps Hubert told Henry this story to put him on his guard now that, on account of him, Henry is moving in a fancy Belgian milieu. Then again, he may have simply wanted to show Henry how he is condescending for the sake of their friendship. I wouldn't put it past him.

XXIX

HENRY HAD TOLD ME some years before that, contrary to what he had expected, the chagrin and sense of disorientation he experienced when his mother and then his father died did not give way to a feeling that he was at last a free man.

Sure, he said, no one contradicts me now when I talk about what happened in EBH—Era Before Harvard—and now I no longer have to make those odious and pointless telephone calls or ask myself whether this time my mother has really gone nuts or wonder whether my father is faking his angina. But what kind of liberation is it to be left staring at what I've botched? At things done ill and to another's harm?

I had no such feelings of remorse about my father. The number he had done on himself right up to the cancer, which he might as well have grafted onto his gut, was his responsibility. Of that I was certain. One could speculate about whether he would have turned into such an ineffectual drunk if he had been fortunate enough to have a real son instead of a facsimile, and whether he could have been a good father to his flesh and blood, but what did that have to do with me? One could just as usefully wonder whether my mother might have been a faithful wife if her marriage had not been a cold and clammy void. I told myself that they had deserved each other. Had I done harm by fleeing them, hiding behind screens, first of indifference, and then illness? I didn't doubt it any more than I doubted the thrill they got in earlier times seeing their masochistic foundling crawl back each time they'd kicked him in the teeth. How was the harm thus done to them to be weighed against the harm done to me? By a cuckoo couple who'd had the gall to take someone else's kid into their house, fuck it up, and pretend it was their own? Our accounts were square; any incidental damage I had caused was paid and overpaid when I bought the house from my mother. That she should take her Greg away was an unhoped-for boon, as Henry might have said, a special dividend. Henceforth, I said to myself, it would be my pleasure to refer well-wishers with smarmy questions about my dear mother straight to her PO box in Maui. Other demons would no doubt sink their meat hooks into my flank, but once the exorcism of the place by plumbers and painters had been performed, the house that had been my father's and mother's would start on its new career: that of a handsome late-eighteenth-century gabled structure that happened to be owned by a well-known novelist called, like all its previous owners, Standish.

The presence of workmen did not prevent my spending August there, which was when George took his vacation. We played tennis regularly, George and Edie against May Standish and me, and often I stayed on for lunch. Over a gin and tonic or chicken salad George explained his plans for a modern international trusts and estate practice that would help superrich foreigners shelter their dollars, shares of American companies, and U.S. real estate from every legally avoidable cent of tax. His model for how this could be done was what Henry had accomplished with Hubert de Sainte-Terre. Not only had he been given responsibility for legal problems of Sainte-Terre businesses, but somehow he had also succeeded in snaring his estate plan and other personal matters. That work alone kept half the firm's trust lawyers busy, and now Hubert's cousins and associates were bringing their problems to the firm as well.

The rule is, George said, that the firm should take care of the private money of all the heads of large business groups that are its clients. It's the best way to make sure you get to do the corporate work. LBJ had it right: if you get them by their balls their hearts and minds will follow!

At some point I must have asked him how the firm was responding to Henry's accomplishments.

George became very serious and said there wasn't a real consensus among the partners. If you listened to one of the most senior partners, a big rainmaker, a lawyer should never have the ambition to do all of a major client's legal work. The risk is too great that the client will begin to take the high level of the lawyer's service for granted. From there it's a short slide to asking why the lawyer's charges for routine work are so high. Never mind whether the work is really routine. The client reasons that if the lawyer does it so quickly and all the same so well it must be routine. Therefore, from that senior partner's point of view, it's better to encourage the client to use other lawyers too; that way he can compare. After that, if you still look good, you will keep the client and his respect. I agree with that as a general principle, but Henry's case is exceptional because he and Hubert have become so close. It's only natural that Hubert should want Henry's advice on practically everything. At the same time, there is something excessive about it. Old Derek de Rham swears that Henry now speaks French with a Belgian accent.

I said that was very funny if true; in my opinion Henry had less of a foreign accent in French than in English. Perhaps in time he could pass for Belgian.

Another issue, George continued, is whether Henry is going native. A couple of partners from the New York office went with him to a reception in Paris given by one of the Sainte-Terre companies. After their return to New York, one of them reported at firm lunch that Henry was scooting around the room kissing women's hands. Some people laughed, but old Mr. Allen, who still comes to firm lunch every Thursday, said that Henry is American and Americans have no business behaving like Frenchmen. Believe it or not, quite a few of the partners around the table cried, Hear! Hear!

I LIKED MY APARTMENT in rue de Tournon and had gotten thoroughly used to the neighborhood. Nonetheless, I knew that I was likely to spend summers in the Berkshires. A bond I had formed with a Japanese writer causing me to spend the winter and early spring in Kyoto, I was in rue de Tournon not more than three months a year. That made the high rent seem an unjustifiable expense. Since I happened to be in New York that fall and had a book coming out in time for the Christmas shopping season—which meant that the publisher would want me to help peddle it in November—I decided to go to Paris in September to close my apartment. There was every reason to think that the new book would do well. If it did, I might feel encouraged to buy something small that a concierge could look after when I was away from Paris and perhaps even when I was there.

I had missed Henry during several of my recent visits. This time he was in town, and I invited him to dinner. He looked rested and suntanned—the result, he told me, of two weeks on Hubert de Sainte-Terre's caique, sailing from Bodrum due south along the Anatolian coast. The progress of the yacht had been stately, with swimming at lunchtime and beautifully organized excursions to ruins and archaeological sites. An expert on Hellenic antiquities would meet the launch at each site, along with cars and drivers.

Etienne and his wife were the only other guests, he added after a pause. I was really very flattered to have been included.

I said that in his place I would have been as well.

That's what I wanted to talk about, he replied. I spoke to Hubert right after we hung up and told him you were here. He'd like to invite you to dinner here in Paris tomorrow or, if you're game, a more festive one in Brussels on Friday. He'll send his plane to get us and fly us back on Saturday—unless you want to stay longer in Brussels. I might.

I was curious to meet Goldfinger, especially on his home turf, and told Henry that I'd be delighted to go to Brussels. Then I asked how the work for the Banque de Sainte-Terre was coming along.

It's the most fun I've had as a lawyer, perhaps in my whole life, he said. First, I have this hard-to-believe bond with Hubert, whom I really admire. If you can imagine it, at one point he took to writing to me in Latin. It's no sweat to compose replies on subjects such as what a good time we had at the theater and the refinement of the supper that followed. But he also wrote about business! At first I couldn't understand where he got the words for things and concepts that didn't exist in the pagan era or in medieval Latin, and then Margot asked, Well how does the Vatican do it, not just in papal bulls or other pastoral letters, but also in everyday correspondence? Fortunately, I remembered that there is some sort of office in the curia that makes up new words, and it occurred to me that they must publish a dictionary. In fact they do. I got the Italian-to-Latin version and, believe me, there isn't a single word that I've needed for discourse about the modern world that the Church hasn't invented. It's all in that diction-ary. The funny thing is that as soon as I demonstrated my mastery Hubert stopped writing to me in Latin. So once in a while I send him an episto-lary puzzle. Never on firm business, of course. Actually, more and more of my time is taken up by Banque de l'Occident right here in Paris, which Banque de Sainte-Terre controls. It's a part of the business Hubert cares about passionately. The local man in charge is a Frenchman called Jacques Blondet; he's been with Sainte-Terre since the beginning of time. He's very sharp and very deep. At times disturbingly deep.

At some point in the conversation Henry told me that Margot hadn't yet returned to Paris from the South of France. Jean was living alone in the apartment on rue Barbet de Jouy. The boy was at a boarding school in Switzerland.

I was humiliated by the thought of my self-absorption and inattentive-ness. I had been out of touch for years. Beyond a vague memory of receiv-ing some sort of announcement, perhaps a year after their marriage, that Margot and Jean had had a baby, I was in the dark. Probably I hadn't even sent a baby present, much less written.

Ah yes, said Henry. Margot insisted on having a child right away. You do know his name?

I confessed that I hadn't noticed.

Henry, he said, blushing. Spelled with *y,* in honor of Henry de Mon-therlant. That's what she told Jean. I don't think that Jean bought it, but for once Margot put her foot down. I'm also Henry's godfather.

How did you manage that? I asked. Have you converted?

That hasn't been necessary. I arranged to be out of town, and Margot got a *Paris Match* photographer who'd been hanging around her and Jean to represent me.

Admirable.

You could call it that, he said. If you connect with Margot you should make a point of seeing the apartment and the eighteenth-century hunting lodge they've bought outside of Chantilly. Ever since Mr. Hornung learned that a grandchild was on the way, no extravagance has been too great.

That must be very satisfying for Jean, I suggested.

Yes, Henry said. Lap of luxury and Margot too: for a conceited pompous ass with a mean streak, he has done very well for himself. But I shouldn't complain. He doesn't mind all the time I spend with Margot. I'm welcome to the scrapings from his table. I suppose I should even be grateful that he doesn't treat her well. If he did, she might have less use for me.

Henry, I asked, is there no one apart from Margot?

He shook his head. I take out other women, go to bed with them, of course I do. Some are nice; some aren't so nice. These are barren relationships. I can't tell any of those ladies, even the ones I like most and respect, that I love her more than anything else on earth and want to marry her. Not with Margot in the rue Barbet de Jouy.

Perhaps she'll leave him, I ventured. She hasn't been brought up to turn the other cheek.

It hasn't gone quite that far, Henry said slowly, but it may if he goes on interfering with her effort to be a good mother. Whatever happens, it won't help me.

Why? I asked.

Because we've been on the wrong track too long.

I pressed him to explain, but he shook his head and said he didn't want to talk about it. It's enough that I'm always there when I'm wanted and that I'm wanted. That's how it is, and there is nothing to be done about it.

THE EMPAIN EFFECT, Henry said. That's why we're traveling in a goddamn Sherman tank.

The Sherman tank was a clunky Mercedes limousine, armored to resist heavy machine gun and bazooka fire and all car bombs known to be used by terrorists. Hubert de Sainte-Terre had sent it to the Brussels airport to pick us up and convey us to his huge villa. Henry pointed out certain special features: tires as resistant as the body of the car and a control panel with four buttons that permitted the count to stop the engine and lock the brakes, activate an alarm siren, lower and raise the pane of bulletproof glass separating the passengers' seat from the chauffeur, and lock and unlock the car doors and the trunk without being overridden by the chauffeur.

Primitive, he said, if you compare this with what Q serves up for 007, but it makes Hubert less nervous. He's determined to keep his fingers.

On the way he told me the story of Baron Empain, the head of Empain-Schneider, a big French steel and heavy machinery producer, whose namesake had built the palace at Heliopolis. The present baron had been kidnapped early that year as he was leaving his apartment on the Avenue Foch. At one point during the negotiations over ransom, the kidnappers sent the baron's little finger by mail to the baroness to make clear to her and company officials that they really meant business. I had seen a mention of *l'affaire* Empain in the *Herald* or *Time* while I was in Kyoto but had forgotten or had never read about the details, which Henry related with apparent delectation. According to him, the baron was eventually released, minus his little finger, at a metro station in Paris after the kidnapping ring had been cracked by the police, with no money having been paid. No one wanted him back that much, Henry said. There had been many sleazy aspects to the case and the way the baron lived, including huge gambling debts at the casino in Aix-les-Bains or perhaps Enghien, laundered drug money, and so forth. His sexual inclinations were another subject of gossip.

Nothing in the Empain case applies to Hubert even remotely, Henry continued, speaking carefully and lowering his voice because, as he said, he wasn't sure that the chauffeur's intercom had been turned off, though of course people immediately remark that he is another very important titled Belgian businessman. Hubert has so far kept his personal life free of scandal. It's no small help that the women he has flings with are mostly ladies. And he operates within the law. I wouldn't be advising him if he didn't. Of course he is incredibly persistent when he has settled on a goal—usually buying a business that isn't up for sale. Beyond that, he'd like to be known as the richest man on the Continent, perhaps in all Europe. He's already the richest by far in Belgium and probably France. I should know how he measures up in Germany, but I don't. Luckily we don't all have the same ambitions.

That Hubert, as he immediately asked me to call him, was a ringer for Gert Fröbe was certain, except that, unlike Goldfinger in the movie, Hubert had a full head of blond hair cut in an old-fashioned military brush. It stood up so straight that I decided he must use a wax pomade. The effect when his face turned red, not a rare occurrence, was striking. So long as Bond didn't bait him, Goldfinger was possessed of a backslapping and backstabbing kind of politeness. Hubert's was mechanical and very efficient. He introduced me to Gilberte, his unicorn tapestry countess, and then marched me from guest to guest explaining to each, in identical terms, that, in addition to being the renowned American author of many novels, I was Henry's college roommate and his friend. The almost invariable response to my literary activities of these elegant figures, most of whom had titles that Hubert pronounced as distinctly as their double- or triple-barreled names, was a well-bred smile and a promise to be on the lookout for my new novel. Gilberte, however, sounded sincere when she said that my most recent novel had appealed to her no less than to Corinne, the wife of Etienne, who was also at the party. I knew that Corinne was a real fan of my work; she had been writing to me for years in her lovely English astute letters about it.

If Henry or Hubert had been naive enough to think that my literary achievements would impress the Sainte-Terre guests, I disappointed them. Indeed, that may have been true of Henry; he had been hopelessly starry-eyed about my minor celebrity for too many years. As for Hubert, it suddenly occurred to me that he was just cunning enough to have concocted the invitation for the precise purpose of showing Henry that his own weight might be greater than mine in the context of this sort of high-society occasion, and that, having become a man of the world under Hubert's tutelage, he need not let himself be impressed by me quite so much. That theory fit with Hubert's words as he was beginning to parade me through his salon. Not only had Henry become his principal adviser, he told me, but in time he planned to dispute my claim to being his best friend. I was amused and answered that, in my long experience with Henry, there had never been only one claimant to that position; he would have to deal with at least two other contenders. Good, he said, giving my elbow a squeeze. I will enjoy the fight. I have never won a prize only to share it.

If my impact as a novelist on Hubert's guests was imperceptible, the same could not be said of the aura of power and importance with which Hubert had invested Henry. The way men whom Hubert introduced as his partners perked up at the mention of my long-standing connection with Henry was striking proof. It made me imagine a like alertness that the ancestors of these Walloon nobles would have displayed finding themselves in the presence of a close ally of one of the king's favorites. I knew just enough about powerful businessmen's patterns of speech to understand that when Hubert said partner he was using that word as an honorific, an accolade reserved for his high-ranking employees and certain investors in his businesses. One such "partner," who did not appear to feel the same frisson of delight at meeting me as his colleagues, was Jacques Blondet, head of the Paris bank, whom Henry had mentioned. Blondet examined me quizzically and assured me that he had read every word I had written—looking for clues, clues: revelation of personality. We should find a moment to talk, he said. Perhaps over a Cognac after dinner. I bowed slightly without comment. When he left me, I drifted over to Corinne and stayed at her side until we were called to dinner. I had expected to be placed on Gilberte's right. That I should be between Corinne and Gilberte was a pleasant surprise. I began to look forward to our conversation. However, we were not able to exchange more than a few words before conversation at the table became general and very animated, the subject being the Camp David agreements that Sadat and Begin had just signed. Perhaps out of regard for Henry, perhaps out of admiration for Sadat, if any anti-Semites were present at this gathering of Belgium's ruling class, they held their tongues.

After dessert, at a signal from Gilberte, the ladies rose and followed her to the sitting room. The men were shepherded by Hubert into the library. Disliking the smell of cigars, I found an armchair near an open window and settled down to drink my coffee. I thought about the ease with which Henry had handled himself in this setting, manifestly enjoying the world into which Hubert had brought him. Or into which he had made his way. He had not changed physically—I thought that of my college classmates he had changed the least—and in other respects, except for having become over the ten years since he was made a partner almost terrifyingly adroit and competent, he was still the old Henry who had been my friend for almost thirty years. He wanted to be in charge and he was, and it little mattered that in this particular setting the power derived from Hubert.

His position was the fruit of his own efforts and his own merit; the intervention of the van Dammes, *mère et fils,* had given him a leg up, but no more than that. The one big failure was in his relationship with Margot. They were both stuck in quicksand.

My train of thought was interrupted by Jacques Blondet, who pulled up a chair next to me and, without preliminaries, said that he imagined that I knew Henry better than anyone. He waited for an answer, and, seeing that I wasn't about to offer one, he added that he was forcing me to make a statement that could be thought of as lacking in modesty. For him, it was a conclusion supported by clear evidence: an acquaintance going back so many years, one that had included Henry's late parents, and the general sense that I stood by Henry's side and always had. He paused again, as though to give me time to make a statement, and then told me that in his experience with Hubert de Sainte-Terre, which went back to when Hubert's father died and Hubert took over the business, no one had gained Hubert's confidence so completely, not even he, Jacques, although he had gone to work for the old Comte de Sainte-Terre directly after finishing his studies—he was a graduate of the École Polytechnique in Paris—or had as good a grasp of the structure and dynamics of the Sainte-Terre businesses. It was in his opinion a virtuoso performance.

I liked Monsieur Blondet less the more he spoke, but I said that Henry indeed was unusually intelligent and hardworking, as well as loyal as a friend.

Characteristics you and he share, Blondet observed. Then he told me that sometimes these invaluable traits engendered a certain lack of measure in pursuing the objectives of the client, who is also the adviser's friend. Do you see what I mean? he asked.

I shook my head.

I'll give you an example, he said. A skilled and very tough negotiator may quite correctly decide not to pick every bit of flesh from an adversary's carcass. Why? Because he is careful of his reputation. He'd rather lose a few points that he knows aren't essential than acquire a reputation for ruthlessness. Is that putting his own interest ahead of the client's? Perhaps, but if he has obtained for the client substantially all that the client needs, there is no harm, and there may be a benefit to the client as well. The adviser's reputation for ruthlessness might begin to stick to the client, and that is something to be avoided. But once the adviser loses the detachment that should allow him to make this sort of calculation, he will insist on having the last bit of flesh and the last drop of blood. Do you now see what I mean?

More or less, I said.

Less zeal, said Blondet, less zeal. If only you would whisper those two little words into our friend Henry's ear.

Are you suggesting that Henry pushes too hard on Hubert's behalf?

You've put it very well.

Then I think you should tell him so, I replied. If I were to speak to him about it, I would have to tell him what you have told me, and he would want to know why you haven't spoken to him yourself, and I would have to tell him that I don't know.

A fair point, said Blondet, a fair point. In any case, I am very happy that we have talked.

XXX

MY FRIENDSHIP with the Japanese writer and sojourns in Kyoto came to an abrupt end. I returned to New York sooner than had been my custom. During the summer, Tom collapsed on the tennis court at the Standishes' playing singles as Edie and I watched. I got him to the Pittsfield hospital and then to the Mass General in Boston. After three weeks in a coma he was dead. Thus disappeared the one older friend on whose advice and affection I had always counted. After Dr. Kalman retired, I began seeing a new analyst in Manhattan, who like his predecessor seemed willing to put up with my erratic schedule, but I thought that in this time of grief I should stay near him and plunge into work. The company of George and Edie was another reason for making East Seventieth Street again my principal abode, with occasional long weekends in Lenox. Although I had followed my plan and acquired a small apartment in Paris, nothing drew me there. I couldn't even say that I missed Henry, because his visits to New York were frequent, and he always made time to see me over dinner or lunch. In fact, he came to the city a couple of months after Tom's death. I hadn't written to him about it, and he had missed the obituary in *The New York Times,* which the *Herald Tribune* hadn't reprinted. When I told him about it over dinner he cried. He regained his self-possession quickly and talked about how amusing Tom had been in the old days at the house, regaling us with his Carolingian and Merovingian anecdotes. A short time later, I learned that Henry had made a sizable contribution to the scholarship fund established in Tom's memory for which I had provided the seed money.

That he was doing very well as a lawyer was evident from what he told me about Hubert de Sainte-Terre's businesses, his air of contented prosperity, and George Standish's occasional slightly envious asides. What I knew about his personal life was limited by his reticence and my absence from Paris. I did know that he continued to live on rue de Rivoli and that, in the company of Hubert and Gilberte and their instructor, he had become a proficient skier. George thought that he must have bought a house in some French province. That was the gossip at the Paris office, in which curiosity was mixed with mild vexation because he hadn't said a word about it to anyone. All the same, the weekends when he was presumed to be at his hideaway were immediately noticed. Instead of the telephone number of one of the Sainte-Terre residences or of a hotel in London or Venice, he would leave in his absence memorandum only a telephone number—always the same—in Tours, with none of the other usual information. The office had on occasion tried to reach him at that number. An answering service picked up and offered to take the message, disclaiming any knowledge of the whereabouts of the subscriber. Usually, Henry called back within minutes. I found this intriguing. It seemed to me that if he were living with some woman George and I would know it. Whether he and Margot were having an affair was a question that occurred to me more than once, and perhaps it was conducted at that hideaway, but he had volunteered no information, and I drew no conclusions from the sadness with which he talked of the Hornung parents. By one of those meaningless but painful coincidences, Mr. Hornung died in the same week as Tom; from his obituary I learned that Mrs. Hornung had preceded him by less than a year. I wrote to Margot at once, offering my condolences on both losses. She wrote two sentences in reply, or perhaps rebuke, to the effect that the loyalty of her friends had sustained her.

QUITE APART from Henry and Margot, Paris was once again on my mind two years later, principally because of the election in May that had carried François Mitterrand to the Élysée. The change of political direction to him after Giscard was in neat contrast to the one recently effected in our country, with the defeat of Jimmy Carter by Ronald Reagan. Taken together, they illustrated my thesis that we lived in an Age of Un-Reason. I had not much liked Giscard's regime or the class he represented. But Mitterrand troubled me because of the skullduggery in the *affaire de l'Observa-*

toire and also for a subsidiary reason that I kept to myself: the appalling condition of his teeth: I had the opportunity to inspect them from up close a few years earlier at a small dinner given by the French consul general in New York. Would I have thought much better of him had he something resembling President Reagan's porcelain choppers? I can't say. But I followed with more than usual vigilance *The New York Times*'s spotty coverage of France. I even subscribed to the airmail edition of *Le Point*. It was thus that, among a number of articles dealing with the program adopted by the Left, I came across the controversy concerning Banque de l'Occident, the French bank controlled by Hubert de Sainte-Terre, which had been scheduled for the first wave of nationalizations. Jacques Blondet was taking every opportunity to make public his conviction that having the state as owner would lead to the ruin of a bank like l'Occident that did most of its business outside of France. Non-French banks and clients would shun it; they wouldn't tolerate having the French state stick its nose into their transactions. This position was echoed by Hubert more pungently and with equal vigor. The attacks by French government spokesmen and left-leaning journalists—in these instances one could hardly distinguish French reporters from editorialists—against the forces of international capital were equally energetic. With other privately owned French banks as well as the most important industrial firms under the same nationalization threat, it was easy to gain the impression that the French bourgeoisie, foreseeing a new reign of terror, had decided to emigrate, London and New York being the refuges of choice. I was not in the habit of making transatlantic calls. Nonetheless, I telephoned Henry to ask him what was going on—not so much in general as in relation to Hubert's bank and to him. He was in a meeting and his secretary told me he would be in touch as soon as he was free.

Hah! he said when he called back, what's going on is that Monsieur le comte and his Figaro Blondet want to stop the French state in its tracks. They want to derail the nationalization of l'Occident. So they have asked—or, to be more precise, ordered—me to figure out how to do it, and one or the other is on the telephone just about every hour to check on my progress. I wonder what dreadful punishment awaits me if there is no solution or if I can't find it. There are things that were done in Rome to slaves if the *dominus* caught them screwing up: mutilation for a broken plate, whipping for spilled wine, etc., etc. Perhaps there is a similar custom handed down by the Sainte-Terres from father to son since the Crusades that applies to clerks in their service.

But do you think there is no solution? I asked.

Of course there is one, he said, I have it. It came to me a couple of days ago, on the way home from the office. I was turning the problem over in my mind as I walked, and bingo, I had it. I am quite sure it works. There's even a nice tax angle that looks very promising.

And have you told them?

Not yet. I want to put the scheme out of my head for a few days and then look at it again with a cold eye. And there is another reason: I think they will love my idea, but, even if it works as well as I believe, it's political poison. So I also have to figure out how to show them that I have found what they wanted while counseling them that for the sake of their own self-interest they must abstain from using it.

Afterward, as we were talking about politics in France and at home, he asked abruptly whether I would come to Paris. He wanted to have a real friend at his side at this time as he faced the most difficult legal and moral issues of his career. There had been occasions in the past when I thought I had abandoned him in a moment of need, each of which I later regretted. I didn't want to repeat the mistake. I was hard at work on a novel, but it seemed to me that if I opened my apartment I would be able to work in Paris. I told him that I'd be over in a couple of days. First thing in the morning, I called George at the office and told him what I was doing.

HENRY AND I had dinner the day I arrived, and right away he said, I am now sure that I know how to do it, and I am equally sure that I can't let it be done. The only unknown is how the firm will feel about my taking that position—telling a client like Hubert that you know how to solve his problem but don't want to use the solution—and how on earth I am going to get Hubert and that madman Blondet to stay put. Blondet, you know, has been squealing like a stuck pig all over town, as though anyone gave a damn about what he thinks. He's a *polytechnicien*, like a lot of the top guys in the government, and they all say *tu* to each other if they're not in the least intimate, like dukes in Balzac. Anyway, he's been to see the important bureaucrats to lay out his case, and they've all told him to stuff it—or whatever one French *fonctionnaire* says to another. What do you think I should do about my problem?

I said that for the moment I didn't know enough to have an opinion. I wasn't even sure I understood why he was in a quandary. Fair enough, Henry said. I was hoping to spare you the arcana; I couldn't make them comprehensible without a blackboard anyway. The essential facts. One: most of the value of l'Occident is in the non-French businesses, which, with a couple of negligible exceptions, are owned by a Dutch company owned by the French bank, and not by the French bank directly. I'll call that Dutch company Dutch Occident. Two: Hubert de Sainte-Terre personally or through the Banque de Sainte-Terre, of which he is the majority shareholder, owns fifty-five percent of Banque de l'Occident. He has been buying additional shares as rapidly as market conditions permitted. Three: the French government has announced a price for the purpose of the nationalization, that is to say the price at which the shareholders of l'Occident will be forced to sell their shares to the state, that is much too low, no more than one-half to two-thirds of the real value. He paused and asked whether I was following him so far.

I nodded. All right, he said, now he was moving to the basic legal rules. One: under the nationalization law, the French state has the power to force all shareholders, including foreign shareholders, to sell at the price it set, subject, of course, to litigation of fair value before French courts. Two: there is a loophole. The state didn't make it illegal for a French company on the nationalization list to sell its assets and, in particular, its foreign assets just ahead of the nationalization.

Here I want to open parentheses, Henry said. Only an imbecile would buy the French business—that is to say, the French bank and all its French assets including shares in its foreign businesses—he'd be throwing money out of the window because once he came to own the French bank he'd be in the same mess as the current shareholders. The state would be able to force him to sell the bank. He would have gotten exactly nowhere.

Here he announced that he was closing parentheses and would tell me rule three: the directors of the French bank have a duty to act in the best interest of the shareholders. More concretely, if the directors have a choice between two transactions, they must choose the one that gets more money to the shareholders or face having to pay damages. That's pretty much the same as the American rule, he added, with some important differences that don't matter here.

He asked again whether I had followed him, and once more I nodded helplessly.

This isn't simple stuff, said Henry, but now I will show you the solution to Hubert's problem, which I am quite sure the government won't be able to defeat by any legal measure. Are you sure you want to hear it?

I said I couldn't wait.

Here it is, he said. Banque de Sainte-Terre and Hubert and possibly some friends organize a Dutch company, which we will call Dutch Sainte-Terre—it should be a Dutch company for tax reasons I won't get into because they'd really bore you. Hubert's gang gives their Dutch company access to enough cash to buy from Banque de l'Occident its subsidiary Dutch Occident, which I'm sure you remember is the company that owns most of the non-French business of l'Occident. The offer goes before the board of directors of l'Occident. Obviously the directors who were appointed by the Sainte-Terre interests approve it. But the beauty of my scheme is that the independent directors are forced to vote for it too or abstain, once it has been pointed out to them that if they vote against the sale they will be liable for huge damages. Why?

Why indeed?

Simple: because Dutch Sainte-Terre will be paying the real value, and not the low-ball share price that can be derived from the government's offer for all of l'Occident. Beautiful, isn't it?

Brilliant! I said, and I really meant it.

Airtight. It's a shame that I can't recommend it to Hubert.

Now you've lost me. Why in heaven's name can't you? I asked.

Because it would be very dangerous. Hubert, the Sainte-Terre bank, Blondet too, not that he matters, would be pariahs in France until the Socialists are voted out of power and who knows when that day will come. The government will use every trick in the book to hound them. Yes, as a legal matter, the Socialists won't be able to undo the transaction, but, as for doing business in France, or anything else that the current government might have a say in, they can forget it. Theoretically they could tough it out, but only if they aren't spooked by the government's antics and if they are resigned to not doing deals in France that require the government's consent—tacit or official. The truth is that most deals of any size do.

So what can you do, Henry?

He said he would like to explain his scheme—and the interesting tax advantages that he hadn't described to me—to Hubert and, if Hubert wished, to Blondet as well. If they use their heads, Henry said, they will see the dangers and let l'Occident be nationalized. But these guys are greedy. They've gotten themselves to believe that they don't scare easily so they may want to go for it, regardless of the consequences. In that case, I would lay out enough of my reasoning and research to enable them to hire another lawyer—preferably a Dutch lawyer—to take my scheme and carry it out. I've have done my part, he said. Anyone normally competent can execute the rest.

If you do that, why not do the rest yourself? I asked. I'm not sure I see the reason.

It's the good name of the firm, was his answer.

He added that, given the prominence of the Paris office, it wouldn't do for Wiggins & O'Reilly to get tarred with the pitch of this transaction. He was prepared to ask the firm not to charge Hubert and the Sainte-Terre group any fee for the work he had done if Sainte-Terre went forward with counsel from some other firm.

There is one more thing that has to do with Hubert, he said after a moment. I'm not able to discuss it.

And what if they listen to you and drop the scheme? I asked.

Then I would have done my work perfectly, and naturally I should be paid, he answered.

I could see his logic, but I was still left with one simple question: Wasn't telling Hubert that there was no way around the nationalization the simplest solution? Who has ever said that all problems can be solved? Was Henry White's pride preventing his saying that he'd been defeated when in fact he hadn't?

Henry said he had asked himself that same question more than once. But his conscience was clear. Whatever might be the urgings of his *amour propre,* in his opinion he had a professional duty to tell the client his findings. He couldn't hide them for the client's good, because in the end it was for the client to decide where his good lay. It was utterly irrelevant that this result indeed coincided with the urgings of his *amour propre.* But, he added, I can't have that talk with Hubert without discussing it first with the firm's senior committee. He didn't think that could be done over the telephone. He had decided—in fact while we talked—to go to New York the next morning. It would be just a day trip, and he hoped I would forgive him for running out on me. He'd take the Concorde both ways.

One day stretched into three. We had dinner as soon as he had cleaned up from his supersonic ride. He was very solemn; the committee had not had an easy time coming to a decision. Wouldn't Hubert resent Henry's unwillingness to carry out his own scheme, and how was that going to affect the flow of business from Sainte-Terre? That had been the big question. But, in the end, approval was given, including, if necessary, not charging for the work, although several partners had implored him to get paid something, even if the fee was deeply discounted. All expressed the hope that a generous gesture would placate Hubert. He'd talk to Hubert the next day. As it happened, he was in Paris.

I was relieved that he didn't seem to want to go on talking about l'Occident, but I asked whether he had spoken to Margot.

I can't just now, he said. She has too many worries of her own. Ever since du Roc found out that Margot's inheritance was tied up in a trust for the exclusive benefit of her and her children—with no distributions to Jean while she was alive, and nothing coming to him if he survived her— he's put his mind, possibly to the detriment of his literary production, to using her money to buy major works of art (coals to Newcastle, considering the collection Margot has inherited but plans to leave to the Metropolitan Museum) and more very fancy real estate. He has gotten her to pay for another manor in Normandy and a magnificent town house in Versailles that once belonged to one of the ministers of Louis XIV. The game is painfully transparent: those assets, which are out of the trust, can potentially become his if Margot dies or in case of divorce if he negotiates a rich settlement. Margot's feelings are hurt; this insult—that's really what it is—may be the last straw.

And your hopes? I asked.

I have no hopes, he answered. Margot may have one though: an American moviemaker she has recently met through Jean, ten years her junior. She's quite taken with him. I can always tell.

I told him I was sorry.

There was a message from Henry on my answering machine when I got home. He thought he should keep the next day open for Hubert. Could we have lunch the day after? I called back, said yes, and wished him luck.

XXXI

IT WAS the strangest meeting, Henry said. I've already reported to the firm. Yours will be an abbreviated version. I won't ask you to keep it to yourself; I know you will. The fact that crowds out everything else is that, as soon as I began to explain the scheme to them, their eyes lit up. I thought Hubert was going to get up from the sofa—he's never behind his desk when he receives you in his office—and dance a little jig. The effect on Jacques was as impressive, except that Jacques being Jacques it seemed more likely that he would merely levitate: remain in a seated position, arms crossed on his chest, floating down occasionally only to be lofted up again by his delight. After I had finished laying out the details, I launched into an impassioned speech about the political realities that dictate consigning my brilliant plan to the dustbin. I hadn't gotten far before Hubert stopped me. Henry, he said, is the transaction we've been hearing about illegal? No, I said. Then Jacques asked: Do you mean that there is no legal risk in it for us if we carry it out? I said that the transaction posed no legal risk of liability for engaging in it and couldn't be undone by government action on the counts, because it involved no violation of the law. But then I inventoried all the things that the French government could do if the prime minister or the minister of finance got mad enough, or the president expressed to them his displeasure. Of necessity, I repeated some of the points I had made before. Jacques looked bored and tried to shut me up, but Hubert said, Let him finish. They listened, but I knew I'd lost them. And then Hubert said very gently, because he is, after all, my friend and a gentleman: Look Henry, don't you think that you should leave the assessment of French politics to Jacques, who is French as well as the

chief executive of l'Occident? And let me worry about the broader consequences; it's my money that's at stake.

There was only one answer to that. I conceded as pleasantly as I knew
how, adding only that there was another issue, which involved me and my
firm. I could not assist in executing a transaction that in my professional
judgment was against the long-term interests of my client and would
bring down the wrath of the French government on everyone involved in
it. As a practical matter, I added, if they wanted to disregard my advice
and go ahead, they might engage for that purpose, instead of me, another
lawyer—preferably Dutch but certainly not French. Faced with their
stony silence I finally said that there would be no fee for the idea I had
presented to them. I guess that Jacques had just about had enough of me,
because he exclaimed that paying me was out of the question. Hubert
jumped in and told him that was his decision to make, and he directed me
to send the bill right away. Thereupon, without pause, Hubert and Jacques
began discussing how to organize themselves for the transaction with the
Banque Sainte-Terre's usual Belgian lawyer—not a Dutch lawyer, Hubert
said, because he wanted someone who would be right there at his side—
and as they went on laying their plans I got the peculiar feeling that I had
become invisible to them. I had ceased to exist. An odd feeling, don't you
think, for someone who had worked so long and so very hard on a client's
problems and had solved this one, which in my opinion would have
defeated ninety-nine percent of lawyers. In any event, I stood up and,
wishing them luck, undertook to shake Hubert's hand. No, don't leave
that way, he cried out, Gilberte is in Paris with me, let's have dinner at the
Grand Véfour, this is an occasion to celebrate. Once we get the hard work
behind us I think we'll be grateful to Mitterrand. I never cared much for
the French part of l'Occident. France is an overbanked, sclerotic environ-
ment. Then he asked Jacques whether he and his wife would join us, but
Jacques said they were dining at his mother-in-law's. And guess what, said
Henry, shaking his head. I had a very pleasant dinner with Hubert and
Gilberte. We didn't talk about business for a moment—something that is
unusual for him in any circumstances and made me wonder all at once
whether he would ever again discuss with me anything concerning his
affairs. When dessert came he gave me a present. A beautifully bound first

edition of *Les illusions perdues*. He knows how much I like that novel; we've talked about it often. It's a lovely thing to have and to hold in one's hand, but I would have been even more grateful, since he always thinks this sort of thing through very carefully, if I hadn't been certain that it was intended to set me to wonder who had lost his illusions: he or I or both of us.

VERY LATE THAT EVENING the telephone rang. It was Greg Richardson. My mother was dead, of blood poisoning, the consequence of a puncture wound. She had stepped on a rusty nail walking barefoot in the yard where they had some construction going on. The doctors hadn't realized how serious it was until the night before; he knew he should have called right away. Her wish had been to be cremated, and that was going to be done later in the day, but she had also asked to have the urn placed in the Standish family plot in Lenox. Did I see any obstacle? I said that there wasn't any I knew. We agreed that I would get in touch with the church in Lenox and arrange for a memorial service in ten days' time. He said he knew who her friends were and would notify them. I called Jack and May and George and Edie myself, and on the appointed morning followed what was left of my mother to the cemetery. I had been a fool to think that her removal to Hawaii had freed me; having allowed that ghoulish idea, irresponsibly encouraged by Madame Bernard, to take root had merely given me another reason to mourn. Not because I loved her. Probably I had when I was little, before the rancor, and before I had become what I was. No matter how hard I tried, I couldn't remember, and was no longer certain that I knew, what love for her might have meant. Nor was I sure that Mr. Hibble's revelation had been more than a shabby pretext for my hostility. I did see, however, that I had failed in one basic duty, the duty to treat with kindness a woman who thought she had a right to rely on me. That the duty had been derived from the legal process of adoption rather than an accident of birth didn't lessen it. If anything, the bond of duty to her and my father should have been stronger, for hadn't they given me a life almost certainly far better than the unwanted childhood that I might otherwise have had, stronger than any I would have owed to my natural parents, had I known them, for the poisoned gift of life they had bestowed? If there was a circle in hell reserved for such ingrates, Henry and I belonged there. We would have the company of many of our friends, I supposed.

Because I tried to make some reparation by helping out Greg, my stay in the U.S. lasted longer than I had expected. By the time I returned to Paris, the rape of l'Occident, as the French press called it, had been approved by the board of directors and the shareholders; and the prime minister, the minister of finance, as well as the minister of justice, and the governor of the Bank of France had all condemned the dastardly scheme, which, the government spokesman acknowledged, the authorities were powerless to prevent. The nationalization law was imperfect; the devilish advisers of Banque de Sainte-Terre had not scrupled to take advantage of it. All three ministers promised retribution. I supposed that Henry must be in seventh heaven: his scheme had worked, and it was indeed political poison. He had been remarkably prescient. I called him from the airport as soon as I had cleared customs. Having slept surprisingly well in the plane, I wasn't tired and proposed we lunch in a couple of hours. He was all too free, he said, and asked me to meet him at a restaurant on rue de Bellechasse, a few steps away from my apartment.

How does it feel to be right on all counts? I asked him.

Do you know, he said, even in my worst attacks of self-doubt I have never put in question my intelligence or my legal ability. But if you want to know whether I take any joy in this particular situation, the answer is no. Whether he now realizes it or not, Hubert is going to suffer, and that pains me. He still calls me all the time to ask whether they have done this or that right. I can't answer the questions. Not specifically, in any event: I have to say things like if you have followed Jean-Louis Lièvre's advice—he's the Belgian lawyer—I'm sure you've done it right. Anything else and I couldn't deny that I was representing them in this caper. Anyway I don't like second-guessing colleagues. I couldn't resist, though, pointing out the government's humiliating acknowledgment that my scheme was unbeatable, and the government's fury, which I had predicted.

Henry concentrated for a moment on his food and then continued. Not a week goes by when a new legal project isn't taking form in the Holy Land, and there isn't a day when Hubert doesn't have five important questions demanding serious legal skills and common sense. That is what has kept me hopping since Hubert became a client. None of these projects or questions comes to me, and not a word of explanation has been given. You know me, I'll never ask the reason. I'm too proud. Is Lièvre running so fast that he can handle the Occident transaction and everything else as well? It's possible, although it's a small firm—they must be up to their ears in l'Occident. Another American firm? I haven't heard anything through the grapevine. Or maybe I have. A week ago, Blondet suggested we have dinner alone, and some time *entre la poire et le fromage* he asked me about the state of my relations with Hubert. I replied that I supposed they were excellent; I considered us to be close friends despite having agreed to disagree over l'Occident. Ah, said Blondet, *mon pauvre ami,* the friendship of princes, why it's like trying to hold water in your cupped hands. Do you not ask yourself whether *cet excellent* Hubert hasn't concluded that you're no longer the loyal servant, that you left his side afraid to find yourself under fire?

I got hot under the collar, Henry continued, and told Blondet that such a view would be pure nonsense. I had been vindicated on every point: the flawlessness of the scheme and its prohibitive political cost to Hubert and everyone associated with it, and the ability of any good lawyer to whom my solution was given to carry it out. All that, I said, has turned out to be exactly true. Being right isn't everything, said Blondet, although it would have been truly disastrous if you had been wrong about the legal aspect. Just accept the possibility that what Hubert might have liked even more than your brilliant idea was a show of your willingness to fall on your sword. And what can I do about that, I asked, short of hanging myself or borrowing a sword somewhere or other and trying the Roman maneuver? Oh no, said Blondet, that would be useless. When a bowl shatters you can't put it back together. Of course princes do have to be practical—at times— and they can pretend they don't see the shards on the marble floor. As you can imagine, we didn't linger at table. In the meantime, in spite of this nasty twaddle, invitations to dinner in Paris and Brussels continue at the old pace; Gilberte has been talking to me about Christmas and all the other usual stuff. I am at my wits' end.

He did look distraught, and when he apologized for having carried on about himself before saying a word about my mother, I was able to tell him sincerely that I understood and had not minded. Then I asked about Margot. Henry said she was in Paris; he had been to dinner at her house, with both Jean and the moviemaker. It was possible that Jean didn't know, and equally possible that he didn't care, so long as Margot didn't rock the boat.

And what happens now? I asked.

Between me and Hubert? With Margot? Or on some other front?

All three, I said.

A tall order, he said, but as I am underemployed, why not? The Occident transaction closes in ten days. That's when the other shoe will drop. Perhaps I will find an opportunity to see Hubert alone and test the truth of Blondet's insinuations. I don't like the game he's playing. Other than that, I'll sit tight and attend to such work as I have. Margot? I really meant it when I told you last time: she and I have missed the boat. Why don't you look her up yourself? A third front? There isn't one. As you know I like women and I like sex. Nowadays in Paris, if I go to a cocktail party or some business reception with unaccompanied women in attendance, and that happens often enough, my batting average is quite impressive. And if she proves any good the first night, I'll have her come back until we get bored with each other. None of them expect anything more and I don't either.

Pretty decadent, I said.

Really, he answered, I thought that you of all people would understand.

A couple of days later, following Henry's suggestion, I had lunch with Margot at her apartment. She showed me photographs of little Henry, who didn't look so little in the recent ones. He was attending a school in Gstaad, the name of which was familiar to me as that of an incubator for future playboys. Naturally, I told her that I had seen big Henry as soon as I arrived in Paris. Really, she said. Did he tell you that there is a good deal of talk about him? I shook my head. Yes, she continued, it hasn't hit the papers yet, except for a tiny squib in the *Canard,* but people know—certainly the government knows—that he masterminded the hijacking of l'Occident. The deal hasn't gone through yet. I saw a commentator on television who claimed that the minister of finance is still hammering at

Hubert de Sainte-Terre and that pompous man who works for him in Paris, trying to get them to back off. But no one thinks anything will come of that, and soon the fat will be in the fire.

I admitted that Henry had not mentioned being the subject of news and asked whether she thought he was at any risk personally. She made a face and said, If you play with fire. . . .

Henry had called it right.

The foreign business of l'Occident was sold to the Sainte-Terre subsidiary on a Tuesday. That night Hubert gave a celebratory dinner at the Grand Véfour, apparently his favorite restaurant—unless he chose it tauntingly for its location, a mere stone's throw from the Ministry of Finance. Grands-Echézeaux '71 followed by La Tâche '62 and Krug '75 flowed like Stella d'Artois. Henry and I were at Hubert's table. It was his idea to invite you, Henry told me. He said that since you witnessed my first triumphs you should likewise be present at this most recent one. I can't imagine what he's talking about.

It was difficult for me to gauge the sentiment for Henry among the guests who filled the salon where drinks were served before dinner. I knew none of them except Blondet, who seemed to avoid me. At table, however, I found myself seated next to Gilberte, and she spoke to me about Henry with the same warmth as she had at her own house. The meal dragged on—Hubert had ordered one of those menus de dégustation—and for me so did the conversation because Gilberte was very attentive to the man at her right, whose name I never caught, and the woman to my left was a titled Englishwoman who spoke as though with a hot potato in her mouth. I understood one word in three and couldn't be sure whether she understood me at all. At last we reached the baked Alaska. As soon as it had been served, Hubert stood up, stepped back from the table, rang a little bell that he had extracted from the pocket of his jacket, and announced that as a matter of chairman's privilege he was going to offer the first toast, to our friend Henry White. The usual sort of approving and expectant noise followed. He stilled it, saying that he was far from having finished, and began a speech that was at first an orotund and pedantic ramble about his ancestors, their ancient seigneurial rights in Burgundy and sometime possessions there, not unrelated to the choice he had made of the magnificent wines we had all had the good fortune to drink. From there he moved on to a discussion of relations of force and mutual dependence between the Lowlands and Britain, as demonstrated by their having so often stood shoulder to shoulder in opposition to the French. In this connection he noted the presence at his table of his great friend and partner, Lord Cholmondeley. It occurred to me that he might be drunk. His face was certainly flushed. The resemblance to Goldfinger was disconcerting.

I began to pay close attention when I heard myself named: Hubert was saying that he and his guests were honored to have among them a celebrated American novelist, a spinner of fanciful tales who showed in his fiction no less than in life a fine appreciation of both courage and loyalty. The friendship between this great writer and our friend Henry, whose roots, despite his Anglo-Saxon name and his mastery of Anglo-Saxon as well as continental law, were in Eastern Europe—indeed, it pleased him to think they could be traced to the land from which his own ancient family derived its name—this friendship proved, he insisted, that as a young man Henry must have possessed the gifts of impetuousness and verve without which profound friendships are impossible. Now Henry had given proof of a very different quality—prudence—his *cri de guerre,* his battle cry, but no, that was the wrong term, his murmured password has become "the better part of valor is discretion." An admirable and apt one for a lawyer, he said; his own, however, also borrowed from the great bard, was and had always been "out of this nettle, danger, we pluck this flower, safety." Hubert continued to drive his point home. At the end, he said, I raise my glass to Henry.

The days were long past when I would have thrown Hubert's excellent champagne in his face or hit him, and I was of two minds about what I might do in Henry's place, but, after I had seen my friend half rise from his seat and bow silently in his host's direction, I realized that he had made the right decision. He wasn't a brawler. He kept his mouth shut.

The next day the French government opened fire, the account of its actions dominating that Wednesday's evening news and page 1 of the next day's *Figaro* and *Le Monde.* The *Herald Tribune* and *The New York Times,* the two English-language papers I read, caught up on Friday. The Ministry of

Finance had launched an investigation into possible long-standing violations of currency controls by l'Occident and its top management. This
was a threat of criminal prosecution aimed directly at Jacques Blondet.
Another investigation concerned alleged collusion in such violations by
other French banks with known commercial ties to Banque de Sainte-
Terre. Although no announcement was made, *Le Monde* reported that
Blondet would be made the subject of a tax audit covering all years not
barred by the statute of limitations; the ministry, according to that
reporter, suspected serious infractions. If there was fraud, the statute of
limitations wouldn't apply. Another article discussed likely measures to
curtail the operations of Banque Sainte-Terre in France. Unfortunately
they were insignificant.

I tried to get hold of Henry, but his secretary told me he was away and
couldn't be reached. She offered, however, to make a date for lunch on
Monday, the first day he would be back at the office. We agreed on a
restaurant near the Madeleine. I called Margot to ask whether she had
spoken with him or knew where he was. The butler told me she was out
of town.

Monday came, and I was at the point of leaving my apartment for the
restaurant when Henry called. He said he was glad to catch me. The police
were attempting to search Wiggins & O'Reilly's office for documents
relating to the legal advice that he had given to the Banque de Sainte-
Terre. That was a scandalous move, and he wasn't planning to tell them
anything or surrender a single scrap of paper. Let's have dinner tomorrow,
he said, assuming that I'm not in jail for disobeying a lawful order of the
forces of the law. I asked whether he was joking. Not entirely, he said, but
I'm not worried either.

There was some roast chicken in my refrigerator. I had lunch, worked
until late afternoon, and then watched the news. The lead national story
concerned the arrest of Jacques Blondet on charges of numerous currency
control violations including illegal export of gold coins. His lawyer
appeared on the screen, very vehement about the outrageous nature of the
proceedings, including the refusal to release his client immediately on
bail.

XXXII

THE NEXT DAY'S PAPERS were once more full of *l'affaire* l'Occident. Henry called in midafternoon and said that Blondet had been released on bail that morning and that with the assistance of the president of the Paris bar association he had succeeded in getting the police out of the Wiggins & O'Reilly office empty-handed. The prosecutor made some noises afterward about seeking testimony from him as the stage manager of the transaction, but, in Henry's opinion, that was pure bluster. A lawyer couldn't be obliged to reveal the advice he had given to a client unless he had been advising him on how to violate the law, something that he had never done and certainly hadn't done in the Occident case. Still, he wanted to postpone our meal again, until the following evening. Hubert was coming to Paris late that evening and had asked him to a meeting at his office first thing next morning; Blondet would be present as well. Henry thought he had better prepare and go over policy issues with New York.

The following morning in *Le Figaro* I read an editorial on the tawdriness of the government's attempt to take revenge on Blondet only to obscure its own mistakes in drafting the nationalization law. There was a mention as well of the obloquy to which the prosecutor would be exposed after the ill-considered and futile raid on the Paris office of a famous international law firm. *Le Monde* had relegated l'Occident to a short paragraph in the business section. All this boded well for Henry, I decided, and called his secretary to say that we would have dinner at Lucas Carton and that he was my guest. It was, in my opinion, the one great restaurant in Paris where tables were sufficiently far apart for truly private conversation. Arriving at the restaurant five minutes late, I found him at table, staring grimly at his martini. How did it go? I asked him.

He told me I would be able to judge for myself after he had had another drink and we had ordered dinner. As it turned out, he had two more martinis before he began his story.

I'm sick of these people, he said. It was the usual setting: Hubert's private office, he on the sofa next to the telephone—I'm not sure whether I ever told you that he can't keep his hands off it—Jacques Blondet in the armchair at a right angle to the sofa also within reach of a telephone, and I in an armchair directly across the coffee table from Hubert. Hubert asked the Cambodian fellow who serves coffee at the office and also occasionally runs errands to tell Madame Ginette—that's the head secretary—that he won't take any calls. Of course we all know that if his private line rings he'll answer anyway. But we're used to it. Hubert leads off with a speech about how I have always had a special place in his business life as well as in his heart and how he has relied on me implicitly. I nod modestly. But, he says, I have disappointed him bitterly. He remembers—and so does Jacques—having asked me repeatedly whether the Occident transaction was legal, and my assurances that it was. And yet Jacques has been arrested and actually spent the night at the Santé. Could I explain that? I answer that indeed I can, quite simply. Jacques hasn't been arrested because of any illegality in the Occident transaction; he was arrested—take your choice—on his own merits or for his own misdeeds. That's not how I put it, but you get the idea.

But didn't it happen because of the Occident? Hubert asks. Most probably, I answer. The government is furious at you both, and it might not have had any interest in currency control violations if you hadn't pulled a fast one. That's what I tried to warn you about: the government would be out for blood.

At this point Jacques jumps in and says, That's all very well, but you didn't tell Hubert and you didn't tell me that anyone would go to jail.

I guess I'm still not getting the message across, Henry continued, so I say, beginning to feel annoyed at this point, Look Hubert, the government isn't even trying to set the Occident transaction aside or to prosecute you for engaging in it. They know they can't. But they'll get you on anything they can make stick. You can bet that the tax inspector auditing Jacques's tax returns has been ordered to crucify him. And you, Hubert:

Who doesn't know that you drive your Lamborghini too fast? I wouldn't be surprised if a police car were staked out somewhere near your house with strict orders to nail you.

There's a moment of silence after that, during which I ask for another cup of coffee. Hubert presses a button, and the Cambodian reappears, brings the coffee, and leaves. Finally, Jacques repeats, You should have warned us that someone could be arrested. I would have never taken that risk. I was beside myself so I didn't answer; I just sat there. Hubert too says nothing. We remained in silence for a few more minutes, and then I say, addressing myself to Hubert: Surely you agree that you and Jacques have done business in France long enough to know that the government can apply many legal and extralegal pressures to get its way or to punish. I tried to warn you, even to the point of telling you I wouldn't implement the deal. You basically told me to shut up. I don't see what more I could have done.

Thereupon Hubert says he and Jacques need to talk, and they withdraw into his small conference room. I stay in my armchair and pick up an issue of *The New Yorker* on his coffee table. After about twenty minutes Hubert returns alone and tells me that he's disappointed. All things considered he doesn't think that our relationship can continue on the same basis as before. I ask him to explain in simple French what that means. He said he isn't completely sure, but he no longer has complete confidence in my advice, so certainly I can't be his personal adviser. At the same time, he doesn't think I could work well with Jacques Blondet, who's moving to Brussels anyway to run the former foreign business of l'Occident for Sainte-Terre from there. That leaves him at a loss, and, in any case, he wants to tell me once again that he's deeply hurt. How could I have abandoned him in the Occident transaction? My place was at his side. I asked whether he truly believed the logic of his statements. I don't know, he tells me. I am a very emotional man. That's when I finally take the hint and say, I have just figured out what you've been telling me. Our relationship, professional and personal, is over. He doesn't say anything so I stand up, say goodbye, and ask him to say goodbye to Jacques for me. As I'm going out the door, he calls out, Henry, there's one more thing. Shut the door. I didn't want to tell you this in front of Jacques, he says, but there has been one other unpleasant development. The French ambassador in Brussels called me this morning and said that, unfortunately, in view of what has happened, I won't be promoted to the grade of commander in the Legion of Honor. When I heard that, Henry said, I couldn't restrain myself anymore and I burst out laughing. You can't imagine Hubert's face. It was as though I had thrown a pie at him.

That was the end of any serious talk that evening at Lucas Carton. Henry was dead tired. Besides, the wine may have gone to his head. He did say he'd have more to tell me in the next couple of days and promised to call me. Before that happened, however, George telephoned.

It's a mess, said George, and Henry's taking it very hard. People here are worried. It's understood that his relationship with Sainte-Terre is over, which is pretty ironic given that Henry has just pulled off the coup of the century for him. Unfortunately there is no one either in Paris or in New York who can step in and hold on to Hubert as a client until he comes to his senses. Anyway, Henry is making rather theatrical statements about the future. I don't want to get into just what he is saying because it may all blow over. But I wanted to alert you to the fact that Henry is in trouble.

I asked whether Henry had any work other than that for Sainte-Terre. From the outside, I said, it seemed as though he had been spending all his time on that one client.

That's the problem, replied George, people are asking whether he can be effective in Paris without that work, and it's not clear how he would manage a transition to New York. The management thinks it will work out, if he is patient and doesn't fly off the handle. It's some of the younger guys who are worked up. Call me if you find out anything you think I should know.

There was an article I was doing for a U.S. weekly on the debut year of French socialism. But what I hoped would be a distraction only reminded me of Henry and his troubles. I once again called Margot. There was no answer, and no answering machine, although I tried a number of times. I asked my editor whether he knew where Margot and Jean might be. He expressed surprise at my ignorance and said that he didn't think he would betray any confidence by telling me what was quite generally talked about in literary circles: Margot had gone off with an American moviemaker—he mentioned a name with which I was unfamiliar—the boy was in Switzerland, and Jean was traveling. Some sort of program of readings and lectures in Quebec. He had no more specific notion of Margot's whereabouts.

Four days later, I did hear from Henry.

Look, he said. You're my oldest friend. I can't be evasive with you. The truth is that I have decided to make a drastic change in my life—to be more precise, I am inches away from it—I need to think, and a lot of day-to-day stuff, most of it office stuff, is interfering with my coming to a conclusion. Don't take it amiss if I go off the air for a bit; I may need as much as three weeks. As soon as "the intellect grows sure that all's arranged in one clear view," you and I will meet.

I didn't know whether this was good news or bad; in any case it was important. And yet so imprecise that I didn't think I would violate Henry's confidence if I reported it at once to George.

He said, That's pretty much what he told our new presiding partner, Jake Weir. It's a good thing that Henry has a real fan in Jake.

My agent telephoned me the same day to inform me that a well-known director wanted to do a film based on a trilogy I had written in the late sixties and early seventies. He wanted to meet me before committing, and the feeling was mutual. I left a message with Henry's secretary telling him that I was going to the West Coast, that he could reach me by telephone, and that, in any event, I would be back in a week's time. I left a note to the same effect at his apartment. As an additional precaution, I called my French publisher and asked him to tell Margot how I could be reached, if she reappeared.

Meetings dragged on, and I extended my stay on the West Coast by another week. However, my anxiety about Henry was growing, and I called his apartment every evening Paris time and his office during the day. Either he was still away thinking or he had asked his admirably collected and polite secretary to lie. Obviously it would have been sensible to break up my trip by spending a couple of days in New York, but I decided against it and arrived in Paris on the Day of the Dead. The city was empty and slick with rain.

XXXIII

I suppose there is very little that you don't know about yourself, Henry said when we next saw each other. You started writing so early—and you've been seeing a shrink forever. Between the analysis and your novels, I can't imagine that you have left one square millimeter of your self unexplored.

It's not that simple, I told him. We change. We practice to deceive. The moment you get past one ingenious disguise you discover another one behind it. I'm not even sure that there ever was a true self for me to unmask—unless it's the sum of my private lies and appropriations.

Perhaps one day I'll come to some such conclusion, Henry said; I'm only getting started. This shameful business with Hubert de Sainte-Terre and l'Occident has left me disgusted and exhausted, but it's had one welcome consequence: I've had no work to do, so for once I've thought about myself rather than my clients and the wondrous results I can achieve for them. I don't want to mislead you. As you know, for a long time now to me "clients" has meant Hubert and his businesses. I've given you blow-by-blow descriptions of his behavior over l'Occident. Over the years we've talked about the kind of work I was doing for him and the friendship that had developed between us. George has probably filled in many gaps; he's always loved office gossip. All the same, I don't see why you'd realize what I'll immodestly call the scope of my achievement. I'll give you an idea of it—even at the risk of seeming to boast. Until a couple of weeks?—a month?—ago not even one of Hubert's sycophants would have even thought of denying that I've given the boss impeccable advice. Indeed I had. I've saved him millions upon millions by making sense of how his companies are owned. I've put the kibosh on any number of harebrained schemes in which he would have been rolled if not defrauded. I've gotten him out of unpleasant and sticky messes that threatened his reputation. In this l'Occident gambit alone he will double his stake within two years, and that's a lot of money. I realize that since I refused to do the Occident deal my taking credit for it can be disputed, but without me there wouldn't have been a deal. So perhaps I'm entitled to fifty percent of the credit. I could add other examples, but that's enough to put the ingratitude in context. On the minus side, there's an incalculable loss. I don't know what money value to put on Hubert's having to wait until the next government change before he gets to be commander in the Legion of Honor. The initial cost in wounded pride must have been considerable. I would have hated to see the tantrum he threw after that telephone call with the French ambassador. On the other hand, he can blame the Socialists for the insult and that should take some of the sting out. Well, I too am capable of throwing a fit. Do you remember Hubert's gift at the Grand Véfour of *Les illusions perdues*? I told you about it.

I nodded.

It showed his intelligence, which is powerful and eerily subtle. He understands me. You see, I'm giving him his due. He knew that for all my own intelligence, experience as a lawyer, and personal history—my less-than-happy childhood and the accelerated Americanization I have undergone, about both of which he has grilled me—I was in secret a starry-eyed romantic! Full of illusions, including illusions about where I stood in relation to him! I've done some growing up in this and some other departments, but for the moment I am just reporting where I was and where I am now in this particular regard. I no longer have any illusions about Hubert. Actually I began losing them before he kicked me in the teeth, but obviously I wasn't ready to put a name on what I was seeing. So there were incidents that sent a chill through me that I duly noted but did nothing about. I'll give you two examples, one serious and one comical. Jacques Blondet is another ungrateful SOB whose neck I've saved countless times, mainly by renegotiating deals in which he left too much of the boss's money on the table, which in Hubert's eyes is a capital offense. Usually I'd manage to get some of the cash back so that the deal looked better. To my surprise, I learned that in connection with those very deals

Jacques was spreading the word that I'm a Shylock, always looking to take my pound of flesh, while he's the guardian of Hubert's elegant style of fair dealing.

I nodded, remembering Blondet's remarks to me in Brussels.

That's the sort of twaddle to which ordinarily I wouldn't have paid any mind, and certainly it wouldn't have had any bearing on feelings toward Hubert. But I learned from another one of Hubert's flunkies that Hubert was perfectly au courant of Blondet's game and in fact got a big kick out of it. One thing led to another, and I discovered that setting people who work for him against each other like fighting cocks is one of the count's preferred pastimes—right up there with skiing. It is perfectly possible that he arranged for me to be told that he was watching. There are other such sadistic pastimes. I'll return to one in particular. But here is the funny story: Remember the Latin correspondence Hubert conducted with me? It turns out that, like the pope, he has a Latin secretary, who ghostwrites his Latin letters and verse. Of course, Hubert reads Latin well, in fact, better than many people who have at some point been serious about Latin, and has memorized snatches of poems, but that isn't enough to enable you to write. That's a different skill. So he fakes it. Incidentally, after I told him about my dictionary his Latin letters stopped. He knew that his letters were no longer a torment. By the way, I suppose you know that he cheats on Gilberte.

I said that years ago George had told me something along those lines that he had heard from Derek de Rham.

Ah, yes, said Henry. I know Derek's stories. There are dozens and dozens like them, most of them true. Hubert used to regale me with them—especially about ongoing messes—with emphasis on the more sordid details. At first I thought that this was the high-class Belgian equivalent of guys in the barracks telling tall stories about the pussy they'd got themselves in Pigalle on a Saturday evening pass, but no, this was the real stuff, about women who weren't professionals. In fact, I know some of them. All right, I guess that if a man wants to lay women about whom he says such things that's his affair, and if he wants to tell them to his lawyer it's up to the lawyer to stop him if he feels disgusted. I didn't; it seemed part of our intimacy. But Hubert's indiscretion is such that I found Gilberte occasionally revealing, by a phrase she'd drop in what had to be moments of distraction, and by certain silences, that she too was au courant. Poor woman! Hubert impressed me so much, I was so stagestruck, so flattered by the attention he paid to me, so wrapped up in my work for him, that I was inexcusably slow to wake up. I had too much at stake, both professionally and in my personal life, to say to myself in so many words that Hubert is a shit and can't be my friend even if he can be a client. But when I did awaken—paradoxically, since my own relations with women haven't always been what they should be—it was this instance of Hubert's misconduct, his disloyalty and appalling treatment of Gilberte, that put the ugly Hubert in focus: the sadist and overbearing bully preying on whoever can't stand up to him. So much for my admired *rapace*!

He caught his breath and continued. So, while final ingratitude and the kick in the teeth hurt, there was no way that I could, without loss of honor, continue to serve him as a lawyer. A lawyer has to be in his client's corner and defend his interests zealously, and I was, alas, at the point of not being sure whether I still respected Hubert or wished him well. Not that I am at all convinced that I could have gone on serving him as a client if what has passed for friendship were withdrawn by him or by me: that's not the way he works.

He asked the sommelier for another bottle of burgundy and was silent until the wine had been brought to the table, decanted, and poured into glasses.

I've spoken with a good deal of warmth, he said, about this ghastly disappointment, and I want to be sure that you don't draw the wrong conclusion. Losing Hubert's business hasn't rattled me, however much it may have upset my firm. If I want to, I can replace Hubert by other clients who will bring the firm as large a stream of revenues or greater. The specialty I have is putting together jigsaw puzzles made of bits and pieces of legal systems that were never meant to fit together. There isn't anyone in Europe or New York who can do it as well as I can; that's a simple and unchallengeable fact. I gather that some young Turks in New York think that I have thoughtlessly killed the golden goose. Fortunately Jake Weir, who is now the head of the firm, doesn't buy it. We both know they're wrong. We're in agreement that after the few months I might need to regroup, I'd have new work fully as challenging and profitable as Hubert's. For better or worse it's an open secret that I am the author of the Occident transaction, and many heads of large financial institutions wouldn't mind having someone who can invent such strategies advise them. Nor is my falling-out with Hubert a stain on my reputation; clients I'd be interested in and their advisers realize that Hubert has behaved like a horse's ass.

I said, I'm so happy and so relieved. Let's drink to bigger and better puzzles!

Not so fast, said Henry. I told you that I've been thinking. That has included asking myself about the satisfactions I derive from the exercise of my profession. They've been numerous and very intense. In fact, I've been very much happier at Wiggins & O'Reilly than I would have imagined possible, given the special—or shall we call them tenebrous—circumstances that led to my being hired. I was truly proud to become a partner. But satisfactions one gets from a job well done don't increase with each completed assignment no matter how much fuss clients and colleagues make over you. On the other hand, the price you pay for success day in and day out, which is to put other people's concerns ahead of your own, turns out to be very high. You might even say exorbitant. I've read somewhere that survival of the species—at least of the higher orders—reposes on a single anomaly: until senescence, neither the male nor the female tires of orgasms. But I can assure you that nothing I have done as a lawyer has ever come close to giving me a hard-on, never mind the rest.

Was it possible that Henry was aware of Jim Hershey's intervention on his behalf, or that he wanted to reveal to me Margot's role in that defining event of his life? When and by what means had he gained this knowledge? And why did he seem to assume that I too possessed it? These were questions I could not put to him. If, as was quite possible, he had blurted out those words, without intending me to understand, just as Margot's indiscretion, from which I had drawn an unproved inference, was probably involuntary, or if indeed I had misunderstood Margot, there was a risk that, by replying to what I thought he had said, I would humiliate him at the worst possible time, at a moment of great vulnerability. Instead, I raised my hand hoping to slow him down. I wanted to absorb what I had heard.

Henry paid no attention to my gesture or what was surely my pained expression. Hear me out, he said. I am still on the subject of my exercise of free will. I mean to do everything I can to make sure that you understand that I'm not under any obligation to give up my profession or the life I lead. But that's exactly what I am about to do, as a matter of my own choice, and not because these circumstances have forced the decision on me.

Sam, he continued, with poor Archie dead, with my parents dead, you are the person who has known me the longest and the best. Not even Margot has ever known me so well, because for many years I was putting on an act for her. I've never done that with you. You've seen me for what I am from the day we met, that first day in the dorm, and you've accepted me just as I am. Please accept what I am going to do and promise that you'll think of me as fondly in the future as you do now.

What are you talking about, I cried out, what are you thinking of doing?

Shh, shh, he said. Let me catch my breath and I will tell you.

When he spoke again, he asked: Have I said in the course of this tirade that I loathe my life?

I shook my head.

The fact is that I do, he said. As I've just told you, you've seen right through me, from the first. You realized that I didn't want to be what I was: a Jewish refugee from Poland with a Brooklyn address and a Brooklyn high school diploma. Archie told me that you put it very succinctly: Henry is trying to pass. Or perhaps he said that to you; it doesn't matter, in either case it was said without malice and it was true. I had come to the land of the free so I wanted to be free, and that meant ridding myself of the chains, the weight that held me back: Krakow and the morass of Jewish history and Jewish suffering before, during, and after the war. All of it. All the Jewism.

That was a word I had not heard him use since college, and I couldn't help smiling.

He nodded and said, That seems heartless and immoral, doesn't it? Well, nothing's changed. You try living with something like that and we'll see how much piety you'll have left. My parents had to be immolated too; otherwise the rest was impossible. They personified my past, barred my way, called me to account. I wouldn't have changed places with Archie— he too was a misfit but with one advantage over me: he didn't have a refugee skin to shed. You and your cousin George were another matter. If only I could have stolen from you the way you looked, the way you spoke, the way you dressed, the schools you had gone to, in fact every single one of your credentials, each of the trappings that made the unfair difference between you and me. Your stronger, tougher bodies too. After that beating in New Orleans, you told me you hadn't been changed by it. Can you imagine what that meant to me? How much higher you stood? I would have probably wanted to keep my brain, because I thought it was better than anyone else's. If I had known about your talent, though, I might have settled for your brain too, and taken everything else that would entail.

Having said that, Henry giggled.

I raised my eyebrows.

Forgive me, Henry said, it's just me, you know that, and held out his hand, which I shook.

You might rightly ask what has my self-negation got me. My Jewism is still with me, like bad breath. Then what have I gained by betraying my parents? We've talked about my career as a lawyer. They would have approved, after some indoctrination. For instance, I don't believe they had ever heard of Wiggins & O'Reilly. But they would have understood that I'm earning a lot of money and would have been glad to be told that my job is secure, even though Hubert de Sainte-Terre has recently dispensed with my services and other clients may do so in the future. Come to think of it, I am not sure that they would have bought that. One or the other might have said, Be careful, Rysiek. Once you're no longer useful, those goyim will kick you out. The fact is that, for better or worse, I will not be putting the firm to that test. And my apartment, my furniture, my fine English suits? I can hear my mother saying, You need such a big apartment? For what? You've got no children; you haven't even got a wife! How would I answer? I can't imagine trying to make sense out of Margot for them. I'm not sure that I can make sense out of what happened to us either. That leaves on my balance sheet friendships. I have valued yours above all, but I hope you will forgive me when I say something you know better than anyone: Like books, friendships do furnish a room. They don't put life into it. So to answer the question I put in your mouth, I have gotten nothing, zero, or less than zero. My wages are disgrace and shame.

We spoke very little during the rest of the dinner, each lost in his thoughts. Mine had put me in a state bordering on panic.

I declined the offer of coffee, but there was something solemn about Henry's suggestion that we have a brandy, and I didn't object when, after another consultation with the sommelier, he ordered two glasses of a very old Armagnac. He drank his quickly, asked for another, and then said, I will now tell you the conclusion I have come to. I am going to leave this loathsome life. I am saying adieu.

Henry, I cried out, you are insane. You've been ill treated by that swinish Belgian, you're exhausted and overwrought, you need to rest and clear your head. Or see a doctor—I'll get a reliable recommendation.

I'm not insane, he replied, and unlike my mother I'm not obsessed by thoughts of suicide. I don't suffer from depressions. If I am obsessed, it's by the vision of a completely different life. I want it desperately. But I can't conceive of starting it without shutting the door on this one. My way will be to disappear. I will miss you, Sam—probably only you—but that's how it must be. Please don't try to see me after we have parted tonight. Of necessity, you will hear about what I have done from George. Do not come looking for me. If I'm as good a lawyer as I think, you won't be able to find me anyway. And if by some fluke you do succeed, leave me in peace. Otherwise you'll do me harm. If you want to stay in touch with me, go on writing your books. You may be sure that I will read them and that you will have fan letters from me. Of course, you'll have no obvious way of recognizing them as mine.

With that, he stood up. We embraced and he signaled for me to leave. His evident emotion had choked him into silence.

I went home to cry. The next day I spoke to George. Henry had not asked me to keep his decision secret, but I thought I should be careful not to say anything that might affect his position at his law firm. As soon as

I mentioned Henry's name, however, George told me that he had been about to call to tell me about an early morning emergency meeting of Wiggins partners that had just ended, at which Jake Weir announced that he had been secretly negotiating Henry's withdrawal from the firm. This had been done at Henry's insistence, against Jake's will and best judgment—he made that very clear. He asked the partners to approve the financial package as well as a letter from him to Henry expressing the firm's wish to have him come back. He's nuts, George concluded. Were you aware of any of this?

His decision to leave Wiggins, and somehow go underground, yes—since yesterday evening, when he told me at dinner.

He's nuts, George repeated, completely nuts.

I asked whether Henry would be able to live comfortably without working.

That's the least of his problems, George answered. He has savings; he has what he inherited from his father, which turned out to be a tidy sum of money; and the deal he made with Jake is rich. Put it all together, he's got a lot of money. I don't know whether you realize it, but he has lived very frugally. That fancy apartment in Paris, for instance, has always been paid for by the firm.

What are we going to do? I asked.

Try to see him, I suppose, said George. He called me minutes before the partners' meeting to give me the heads up. Very decent of him. As soon as we get off the line, I'll try to get him and ask whether the three of us can meet next week.

Within the hour, George telephoned. He said, It's too late. He cleared out his office during the night. When his secretary came to work this morning, she found boxes all ready to be shipped lined up along the walls. Henry was in his office having coffee and reading a newspaper. He asked her to sit down and told her very nicely how he had decided to retire. A plan he had been preparing for some time, he said, but he didn't want anyone to know until he was ready, and this was the day he was going to leave. He gave her a generous present—one hundred thousand francs in cash and a round-trip first-class airplane ticket to Tahiti, which is a place she has wanted to visit. And he asked her to send the boxes and all personal mail to his *notaire*. As to business mail, he told her to give it to the junior partner who had been working with him. There wouldn't be much, he said, and it would dry up altogether when the firm announced his retirement.

I was struck by a premonition and told George we should hang up so that I could try Henry at home. A phone company message told me that the line had been disconnected at the subscriber's request. I got George and told him I was taking a taxi to Henry's apartment. The familiar houseman opened the door. Ah Monsieur Standish, he said, Monsieur White has left. I am here to clean everything before we surrender the apartment to the landlord.

And the furniture, and Monsieur White's clothes?

What's left here has been given away or will go next week to the Salle Drouot.

I shook the man's hand and, suddenly feeling very weary, went home to speak to George. But we found it difficult to talk. He too felt tired and discouraged. I asked whether he knew anything about Henry's *notaire*. He said he didn't but would find someone to talk to him. When George and I spoke next, the following week, he had nothing new to report except that the *notaire* had been quite firm: his professional duty made it impossible for him to disclose anything about Monsieur White or his arrangements.

But for God's sake, I said, your firm must be making payments to him, and probably needs to communicate for other reasons. What are you doing about it?

Actually that has all been taken care of, said George. It's basically a lump sum settlement. The money was paid into Henry's bank account in New York—which I suppose he has closed or will close soon if I understand the pattern of what he's doing. He and Jake have a deal that if Jake or anyone else in the firm needs something important from Henry, for instance in case we get sued and he has unique knowledge of the facts, he is to send a letter to Henry, labeled urgent, in care of the *notaire*. He will respond promptly.

There was no reason to prolong my stay in Paris. I returned to New York. At George and Edie's a couple of days later, our conversation at table was about Henry—the old times and also the torrent of letters from clients and lawyers who had worked with him at one time or another expressing shock at the news of his retirement. The firm acknowledges these letters on Henry's behalf, George said, and forwards them to the *notaire*. It's unlikely that he will answer any of them himself. It was one of the subjects Jake discussed with him in detail. They agreed on this procedure as most likely to make Henry's silence least offensive.

DESPITE HENRY'S PLEA, I made many attempts over the following years to reestablish contact with him. Armed with a letter of introduction from a member of the Conseil de l'Ordre of the Paris bar, I visited the *notaire* in Paris only to run into a wall of polite silence. I wrote to the Harvard alumni office requesting his address, and, having been told that there was none, I took advantage of a stay in Cambridge—I was giving the Charles Eliot Norton lectures—to comb through the files myself. One day it occurred to me that surely Henry continued to read *The New Yorker* and *The New York Review of Books*. I knew the editors of both periodicals well enough to ask whether Henry was a subscriber. Both came back with the answer that Henry's subscription expired in 1983 and had not been renewed. Minitel, an extraordinary computerized means of searching addresses and telephone numbers, had been launched in France by the telephone company. An editorial assistant at my French publisher, who was reputed to be a crack in using this new technology, conducted several searches designed to zero in on Henry's name if it appeared on any list in France. Finally, during a prolonged stay in Paris, I found the telephone number of Henry's old secretary, who no longer worked at Wiggins, arranged to meet her for a drink, and tried to worm out of her a clue as to what Henry did and where he had gone during his incognito absences. She assured me with evident sincerity that she didn't know. He was very discreet, Monsieur White, she told me, very discreet.

Margot seemed another road that should lead to Henry. My publisher didn't know where she was living but doubted it was anywhere in France. Jean du Roc, like many other French writers, had left in search of a more favorable tax regime. Ireland was especially suitable for creative artists; I was able to find out that he was living in County Clare. I telephoned and wrote. He wouldn't agree to see me or to tell me where I might find Margot. Unwilling to give up, I tried the Radcliffe alumnae office, only to be told what I should have known, that it had ceased to exist, having been folded into the Harvard administration. The Harvard alumni office drew another blank.

Henry's silence, his fate, and the most recent efforts that George or I had made to connect with him preempted all other subjects of conversation between us. But there was nothing to report, unless, perhaps, those single-spaced letters showing a remarkable knowledge of my literary production that I received following the publication of my new novels were from him. They were signed with an illegible initial, bore no return address, and were postmarked from Paris. As a rule, readers who go to the trouble of writing a careful letter to the author hope for an answer. These were the only effectively anonymous fan letters I had ever received. The anomaly made me think they were from Henry.

XXXIV

So MATTERS STOOD for many years, in the course of which I drifted into the habit of living away from New York, my time divided between Venice and the Berkshires, to which I escaped from heat and tourists of the Venetian summer. Then, for various reasons, the sour anti-American mood George W. Bush's presidency had engendered in much of Europe being foremost among them, I decided to spend the winters once again in New York. Out of inertia or perhaps an instinct for good real estate value, I had never given up my place on East Seventieth Street. I was still living haphazardly out of suitcases when Edie telephoned with an invitation to a surprise birthday party for George's seventieth. It would be held at her club; before she realized what she was doing, she had invited more guests than she could feed comfortably at home. She was counting on me for a speech.

It turned out to be a large gathering of what at first seemed to be strangers. With Edie's help, however, I gradually placed a number of the faces, relating them to people I had once known, some at college and some when George was an associate and then a young partner at his law firm, and he and Edie were a bright young couple. One woman I recognized without difficulty was Peggy O'Neill—now, as I found out, Mrs. Gordon Lattimore. We had both been in Renato Poggioli's formidable course on symbolist poets when I was a junior at Harvard and she a senior at Radcliffe. She said that she had a welcome-home present for me, having heard from Edie that I was living again in New York and would be at the party. The present was inside a large manila envelope on which was written "Don't Bend—Open When You Get Home."

Call me in the morning, after you've looked at it, she said.

I got home late. Inside the envelope was a grainy black-and-white enlargement of a snapshot of a group of young people posing in the stern of what I supposed was some sort of excursion boat. A young woman wearing a straw boater, a tall glass in her hand, seemed to be executing a dance step. To her left, a young man had raised his glass to make a toast. The shoreline was blurred, but I thought I recognized the Charles, east of Harvard Bridge, where the riverbed has been widened. Small sailboats, all of the same class, were to be seen off to the side, indicating that a regatta might have been in progress. As for the revelers on deck, I couldn't identify any of them even when I peered at the photograph through a magnifying glass.

I called Peggy and confessed that I was mystified.

But it's a great shot of Henry White just before Commencement, she wailed. I thought you'd love it. That's why I so wanted to give it to you.

Henry, I asked, where do you see him?

He is the one in profile, she said, making a toast. And next to him, with his hand on his shoulder, is poor Archie.

Suddenly, I felt very sad. It should have been impossible for me not to recognize him. I asked whether she was the dancing girl.

What a silly idea, she answered laughing. My legs were never that good. I don't even think that girl was at Radcliffe. I must be somewhere in the back. The funny thing is that I can't find Margot. Of all people she should have been there.

If this picture had really been taken at the end of Henry's senior year that would have been impossible, I said. She left Cambridge a month or two before.

Oh that's right, Peggy said, after I had reminded her of the circumstances. I'd forgotten all that. But you're there, she added, behind Henry.

Again she was right. She told me she had found the original snapshot in a shoebox full of photographs that had never made it into one of her albums and confirmed what I had guessed. We had been aboard a chartered boat, on the Charles. The point of the expedition was to root for the Harvard crew, which explained why George wasn't in the picture. He would have been in the Harvard eight, pulling his oar. She thought Archie was one of the hosts, and that sounded right; it was the sort of party he and his high-living rugby and Latino friends had liked to organize.

Then Peggy told me how her younger son, the curator of photographs at the fine arts museum in Philadelphia, had scanned the snapshot and after cleaning the image and sharpening the focus on his computer blew it up to this size. Isn't it extraordinary? she asked.

It was, and not only because her son's manipulation had made it haunting and otherworldly, reminding me of images of the earth taken by orbiting satellites, but also for a personal reason that I didn't want to discuss with Peggy. It was objective visual evidence of the apogee of Henry's first great transformation, into an elegant and graceful young man disporting himself on the river, apparently completely at ease in this company of gilded youths. It was also a painful reminder of his disappearance.

Certainly until the end of the 1980s Henry had been very much on my mind, in part, no doubt, because of the intermittent but sometimes almost compulsive efforts I made to find him. Then, at first without acknowledging it to myself, I accepted defeat. Except for those fan letters that continued to arrive, there was no reason to believe that he was alive, and no reason to assume that he was dead. George's firm either knew nothing or persisted in making that claim and keeping secret from George whatever information it had. I thought about Henry less and less often and, when I did, it was with the sort of piety that expresses itself in metaphors—untended graves, friendless bodies of unburied men, and such like. Nothing is more soothing. One mumbles this verse or that, and presto, the quotation usurps the place of memory, and once again the pale ghosts of the dead have been kept at bay. But the jolt delivered by Peggy's photograph was both powerful and timely. I resolved to press my search for Henry to a more certain conclusion.

I had given up hope of finding Margot after inquiries at her school and the Harvard alumni office proved futile. The Internet now offered new ways to find people. My assistant was an adept, and I asked him to search for Henry first. When he found nothing, I asked him to go through the process again, for Margot, using her maiden and her married names. Again, he reported failure. There were people, he said, who conscientiously took all the steps required to shield themselves from search engines. A new wave of discouragement came over me. Then I remembered Henry's account of his reconciliation with Margot and her telling him that she wouldn't even try to persuade Radcliffe to readmit her. She would go to Sarah Lawrence. I had been looking in the wrong place. Less than two weeks later a letter—a telephone call to Sarah Lawrence had proved insufficient—produced Margot's address in California. She was living in La Jolla. The college claimed to have no telephone number. I tried information and was told the number was unlisted. I wrote promptly, explaining how hard it had been to find her and asking whether she could direct me to Henry. Her answer reached me some weeks later. It was to the effect that she wasn't sure whether she could or should help. Did I ever come to California? If I did, we might discuss face to face what could be done. She gave me her telephone number. I called the day I received the letter, and a week later I drove a rented car from the Los Angeles airport to the lemon grove above which stood Margot's house.

A coarsened Margot gave me her cheek to kiss. Her mouth was puckered. She was literally long in the tooth. What hadn't changed was her bearing: she had the posture and agility of a young girl. A late lunch was served on the terrace.

I expected her to speak about Henry right away, but she said nothing. It occurred to me that she might want first to talk about herself. I asked her to tell me something about what her life had been. So many years had passed.

Fair enough, she said. I certainly don't need to ask what you've been up to. The press keeps me up to date on all that. All those photographs, all those profiles—what a star you have become.

Then she told me that Jean had surprised her: when she left him to go to California with Steve—that was the filmmaker's name—she was sure that she would face an uphill fight over custody, French courts as a rule favoring fathers, especially if the father is French and the mother isn't. It turned out, however, that Jean wasn't interested in little Henry at all—if the price was right. She paid him an amount that she supposed made her son the most expensive child ever. Of late, she had been wondering whether she hadn't overpaid. Those fights over who gets to keep the kid are pretty silly, she said. A few years pass, the kid is no longer a kid, and, in six cases out of ten, he is more attentive to the parent who didn't care much about him or didn't treat him all that well. There is a hidden principle of justice in this, she said, but I haven't been able to distill it.

By the way, she added, the prize for being attentive goes to the absent godfather Henry White. He opened an investment account for my Henry when he was born, and ever since not one of his birthdays has passed without a big check being deposited in the account. But only money; never a word or other sign of life. I know, because I ask him.

So he's alive, I exclaimed.

Ah yes, she said, at least I assume he is. Somehow I think that if he had died Henry the younger would have received something even more substantial. Or some indication about his prospects.

Tell me how I can find him, I said.

Why? she asked. I'd be giving away his secret. The only memento I have.

He was my best friend, I answered. It's late in our lives. I would like to see him again.

And then I told her about the failed attempts George and I had made over the years.

She thought for a moment and said that she didn't have his address and hadn't tried to obtain it, but could tell me enough so that some simple research would lead me to it. But hadn't I meddled enough in Henry's life? Didn't I understand that I was as much to blame as she?

For what? I asked.

Don't you know even that? It's so simple, she replied. You and Archie taught him all these tricks. Like a bear in the circus. Archie not so much—even if deep down Henry sometimes liked him better, you were the one he took seriously, you were what he wanted to become, you with a little of your Cousin George thrown in. That odious troglodyte! Why didn't you all leave him alone? Why did you help him become an honorary Aryan? Why did you encourage him to keep after me? I was stupid to thank you for it that time in my ridiculous little apartment. He would have been better off with a girl more like him, one of his own kind.

Rubbish, I said, and asked whether she imagined that anything short of the Nuremberg laws could have kept Henry from his own sort of Americanization. And had she ever met any of Henry's kind? It was his own opinion in fact that no such kind existed. You're talking like Mrs. White.

Mrs. White was right, she replied. You and I and Harvard corrupted her little boy. It would have been better if he had stayed away: stayed away from you and from me.

Her eyes filled with tears. I took her hand and said we've talked about this before, but why, why in the world did you and he not make a go of it? You had so many second chances, even in Paris, when things didn't go well between you and du Roc. Henry was right there, yours for the taking. You did love each other.

Love, she said, love wasn't the problem or the solution. Perhaps we could have had a marriage of convenience with sex thrown in—that's what my poor father would have recommended, not that we ever discussed it. But it wouldn't have been physically satisfying for me, I told you that so long ago. That never changed. But he changed.

She stopped, bit her lip, and said, Is it possible that there is one thing that you don't know about what went on between us? You really don't know what he did?

I told her I truly didn't know what she was talking about.

All right, she said, I'll tell you, just to make sure you have a complete dossier. I'm not completely crazy, you know, so eventually, when I knew I would have to leave Jean sooner or later, I thought of the marriage of convenience. I proposed it to Henry, though not in those words, I proposed to him nicely, to an old friend, an old lover, the man who'd been screwing me since I was nineteen up to and including right then. You do know that both before little Henry—I had been amused to notice that she actually pronounced it Henri—and afterward we kept on having our old five to sevens or whatever other hours he happened to be free, and that I could manage. But I guess you don't know, but maybe you do—he told you the damnedest things—how he answered my proposal. You really don't? Well, here is what he said: We've gotten old, Margot, you're past the age when we could have had a child together. We're doing fine as we are. You could have knocked me over with a feather. But then, as though nothing had happened, he unbuttoned my dress, undid the snaps of the bra, and put my hand on his erection. That's when I slapped his face—really hard—for the second time in his life. And you know what he said then? I'm sorry you take it like that. I thought I was stating the obvious. And here's one more tidbit, to complete the picture. I took his hand and kissed it. Because we were equally at fault.

What a waste, I said.

Of course, she answered, if I had been different, less capricious, less nihilistic, if I hadn't needed—anyway, wanted—those other men. But if I had been different, would he have become hooked? Until he couldn't do without me? We should have gotten together while he was still in law school.

That would have been best, I said.

She shook her head and said, What a square you are. All right, I didn't marry him but I served him in other ways, and I don't just mean free sex. Though I kept that up with him as well, while I had other men, and when I was married to Jean, not only because I enjoyed it but because that was the one thing he wanted that I knew I could give him.

Margot, I asked suddenly, because I thought I had understood her, did you tell him how he got the job at Wiggins or did he figure it out?

You know about that too?

I nodded.

Did he tell you?

Oh no, I said, I began to think that there might have been something of the sort because of an offhand remark you made at lunch. I wasn't sure whether you had blurted it out unintentionally or were trying to give me a hint.

Unintentionally, she told me, unintentionally, that business was between that man and me, and I never told Henry. Sure, I teased him about his great patron and mentor, because he was always telling me these marvelous things Jim had said and done. Perhaps I overdid it. Or perhaps poor Jim let something slip out during all those hours and hours they spent together working, though I wonder whether that's possible, Jim was so careful, kept each thing in its own little compartment. But one day I realized that Henry knew or almost knew. Something to the effect that he would never forget that he was in my debt. I began to feel that the knowledge gnawed at him, but there was really nothing I could do about it. We've never discussed it.

I nodded.

She opened another half bottle of wine and poured me a glass. We drank in silence until I returned to the purpose of my visit and said that I hoped she would tell me how I could reach him. She assured me she had told the truth when she said that she didn't have his address, but, in the end, gave me all I needed to know. Henry White had transformed himself into Henri Leblanc, and he lived not far from Avignon.

How did you find out? I asked.

She laughed and said that during those five to sevens there are also moments when one rests and talks nonsense about what isn't and what might be.

A NEW MINITEL SEARCH yielded Henri Leblanc's telephone number and address in a village southwest of Avignon. I didn't think it would be any use to call him in advance. Instead, I flew to Paris, rested for a couple of days, and took the high-speed train to Avignon. By five in the afternoon I was at the station. There was a café across the street and I called from there. He answered the telephone in French, but there was no mistaking his voice. Henry, I said, I am less than thirty minutes away from you. That gives you just enough time to get out some ice. I'll want a pastis after my train ride.

There was a long hesitation. Then he said, in English, I asked you not to do this.

Never mind all that, I answered. That was long ago. I'm here now and I want to see you.

After another hesitation he said all right and dictated the directions.

The taxi deposited me at a large *bastide*. He came to the door, and I was relieved to see that he hadn't changed much, except that his hair had gone from red to an odd shade of blond. We shook hands and then—as though he had been struck by the formality of the greeting—he held out his arms and embraced me.

I'm glad you're here, you old rascal, he said, come in. Let's sit on the terrace on the other side of the house. Mireille will be home soon. I had better clue you in so you won't say anything stupid. But first I'll see about that pastis.

He went into the house and returned minutes later followed by an old lady dressed in black who brought the drinks. We sat down, and he told his story with the seriousness and concision I had known so well.

He had bought the house three years after he became a partner— bought it for a song and spent considerably more, a sum that was for him then a fortune, on restoring it. The idea was to have a hideaway from everyone, including Margot and me, and everything. Once the work on the house was done, he came down as often as he could, which certainly wasn't every weekend since at the time it was a five-to-six-hour drive over dangerous roads. Going by train for just a couple of days was impractical. Sometimes he cooked for himself and sometimes he went out to a restaurant, and, when he went out, he liked company. He fell into the habit of inviting the real estate agent who had sold him the house, a very young woman, really a girl, recently divorced, with two little boys. Then he fell in love. What to do about it tormented him, because she was not meant for the life of a Wiggins partner's wife, in Paris or New York, and she had no intention of uprooting the children. That would have been, in any event, impossible because of the custody rights of the father, who lives in Aix. At the same time the feelings he had about the fundamental falseness—no, hideousness—of the life he led, which he had expressed to me with so much feeling at our last dinner, were percolating. How he would have resolved the conflict between Paris and the need to be near Aix if Hubert hadn't proved such a prick he couldn't really tell. Probably he would have cobbled together some weekend husband arrangement, but, knowing himself and Mireille as a couple as well as he did now, he was certain it wouldn't have worked. Neither of them would have put up with such constraints. The kick in the ass arrived just in time. Within months they were married. They had one child together, a boy now in the *lycée* in Avignon. I would see him, because Mireille was picking him up on her way home from work. She insisted on working—real estate in the region was booming—and he had helped her financially to open an agency of her own.

It's a terrific business, he said, the best thing I could have done with that money. The odd consequence is that it has gotten me into the part-time practice of law. Mireille thought it would be unhealthy for me to sit around at home all day reading books and playing with little Sam while she worked. As a majority of her clients are foreigners—I mean not French—she came up with the idea that I might give them tax advice on setting themselves up in France in a way that works well here and in whatever country they're from. That happens to be something I know how to do exceedingly well. The result is that I have a five-star clientele of international oddballs. I call myself a *conseil fiscal,* tax counsel, which I have a perfect right to do.

Henry, I said, you sound pretty happy, you look happy too. Are you? Is this the life you wanted?

He smiled at me benignly. I am very happy, he told me. Two-thirds of it is Mireille, one-third is Sam, and then, as a dividend, I have all this. He made a gesture encompassing the house, his olive trees, the hills on the horizon, perhaps the entire world. It's wonderful here, don't you think? And for the first time I am absolutely myself. Leblanc is no more my name than White, but everyone here knows that I wasn't born Leblanc and no one cares. Although my French is easily as good as my English, people realize that I am a foreigner. That defines me. There's nothing to explain; no one to betray. I've behaved well here, and I've been treated with great discretion and indulgence. When I don't feel like eating what Madame Susanne wants to prepare for lunch, I take my bicycle and go to the café in the village. I even play *pétanque* with the locals. Finally a use for what I learned during my rare visits to a bowling alley in Brooklyn. They are glad to have a pastis with me after the game, and they don't ask any questions. If they did, I'd tell them the truth. Simplified perhaps, but still the truth.

And what happens when you meet Americans? Aren't you likely to run into Americans in this practice of yours, even people who might know you?

It hasn't happened yet, but if it does, and someone recognizes me, I'll deal with it. It isn't as though I'd escaped from Devil's Island! By the way, you've received my letters, haven't you?

Yes. But I couldn't thank you for them.

In the future you will.

And you called him Sam.

Yes, he answered, and smiled.

Henry, I asked, why did you have to cut yourself off from me, from George, from your friends and partners, why have you done this to people who cared about you so much?

He became very serious. You had all been my accomplices, always busy aiding and abetting. There was no leaving my old life of crime with you at my side. I had to leave you behind.

He stopped speaking and listened. I listened too. It was the sound of wheels on the gravel.

It's Mireille, he said. She knows all about me and a great deal about you, including your novels. I am so glad that you will finally be able to meet her. Briefly. After that you'll have to leave.

She was short and cheerful looking, with the kind of strong Mediterranean face one associates with the region, and lustrous black hair. Her laugh was like a young girl's. Little Sam was as tall as his father. He had his mother's coloring. We talked pleasantly for a few minutes and then I said that I must go. Henry asked where I was staying. In Villeneuve, I told him. In that case, he replied, Sam will drive you.

Night had fallen. As Sam and I walked to the car, I looked up at the sky. It was full of stars.

Matters of Honor

LOUIS BEGLEY

A Reader's Guide

BETWEEN FACT AND FICTION

> *Tell me where is fancy bred,*
> *Or in the heart, or in the head?*
> *How begot, how nourished?*
> > *Reply, reply.*
> *It is engendered in the eyes,*
> *With gazing fed, and fancy dies*
> *In the cradle, where it lies.*
> > *Let us all ring fancy's knell.*
> > *I'll begin it—Ding dong bell.*

> —William Shakespeare,
> *The Merchant of Venice*

So sing Portia's musicians, at Belmont, her vast domain, while Bassanio ponders which casket he must open—gold, silver, or lead—if he is to win Portia's hand and fortune. Their questions are not unlike those that readers ask of novelists about their novels: How did the idea of writing your book occur to you? How much of it is based on your life? *Matters of Honor* has provoked its fair share of them, most frequently put to me after readings I have given from that book. I rejoice in contacts with my readers, so I have answered them extemporaneously with results that have seemed to me uneven. This is my first attempt to provide a coherent response.

Some time after I had published my first novel, *Wartime Lies,* my wife, Anka Muhlstein, who is a French historian and biographer, suggested that I should consider writing about how I had set about becoming an American after I arrived in the United States from Poland in

March 1947, at the age of thirteen. I replied that I liked her idea, and was already working on it. I was referring to my second novel, *The Man Who Was Late,* the protagonist of which is Ben, a brilliantly successful and tormented young man, Jewish like me, who after surviving the war in an unnamed Central European country streaks like a comet through the firmament of Harvard College, the Marine Corps, and Wall Street only to crash disastrously in consequence of an unhappy and impossible love affair. That novel, of which I am inordinately fond, could have been the sort of book my wife had in mind, but I had become too engrossed by the destructive relationship between Ben and the woman he loves, and too obsessed by aesthetic concerns—the need I felt for the action of that novel to proceed at a gallop—to pay sufficient attention to the great theme of Americanization. I suppose that I thought, correctly as it turned out, that I would one day turn to it.

An opportunity presented itself in the period that followed the completion of my seventh novel, *Shipwreck.* My mother's health had been declining steeply; in fact, she would die soon afterward. I couldn't avoid thinking intensively about the past, not only the wartime years in Poland but also the years that followed my family's and my arrival sixty years ago in New York City; Harvard College, which I entered in 1950; army service from 1954 to 1956; Harvard Law School; and the slow resolution of many internal conflicts tearing at me that had their roots in my early youth. As I immersed myself in those memories I began to see that my efforts to become an American had been only one facet of a larger experience that I had shared with others. I was thinking in particular of the man who was my Harvard College roommate from our freshman year until graduation, whose background, ambitions, and destiny were totally different from mine, as well as of other students who had been close friends. We had all embarked on the great adventure of self-reinvention, of remaking ourselves as nearly as such a thing was possible in the likeness of the secret or not-so-secret imago we had chosen. My own reinvention was complicated by the anti-Semitism that was then prevalent in the United States, and the impression I had that normal Americans couldn't comprehend my experiences during the war and weren't especially interested in hearing about them.

These assertions may sound strange in the first decade of the twenty-first century, but I am speaking of a time—end of the 1940s and beginning of the 1950s—when the word "Holocaust" had not yet been applied to the slaughter of European Jews, and it wasn't clear that Auschwitz, Treblinka, Majdanek, and the other furnaces of Moloch were a fit subject for polite conversation.

Thus I came gradually to the decision that the novel about Americanization my wife had "commissioned" and I had in mind would need a wider focus. That a young man whose origins were like mine—Henry White in *Matters of Honor*—would be at the center of the stage could be taken for granted; I wanted also a personage not unlike my roommate during the four years at Harvard College. He became Archibald P. Palmer III, or Archie, as he wished to be called. I could see fairly distinctly the trajectories of those two young men, including the rather surprising dénouement of Henry's career. But I didn't know how the story should be told. When I first tried to write it in the first person, from the point of view of Henry, the result dismayed me. What I had set down was flat and lifeless. I wondered whether I shouldn't abandon Henry and Archie and move on to a different story. Then Sam Standish, the third roommate, came into my life and I realized that he was the inevitable narrator. He gave me the opening to speak of a milieu I know and find amusing: the "good" families in the Berkshires. Ostensibly a WASP with the right name and the right manners, he could provide the distance from Henry's specific preoccupations that I thought was necessary. At the same time, he would be secretly as much an outsider as Henry. I would accomplish that by making him an adopted son of parents he doesn't respect and by raising a doubt about his sexual orientation. To top it off, Sam would be a novelist, therefore qualified professionally to tell this complex story in which he is an actor as well as an observer.

My biography is available to all. Every reader is in a position to draw the obvious conclusion, that Henry's curriculum vitae on the surface corresponds to mine: We were both Jewish children born in Poland in the early 1930s, and during World War II were in great danger of being killed by Germans; both of us came to the United States in the late

1940s, settled in Brooklyn, N.Y., and after a passage at a Brooklyn public high school moved on to Harvard College and Harvard Law School; we served in the U.S. army. After law school, like Henry, I went to work for a first-class New York law firm, and like Henry I had what I might describe, if modesty didn't prevent it, as a brilliant legal career. But the superficial resemblance stops when Henry and I go to work: Unlike Henry, I was hired by my firm on my merits, and welcomed with open arms; unlike Henry, I did not find that I had reached the apogee of professional success only to look into an abyss. Like Sam, I have become a novelist; Henry didn't.

There are innumerable other fundamental differences between Henry and me. They include relations with my parents—to whose memory I dedicated *Matters of Honor*—the women I have loved, and my children and the joy they have brought into my life. If I were to attempt to list them I would probably obscure the essential point, which the reader is invited to take on faith: I am not a character in a novel, and Henry is not me. I invented him—as I have invented everyone else, with the exception of historical figures, in *Matters of Honor* and in my other works—using materials taken from my life and from the lives of others whom I have known, but all such materials have been deconstructed and reformed by my imagination. Of course, some personages owe more to living models than others. Archie is greatly indebted to my college roommate; I have intimated as much. Henry's parents resemble my parents, albeit imperfectly. Sam Standish is not modeled on anyone in particular. He is a pure product of my fancy, but I have poured into him a great deal of myself. That infusion was dictated in part by his having become a writer; a similar case is John North, the novelist narrator of my novel *Shipwreck* who, in that novel, speaks for me on all literary matters. Sam's parents are almost completely invented, except for one or two indispensable traits. Many years ago I knew in the Berkshires a stoop-shouldered, sexily thin woman whom I had in mind when I wrote about Sam's mother, while a Texan I knew slightly provided me with the diction of Sam's father. There are no identifiable models for Sam's very proper cousin, George Standish, or for the fascinating and dangerous Margot. No doubt I have known people George and Margot resemble in one detail or another, cases in point being the clothes Margot wears and her half lazy and half haughty way of talking through her nose. Harvard College in *Matters of Honor* is very much like the college I remember. In three instances I refer to real people who were very prominent there at the time: Harry Levin, Renato Poggioli, and Bob Chapman, each of them an admired member of the faculty. There is no single model for the odious Belgian magnate, Hubert de Sainte-Terre. Like his billionaire colleague, Mike Mansour, who prowls the pages of my *Schmidt Delivered,* he was derived from several hugely rich men I have known. However, unlike Mansour and Sainte-Terre, none of those men was any good at business. The most striking characteristics that those real-life moguls share with my characters are their egotism, conceit, and frivolity. I am especially proud of the moment when Sainte-Terre reveals the consequence of thumbing his figurative nose at the French government that has really gotten to him: He won't be promoted to the next higher grade in the Légion d'honneur! This mishap is 100 percent invented and yet I believe that it is also 100 percent accurate. Each of the moguls I have known would have found it to be the unkindest cut of them all.

So this is how fancy is bred and nourished. I could carry the investigation of the real-life content of my novel further, and it is safe to say that every detail in my descriptions, every personality trait of my characters has some real-life antecedent. The question I have to put to myself, however, is whether research of this sort, amusing for me because it is so much like gossip about acquaintances and friends I haven't seen for a long time, is of any value to the reader. The truth it reveals, that I am present in my novel, should be obvious without it. How could it be otherwise? As Franz Kafka put it to his fiancée, Felice Bauer, urging her half seriously not to be jealous of his characters, the creation of whom he devoted so much of his time, "the novel is me, the stories are me. . . ."

READER'S GUIDE
QUESTIONS AND TOPICS FOR DISCUSSION

1. Harvard College in the 1950s is a vivid setting for the first part of *Matters of Honor*. Could this novel have taken place at another institution, or does Harvard have a unique significance?

2. Henry says: "Margot and Margot's parents are way up at the top of the tree. We're way down here at the roots. But that's the one tree I will learn to climb. Otherwise there is no point in my being here" (p. 51). How would you describe the social hierarchy portrayed in this novel? What do you think Henry means by "here"? Harvard? America? Or something else?

3. Archie's ambitions seem to reflect the values not of his own parents, but of Sam's. He aspires to their 100 percent respectability. That status being unattainable to him, he settles for the trappings of high society, and the reckless, irresponsible behavior that tends to follow them. Why, then, do you think Sam is drawn to Archie as a friend? What makes Archie different from the Standishes?

4. Before matriculating at Harvard, Sam learns that he had been adopted. What is Sam's reaction to this startling revelation? Both his physical appearance and the secret trust fund paying for his education suggest that he might still have blood ties to the Standish family. Why do you think Begley included these details?

5. On a weekend vacation at the Standish household, George forces himself on Margot while she is sleeping. How does she handle the sit-

uation? Does he take responsibility for his actions and feel that he has done something wrong? If this incident had taken place today instead of back in the 1950s do you think Margot might have responded differently?

6. Sam's romantic life is not spelled out in the novel, but it is implied that he is a homosexual. Why do you think he is so guarded about his sexuality? Why do think that Begley chose not to explore these undertones further? Are there any similarities between Sam's relationship with sex and Henry's relationship with Judaism?

7. Sam develops a long-standing dependancy on psychoanalysis, stemming from his "nervous breakdown" at Harvard. Why is he so drawn to this kind of therapy? How, if at all, do you think it helps him?

8. At the beginning of the novel, the trio of roommates share an important relationship. How do things change after Archie's death? What do you think is Archie's role in the novel? How was Archie important to the development of Sam and Henry's relationship?

9. At the beginning of the novel, Henry says: "I feel no more Jewish than a smoked ham" (p. 31). And at the end he says, "You might rightly ask what my self-negation got me. My Jewism is still with me, like bad breath . . . I have gotten nothing, zero, or less than zero" (p. 291). What part do you think Henry's unease with his past and identity played in the destructive relationship between him and Hubert de Sainte-Terre? Do you think Henry could have shaped his life differently once he had arrived at Harvard?

10. Henry's lifelong infatuation with Margot is one of his most defining characteristics. Even after she marries, Henry finds himself unable to move on. "I can't tell any of those ladies, even the ones I like most and respect, that I love her more than anything else on earth and want to marry her. Not with Margot in the rue Barbet de Jouy" (256). Why

do you think Henry is so drawn to Margot? Why is she drawn to him? Why does their relationship consistently fail?

11. Near the end of the novel, Margot blames Sam for Henry's unhappiness, saying: "You and Archie taught him all those tricks. Like a bear in the circus. Why didn't you all leave him alone? Why did you help him become an honorary Aryan?" (301) Do you agree with her? Would Henry have been better off without Sam? Without Margot?

12. Names are significant in *Matters of Honor,* often representing the personal struggles that the characters face. Sam's surname, for example, ties him to a family about whom he feels ambivalent. Archie's name has a deceptively aristocratic ring to it. And Henry's name has the ability to adapt in whatever way he chooses. At the end of the novel, he tells Sam that "Leblanc is no more my name than White, but everyone here knows that I wasn't born Leblanc and no one cares. Although my French is easily as good as my English, people realize that I'm a foreigner. That defines me. There's nothing to explain; no one to betray" (306). As the novel concludes, how do you think each character has lived up to or forsaken his name? What does the future hold for the next generation of characters—Margot's Henry and Henry's Sam?

ABOUT THE AUTHOR

Louis Begley lives in New York City. His previous novels are *Wartime Lies, The Man Who Was Late, As Max Saw It, About Schmidt, Mistler's Exit, Schmidt Delivered,* and *Shipwreck.*

A NOTE ON THE TYPE

This book was set in Garamond, a font named for the sixteenth-century French typographer Claude Garamond. The version used here is a revival of his famous type issued by the Lanston Monotype Company in 1922.

Composed by Stratford Publishing Services, Brattleboro, Vermont
Printed and bound by Berryville Graphics, Berryville, Virginia
Designed by Peter A. Andersen